MW00981191

AUSTRALIAN LOVE STORIES

SELECTED BY KERRYN
GOLDSWORTHY

Melbourne

OXFORD UNIVERSITY PRESS

Oxford   Auckland   New York

OXFORD UNIVERSITY PRESS AUSTRALIA

Oxford   New York
Athens   Auckland   Bangkok   Bombay
Calcutta   Cape Town   Dar es Salaam   Delhi
Florence   Hong Kong   Istanbul   Karachi
Kuala Lumpur   Madras   Madrid   Melbourne
Mexico City   Nairobi   Paris   Singapore
Taipei   Tokyo   Toronto

and associated companies in
Berlin   Ibadan

OXFORD is a trade mark of Oxford University Press

National Library of Australia
Cataloguing-in-Publication data:

Australian love stories: an anthology.

Includes index.
ISBN 0 19 553 772 6.

1. Love stories, Australian. I. Goldsworthy, Kerryn,
1953–.

A823.085

Edited by Jo McMillan
Cover design by Steve Randles
Text design by Steve Randles
Cover photograph from Arthur Boyd born Australia 1920
   Romeo and Juliet Polyptych: detail 1963–64
   earthenware. Presented by the National Gallery of
   Victoria Women's Association, 1965.
   National Gallery of Victoria, Melbourne
Typeset by Desktop Concepts P/L, Melbourne
Printed through OUP China
Published by Oxford University Press,
253 Normanby Road, South Melbourne, Australia

Contents

Introduction

At first the words 'love story' suggest the kind of story that begins with 'boy meets girl' and ends with 'happily ever after'. The harnessing of desire, and of desire's great powers, in the service of the social order is celebrated in such stories: in them the dangerous forces of sexuality are contained, or at least seen to be contained, within the family and within the social structures of which the family is a basic unit.

But a bit more thought calls to mind Cathy and Heathcliff, Romeo and Juliet, Rhett and Scarlett, Tristan and Isolde, Othello and Desdemona, Oscar Wilde and Lord Alfred Douglas, Edward VIII of England and Wallis Simpson: famous lovers, real or imagined, who could not be further from the happy stereotype that most people hanker after and that most, at least for a while, achieve. The great love stories that everyone remembers are those in which desire confronts and challenges the social order and eventually, sometimes spectacularly, loses.

This book contain both kinds of stories, and some others as well. Many quite deliberately confront or subvert the conventions of the happy ending or of the grand tragedy, and use that confrontation as a way of saying something about love, or about storytelling, or about Australia. Distance, hardship, landscape, and the particulars of history have all played their part in the evolution of Australian gender roles and relations.

It has been argued that the short story in general, and the love story in particular, are forms that privilege the personal over the political, and the private over the public. But there is a limit to the usefulness of such simple divisions. The personal — as the last few decades have taught us, if we didn't already know — *is* political, and public and private life cannot be so neatly disentangled; apart from anything else, the conditions of the former usually determine the quality of the latter, sometimes (as, for example, in the case of the several stories in this book that deal with the Second World War) to a dramatic extent. As these and other stories here demonstrate, the developments, trajectories and resolutions of romantic love all constitute a process of continuing negotiation between private, personal or emotional issues, and public, political or social ones. And, far from being any kind of timeless human universal, romantic love as represented in these stories is firmly grounded in time, place, and society.

The literary theorist and critic Terry Eagleton, writing about *Wuthering Heights*, has pointed out that 'the institution of the family is founded upon a potentially anarchic force — sexual desire — which it must nevertheless strictly regulate':[1] this is the paradox at the heart of romantic love. Marriage and family are its sanctioned and usually wished-for end, yet marriage and family sanitise, domesticate and regulate it, and in the process often kill it off altogether; and 'unregulated' or illicit desire can destroy marriage as surely as marriage can destroy desire. Many love stories, and many of those in this book, present marriage quite directly as somehow the opposite of sexual and romantic love; the romantic or erotic ideal is remote from the concerns of everyday domestic life. It seems profoundly unlikely, for example, that James Pratt in Hugh Atkinson's story 'The Jumping Jeweller of Lavender Bay' will ever settle down in the suburbs with the naked blonde, or, if he does, that she will be willing or able to cook his breakfast egg correctly. 'I am gunna get married,' says Miss Slattery to her exotic demon lover in Patrick White's story, 'and have a washing-machine'.

These somewhat gloomy representations of marriage may be partly a result of the literary form involved. Love poetry is usually a lyric expression of emotion or thought at a single point in time, but a story has a sequence of events and things have to happen in it, and most love stories track some point of crisis and resolution in the narrative of love. In a number of the stories presented here, one of the protagonists is already married (usually the man; could it be that, even today, writers find it harder to elicit readerly sympathy for an unfaithful wife?), and the love affair is leading away from marriage rather than towards it. Of course, there are exceptions: Ethel Anderson's 'Murder!' and Christina Stead's 'Street Idyll' celebrate married love, while Brian Matthews's 'Crested Pigeons' and Carmel Bird's 'Maytime Fair' mourn its passing. But on the whole, a 'happy marriage' has few crises of the kind that might provide the stuff of love stories; the best way to get a plot out of love is to give it something to struggle against, and that is usually some kind of rule or law. It can be the rules of marriage, or, as in Tim Herbert's 'Pumpkin Max', the rules of an already transgressive sub-culture. It can be the law of a stern father, as in John Morrison's 'To Margaret'; of a socially ambitious mother, as in Olga Masters's 'Stan and Mary, Mary and Stan'; or of the police, the judiciary and the empire, as in Delia Falconer's 'Republic of Love'.

Transgression, then, makes for a good love story, as do disorder and anarchy. *'Prohibeo'*, writes the Catholic schoolgirl on her way to meet the dark, middle-aged stranger in Thea Astley's 'Getting There', *'prohibere, prohibui, prohibitum'*. 'There is danger in such disorder,' reflects Jenny in Christina Stead's 'Street Idyll', thinking of the strength of her passion for her beloved husband of almost forty years. 'Was it my fault?' asks the narrator of Helen Garner's 'What the Soul Wants': forbidden to look at her lover, she has disobeyed and held up the candle to his sleeping face; and she will be ferociously punished, as will he. In Beth Yahp's 'The Red Pearl', transitional characters on the mysterious fringes of society make love in a room above a bar 'with the promise of *transposition*: of anonymity, abandonment, delirium, dream'.

Perhaps the clearest example of rule-breaking in love and its consequences for the social order can be found in William Ferguson's 'Nanya', an extraordinary and apparently true story in which the runaway lovers, prevented by tribal law from marrying, found an inbred and degenerate lost tribe. 'We both know,' says Nanya to his lover, 'that it is against the law'. The converse, as it were, of this story is M. Barnard Eldershaw's 'Christmas', set in Canberra at the arid and sterile seat of government, which argues the drought-breaking power of love to transform an ailing society.

Other stories show lovers struggling and failing to cross barriers of class or race: in Murray Bail's 'A, B, C, D, E...' and, less obviously, Patrick White's 'Miss Slattery and Her Demon Lover', cultural contrasts first bring the lovers together and then push them apart. In 'To Margaret' and Lily Brett's 'Something Shocking', illicit love is revealed in acts of writing that are themselves transgressive: the humble Dutch gardener in 'To Margaret' writes a floral message to his employer's daughter, while the betrayed wife in 'Something Shocking' writes her wrongs in Hot Ochre gloss paint on the outside front wall of the marital home: 'My husband is shtooping a shikse'. In both stories, unacceptable truths about forbidden love are written like graffiti across the surface of respectable Melbourne suburbs.

The 'Australianness' of these stories is rarely obtrusive, but many of them are strongly evocative of place and landscape. 'Republic of Love' maps the geography of Ned Kelly country through the stages of his outlaw career: Jerilderie, Glenrowan, Mount Disappointment and the Puzzle Ranges; lorikeets and lightning and Salvation Jane. The houses, gardens and weather in Venero Armanno's 'I Asked the Angels for Inspiration' couldn't be anywhere but Queensland. Sydney Harbour is practically a character in this book: in 'The Jumping Jeweller of Lavender Bay', James Pratt disappears into it; in 'Miss Slattery and Her Demon Lover', Tibor Szabo hurls into it an entire roast leg of lamb ('with pumpkin and two other veg'); in Amy Witting's 'A Bottle of Tears', a nameless woman looks down at it from the zoo and says '*Wunderschön*' — wondrous, beautiful — and, in doing so, unknowingly changes the course of a stranger's life.

The stories were initially chosen on broadly based grounds of literary quality and general appeal from a large number found by systematic searching through bibliographies, journals, anthologies, and collections. Once I had amassed a large pile of material that qualified as love stories, had decided to include only one story per writer, and had got over my discomfort at the comparatively small number of male writers represented in the pile, some oddly assorted criteria for further choice came into play. A few of the stories were simply too long, and not quite effective or gripping enough to justify the space. The late-nineteenth-century stories, in particular, were told at a very leisurely pace, and this is why Rosa Praed's 'The Bushman's Love Story', and Tasma's 'How a Claim was Nearly Jumped in Gum-Tree Gully' (which also contained numerous obscure classical references requiring extensive footnotes to make sense of the story) were weeded out in the final round. Yvonne Rousseau's recent story 'Possum Lover', a wonderful but very long piece of speculative fiction about a were-possum (and I mean a were-possum in labour), was also reluctantly omitted in the final stages lest it squeeze out too many other things, as was Elizabeth Jolley's 'Adam's Bride'.

Sometimes, in the original pile, whole decades went unrepresented, while single years yielded up five or six stories; here I did further searching and tried to make choices that would render chronological representation as even as possible without affecting the quality of the collection. Some stories I would have liked to include had been anthologised many times before; given the choice of several Helen Garner stories, I went for the most mysterious and troubling, which is also the one that has had the least exposure.

Some readers may find the gay and lesbian writing quite confronting, particularly the explicitness and violence of the Frank Moorhouse story: Moorhouse, like Garner, provided me with several possible choices — most of them 'straight' stories — but in the end 'The Letters' was irresistible, partly because of its uncompromising treatment of powerful material and partly because the issue of sexual identity in writing is a complicated one and I wanted to represent it that way here. Who's queer, who's straight, who's doing what with whom and who's writing about it can all be very hard questions to answer — as 'The Letters' and Susan Hampton's 'The Lobster Queen', as well as the stories by Tim Herbert, Robert Dessaix, and Patrick White all demonstrate. And the seventeen-year-old female narrator's announcement in Judith Wright's 'The Nature of Love' that she has 'fallen in love

... with Lisa' would have been unconsciously, effortlessly nor-malised by the reading practices of 1966 as 'only a manner of speaking', but would be read quite differently today.

Since romance fiction is a genre usually associated in both its popular-culture and high-culture forms with women writers (and readers), I suppose I should have been less surprised at how hard it was to find good love stories by contemporary male writers. Frank Dalby Davison's 'Lady With a Scar' offers one possible rea-son for this, showing a boy unable to express feeling except through non-verbal — and, here, permanently damaging — means. A number of male writers whose work I like very much do not appear in this collection because I simply couldn't find one good love story among the lot. There were some powerful, if rather hard-boiled, stories about sex and desire, but their emo-tional basis was usually negative: self-loathing, hostility, fear or rage. One hopes that this gap is only generational (and fears that Hemingway has a lot to answer for); Venero Armanno, the only contemporary male writer in this collection writing about love in a loving way as well as in lush, unselfconscious, erotically charged detail, is well under forty years old.

The Aboriginal material included here struck me as having a special kind of integrity; rather than include 'love stories' by Aboriginal writers trying to work within the confines of the Western genre (of which, in any case, there are few; it was easier to find autobiographical writing about love by writers like Ruby Langford and Archie Weller, but autobiography was not what I was looking for), I chose the two very different pieces by Jimmy Pike and William Ferguson, both of which are working within generic, and other, rules of their own.

If the collection seems heavily weighted at the contemporary end it must be remembered that the number of writers and the quantity and variety of writing in Australia continued to increase throughout the nineteenth and twentieth centuries and then underwent a population explosion in the mid-1970s after the establishment of the Australia Council, while the lifting of cen-sorship restrictions at around the same time provided new freedoms in the writing of love stories. There is, in the writing of the last twenty years, simply a great deal more from which to choose.

Finally, like all anthologists, I consulted my own feelings and experience and made choices accordingly. Some of the stories contained an unforgettable image: the lover's initials bloodily carved into the flesh of a young arm; the warm loaf of bread scooped out to make a baby's cradle; the flower seeds planted to spell out, once they come up, a woman's name. Others had a phrase or sentence about love that grabbed the heart, or the memory, or both. 'Harry didn't understand why he had put his hand on Diane's shoulder that night at Florentino's.' 'I am singing to myself.' 'His hair so heavy and black.' 'By the air they carry with them, and the look of gold, I know that is how they feel.' 'She did not know she was singing.' 'It's a dark thing he feels for her.' 'Night of beauty, night of miracles.' 'In the twilight he saw a relationship of chin and shoulder that was like the first glimpse of the person one is going to love.' 'Was it my fault?' ' "Let's go back to the hotel," he said.' 'I didn't mean to hurt you, sweetheart.' 'Because everything about her — her legs sheathed in stockings, her pale fingers, her baby-talk, her rhythmic walk, the way she put spectacles on to read a book, her yawns, her shoulder-blades, everything, everything, everything was utterly beautiful.'

As this is intended to be an anthology of stories, rather than of writers, and as one of my concerns was to map changes and shifts in the genre and in various aspects of Australian literary production, the stories have been ordered chronologically according to the date they were published. Because many writers make major changes to stories between their publication in a magazine or journal and their appearance in a collection of stories, I have used the final version of the story and given the date of publication as the year it was published in a collection of stories by the writer, in order to give the version that the writer preferred. Where the story has not been published in a collection, the date given is that of first publication.

A few stories, however, resisted this kind of ordering. William Ferguson's 'Nanya' is his version of a story that was told to him in 1920, which is therefore in a sense the 'date' of the story and I have ordered it accordingly. Christina Stead's 'Street Idyll' and M. Barnard Eldershaw's 'Christmas' were both published in posthumous collections; the former story was thirteen years old and the latter at least fifty-six, so for the sake of historical coherence they have been placed differently. 'Street Idyll' has been ordered by the date of its first publication, 1972. 'Christmas', according to the scrupulous scholarship of Robert Darby, was intended to be published around 1932, in a short-story collection that never materialised. In the end, 'Christmas' was not published until 1988, when Darby edited a collection of M. Barnard Eldershaw stories called *But Not for Love*; Darby's introduction to this collection contains a detailed account of the provenance of these stories. 'Christmas', an undated manuscript in the Mitchell Library in Sydney, was probably written around 1931 and has been ordered here according to that date. Delia Falconer's 'Republic of Love' was written in 1995 for inclusion in this collection, and is published here for the first time.

My warmest thanks go to Peter Rose for his enthusiasm when (and since) I first suggested putting this book together, and for his support, advice and readiness to confer. For suggestions about the book's contents I am also grateful to numerous colleagues from ASAL, AUSTLIT and the Melbourne University English Department, particularly Patrick Buckridge, Ra Foxton, Tseen Ling Khoo, Alan Lawson, Chris Lee, Sue Martin, Philip Morrissey, Paul Salzman, Lucy Sussex, and Meg Tasker. Delia Falconer was grace itself under relentless editorial pressure to produce a story especially for this collection. In this project, as in all projects, I have been supported by the generous friendship and wise counsel of Paul Salzman and Susan Bye, of Judy Brett, and of Robyn Groves.

In return for the copy of Colin Thiele's *Favourite Australian Stories* that Santa brought me in 1965, this collection of Australian love stories is dedicated to my parents, who met in Sydney in 1945, both in uniform, both eighteen, and who have been together ever since.

Note

[1] Quoted in James Kavanagh, *Emily Brontë*, Basil Blackwell, Oxford, 1985, p. x.

Poor Jo

He was the ostler at Coppinger's, and they called him Poor Jo.

Nobody knew whence he came; nobody knew what misery of early mutilation had been his. He had appeared one evening, a wandering swag-man, unable to speak, and so explain his journey's aim or end — able only to mutter and gesticulate, making signs that he was cold and hungry, and needed fire and food. The rough crowd in Coppinger's bar looked on him kindly, having for him that sympathy which marked physical affliction commands in the rudest natures. Poor Jo needed all their sympathy: he was a dwarf, and dumb.

Coppinger — bluff, blasphemous, and good-hearted soul dispatched him with many oaths to the kitchen, and when the next morning the deformed creature volunteered in his strange sign-speech to do some work that might 'pay of his lodging', sent him to help the ostler that ministered to King Cobb's coach horses. The ostler — for lack of a better name perhaps — called him 'Jo', and Coppinger, finding that the limping mute, though he could speak no word of human language, yet had a marvellous power of communication with horseflesh, installed him as under-ostler and stable-helper, with a seat at the social board and a wisp of clean straw in King Cobb's stable.

'I have taken him on,' said Coppinger, when the township cronies met the next night in the bar.

'Who?' asked the cronies, bibulously disregarding grammar.

'Poor Jo,' said Coppinger.

The sympathetic world of Bullocktown approved the epithet, and the deformed vagabond, thus baptised, was known as Poor Jo ever after.

He was a quiet fellow enough. His utmost wrath never sufficed to ruffle a hair on the sleek back of King Cobb's horses. His utmost mirth never went beyond an ape-like chuckle that irradiated his pain-stricken face, as a stray gleam of sunshine lights up the hideousness of the gargoyle on some old cathedral tower. It was only when 'in drink' that Poor Jo became a spectacle for strangers to wonder at. Brandy maddened him, and when thus excited his misshapen soul would peep out of his sunken fiery eyes, force his grotesque legs to dance unseemly sarabands, and compel his pigeon breast to give forth monstrous and ghastly utterances, that might have been laughs were they not so much like groans of a brutish despair that had in it a strange chord of human suffering. Coppinger was angry when the poor dwarf was thus tortured for the sport of the whiskey-drinkers, and once threw Frolicksome Fitz into the muck-midden for inciting the cripple to sputter forth his grotesque croonings and snatches of gruesome merriment. 'He won't be fit for nothin' to-morrer,' was the excuse Coppinger made for his display of feeling. Indeed, on the days that followed these debauches, Poor Jo was sadly downcast. Even his beloved horses failed to cheer him, and he would sit red-eyed and woe-begone on the post-and-rail fence, like some dissipated bird of evil omen.

The only thing he seemed to love, save his horses, was Coppinger, and Coppinger was proud of this simple affection. So proud was he, that when he discovered that whenever Miss Jane, the sister of Young Barham, from Seven Creeks, put her pony into the stable, the said pony was fondled and slobbered over and caressed by Poor Jo, he felt something like a pang of jealousy.

Miss Jane was a fair maiden, with pale gold hair, and lips like the two streaks of crimson in the leaf of the white poppy. Young Barham, owner of Seven Creeks Station — you could see the lights in the house windows from Coppinger's — had brought her from town to 'keep house for him', and she was the beauty of the country side. Frolicksome Fitz, the pound-keeper, was at first inclined to toast an opposition belle (Miss Kate Ryder, of Ryder's Mount), but when returning home one evening by the new dam he saw Miss Jane jump Black Jack over the post and wire into [the] home station paddock, he forswore his allegiance.

'She rides like an angel,' said pious Fitz, and next time he met her told her so. She stared, smiled, and cantered away.

Now, this young maiden, so fair, so daring, and so silent, came upon the Bullocktown folk like a new revelation. The old Frenchman at the Melon Patch vowed tearfully that she had talked French to him like one of his countrywomen, and the school-master, Mr Frank Smith — duly certificated under the Board of Education — reported that she played the piano divinely, singing like a seraph the while. As nobody played (except at euker) in Bullocktown, this judgment was undisputed. Coppinger swore, slapping with emphasis his mighty thigh, that Miss Jane was a lady, and when he said that he said everything. So whenever Miss Jane visited the township she was received with admiration. Coppinger took off his hat to her, Mr Frank Smith walked to the station every Sunday afternoon to see her, and Poor Jo stood afar off, and worshipped her, happy if she bestowed a smile upon him once out of every five times that he held her tiny stirrup.

This taming of Poor Jo was not unnoticed by the whiskey-drinkers, and they came in the course of a month or so to regard the cripple as part of the property of Miss Jane — as they regarded her dog for instance. The schoolmaster, moreover, did not escape taproom comment. He was frequently at Seven Creeks. He bought flowers from the garden there. He sent for some new clothes from Melbourne. He even borrowed Coppinger's bay mare Flirt to ride over to the Sheepwash, and Dick the mailboy — who knew that Coppinger's mare was pigeon-toed — vowed that he had seen another horse's tracks beside hers in the sand of the Rose Gap Road.

'You're a deep-un, Mr Smith,' said Coppinger. 'I found yer out sparking Miss Jane along the Mountain Track. Deny it if yer can?'

But Frank Smith's pale cheek only flushed, and he turned off the question with a laugh. It was Poor Jo's eyes that snapped fire in the corner.

So matters held themselves until the winter, when the unusually wet season forbade riding parties of pleasure. It rained savagely that year, as we all remember, and Bullocktown in rainy weather is not a cheerful place. Miss Jane kept at home, and Poor Jo's little eyes, wistfully turned to the station on the hill, saw never her black pony cantering round the corner of Archy Cameron's hayrick.

A deeper melancholy seemed to fall on the always melancholy township. Coppinger's cronies took their 'tots' in silence, steaming the while, and Coppinger himself would come gloomily to the door, speculating upon evil unless the leaden rain curtain lifted.

But it did not lift, and rumour of evil came. Up the country, by Parsham and Merrydale, and Black Adder's Gully, there were whole tracts of grassland under water. The neighbouring station of Hall's, in the mountains, was a swamp. The roads were bogged for miles — Tim Doolan was compelled to leave his dray and bullocks at Tom and Jerry's, and ride for his life before the advancing waters. The dams were brimming at Quartzborough, St Roy reservoir was running over. It was reported by little M'Cleod, the sheep-dealer, that the old bridge at the Little Glimmera had been carried away. It was reported that Old Man Horn, whose residence overlooked the river, had fastened a bigger hook to a longer pole (there was a legend extant to the effect that Old Man Horn had once hooked a body from the greedy river, and after emptying its pockets, had softly started it down stream again), and was waiting behind his rickety door, rubbing his withered hands gleefully. Young Barham rode over to Quartzborough to get M'Compass, the shire engineer, to look at his new dam. Then the coach stopped running, and then Flash Harry, galloping through the township at night, like the ghost rider in Bürger's ghastly ballad, brought the terrible news — THE FLOODS WERE UP, AND THE GLIMMERA BANK AND BANK AT THE OLD CROSSING PLACE! [*sic*]

'It will be here in less than an hour,' he shouted, under Coppinger's red lamps; 'make for the high ground if you love your lives;' and so, wet, wild-eyed, and white, splashed off into the darkness, if haply he might warn the poor folk down the river of the rushing death that was coming upon them.

Those who were there have told of the horrors of that night. How the muddy street, scarce reclaimed from the river bed, was suddenly full of startled half-dressed folk. How Coppinger's was crowded to the garret. How the schoolmaster dashed off, stumbling through the rain, to warn them at Seven Creeks. How bullies grew pale with fear, and men hitherto mild of speech and modest of mien, waxed fiery-hot with wrath at incapacity, and fiercely self-assertive in relegating fools to their place in the bewildered social economy of that general Overturn. How when the roaring flood came down, bearing huge trees, fragments of houses, grotesquely terrible waifs and strays of household furniture, upon its yellow and turbid bosom, timid women grew brave, and brave men hid their faces for a while. How Old Man Horn saved two lives that night. How Widow Ray's cottage — with her light still burning in the window sill — was swept off, and carried miles down stream. How Archy Cameron's hayrick stranded in the middle of the township. How forty drowned sheep were floated into the upper windows of the Royal Mail. How Patsy Barnes' cradle, with its new-born occupant sucking an unconscious thumb, was found jammed into the bight of the windlass in Magby's killing-yard. How all this took place has been told, I say, by those who were present, and needs not repeating. But one thing which took place shall be chronicled here. When the terror and confusion were somewhat stilled, and Coppinger, by dint of brandy and blankets, had got some strength and courage into the half-naked, shivering creatures clustered in his ark, a sudden terrible tremor went through the crowd like an electric current. In some mysterious way, no one knew how originating or by what fed and fostered, men came to hear that Barham's dam was breaking! That is to say, that in ten minutes or less all the land that lay between Coppinger's and the river would be a roaring waste of water — that in less than ten minutes the Seven Creeks Station, with all its inmates, would be swept off the face of the earth, and that if Coppinger's escaped it would be a thing to thank God for.

After the first sharp agony of self-apprehension, one thought came to each — Miss Jane.

'Good God,' cries Coppinger, 'can nobody go to her?'

Two men volunteered to go.

'It's no good,' said faint-hearted Riley, the bully of the bar. 'The dam'll burst twice over 'fore you reach the station.'

It was likely.

'I'll go myself,' cries brave old Coppinger; but his wife clung to his arm, and held him back with all the weight of her maternity.

'I have it,' says Coppinger; 'Poor Jo'll go. Where is he?'

No one had seen him. Coppinger dashed down the stairs, splashed through the yard into the stable. The door was open, and Blackboy, the strongest of King Cobb's horses, was missing. Coppinger flashed round the lantern he held. The mail boy's saddle had disappeared and faintly mingling with the raging wind and roaring water, died the rapid strokes of a horse's feet.

Poor Jo had gone.

The house was already flooded out, and they were sitting — so I was told — with their arms around each other, not far from where poor Barham's body was found, when the strange mis-shapen figure bestriding the huge horse splashed desperately through the water that was once the garden.

'Rescue!' cried Frank, but she only clung to him the closer.

Poor Jo bit his lips at sight of the pair, and then, so Frank Smith averred, flung him one bitter glance of agony and dropping his deformed body from the back of the reeking horse, held out the bridle with a groan.

In moments of supreme danger one divines quickly. Frank placed his betrothed upon the saddle, and sprang up behind her. If ever Blackboy was to prove his mettle he must prove it then, for already the lightning revealed a thin stream of water trickling over the surface of the dam.

'But what is to become of *you*?' cries Miss Jane.

Poor Jo, rejecting Frank's offered hand, took that of Miss Jane, patted it softly, and let it fall. He pointed to Coppinger's red light, and then to the black wall of the dam. No man could mistake the meaning of that trembling finger and those widely-opened eyes. They said, 'Ride for your lives! ride!' plainer than the most eloquent tongue owned by Schoolmaster could speak.

It was no time for sentiment, and for the schoolmaster there was but one life to be saved or lost that night. He drove his bare heels into the good horse's sides, and galloped down the hill. 'God bless you, Jo!' cried Miss Jane. Poor Jo smiled, and then falling on his knees waited, straining his ears to listen. It was not ten minutes, but it seemed ten hours, when through the roar he heard a distant shout go up. They were saved. Thank God! And then the dam burst with a roar like thunder, and he was whirled away amid a chaos of tree trunks.

They found his little weak body four days afterwards, battered and bruised almost out of recognition; but his great brave soul had gone on to Judgment.

Miss Jackson

He stopped suddenly and stared in front of him. Then he turned to me and said: 'Do you see that girl?'

We were in King Street, Sydney; it was about four o'clock on a lovely autumn afternoon, and Murdoch and I were taking a stroll. Murdoch is a very old friend of mine. We were at Marlborough together, and again at University College, London, when he was a student of medicine and I a student of all things in general and nothing in particular. I had just lit on him in Sydney, lately married, and a flourishing young suburban medico, and we were full of reminiscence and narrative. We had lunch at Compagnoni's, and were sauntering along when, turning round one of the corners of Pitt and King Streets, he stopped suddenly, stared in front of him, turned to me and said:

'Do you see that girl?'

I glanced in the direction indicated by his eyes and the wave of the hand holding his cigar, and saw a lady standing in front of a jeweller's window looking carelessly in, rather with the air of a person who was whiling away the moments of an expected rendezvous than of a passer-by attracted by the wares exposed. I knew her at once. It was Mrs Medwin. Mrs Medwin is the wife — the young second wife — of one of our best-known Victorian squatters and politicians. Perhaps she was here on the return from her honeymoon. It was only six or seven months ago that Medwin married her, and the two went off at once for a trip to England, purposing to return by New York and San Francisco.

We were now directly opposite her, and, as she was still looking in at the window, it seemed improbable that she would see us. A small group of pedestrians, coming from the opposite direction upon us, compelled me to step ahead of Murdoch. At that very moment I saw, by the glance I cast over my left shoulder as I advanced, that she turned rather suddenly. She almost ran into him. By the time I had wheeled round it was all over. Their eyes had met; an extraordinary expression had flashed over her beautiful face; he had raised his hat, she had bowed her head slightly, and then he was with me and we were walking on together again and away from her. That impression of her face as their eyes met is as vivid to me at this moment as it was then.

I behold her before me as I write. She never had much colour, but you could not call her pale. I have seen Italian women at Naples with just her warm, moulded features, like olive-hued marble. Her eyes had a singular look that reminded me of the jewelled, enamelled eyes in certain statues. Whenever I saw her the prevalent colour of her dress was always something metallic — golden or silver or bronze. Probably she did it on purpose. She knew it suited her peculiar style of beauty. I saw her married, and the orange and glistering while of her toilet were like solid bronze and silver. I never thought her cold. She gave me the impression of passion in a calm and deep slumber, but I confess that that sudden glimpse of her face as she saw Murdoch, and the subtle heightening of its colour — not a blush or even a flush, it was so faint and evenly distributed — made her, for the first time, strike me as not only a beautiful statue, but a lovely woman.

He did not repeat his question, and I did not answer it for quite a minute. We walked on side by side. Then I said:

'Girl? You would scarcely call her a girl. She is every inch of her a woman. She is Mrs Medwin.'

'Mrs Medwin? Mrs Medwin?' he repeated, vaguely. 'I know the name somehow.'

'Medwin is one of the richest men in Victoria or Australia. His first wife was, perhaps, the best-known personage in Melbourne "society". She ruled it like an empress. Imagine the luck of that great, hulking brute to have found such a woman as that as her successor! Did you know her in England?' I asked mildly, after having eased him off with this.

But he still refused to be communicative.

I tried a second flight.

'It seems amazing,' I said, 'to light on a face or form like hers here. She is the sort of feminine type one meets in the drawing-rooms of old superb civilisations, one of the ladies of Imperial Rome, or mediæval Florence or Venice, at the court of Henri Quatre, or, perchance, at some Viennese embassy. What has fecund splendour like this to do with the "ghastly, thin-cheeked" aperies of this tenth-rate pseudo-civilisation of ours here in Australia? The music to which such a woman walks is that of a Galuppi or a Chopin; and, lo, Australian social life thrills to the vulgar temerity of barbarous iron-framed pianos, usually bought on the time-payment system! She seemed quite unconscious of us all, thank Heaven! Everyone was looking at her, and she paid about as much heed to them as Faustina did when she sat with poor dear Marcus Aurelius in the Imperial box at the amphitheatre, and the Roman mob united with Roman "society" in canvassing her character.'

'That is beastly high-flown,' he said, a little irritably, 'I should have thought five years of Australia would have toned down your exuberant fancy a bit more, old man.'

We went on right up King Street, and, following some imperceptible impulse, passed over into Hyde Park. We entered a shady alley and paced on side by side, smoking in silence.

'How she is changed,' he said reflectively, 'and yet not changed. She is just the same — exactly the same. It is only that she is richer, riper. She has finer clothes now, and has been living well. She was inclined to be even a bit skinny then. I came out in the same ship with that girl,' he added, to me more particularly. 'Her name was Jackson, Miss Jackson.'

'It was,' I said.

'I was doctor on the ship — a sailer, one of the old Blackwall liners. We came by the Cape, of course. There were thirteen of us in the saloon, and the skipper and first and second mates. Miss Jackson was one. She came out alone in the skipper's charge, or his wife's, or both, and she had a cabin to herself. The ship had many cabins but few passengers.'

He paused for a moment. He was speaking in rather a dreamy way now, looking in front of him as if at the rising shapes of his memories. Then he suddenly seemed to decide to sit down on an empty bench under a dense-leaved Moreton Bay fig, and I took my place beside him.

'I will tell you about her,' he said, 'what I know. It isn't much. We were rather above the average collection of people on board — for a sailer. There were only five women; the rest men. There was the skipper's wife, a stout, rather showy, but at bottom motherly old soul; the wife of one of the passengers, also stout and showy, and addicted to divers liquors; an old maid of a long and lean but rather nice type, reading nice books and playing nice music; her cabin-companion, the grown-up daughter of another of the passengers, an old colonist who had made his pile; and, lastly, Miss Jackson. Among the men there were two sets, both of which, however, were on very good terms with each other. There was the sporting set, the fellows who played "nap" perpetually; got up deck games; fished for sharks or albatrosses, and the rest. And there was another set that was quieter, read the better class of novels, played chess, and talked rather "intelektooal." The women had a tendency to keep to themselves. There was one fellow who understood the whole lot, and in his quiet way got on with the whole lot. His name was Allenson.'

He paused again. Then, turning and looking at me, said:

'Allenson was just a devil. He was rather like you.'

I laughed.

'Thank you,' I said.

'Not like what you are *now*,' he proceeded, 'but like what you were at Marlborough, and even a bit at the College. He was what you call a thorough gentleman. He was always quite at his ease, calm, courteous, with lots of tact. He never showed you he despised you, or, rather, did not consider you of the very least importance — in fact, thought himself almost of another flesh and blood to you; but that was what in his heart he must have felt. He never said so, but I am quite certain he was of some swell family. I have no idea what was bringing him out in a Blackwall liner to Australia. Perhaps he had been overdoing things in town, and had made up his mind to a health-voyage and some quiet travel at the other end. I'll admit that he was the best-looking man I ever saw. He was a bit "intelektooal" too. When he came on board he looked pale and rather worn, but this soon passed and presently he was magnificent. He dressed finely — in the very best taste, and he was the only perfectly made man I ever met. I can't tell you how I hated him!'

He looked at me again.

'If you could have been like him,' he said, 'you would have been happy. He was your ideal — your ideal in the old school and college days. And this Allenson turned his eyes on Miss Jackson.'

He threw away the end of his cigar, frowned, and drove his hands into his pockets.

'You know her?' he said. 'You met her, perhaps, before she married Medwin?'

'I met her once or twice,' I said, 'but it was nothing.'

'Well,' he proceeded, 'I think she was even nicer then than she is now. She wasn't so beautiful. She has bloomed out since. She was rather thin, and did not seem robust. She was poor, going out, an orphan, to a new land, to a strange home, with a distant relation who had agreed to take her. The skipper knew the man — a half-uncle or something. He lived up near Sandhurst, and was manager of a mine. Her outlook was far from bright. I myself,' he said, with a sudden rapidity, 'had no notion of what might be in store for me, for I wasn't such a fool as to think fortunes were to be got for the mere seeking in Australia nowadays — but — but — Well, what am I talking about?'

'You were talking about Miss Jackson,' I said, incidentally wondering to myself what sort of 'girl' was the 'girl' who presided over the domestic arrangements in that medical suburban home where I was to partake of dinner that evening.

'Allenson,' he proceeded again, 'was a terribly dangerous sort of man for women. No woman can ever get over the fact of a genuinely good-looking man. Even if he's a fool and a stick, they can't get over it — and what can they do, what *do* they do, when he is the very reverse of a fool and a stick? I watched the devil drop his meshes round that girl day by day, and could effect nothing. I couldn't even quarrel with him. The man witched me as he did everybody. Even the stupid brewer lot — there were three of them — swore by him. They said he was very "affable!" It was sickening!'

He drew his hands out of his pockets in a quick, nervous manner; leant his elbows on his knees, and bent forward.

'She got a way, presently,' he said, 'of looking up with a curious expression whenever he came to her or spoke to her. I knew what that meant. And yet she was as proud as Lucifer. Anyone could see that. It came out over and over again. I never for a moment imagined that he intended marrying her. Men like that don't marry till they begin to get bald and take an infatuation, a *grande passion* — (you know) — or else they wait till they've got heads as bare as billiard-balls and make fools of themselves. Perhaps he wasn't rich enough. He might have sought the earth through to get a girl to equal her, anyway! I thought he was amusing himself with her — creating an "interest" on the voyage. Not that he seemed bored, but he had a way of sitting in his deck-chair, motionless like a statue, looking in front of him, and I know he must have found us dreadful poor company. Then one night in the tropics I got a shock.'

Once more he paused.

'It was a dark warm evening,' he said, 'no moon and the stars not very bright. It wasn't oppressively hot. There was a steady breeze aft, sending us along at five or six knots an hour — the tail-end of the trades. Most of the passengers were down in the saloon, playing cards, singing or reading. There was nobody on the poop but the man at the wheel and the officer of the watch. I came up for a breath of air and walked down one side of the poop and round by the helm and up the other. I had on indiarubber-soled deck-shoes, and it was so dark, outside of the glare coming from the sides of the saloon sky-lights, that I was upon them before I was aware of it. They were standing below the boat, leaning together, their elbows on the taffrail, and his hand holding hers. I passed on immediately and went below.'

He sat up.

'That was all,' he said 'all I saw of their love-making. I don't know how it went. I could only guess, but that guessing process used to drive me wild. For about a fortnight she looked a different girl, like a rose-bud that had bloomed out into a rose. Then came another change. I could see her day by day suffering torture. And I could say nothing — do nothing. I tried once. It was merely the vaguest expression of sympathy, of kindly feeling. She would not look at me for a week. I suffered torture too. I can't describe it. Especially at nights.'

He paused.

'And so,' he said with a sigh, 'day followed day, and week week, and things went from bad to worse. I saw he was getting tired of her. I used to long to smash his face in. Not that he behaved brutally or rudely to her: I should have done it if he had. No, he was just the same, calm and courteous, only to her it was a little cold and distant, and, so to say, oblivious. We were round the Cape now, and into the roaring forties. Some days we made great runs — 280 or even 300 miles. We had the wind right behind us, bowling us along to Australia at full speed. Then we had a taste of storm for two days with heavy rain.'

He paused once more, and longer than before, sitting looking in front of him at the asphalt of the walk.

'It was the second evening after the storm,' he went on slowly. 'The ship was close-hauled, and heeled over very considerably to leeward. The rain had drawn off a little towards sunset, and three or four of them — the skipper, his wife and the old maid, with one or two of the men — were walking up and down the weather-side of the poop, getting up an appetite for dinner. It grew so dark that you couldn't see more than a few yards clearly in front of you. Every now and then a shower of spray broke over the poop, and this ended in driving the ladies below, but the skipper, one of the young brewers and myself still kept up our walk. At last I had had enough for the nonce, and turned off between the sky-lights and was passing down to the lee-side of the deck when I almost lurched up against Miss Jackson. She was standing with her back to me in just the position as that other time. I did not dare to speak to her, and went on to the ladder. Allenson was coming up it. I drew back without a word, and he mounted and passed me. I went down onto the main deck and hung about, talking with one of the mates. The first bell for dinner hadn't gone yet; so having nothing to do, I went up again by the other ladder on the poop to the skipper and the young brewer, who were still tramping up and down, and fell in with them. We staggered along on the oblique deck and discussed the construction of iron ships, and the future of sail as against steam. About a minute later, as we were all turning by the ladder, we saw the form of a woman come out from round the first sky-light. It was so dark that it was possible only to guess even so much as that. She came along steadily to us, and was with us as we made our first few steps forward together. I knew who it was of course, at once. It was Miss Jackson. She addressed the skipper.

'Captain,' she said in a quiet voice, 'I heard a cry, I think. Is every one on board?'

The skipper was incredulous.

'Where did you hear it?' he asked, in a light tone.

'Along by the helmsman,' she said. 'Someone passed a moment ago, and sat on the rail.'

We left her and went aft to the helmsman.

'If it's any one,' said the skipper, 'it's Mr Allenson. I warned him only yesterday about sitting on the taffrail.'

'The helmsman said that four or five minutes ago someone had come and sat on the taffrail behind him, and then went forward a bit, but it was dark and he'd such a lot to do to keep her head up to the wind that he didn't notice who it was. That was all. No one ever saw any more of Allenson.'

He stopped suddenly and showed no sign of continuing.

'What do you mean?' I asked. 'How did he fall overboard?'

'I don't know. No one ever knew. No one was ever sure, even, that he fell overboard that evening at that time, or when. The last time he was seen (unless the helmsman saw him) was up on the fo'c'sle half-an-hour or so before. Several people saw him there.'

'But how can that be,' I asked, 'since you yourself said you saw him come up the ladder onto the lee side of the poop by Miss Jackson?'

'Did I say so? I never said so at the investigation we held.'

He got up.

'Let's go on,' he said.

We walked away together.

'But, look here,' I said, 'I don't understand. Do you mean to imply that it was an accident, or that he went down behind the helmsman and sat on the taffrail again, talking to her, and she shoved him over?'

He had taken out another cigar.

'What do I know about it anyway?' he said, biting off the end and spitting it out. 'Can you give us a light?'

HENRY LAWSON

'Some Day'

The two travellers had yarned late in their camp, and the moon was getting low down through the mulga. Mitchell's mate had just finished a rather 'racy' yarn, but it seemed to fall flat on Mitchell; he was in a sentimental mood. He smoked a while, and thought, and then said:

'Ah! there was one little girl that I was properly struck on. She came to our place on a visit to my sister. I think she was the best little girl that ever lived, and about the prettiest. She was just eighteen, and didn't come up to my shoulder; the biggest blue eyes you ever saw, and she had hair that reached down to her knees, and so thick you couldn't span it with your two hands — brown and glossy — and her skin was like lilies and roses. Of course, I never thought she'd look at a rough, ugly, ignorant brute like me, and I used to keep out of her way and act a little stiff towards her; I didn't want the others to think I was gone on her, because I knew they'd laugh at me, and maybe she'd laugh at me more than all. She would come and talk to me, and sit near me at table; but I thought that that was on account of her good nature, and she pitied me because I was such a rough, awkward chap. I was gone on that girl, and no joking; and I felt quite proud to think she was a countrywoman of mine. But I wouldn't let her know that, for I felt sure she'd only laugh.

'Well, things went on till I got the offer of two or three years' work on a station up near the border, and I had to go, for I was hard up; besides, I wanted to get away. Stopping round where she was only made me miserable.

'The night I left they were all down at the station to see me off — including the girl I was gone on. When the train was ready to start she was standing away by herself on the dark end of the platform, and my sister kept nudging me and winking, and fooling about, but I didn't know what she was driving at. At last she said:

'"Go and speak to her, you noodle; go and say good-bye to Edie."'

'So I went up to where she was, and, when the others turned their backs —

'"Well, good-bye, Miss Brown," I said, holding out my hand; "I don't suppose I'll ever see you again, for Lord knows when I'll be back. Thank you for coming to see me off."

'Just then she turned her face to the light, and I saw she was crying. She was trembling all over. Suddenly she said, "Jack! Jack!" just like that, and held up her arms like this.'

Mitchell was speaking in a tone of voice that didn't belong to him, and his mate looked up. Mitchell's face was solemn, and his eyes were fixed on the fire.

'I suppose you gave her a good hug then, and a kiss?' asked the mate.

'I s'pose so,' snapped Mitchell. 'There is some things a man doesn't want to joke about ... Well, I think we'll shove on one of the billies, and have a drink of tea before we turn in.'

'I suppose,' said Mitchell's mate, as they drank their tea, 'I suppose you'll go back and marry her some day?'

'Some day! That's it; it looks like it, doesn't it? We all say "Some day." I used to say it ten years ago, and look at me now. I've been knocking round for five years, and the last two years constant on the track, and no show of getting off it unless I go for good, and what have I got for it? I look like going home and getting married, without a penny in my pocket or a rag to my back scarcely, and no show of getting them. I swore I'd never go back home without a cheque, and, what's more, I never will; but the cheque days are past. Look at that boot! If we were down among the settled districts we'd be called tramps and beggars; and what's the difference? I've been a fool, I know, but I've paid for it; and now there's nothing for it but to tramp, tramp, tramp for your tucker, and keep tramping till you get old and careless and dirty, and older, and more careless and dirtier, and you get used to the dust and sand, and heat, and flies, and mosquitoes, just as a bullock does, and lose ambition and hope, and get contented with this animal life, like a dog, and till your swag seems part of yourself, and you'd be lost and uneasy and light-shouldered without it, and you don't care a damn if you'll ever get work again, or live like a Christian; and you go on like this till the spirit of a bullock takes the place of the heart of a man. Who cares? If we hadn't found the track yesterday we might have lain and rotted in that lignum, and no one been any the wiser — or sorrier — who knows? Somebody might have found us in the end, but it mightn't have been worth his while to go out of his way and report us. Damn the world, say I!'

He smoked for a while in savage silence; then he knocked the ashes out of his pipe, felt for his tobacco with a sigh, and said:

'Well, I am a bit out of sorts tonight. I've been thinking ... I think we'd best turn in, old man; we've got a long, dry stretch before us tomorrow.'

They rolled out their swags on the sand, lay down, and wrapped themselves in their blankets. Mitchell covered his face with a piece of calico, because the moonlight and wind kept him awake.

The Wind of Destiny

The yachtsmen of the bay had been jubilant for months: this morning they were simply in ecstasies. Aha! it was their turn now. The sporting landsmen, magnates of the Melbourne Club and the great stations, who had had all the fun of the fair hitherto, were out of it this time. Oh, no doubt the new Governor was fond of his 'bike', and of a good horse, and of golf and polo, and the usual things; and, of course, he would be pleased with the triumphal arches and many gorgeous demonstrations of civic welcome and goodwill. But it was here that his heart would be — here, on the blue water, with the brethren of his craft. The country might not know it, but they knew it — mariners all, with their own freemasonry — they and he.

Every yacht of any consequence had been on the slips quite lately — as lately as was compatible with having paint and varnish dry. One or two of the newer models, wanting extra depth for their bulbous keels, were all but too late in their desire to be spick and span for the great occasion, but happily got a west-wind tide to float them up in time. And here they all were, scores and scores of them, as smart as they could be, with their beautiful sails going up, burgee and ensign flying in the breeze of the loveliest morning that could possibly have been provided for a national festival depending wholly on the weather for success. Yesterday it had been cloudy and gloomy, threatening rain; and to-morrow the north wind was to blow a sultry hurricane, opaque with dust; but today was heavenly. No other adjective, as Fanny Pleydell remarked, could describe its all-round perfection.

She was putting on her new white drill with the blue sailor collar, and her new straw hat with *Kittiwake* in gold letters on its new blue ribbon, and joyously addressed her brother through a passage and two open doors. He shouted back that it — the day — was 'ripping', which meant the same thing. The only doubt about it was whether there would be wind enough. There is always that doubt in yachting forecasts — that and the lesser fear of having too much; without which, however, yachting would be no fun at all. The *Kittiwake* (once the property of Adam Drewe, Esq.) was one of the crack boats, and Herbert Lawson — familiarly 'Bert' — was skipper and owner; and he had no mind to make himself a mere St Kilda decoration, as the land-lubbers in authority desired. Let the others tug at moorings if they chose, like wild birds tied by the legs, for hours and hours; the *Kittiwake* intended to fly when she opened her wings — weather permitting — and not submit to be treated as a slab in a canvas wall. She was going to meet the *Sunbeam* on free water, halfway down the bay, which, with any sort of wind, she could easily do, and still be back in time for the landing ceremony. And so Captain Bert kept an eye on tree branches and the set of anchored craft, while giving keen attention to his *toilette*, arraying himself in ducks like the driven snow and flannels like milk, waxing the curly points of his moustache till they tapered smoothly as a ram's horns, trimming his nails, and choosing a silk handkerchief to foam out of his breast pocket, as with a view to being inspected at close quarters through a strong telescope from the *Sunbeam*'s deck.

But he was not dressing himself for the eyes of his vice-sovereign lady. It was for the sake of Lena Pickersgill and Myra Salter that he took such pains to render his handsome person as attractive as possible — and he did not quite know which.

Let me briefly explain. Old Lawson had died not long ago, leaving Herbert master of a good business in Melbourne, a good old family house at Williamstown (with the *Kittiwake* attached), and a most comfortable and even luxurious income for these post-boom days. Sister and brothers were sufficiently provided for — the former married, the latter studying for professions — and there was no widowed mother to take care of and defer to. Herbert was a man of domestic instincts, and turned thirty, and an arbitrary housekeeper bullied him. In short, every circumstance of the case cried aloud to him to take a wife, and he was as ready as possible to do so. But, of course, he wished to be a lover before becoming a husband, and fate had not yet clearly indicated the object he sought. He was a particular young man, as he had every right to be, and much in dread of making a mistake.

Today he had arrived at the stage of choosing Lena and Myra, out of all the girls he knew, as the only possibles. Before night he hoped to have made up a distracted mind as to which of the two was the right one. Chaperoned by young Mrs Pleydell, both were to be guests of the *Kittiwake* for a long, fine day; and surely no better opportunity for the purpose could possibly have been devised.

Miss Salter was a Williamstown young lady, a schoolmate of Fanny Pleydell's, and was to embark with her hostess early. She was Fanny's candidate for the vacancy in the family, and rather suffered as such from the advocacy of her friend. Miss Pickersgill, belonging to a somewhat higher rank of life, lived in town, and was to be taken off from the St Kilda pier. Fanny had not wanted to have Lena asked, and for that reason Bert had firmly insisted on it. For that reason also he was inclined to promote her to the place of honour, rather than a girl whom he felt was being thrust down his throat.

But when he presently met the latter, and helped her into his dinghy with the tenderest air of strong protection, he thought her very sweet. She was a fair, slim thing, shy, unaffected, and amiable, and looked delicious in her white garb. All the ladies on board had to wear white today, to harmonize with the pearly enamel of the boat and her snowy new Lapthorn sails; and Myra had the neatest frock, and the prettiest figure to set it off. And, moreover, as he very well knew, *she* did not run after him when she was let alone.

He rowed her and his sister to the yacht, on which a numerous white-uniformed crew had made all ready for the start, and he sent the dinghy back in charge of his brother to pick up three more lady guests. These three were nobodies as regards this story — a homely aunt and two plain cousins, who had a family right to the suddenly valuable favours at their kinsman's disposal. They made up the number he thought would fill the cockpit comfortably — three on each side.

Mrs Pleydell, as soon as she had gained the deck, plunged below to investigate the matter of supplies; Miss Salter sat down to survey the scene, and the skipper sat down beside her. They had quite twenty minutes of quiet *tête-à-tête*, and to that extent placed Miss Pickersgill at a disadvantage.

'Isn't it a heavenly morning?' — or 'a ripping day', as the case might be — was what they said; and 'I wonder will the breeze hold?' and 'Didn't you feel certain last night that it was changing for rain?' — conversation that had no literary value to make it worth repeating. However, it is not in words that incipient lovers explain themselves, but in the accompaniment to words played by furtive eyes and the corners of lips, and other instruments of nature inaudible to the outward ear. Myra's varying complexion confessed a lot of things, and the amount of intelligence in the horns of that moustache which had been waxed so carefully was wonderful. Indeed, it really seemed, thus early in the day, as if the die were cast. Both looked so handsome and felt so happy, and the weather and all the circumstances were so especially favourable to the development of kindly sentiments.

'I *am* so glad you were able to come,' the young man remarked, whenever they fell upon a pause, changing the emphasis to a fresh word each time. And the young woman put it in all sorts of modest but convincing ways that he was not more glad than she was. Oh, it was a heavenly morning, truly! And Mrs Pleydell and the crew were more and more careful to do nothing to mar the prospect.

But soon the fat aunt and excited cousins arrived, all in white, and as conscious of it as if dressed for a fancy ball, and it was time to make for the rendezvous across the bay. Thither were the yachts of all clubs converging in dozens and scores, like an immense flock of seabirds skimming the azure water, their sails like silver and white satin in the sun. As Bert Lawson steered his own, proudly convinced that she was queen of the company, he named his would-be rivals to his guest, keeping her so close to him that he had to apologise for touching her elbow with the tiller now and then. Occasionally he exchanged an opinion with the crew that the old so-and-so didn't look so bad, and they continually cocked their eyes aloft to where the blue ensign waved in the languid breeze. It wasn't every boat that could dip that flag to the new governor — no indeed!

'Isn't it a pretty sight?' the ladies cried to one another — and it certainly was. Even the prosaic shore was transfigured and glorious — in one place, at least. The St Kilda pier and the hotel, and the steep slope connecting them, smothered all over in green stuff and bunting, and packed with what appeared to be the whole population of the colony, was a striking spectacle as viewed from the sea. The most bigoted Englishman must acknowledge it.

'Oh,' exclaimed Fanny Pleydell, staring through a strong pair of glasses, 'I wouldn't have had you miss it for the world, Myra dear.'

'And yet I nearly did,' the girl replied, glancing at Bert from under her hat brim as he stood over her, intent on business. 'If mother had not been so much better this morning, I could not possibly have left her.'

The skipper ceased shouting to his too numerous men not to crowd the boat's nose so that he could not see it, and dropped soft eyes on his sister's friend. 'Dear, dutiful, unselfish little soul!' he thought. 'That's the sort of woman to make a good wife. That's the girl for me.' It was still not more than twenty minutes to eleven, and he had got as far as that.

But now Miss Pickersgill intervened. She put off from the gorgeous pier, which was not yet closed to the public, in the dinghy of a local friend, in order that the *Kittiwake* should not be burdened with its own. It afterwards transpired that she had engaged to grace the yacht of the local friend, and had thrown him over for Bert Lawson, having no scruples of pride against making use of him, nevertheless. She was a radiant vision in tailor-made cream serge, a full-blooded, full-bosomed, high-coloured, self-confident young beauty, with bold eyes and a vivacious manner, calculated to make any picnic party lively. As she approached, like a queen enthroned, all the male creatures hung forward to gaze and smile, Bert springing to the side to help her over — which was only what she expected and was accustomed to. And she jumped into the midst of the group around the cockpit — four humble-minded admirers and one firm adversary, — chose her place and settled herself, nodding and waving salutations around, as if she were Mrs Bert already.

Myra's heart sank in the presence of so formidable a rival. Myra was the daughter of a retired sea-captain in rather narrow circumstances; Lena's father was a stock-broker, and reputed to roll in money. She had fat gold bangles on her wrists, and a diamond in each ear. She lifted her smart skirt from a lace-frilled petticoat, and the serge was lined with silk. The dejected observer moved to make way for so unquestionable a superior. But Bert detained her with a quiet hand.

'Sit still,' he said. 'There is plenty of room.'

To her surprise and joy, she found he still preferred her near him. It was not money and gold bracelets that could quench her gentle charm.

And now the fun began. The yacht, with every stitch of canvas spread, set out upon her course, determined to be the first to salute her future commodore. There was just enough wind to waft her along with a motion as soft as feathers, as airy as a dream, and the heavenly morning, on the now wider waters, was more heavenly than ever.

'It's our day out, and no mistake,' quoth Miss Pickersgill, in her hearty way. 'Let's have a song, old chap' — to Bert — 'or do something or other to improve the occasion. What do you say, Mrs Pleydell?'

'I,' said the hostess cheerfully, but with tightened lips, 'am going to get you all something to eat.'

'And I'll go and help you,' said Myra, rising hastily.

'Oh, all right — go on; I'll keep 'em alive till you come back. Now then, tune up, everybody! I'll begin. What shall I sing, Mr Lawson?' with a languishing glance at him over her shoulder. '*You* shall choose.'

'I think you'd better whistle,' said Bert, whose eyes were on his sails, and his nose sniffing anxiously.

'All serene. I can do that too. But why had I better whistle?'

'Wind's dying away to nothing, I grieve to say.'

'By George, it is!' his young men echoed, in sympathetic concern. 'If we don't mind, we shall fall between two stools, and be out of everything.'

'What's the odds, so long as you're happy?' was Miss Lena's philosophic response. And they adopted that view. With every prospect of being ignominiously becalmed, out of the track of events in which they had expected to take a leading and historic part, they lolled about the deck and sang songs with rousing choruses — popular ditties from the comic operas of the day — and professed themselves as jolly as jolly could be.

'How fascinating she is!' signed Myra Salter, listening from the little cabin to the voice of the prima donna overhead. 'I don't wonder they all admire her so much!'

'I am quite sure my brother does not admire her,' said Mrs Pleydell with decision. 'He thinks, as I do, that she is a forward minx — he *must*.' Bert's laugh just then came ringing down the stairs. In an interval between two songs, he and Miss Pickersgill were enjoying a bout of 'chaff' — rough wit that crackled like fireworks. 'Of course she amuses him,' said Fanny grudgingly.

'And isn't it lovely to be able to amuse people?' the girl ejaculated, envious still. 'She charms them so that they forget about the wind and everything. She is just the life and soul of the party, Fanny.'

'*I* think she spoils it, Myra. If we don't look out, we shall be having her serenading the Governor with 'He's a jolly good fellow,' or something of that sort. If she attempts to disgrace us with her vulgarity before him, clap your hand over her mouth, my dear. I shall.'

Myra laughed, and was somewhat comforted. But she still thought how lovely it would be to be able to amuse people and take them out of themselves. 'He would never be dull with her,' she thought sadly. 'I am so stupid that I should bore him to death.'

One of Miss Salter's unusual charms, perfectly appreciated by sensible Mrs Pleydell, and not overlooked by Bert, was a sweet humble-mindedness — a rare virtue in these days.

The first of several light luncheons was served on deck, without interrupting the concert. Between gulps of wine and mouthfuls of sandwich, Miss Pickersgill continued to raise fresh tunes, and the crew to shout the choruses, and the audience of fat aunt and simpering cousins to applaud admiringly. It was a case of youth at the prow and pleasure at the helm, and an abandonment of all responsibility. A dear little catspaw came stealing along, and scarcely excited anybody. The yacht gathered way, and began to make knots again, faster and faster, but even that did not draw the light-hearted young folks from their frivolous pastime. Thanks to the syren [*sic*] of St Kilda, they had almost forgotten the errand they were on. It really did not seem to matter much to any one whether he or she met Lord Brassey or not; he had become an incident of the day, rather than its main feature.

Still, the eyes of the crew continually searched the horizon, and presently one man saw smoke where no one else saw anything, and out of that spot a faint blur grew which resolved itself into the *Aramac* with the Governor on board, and the *Ozone* and the *Hygeia*, its consorts. The three boats in a row advancing steadily, under all the steam they could make, were not unimpressive in their way, but the only thing the *Kittiwake* cared to look at was the lovely pillar of white cloud, shining like a pearl, which was recognised as the *Sunbeam* with all sail set. She was bearing off from the Government flotilla, dismissed from their company, superseded and discarded; but to yachtsman's eyes she was a sort of winged angel, a spirit of the sea, and they but grubby mortals by comparison, common and gross.

'Why, why,' they exclaimed, with groans of regret, gazing on the fairy column as if that were all the picture, '*why* didn't they let him come up in her, and let us bring him? What does he want with a lot of cheap-jack politicians *here*? They just spoil it all.'

'It wouldn't be them if they didn't,' some one said, voicing a rather prevalent opinion. And in fact they were spoiling it rather badly on the *Aramac* just then, if all tales be true. They had not needed Miss Pickersgill to show them how to do it.

It was past the hour fixed for the landing ceremonies — and the poor sun-baked crowds ashore would have been dropping with fatigue if there had been room to fall in — when Bert Lawson shouted 'Dip! dip!' to his brother, who held the ensign halliards, and was confused by the excitement of the moment. After all, the *Kittiwake* was first, and proud was every heart aboard when the cocked-hatted figure on the *Aramac*'s bridge saluted her and the flag as if he had known and loved the one as long as the other. Every man and woman was convinced that he stood lost in admiration of her beauty and the way she was manoeuvred. Bert brought her as close as was compatible with proper respect, and they all posed to the best advantage for the Governor's eye, Miss Pickersgill in front.

'*Now*, you fellows,' she panted breathlessly. 'All at once — "See-ee the conqu'ring he-e-e-e-ero" — '

But Mrs Pleydell's hand was up like a flash, and there was a 'Hsh-sh-sh!' like the protest of a flock of geese. The fair Lena was so taken aback that she nearly fell into the captain's arms. The captain did not seem to mind; his arm went round her waist for a moment almost as if it had the habit of doing it; and he whispered an apology that restored her self-control. At the same instant he signalled to the crew, and they burst into three great solid British cheers. Another signal stopped them from further performances, and the steamers swept by. The crisis of the day was over.

Then the *Kittiwake* turned and followed the fleet, and realized her remaining ambitions. She was back at St Kilda, with the yachts that had been lying there all the morning, by the time his great excellency, transhipped once more, arrived there. Through their glasses the ladies could see the procession of little figures along the pier, and the departure of the carriages after the guns had fired the salute; and they could hear the school children singing. When all was over, a sigh of vast contentment expressed the common thought, 'What a day we're having!' The turn of the landsmen had come, but no one at sea could envy them.

'Now we'll have a look at the *Sunbeam* as she lies,' said Bert, and then headed back for Williamstown.

'And we want some refreshment after what we have gone through,' said the hospitable hostess.

Luncheon was served for the third time, and subsequently two afternoon teas. The yachts, dissolving all formation, swam aimlessly about the bay, more like seabirds than ever, and took snap-shots at each other with their kodak [*sic*] cameras. Miss Pickersgill's singing powers failed somewhat, but she contrived to chaff and chatter with the young men, breaking off at intervals to hail her friends on passing boats. Good-natured Fanny Pleydell laughed with the rest at the fun she made; the admiring aunt and cousins could not remember when they had been so entertained; and Myra Salter was satisfied at heart because Bert had never allowed her to feel 'out of it'. And so the happy day wore through. They had had seven hours together when they began to look for Lena's dinghy, and before separating they testified with one consent that they had never had a more delightful holiday, or, as Lena neatly phrased it, 'such a jolly high old time.'

'Then I'll tell you what we must do,' said the gratified host. 'Go out together — since we suit each other so well — on the sixteenth of next month. That's our opening day, Miss Pickersgill, as of course you know; and, with the Governor for commodore, it ought to be the best we've ever had.'

'All those who are in favour of this motion,' chanted Lena, 'hold up your hands!'

Every hand went up at once, except Myra's. The shy girl looked to Fanny for an endorsement of the free and easy invitation, and Mrs Pleydell was knitting her brows. But soon she smiled consent, to please her brother, who, stealing behind Miss Salter unobserved, seized her two hands and lifted them into the air.

———

They imagined they were going to have their good time over again. They even anticipated a better one, though only of half the length. For whereas the wind had been too light on the 25th

October, it blew like business on the 16th November, when it was of the last importance that it should do so. No more auspicious opening day had ever dawned upon Victorian yachtsmen. The Governor, who was *their* Governor for the first time in history, had consented to direct their evolutions in person. This alone — this and a good wind — assured laurels to the clubs of Hobson's Bay which all other clubs would envy them. The *Sunbeam* had been towed to the chosen anchorage; Government House was on board. All the swells, as Miss Pickersgill termed them, indigenous to the soil, would be lone and lorn at the races, because their Lord and Lady were away. Even if they offered their ears for a place in viceregal company, they could not get it. 'Aha!' said the yachtsmen to one another, 'it is our turn now.'

This time the *Kittiwake* took her own dinghy to St Kilda. She towed it along with her all the afternoon, as a brake upon the pace, which threatened to carry her beyond the position assigned to her in the wheeling line, for she was faster than the boats before and behind her. And so the services of local friends were not required on Miss Lena's behalf. Bert himself, in a very ruffled sea indeed, went off to the pier to fetch her. But not altogether for the sake of paying her special honour; rather, because it was most difficult to bring anything alongside today without bumping off fenders and on to new paint. He had had the kindest feelings for both girls during the past three weeks, but what little love he had fallen into was for Myra Salter. He had just left her deeply in love with him. He had given her the card of sailing directions, taught her how to read the commodore's signals, and told her she was to be his captain for the day, as he was to be the crew's. Down in the small cabin, picking pecks of strawberries, with the assistance of the aunt and cousins, Mrs Pleydell's prophetic eye saw visions of an ideal home and family — that comfortable and prosperous domestic life which is the better and not the worse for having no wildfire passions to inflame and ravage it — and a congenial sister-in-law for all time. Myra lingered on deck to follow the movements of the tossing dinghy through the captain's strong field-glasses, also assigned to her exclusive use for this occasion. He had another pair — not quite so strong — for Miss Pickersgill.

Little did that young lady suppose that she was to play second fiddle for a moment. She wore another new dress and a ravishing peaked cap, much more becoming than the sailor straw. She smiled upon the skipper, struggling to hold the dinghy to the pier, as at a faithful bond-slave merely doing his bounden duty.

'It is our opening day!' she sang, as she flourished a hand to him. 'It — is — our — opening da-ay!'

'It is, indeed,' he shouted back. 'Made on purpose. Only I think we shall have too much of a good thing this time, instead of not enough. Wind keeps getting up, and we've reefed already.'

'Oh, it's stunning!' she rejoined, gaily skipping into the boat; she was a heavy weight, and nearly tipped it over. 'Let it get up! The more the merrier.'

'Yes, if there were going to be racing. I wish there was! We should just run away from everything.'

'Then let's race,' quoth Miss Pickersgill, as if commanding it to be done. 'Let's show the old buffer' — I grieve to say it was his sacred lordship she referred to — 'what the *Kittiwake* can do.'

Bert had to explain. It took him until they reached the yacht to make the young lady who looked so nautical understand what she was talking about. And after all she was inclined to be sentimentally hurt because he would not do such a little thing to please her.

The wind got up, more and more, showing that there was to be no monotonous repetition of the former circumstances. The *Kittiwake* danced and pranced as if the real sea were under her, and half a dozen dinghies trailed astern would hardly have made any difference. There was no sitting round the cockpit, as on drawing-room chairs, to flirt and sing; one side was always in the air, and the other all but under water, see-sawing sharply at uncertain intervals; and the ladies had to give their attention to holding on and keeping their heads out of the way of the swinging boom. Lena shouted to the men, who had to stick to business in spite of her, that it was the jolliest state of things imaginable, and said 'Go it!' to rude Boreas when he smacked her face, to encourage him to further efforts. But her five companions were more or less of the opinion that they had liked the first cruise better. The poor fat aunt was particularly disconcerted by the new conditions; she said she couldn't get used to the feeling of having no floor under her, and the sensation of the sea climbing up her back.

She was the first to say 'No, thank you,' to strawberries and cream, and 'Yes, please,' to whisky.

———

Is there anything funny in having the toothache, that people should laugh at the victim as at some inexhaustible joke? Ask the poor soul whose nerves are thus exquisitely tortured what *his* opinion is. He will tell you that it is one of the gravest elements in the tragedy of human pain; also that the heartless brute who sniggers at it ought to have thumbscrews put on him and twisted tight. Is there anything disgraceful in being sea-sick in rough weather, that those who don't happen to feel so at the moment should turn up their noses at the sufferers in contemptuous disgust? Emphatically not. It is a misfortune that may befall the best of us, and does, instead of being, as one would suppose, the penalty of a degrading vice, like delirium tremens. Why, even the *Sunbeam* was ill that afternoon — the first folks of the land, fresh from the discipline of a long and stormy voyage — which sufficiently proves the fact.

But when Myra Salter was observed to sit silent and rigid, with bleached lips and a corpse-like skin, it was with eyes that slightly hardened at the sight. Yes, even the captain's eyes! It is true he smiled at her, and said 'Poor child!' and peremptorily ordered the useless stimulant, and was generally concerned and kind; but the traditional ignominy of her case affected him; her charm and dignity were impaired — vulgarized; and the flavour of his incipient romance began to go. Of course young men are fools — we all are, for that matter — and young love, just out of the ground, as it were, is like a baby lettuce in a garden full of slugs. And it is no use pretending that things are different from what they are. And if you want to be an artist, and not a fashionable photographer, you must not paint poor human nature, and leave the moles and wrinkles out. It is a pity that an estimable young man cannot be quite perfect, and that an admirable young woman should be unjustly despised; but so it is, and there's no more to be said.

Myra shook her head at the suggestion of whisky; only to imagine the smell of it was to feel worse at once — to feel an instant necessity to hide herself below. But Fanny Pleydell, coming upstairs at the moment when she was beginning to stagger down, caught her in her arms and held her back — a fatal blunder on Fanny's part.

'No, my dear, no!' she cried on the spur of a humane impulse; 'you must *not* go into that horrible hole; it would finish you off at once. Besides, there isn't room for you; aunt and the girls are sprawling all over the place. Have a little spirits, darling — yes, you must; and keep in the fresh air if you want to feel better.'

She pressed whisky and water on the shuddering girl, and cruel consequences ensued. Bert turned his head away, and tried to shut his ears. Lena smiled at him in an arch and confidential manner. *She* was as bright and pretty as ever — more so, indeed, for the wind exhilarated her and deepened her bloom.

'I think,' she said, 'it is a great mistake for people who are not sailors to go to sea in rough weather, don't you?'

Well, Bert almost thought it was. He was a very enthusiastic yachtsman, especially today, when he wanted the *Kittiwake* and all her appurtenances to be as correct as possible.

———

The drill was over, and the regiment of yachts disbanded. The *Sunbeam* had gone to a pier at Williamstown, and the commodore was receiving his new colleagues and entertaining them. The *Kittiwake* was off St Kilda, with her freight of the afflicted on board. The aunt filled up one tiny cabin, the cousins another, and they groaned and wailed and made other unpleasant noises, to the amusement of a callous crew. Myra Salter, too helplessly ill to sit up without support while the boat rushed through the water with a slice of deck submerged, had sagged down to the floor of the

cockpit, and now lay there in a limp heap, propped against
Fanny's knees. She had not spoken for an hour, and during that
time Bert had hardly noticed her. He had been devoting himself
to Miss Pickersgill, so far as the duties of his official post allowed,
as was only natural when she had become practically his sole companion, and when, as a lover of a good breeze and proper sailor-
ing, she had proved herself so sympathetic.

Now he was rowing her home from the yacht to the shore.
She sat facing him in the dinghy, with the yoke lines round her
waist, and he could not keep his eyes from her brilliant person,
nor keep himself from mentally comparing it with that sad wisp
on the cockpit floor. She met his glance, and held it. They were
both excited by the wind, the inspiring flight of the yacht, the var-
ied interests of the opening day.

'Oh, it was splendid!' she exclaimed. 'Whatever the others
may think about it, I know *I* never enjoyed myself so much in my
life. And I *am* so obliged to you for taking me, Mr Lawson.'

'You are the right sort to take,' replied Bert with enthusiasm;
and he imagined a wife who could enter into his favourite pursuits
like a true comrade. 'And I hope we shall have many a good cruise
together.'

'It won't be my fault if we don't,' she said promptly.

'It won't be mine,' he returned. 'Consider yourself asked for
every day that you'll deign to come.'

'What, for ever?'

'For ever.'

She looked at him archly, pensively, meaningly, with her head
on one side. She was really very handsome in her coquettish
peaked cap, and he reflected that she was evidently healthy and
probably rich.

'You don't *mean* that, Mr Lawson?'

'I do mean it, literally and absolutely.'

'For every yachting day as long as I live?'

'For every yachting day, and every day that isn't a yachting day.'

She was so joyously flustered that she ran the dinghy into the
pier. He had to catch her in his arms to prevent her going over-

board. As there were people watching them from above, he could not kiss her, but he gave an earnest of his intention to do so at the first opportunity.

——————

Of course she was the wrong one. He knew it no later than the next day, in his heart of hearts, though never permitting himself to acknowledge it, because he flatters himself that he is a gentleman. Equally, of course, he will go on to render his mistake irrevocable, and be miserable ever after, and make her so, from the highest motives. Already the wedding gown is bought, and they go together to ironmongers and upholsterers to choose new drawing-room furniture and pots and kettles for the kitchen. The marriage will surely take place when the bride has made her preparations, and anybody can foretell what the consequences will be. They will pull against each other by force of nature, and tear their little shred of romance to bits in no time. And then they will sink together to that sordid and common matrimonial state which is the despair and disgrace of civilization. She will grow fat and frowsy as she gets into years — a coarse woman, selfish and petty, and full of legitimate grievances; and he will hate her first, and then cease to care one way or the other, which is infinitely worse than hating. And so two lives will be utterly spoiled, and possibly three or four — not counting the children, who will have no sort of fair start.

And all because there was a bit of a breeze on the opening day of the season!

But such is life.

Nanya

*William Ferguson first heard the story of 'Nanya' as
a young man and later met Harry Mitchell, one of
the trackers sent out to bring in the 'lost tribe' of
Scotia Blacks, This is the story as told to him by
Harry Mitchell around 1920.*

A long time ago, before the white man came to this country, the
Aborigines used to make their camps along the main rivers, and
on any site close to permanent water, hence we find at the time
our story opens, groups, or tribes of dark skinned people scattered at different distances along the Darling River. Each tribe
conducted their own social affairs, by means of a local committee,
with one man as the head, but all tribes and committees and head
men, were subject to one mighty Law, the Bora, or Bulbung.

The Bora controlled all Aborigines throughout Australia. By
means of the Bora the Aborigines have been able to keep the race
clean, without mixed marriages right down through the long ages,
for many thousands of years, which in itself is a great achieve-
ment. I can't say very much about the Bora, only that it represents
a powerful secret society, but I will explain as much as I dare, and
be truthful. Any writer, White or Aboriginal, who dares to go further than I, is either a lunatic or a liar, because all the secret rites
of the Bora are known only to those who have been initiated, and
have never been divulged to outsiders. I know several old men
who had been through the Bora, confirmed old drunkards some
of them were too, and I spent much time and money trying to get
the desired secret information, but whether drunk or sober, they

guarded the secret well. They told me that if they said the things I wanted them to, their life wouldn't be worth living, some of the tribe would find out, and the punishment would be swift, nothing less than the spear. As far as I could find out, the Law centred around one word, Meat, and it is the hardest word in all the different Aboriginal dialects to pronounce. I can pronounce it, but I cannot find letters to spell it, so I will spell it Gingue. The Aborigines with their belief in reincarnation, believe that every soul is born and re-born, each time in different forms. Every baby born therefore, represents some animal or bird, and the marriage laws are fixed, in order that only those named after certain meat can marry only certain other meat. It is very simple, although it may appear complicated.

An illustration — a family of Kangaroo in the far north, say Darwin, start to move south. Thousands of years later they are spread right across the country. A stranger walks up to a camp, and the first thing they ask him 'What meat you?' 'Kangaroo,' he answers. 'Alright,' he is told, 'you my brother, that's your wife over at the next camp,' and so it has always been.

If he didn't tell the truth and said he was Emu, and they let him marry his own meat, that would be breaking the Law, and although his lie might go over for a while, he would be sure to be found out sooner or later, and then the spear.

Our story opens on an ordinary scene at that long forgotten time. About twenty youths are gathered around the camp of the head man, or Chief, and he is speaking to them. The Chief is an old man, and still shows traces of his once fine physique. He is tall, about six foot two inches, and in spite of his years, stands very erect. Rather thin, but strongly built, grey hair and whiskers singed short. The boys grouped around are listening attentively to what he has to say. Their ages are about sixteen years. 'Now you boys, you are going away today to the Bora. There you will be told all the mysteries about life. You will be taught how to hunt for food, how to track animals, and man, how to make all kinds of weapons and tools, and how to use them. You will be told how to respect all people, particularly women, and how to devote your lives to love and not to hate your neighbours. You will go now with the old men who are waiting for you, and stay away until they bring you back.' The boys knew he had finished speaking, and all turned and walked away into the bush, following the six old men who took the lead.

The old Chief watched until they were out of sight, his old eyes following to the last one boy in particular, whom he watched until they were swallowed up by the Bush. Then he sat down beside his fire, and thought: who knows what he thought, but we suppose it was of the time when he as a boy many years ago, went to the Bora, or was he thinking of his own son, who had just left for the Bora, and who was to take his place as Chief of the Tribe when he became too old? Nanya was the boy's name. He was about sixteen years of age, tall like his father, of powerful build and could run faster than any other man of the tribe. Not only his father, the Chief, but all the tribe loved Nanya, old and young, and why shouldn't they? He was always helping the older men, fixing their mia-mias, carrying wood and making them comfortable. Even as a boy he speared more food than any of the others and shared it among the tribe. He was to be seen playing with the children, and making them laugh with his antics. He would carry them on his broad shoulders for miles, and never tire, his endurance was simply marvellous. He had been known to run all day, as a stick carrier. On one occasion, he ran from his camp, about where the Menindie Aboriginal Reserve now stands, six miles above Menindie Town, to another tribe at Cuthrow Station, about 40 miles down the river. That means that Nanya travelled forty miles to Cuthrow and forty miles back in twenty-four hours, without rest.

The Aborigines matured very early in life. A boy of sixteen was as much a man as he ever would be, and girls were women at fourteen — some even younger. They were given in marriage when very young, and often went to live with their older husbands, but the husbands never had intercourse with their wives until they matured to womanhood, about thirteen or fourteen. Among the girls of this tribe was one whom we must turn to for a while. Mimi was fifteen years of age, and she watched with others of the tribe, the departure of the boys. Like the old Chief, she too had eyes for only one, and that one was Nanya. Love shone in her beautiful big eyes, the full young love of a lovely girl. Mimi knew that her love was returned, because Nanya had told her. But oh, the tragedy of it all. They both knew that she was the wrong Gingue. Mimi was not for Nanya, because they were both the same line of Gingue, both belonged to the Kangaroo. She was given when very small to an old man, who died before she was old enough to be his wife. Her next husband elect was among the boys now proceeding to the Bora, and when they returned, the Law said he was to take her. Hearts were not consulted in Aborigine marriages, and it's just as well so, because if they had been allowed to choose for themselves, they would have degenerated hundreds of years before. The one chosen as husband for Mimi was not a very desirable person. He was bad tempered and selfish, short of stature and fat, like all selfish greedy boys are, but the Bora Law gave to him the most beautiful girl of the tribe for wife.

Nobody knew, or even suspected the secret love of Nanya and Mimi, except God, the great master, who knew everything. When the little band of boys led by the old man vanished into the bush, the light died in Mimi's eyes, she knew her life was doomed to emptiness, there would be no happiness for her without Nanya. She turned away from the rest of the people, and walked down by the river to sit and dream of her sorry plight and perhaps to talk and commune with her friend, the black Swan, who swam majestically across the river to where she sat in tears. Whatever the Swan told her is not known, but when she joined the other girls she was her usual self, jovial and bright, and none knew of her hopeless love. She even chaffed with the other girls about their marriages when the boys returned. Although their stay would only be a little more than six months, on their return they would be men and qualified for marriage.

We now follow the boys into the bush. They walked on and on till near sundown. It was springtime and the bush was teeming with life. The ground everywhere was covered with beautiful flowers, the boys enjoyed the walk, and when the old men told them to get some food for supper, they all tried to outdo each other in spearing emu and kangaroo and possum. When they had sufficient food, a place was selected for camp, fires made, bough breaks made and supper prepared. Choice bits of food were given to the old men and the boys ate what was left. After supper they all sat around the fire, in their most comfortable positions and listened to the old legends told by the old men. Great old yarn tellers they were, and they talked and talked until one by one the boys fell asleep. They were roused at daybreak and started on their march, which continued until late in the afternoon, when they arrived at the Bora, about fifty miles from the camp, and situated in a wild scrubby place, well hidden from curious eyes, because the Bora and all pertaining to it is sacred to Aborigines.

The Bora ring is a place in the bush made similar to a circus ring. It is about fifty yards across the ring and worn down to about a foot deep from the tramping of bare feet of many Aborigines over a long period of years. This is the place where the actual ceremony takes place. The knocking out of the two front teeth we know of, but [of] the other part (riding the goat) we know nothing. We won't even try to guess, beyond saying that for six months or more, those boys, who are being trained by the old men in bushcraft during the day, spend the greater part of the night in Sacred Corroboree in the Bora ring. So we will skip over the months and come to the last day of their schooling, and we find a different lot of boys. From continual and careful teaching, they are now experienced men, able to make tools and weapons to perfection, and use them just as perfectly. They have learned how to prepare for and go into war, how to track and kill game, and other mysterious things such as pointing the bone and witchcraft. Only special ones are selected for witchcraft. Those selected are known to possess supernatural powers, inherited from their ancestors. Among this line of gifted men is our hero Nanya, who came from a long line of Wirrugar, or clever men. The Wirrugar is a spirit man, who has been endowed with supernatural powers, given direct from the sky, and anyone with this power, can change from a man to an animal. If his meat of Gingue be a Kangaroo, then he will take the form of a Kangaroo, and his power will take effect for good or evil over any distance. For instance, if a man offends a Wirrugar, he will get a warning, and although the one offended be many miles away, the offender will take sick and die. I suppose it is the power of mind over mind. It is one of the things that the white man makes fun of, so we will leave it to the learned white man and not trespass too much on something sacred to Aborigines. The old men who were in charge of the Bora were Wirrugar, and they imparted some knowledge of spiritcraft to Nanya.

So now on the eve of their return to camp, we behold a different lot of boys, and especially a different Nanya. Almost the perfect man walking, with long springing steps, head slightly thrown back, apparently carefree, but with a deep resolve to marry the girl he loves, with the full knowledge of doing wrong. Great was the jubilation on the night of their return. A big feast was given, and a big Corroboree, natives from hundreds of miles around, had been gathering for weeks. We can imagine the scene. All the mia-mias clustered around, hundreds of camp fires, men in groups talking earnestly, women talking of the coming marriages and children playing at their noisy games. Many a night I have witnessed such scenes.

But there was no happiness for Mimi. The next day, after the Corroboree, all those girls promised in marriage would be claimed by their husbands, and Mimi would be the wife of the man she detested. She cast many a covetous glance at Nanya. It was not allowed that she could walk up openly and speak to him, that would be against the Law, and Nanya avoided looking at her, but I suppose it was instinct, or nature asserting itself, that told them both that they would meet as soon as an opportunity offered. It came just before the Corroboree started. Nanya walked towards the river, Mimi happened to be near the river too. Others were close by, but not close enough to hear Nanya give a command; 'Be waiting for me near the Warwee hole just before dawn.' Mimi just bowed her head, and passed on.

The Warwee hole (means the place where the Bunyip lives) was over two miles from the main camp, and just after midnight we see Mimi walking quietly towards the meeting place, wondering what did her lover mean. She did not belong to him, but she did not care. She would just wait and trust to his wisdom. It might mean just one sweet hour of love, and then death for both.

At the camp all the men painted and decked out with feathers. This was a special Corroboree, which marked not only the return of the Bora men, but also the induction of Nanya as the next head man of the tribe, to succeed his father. Many fine speeches were made and Nanya's name was mentioned often. He was held up as a model of manhood, one whose example could easily be followed to advantage, one who was sworn to obey and uphold the Law, and one day he would be Chief of the tribe. He took his place as leader of the Corroboree and did his part well. Never did a man shake his legs as did Nanya. The people were amazed at his quickness. He seemed to excel at everything, every movement perfect. Like some great actor, he held the people spell-bound, right through to the finish of the Corroboree, when everyone retired to their camps, to rest, and be ready in the afternoon for the big marriage ceremony.

Nanya hurried to the trysting place, his one desire to see Mimi. Her quick ears heard him even before he came in sight. She rose to meet him, before she knew it Nanya had her in his strong arms. No word was spoken between the law-breakers. They loved, and when did ever love wait for Law.

'You belong to me Mimi, we both know it is against the Law and that we must both suffer death.'

'What does it matter now Nanya, so long as we both die together.'

'It is one thing to love and die for each other, but what about loving and living for each other?'

'Impossible,' said Mimi. 'We can't avoid the spear now.'

'Not so impossible' said Nanya, 'we will flee together.'

'We can't get far' said Mimi, 'they will overtake us.'

'No' said Nanya, 'they can't catch us, come on, we will go into the desert. No one can follow us there, they can't get water.' And so commenced one of the strangest elopements known in the history of the world.

Back at the camp, the people are starting a new day. The fires are being poked up, and long spirals of smoke make their way into the sky. Men are calling out greetings to other men at other camps. Women are busy preparing breakfast and children are starting to make a noise. The old Chief scans all the camps within range of his quick eyes, and not seeing his son, calls out to his neighbours. 'Did you see Nanya?' 'No,' and he asks one of the young men, 'Isn't Nanya awake yet?' 'I don't know, he didn't sleep with me last night.' 'Well go and wake him wherever he sleeps and tell him I want him.' A search is made and Nanya can't be found. 'Oh, never mind, perhaps he wanted to be quiet by himself.' At another camp, Mimi's mother and father are concerned about her absence. She might have gone to another camp — a search is made, but without any results. The camp is now all commotion. Whispers are started. Nanya and Mimi are both missing. A council of all the elders and Chiefs of the tribes is called. Witnesses have been called, those who made search for them and the only logical conclusion they can arrive at is that they have broken the Law. All eyes are turned towards the Chief, Nanya's father. How will he act? Will he try to shield his favourite son? The old man stands up bravely and looks them squarely in the eyes. It seems as though he could read their very thoughts. He spoke quietly. 'It is said that my boy, whom you all know is everything in the world to me, has broken the Law. I command that he and the girl be brought to me. If they can't prove their innocence, we will deem them guilty, and although it will break my old heart, the Law of the Bora must be carried out and both will be speared to death tonight — now go.'

And so was given a decree that never was carried out.

Down the river, the runaway pair were making for the desert, which is now known as the Scotia country. This country is a vast scoop of barren waste, sand and mallee, extending from the

Darling River out beyond the South Australian border, and from Broken Hill to the Murray River. The Aborigines had never ventured far into this desert. They told legends of strange animals and spirits who lived out there, but no man had ever lived there. There was no water to keep anyone alive. Once a man had gone in to investigate and five days after he was seen walking and reeling like a drunken man, and when he got to the camp they found he had gone raving mad. He said he met the Mirrie-youla (dog Wirrugar) out there. He died that night and the Mirrie-youla was seen in the river that same night. Nanya had often heard of the spirits that lived in the desert, and as they ran along hand in hand, he told Mimi all about it. 'Don't Nanya, you make me afraid.' 'Have faith in me Mimi, I am not afraid. I, too, am a Wirrugar, I am young and strong, and just as powerful as any spirit or Wirrugar in the desert.' 'But we will die Nanya, we can't live without water.' 'We will die for sure if we are caught,' said Nanya, 'but we have a chance of living if we get into the desert. I have been thinking of this day for the last two years, and preparing for it. Ever since that day when I first told you of my love for you. I studied bush law and signs, I learned how to find water when others couldn't find it. I can travel all night by the stars and not get off course. I can throw a spear straighter than any man living. When you feel tired, say so, and I will carry you because I never get tired.' Mimi believed him.

They had reached a point about twenty miles down the river when Nanya, who had been looking back watching for a signal, at last saw a thin line of smoke rising, followed by other thick black smoke, then repeated. He knew what it meant, and had been expecting it. It meant that their tracks had been picked up, and was a signal for others down the river to intercept them, and hold them, or kill them. The same signal was noticed and interpreted by a party of Aborigines a few miles further down the river, and only for fate interfering, and altering the course of the fugitives, this story would not have been written. Nanya showed Mimi the smoke and laughed to think of them trying to catch him, Nanya the Powerful. He said, 'There is no camp nearer than twenty miles, we will leave the river just this side of the camp and make for the desert.' Hardly had he spoken when right in front of them they saw the strangest sight ever seen by Aborigines.

The sight that startled them was what appeared to be men, with white faces and hands and their bodies and legs and arms covered with something. Even their head and feet were covered, and they were sitting on big four legged animals, unlike any known animal in the bush, and were moving towards the place where Nanya and Mimi stood. Instinct told them to hide in the long grass and they moved on all fours nearer the river, until they found shelter in a big hollow tree. From their hiding place the runaways watched the strange procession, the white men riding the strange animals, and more surprise, two men of their own colour with their bodies and legs partly covered, also sitting on the strange animals and driving other loose animals with packs on their backs following the tracks of the white men. It may have been the Bourke and Wills party.

'What is it?' asked Mimi. 'Wirrugar,' said Nanya. 'Come, we will cross the river here, and head straight into the desert.' This resolve saved them from running into the party of Aborigines waiting just a few miles further on. Here they said goodbye to the river forever.

We cannot but admire the courage of Nanya, when we take into consideration the fact that he was venturing into a wild, unexplored desert, with no other equipment than a strip of Kangaroo skin about his waist in which was stuck a small stone tomahawk. Nothing more. They were both as naked as when they were born and up to that time none of that tribe wore covering, not even the loin cloth. We cannot help comparing the outfit of Nanya and the party of white men. The fugitives ran steadily till about noon, having covered about fifty miles from the main camp. Although it was late summer, the days were still hot, and they were glad to have a few hours rest, so crawling into a low bushy scrub, they lay down and slept till late in the afternoon. Although they had not eaten since the previous night, they felt no hunger and so they continued their flight through the night, mostly running, sometimes walking, having in mind all the time that those who were trailing them were also endowed with great endurance. Nanya left nothing to chance. When Mimi told him she was thirsty, he told her how he could get water by cutting the root of certain trees, many of which they passed in the night, but he advised her to suffer as long as possible until it started to hurt her, then he would give her water. He did not want to let his pursuers know that they would live — the best way to safety was to make them believe that they would perish for water, and his reasoning was right. The two men who were following easily followed the tracks, and they too got quite a scare when they ran into the party of white men, but unlike Nanya and Mimi, they were seen by the whites who tried to speak with them, which only added to their fear, so they ran and dived into the river and swam across to the opposite side, and continued down for about a mile, and then crossed back, but it was hard for them to pick up the tracks, as the horses had been over them and they could only pick them up here and there, until they came to a place where they lost them altogether, and it was just before sundown when they accidentally found where they crossed the river.

So they decided to camp until morning, and take up the trail again. The following morning, as soon as it was light enough, they started on the tracks and at noon they reached the place where the runaways had rested just twenty-four hours before. After talking the matter over, they decided to give up. They reasoned that Nanya and Mimi couldn't last long in the desert. If they got water from the roots, the Wirrugar would get them, so why follow them? Anyhow they might turn back and someone would get them in the end, they can't dodge the Bora. And if we go too far we might die, so they gave up the chase and returned home. Their reasoning was accepted by the tribe, but Nanya's father, the old Chief and medicine man, knew different for he had communion with his Wirrugar. As a consequence a big old man Kangaroo could be seen travelling after the law-breakers, not to wreak vengeance on them, but to safeguard and protect them for all time. The old man lay dead. He was buried next day in the old burying ground near the mission.

So ended a long line of head-men of that tribe. A meeting of the old men resulted in a new Chief, who counselled and advised the tribe, till owing to the advent of the white man, the Bora was finally discontinued altogether and then commenced the degeneration and demoralising of the Aborigines, which has ended in what we have today, a race of unwanted half-castes, who have been deprived of the old Bora Law and given nothing to replace it, refused the rights to proper education, and shunned by their fathers, the white man.

We now return to the fugitives. Mimi was getting thirsty, and from the way she was walking Nanya knew she was tiring. They did not waste much time in talking. The Aborigines are silent people, they convey to one another by means of signs anything they wish to communicate. So, although there was a lot of love and understanding between our two runaways, they spoke little, but each could almost tell what the other was thinking about.

Nanya knew that there was enough distance now between them and their pursuers, so he kept a look-out for suitable trees, but they were travelling over a stretch of sand and spinifex. The sun was just rising. It was the second sunrise since they left home, and they were now a long way from the river, about forty miles into the desert. When Mimi stumbled, without making any complaint, Nanya lifted her on his shoulders, and carried her. The most precious burden he had ever carried. 'I will save you. I won't let you die,' he said. Mile after mile, and hour after hour he walked until he sighted a clump of young needle-wood trees in the distance. He walked straight up and we don't know if he was surprised or not, to see a big red kangaroo lying in the shade of one of the trees. He placed Mimi in the shade of a tree, and at once proceeded to cut a coolamon (a piece of bark off the bump of a tree). He then found the right roots and cut them and by placing one end of the roots in the coolamon and leaning the other end against a tree, standing them almost upright, he soon had about a quart of clear, sweet water. Not until she was told, did Mimi drink. There was plenty of yams growing about so they had their first meal since leaving the camp. Nanya cut more root and cut a larger coolamon, and they rested there all day and that night. Through the night Nanya heard an emu drumming, so early next morning they both set out to find the emu. They both wanted meat. They had not gone far from their first camp, when on looking behind, they saw the big kangaroo go to the coolamon and drink. Did Nanya leave the coolamon full of water for that purpose? And strangest of all, two dingoes — a male and female — both had a drink and started to follow them at a distance of about a hundred yards. Just behind the dingoes came the kangaroo. Nanya had taken his bearings from the sound of the emu drumming in the night and he judged the direction, also the distance so exact that he knew just when he would be close to the emu's nest. Telling Mimi to walk carefully and keep directly behind him, he started to stalk the emu, which he did so effectively that before the emu had time to jump from the nest, he threw the stone tomahawk. His aim was so true that he broke the emu's neck. Great rejoicing. Plenty of meat and nice fresh eggs. Nanya now set to work and dug a hole in the sand. He next filled the hole with pieces of wood and started a fire by rubbing vigorously two pieces of wood together. When the fire burned down, and only coals and ashes were left, he scooped the hole out with a stick cut for that purpose, placed the emu in the hole, and covered it over with coal, and put sand on top to keep the heat in. The eggs were placed in the sand and fire too, and what a feast. The future which but a short time before looked so gloomy, now took on a brighter aspect. Plenty of water, plenty of food and a Kingdom of their own. The dingoes came closer, perhaps the smell of meat coaxed them. Nanya threw some scraps a long distance out, and the wild dogs came nearer, until before the day was through they came quite close and ate up all the scraps, but always retired to about a hundred yards distance. The kangaroo fed on the plain and camped in the shade of a nearby tree by turn, never out of sight. They camped at that place for a few days till they ate up all the meat and eggs, then they moved on. Later on the dingo's howl at night brought other dingoes and later still, the dingoes used to chase the emus and kill them, but always waited for Nanya to cut a piece off for himself, before they would eat of it. Nanya was always close to the kill, for he could run as fast as an emu himself.

So they wandered and lived until once when Nanya had been away all day hunting, on nearing the camp, he heard a strange noise, a baby crying. He just flew over the last few yards. 'Yes Nanya, a son. He is so like you.' 'You alright Mimi?' 'Yes Nanya, I'm alright.' Not much fuss over the birth of their first baby, but in their silence they both knew they were drawn closer to each other. And also by their silence and only speaking in short sentences, they actually forgot their own dialect and learned to speak another language. After a few years their names were not spoken and then forgotten altogether. Another baby, this time a girl, followed by other boys and girls. And because Nanya himself had broken the Law, what was the use of bothering with others? None of them was named because they were all one meat. So it didn't surprise father or mother a few years later, when their first daughter was about 13 years old and the son about 15, that a baby was born to her, and so it went on, they degenerated completely. Fathers cohabiting with daughters, sons having intercourse with their mothers. Mimi was dead, and no one to tell them it was wrong. Only Nanya, and what right had he to reprimand them? Hadn't he set the example in the first place? And so we leave them in their misery, poor unhappy wretches, for surely the way of the transgressor is hard.

About the year 1890 a party of men were erecting the border fence separating two States, South Australia and New South Wales. The border struck through a portion of the Scotia Desert. Water was carted in two four hundred gallon tanks on a bullock wagon. Another wagon was used to cart posts and wire and netting and all the fencing gear. There was no cook but the men took it in turns for one to go to the camp a bit earlier than the rest in order to prepare supper.

One day, the man whose turn it was to cook supper got a suspicion that someone had been at the water tank. Not only was the water a lot lower in the tank, but the lid was not in its proper position. He told his mates about it. Oh no, no one lived out there. If they had been white men they would have camped for company. A search for tracks showed nothing, but the next morning the amount of water was noted and when it was found to be about three or four inches below the mark in the afternoon, they were all satisfied that someone was interfering with their water. So the next morning one stayed back to watch. Soon after the men had gone he was surprised and a bit scared to see a mob of Aborigines walking up to the water wagon. He was too afraid to meet them so he watched from his hiding place. He saw them go straight to the watertank. Some of the men climbed up and the others passed up their water containers (kangaroo-skin bags) which were filled, and as they made off, others brushed the tracks out with bushes, until no sign of a track remained. Word was sent to the police at Broken Hill, who in turn communicated with the police at all outlying police stations advising them of a tribe of lost blacks who were wandering in the Scotia Scrub. The police tried to find out from each camp if any of their number had left camp and wandered away. Enquiries at all camps along the Darling, down the Lower Murray, Lake Victoria, and in fact right around the desert, did not uncover any missing Aborigines.

Word was sent to Melbourne, Sydney and Adelaide, with the result that the New South Wales Government issued instructions to the police at Wentworth to go out and bring them in. The sergeant selected two young troopers and commissioned them to fit out an expedition, to get three of the smartest trackers possible and bring the wandering people in that they might be civilised and protected. So commenced the second manhunt with Nanya, again, the hunted.

The Party consisted of two mounted police and three black-trackers, whose names were Dan McGregor, Harry Mitchell and Bill Bell. The mounted police were both picked men, good horsemen and excellent bushmen. They took along three packhorses, with proper desert water bags, a good supply of food, besides a supply of firearms and ammunition.

For two days they travelled from Wentworth and on the third day a quarrel took place between Dan McGregor, who was the Senior Tracker and a good one too, and the troopers about the route to take. The troopers wanted to go in one direction, but McGregor, with his unerring bush instinct advised a different direction, and the troopers ordered the trackers to continue themselves and they returned to Wentworth. So the trackers journeyed on with only two pack-horses, they themselves were well mounted. For another five days they travelled right into the heart of the desert without seeing any sign of the Aborigines, but on the sixth day, without any warning they rode right onto the tribe. They must have seen the trackers approaching, and lay down in the grass to hide, and watch, and not till the horsemen were within a few yards of them did they jump to their feet and start to run. McGregor ordered the other two trackers to try to surround them. He shouted to Mitchell, 'You go to the right and head them off, and Bell, you go to the left, and on no account will you shoot until I give orders.' So with McGregor riding straight behind and the other two fanning out on either side, the chase began. And what a chase. The men on fast horses racing at top speed and the wild naked people on foot; running in the lead as swift as an emu was an old man with long snow-white hair and beard. He was bearing to the right, and the others following him. He continued to run for about half a mile, when he gave up suddenly and fell down exhausted. The others soon gathered around him, and all the men stood at bay with their spears drawn back ready to defend the old man and women and children.

There were in all thirty-three people. The old man was the tallest of the lot. Some of the other men were well built, others were deformed, as were some of the women. Twelve of the men carried long spears, about twelve to fourteen feet long. The old man carried an old worn-out stone tomahawk. The others carried absolutely nothing. If they had waterbags or food they must have left them behind somewhere. Bell aimed his rifle (a new

Martini-Henry just out). But McGregor made him put it down. Mitchell could speak many native languages so McGregor appointed him as spokesman. Nahndy wa mayjne (What black-fellow you?) he called out, addressing the old man, who still stood with his spear raised. No answer was made. Nahndy wa gingue (What meat?) no answer. The same questions were asked in many languages. Still no answers. The tribe started to talk among themselves in some strange language. The three trackers also conferred. 'Did you ever hear of a man who broke the law, and took the wrong woman,' asked McGregor. 'Yes,' said Mitchell, 'I remember the old people talking about him when I was a boy. It happened when my father was a boy, about sixty years ago.' Mitchell then called out in a loud voice 'Nanya'. The old fellow bent his head as though he was trying to recall some-thing. Mitchell called again 'Nanya'. The old fellow repeated the word Nanya. He put his spear down and spoke to the others, who all put down their spears. Mitchell dismounted and walked towards them. They grabbed their spears again, but Mitchell put his rifle down and continued to advance. Some more talking and the spears were put down again. When Mitchell found he had started a train of thought in the old man's mind, he didn't let up, but continued to talk and talk in Nanya's own language and each word helped to revive Nanya's memory, until he remembered and spoke his own language. Mitchell explained to him that he must come back. 'No', said Nanya, 'the Bora — they will spear me.' 'The Bora is now forgotten' said Mitchell. 'White men have taken our country. We got a good kind Government. Him give us plenty tea, sugar, flour and bacca, also plenty rum. Him give us blanket and clothes and all the women now have white baby, no more black baby.' 'I think we stay here,' said Nanya. 'We happy here, no one to interfere with us, we own this country.' 'Well,' said Mitchell, 'Government now our law. Him tell us to go to desert and bring blackfellow in; if they no come, you shoot them.' He then demonstrated with his rifle. About two hundred yards off there were some kangaroos feeding. 'Look,' said Mitchell, 'I show you how to spear kangaroo,' and he fired. The report of the rifle frightened the wild people, but they were soon quieted again by Mitchell, who called out and showed them a kangaroo lying kicking on the ground. 'Look again' he said, and Bell and McGregor both fired together, and two more kangaroos dropped dead. 'This feller white man spear, him kill anywhere. We not going to spear you. Bora no more, nothing to be frightened of, come and live on river in big camp, plenty fun and tucker.' For a long time Nanya talked to his people, before deciding, and while they were talking the trackers were taking stock of the company. Next to Nanya in age were two old men over sixty years and one woman also old and grey. Those three were the only ones living directly descended from Nanya and Mimi. There was another man over fifty, with a crooked neck and another with a big lump on his neck, others were deformed in legs and arms, and with the exception of a few women, they all suffered more or less from deformity due no doubt to inter-marriage. Just behind was seen an old man kangaroo. The biggest ever seen. And not far from the kangaroo was a pack of about thirty dingoes. Mitchell drew the others' attention to the giant dingo. 'Wirringa' said Mitchell, and they all agreed to go back. After mounting his horse and taking the pack-horse, Mitchell rode off with Nanya walking beside him talking about the tribe he had left years ago. The rest of his people followed while McGregor and Bill rode just behind them and about a hundred yards further back followed the dingoes and the kangaroo. Mitchell told Nanya to get his men to carry the three dead kangaroo for food. 'No,' said Nanya 'that our Gingue.' So they shot two emu that afternoon which was carried on to the night camp. It is sad to relate that no modesty or even moral code was observed by these unfortunate people. They acted more like wild animals than human beings. They obeyed any nature calls as they walked along. They walked in silence and spoke only by signs. Three men had sexual intercourse with one woman that afternoon. There was no fixed mate for any one. Any man had connections with any woman whichever was nearest to him. After the trackers had made their camp, boiled their quarts and cooked some emu, the others just warmed their meat, some ate it raw and all lay just where they happened to be sitting. Nanya sat long into the night and talked to the trackers. He described everything that had happened in that long flight from the Bora. Right up till the time of Mimi's death. Although he must have been over eighty years of age, he could still run but not so long. His eyes were also good and he seemed just as strong and vigorous as ever. An incident occurred that first night which must be recorded. As I stated before some of the women were comely and one girl in particular was really beautiful. As previously stated no names were used for any of the tribe. The custom was for the speaker to look directly at the one addressed. But the trackers for their own convenience named them all. The one with the lump on the neck was called Tom. The one with the crooked neck was named Willie and so on. Now the girl who was most beautiful was about fourteen years old, and they christened her Ada.

From the time the tribe first halted, Bell had been watching Ada with lustful eyes and although he did not know it, McGregor and Mitchell were watching him, and while he was hobbling the horses for the night, these other two discussed the matter. 'I don't like the way he keeps watching her,' said McGregor. 'No,' said Mitchell, 'and although we have seen for ourselves that these people have no moral code, I don't think it would be right for us, who are partly civilised to take advantage of them.' 'Just what I was thinking,' said McGregor, 'and I will watch Bell, and the first sign of interference with that girl, I will stop him.' 'Alright,' said Mitchell, 'I'll back you up in that.'

So after the people laid down to rest and Nanya sat talking with McGregor and Mitchell about the long, long ago, Bell took his swag and settled down, not directly next to Ada, but not far distant, about eight or ten feet away. The others watched him as most of the people fell asleep, edge a little nearer to Ada, who was sound asleep. Still a little closer, now only about a yard away. Mitchell stood up and in his hand he held his rifle. He said 'Bell, come away from there. If you don't I will shoot you like I would a dog.' Bell tried to point out that it didn't matter to them, as they were without any moral code. 'But,' said Mitchell, 'you are not like them.

They have never been told anything about the Bora Law, or white man law. They know only animal law. You lay between McGregor and I, and if you move tonight I will shoot you. Tomorrow morning you will take a fair share of the food and leave us.'

And so in the morning Bell saddled his horse, took his swag and some tucker and started for Wentworth where he arrived after five days' travel. It was he who told the world that the wild Scotia blacks had been found, and were being brought in to Pooncarie by McGregor and Mitchell. The news travelled slowly in those days, and not till a fortnight later did word reach Mr Crosier of Cuthrow Station, who with his wife and family, the residents of Pooncarie and Menindie, made up a big reception party, to meet the Scotia people at Popatar Lake fed by the Annabranch, a Back Station of Cuthrow, that being the place for which the trackers were making, and they told Bell to tell the police to meet them there in two or three weeks' time.

They had to travel slower each day owing to old Nanya getting sick and one of the women, who had one leg shorter than the other, going lame. Although they tried hard to persuade Nanya to ride Mitchell's horse, he steadily refused and insisted on walking the whole distance. Some of the children, and the crippled woman, had a ride for a few days when both the trackers walked, but it took in all ten days to reach the Annabranch, a few miles below Popatar lake, where an old white shepherd was camped in a bark hut, shepherding sheep for Cuthrow Station.

A shepherd's life was very lonely in those days. They were put in charge of a few hundred sheep and stationed in some lonely place far removed from the home station. Their job was to watch the sheep all day and yard them at night. They saw no one from the day they left the station till the ration cart visited them once a month, bringing rations and mail, when newspapers six months old would be eagerly read. Everything contained in the papers would be news.

During the ten days journeying through the desert, Nanya and Mitchell spent a lot of time together. They walked and talked all day and sat and talked late at night. During those talks Nanya, whose memory had become quite clear again, repeated and lived again his life, right back to when he was a small boy. Mitchell told Nanya the story of his flight from the camp, as it was told by Mitchell's mother who was one of the girls of the tribe at that time. When told her name, Nanya remembered her well. Mitchell told Nanya his father died the night after he ran away. Nanya said he knew, because that day the big kangaroo, the one that was still with them, came to him and talked with him when he was cutting roots for their first drink of water. The knowledge that Mitchell already had about Nanya, and other information supplied by Nanya himself, gave Mitchell the full and true history of Nanya. There is not much more to be told, only of the civilising by kindly whites, just a short history of tragedy.

The little party landed on the bank of the Annabranch, a tributary of the Darling. The creek was in flood and with the exception of Nanya, none had ever seen water like this. They must have thought it was a level road or clay pan, for two children, a boy and a girl about eight or ten, ran down the bank and jumped into the water and were not seen again. Nanya had to tell them all about the river and make them be careful, or I suppose others would have done the same, thinking it was level ground. There was no mourning for the loss of the children, so it will be surmised that the loss or death of children was common with them.

A suitable camp was chosen and McGregor rode off up the creek to see if he could find the Lake; they knew they couldn't be far from it because they found signs of sheep and the shepherd's horses tracks. He discovered they were only about four miles from the Lake. He visited the shepherd who was surprised, but pleased, to see and talk with someone. He had very little tucker, but was expecting the ration cart any day. He invited them to bring the tribe up close to camp while they were waiting for the police to come. When McGregor returned to the party, Mitchell told him that Nanya had taken a bad turn, so they laid him on a blanket by the fire, when he asked them all to come close. He spoke in the new language, the one he and Mimi made by cutting short long words and making short sounds like grunts, to convey certain messages to each other. Lumpy neck, who had learned some of the original language, told Mitchell parts of the conversation which he, Mitchell, couldn't follow. Nanya spoke as follows. 'Now children, I am going to leave you tonight to join my father. When I was a young man I committed the greatest sin our people can commit. I broke the Bora Law, but I did what no other man ever did, I evaded the punishment of the spear. Your mother and I both knew we were doing wrong, but we were both young and we loved. We both thought at the time that we had done something clever, by dodging the Bora. It wasn't many years after that we both wished we hadn't been so clever, for although we dodged the spear, the 'gingue' law was too strong for us, the Bora sent Wirrugar after us, we were punished through our children. We saw you marry each other and have deformed children. Then when Mimi died, I was left alone to watch you turn into animals, not like man, but I couldn't tell you because I did the same thing. I am going back to the desert and I hope you will soon follow.' The very minute that Nanya breathed his last, two big kangaroos followed by the dingo pack was seen making straight back to the desert. Kangaroo shooters and dingo-trappers to this day, tell of two old-men kangaroos which live in the heart of Scotia Scrub, and defy leaden bullets. Are they the spirits of Nanya and his father? Who knows.

On the second day after they buried the body of Nanya, the party of squatters, settlers and police arrived, not by motorcar, but on horseback, and some in horse-drawn vehicles, and spring carts loaded with all kinds of food, clothing of all kinds and blankets. Some of the squatters drove in buckboards. The squatters' wives took charge of the women and girls. They gave them each dresses and other clothing and told them by sign to put the clothes on. Some of them put the dresses on upside down, some poked their legs in the sleeves and tried to walk. It took a while to dress them. The same thing was happening with the men who put their arms through the legs of the trousers and their legs in the sleeves of the shirts. Some put both legs in one trouser leg. They jump along and fall, laughing. Everyone was in good spirit.

Food was served out, which the women had prepared with great kindness, such lovely cakes and pies, the result of this feast was the beginning of their death knell, their stomachs were not adapted for such food. The police then read a Proclamation, which none of the Aborigines understood, declaring them subjects of her Majesty the Queen, that they would be taken to Pooncarie, and cared for by the Government. Then commenced the civilising process. After the party of white citizens left, it started to rain and continued for several days. I do not suggest it was the first rain these people ever experienced, but in all their lives they had never worn clothes. They have never seen any shelters, they had never built mia-mias like other natives, so when it started to rain, Mitchell built tents which had been left by the Government and they all packed into three tents. Mitchell and McGregor (who remained with them with orders to escort them to Pooncarie) had a tent to themselves, but before the tents were erected it rained in torrents. The people got wet through and when they packed into the tent with wet clothes and wet blankets, and lay coiled up all night and next day, it is no wonder that they contracted pneumonia and before aid could be brought three women and two children died. That made eight counting the two who got drowned and Nanya, leaving twenty-five souls to be civilised. The nice food brought by the whites and other ailments that were altogether new to them, the two trackers helped all they could [sic]. One went to the shepherd and got two fat wethers. While he was away the other got the flour of which they had a big supply and made 'dampers' and 'johnny cakes'. He showed them how to use the white man's 'tucker' and tea and sugar. The children ate the treacle and jam from the tins with a stick. Some of the natives tried to make damper as they had seen Mitchell do, but instead of making dough, they mixed it on a sheet of bark with water, and then poured it on to the coals, not knowing any better.

When the rain cleared off and they marked the graves of their eight dead ones, McGregor borrowed the spring cart from the shepherd and packed everything into it, together with those who were too sick to walk and they started for Pooncarie. They went around the lake to a place where they could cross the Annabranch, and only travelled about ten miles when another died, so they camped and buried her, a little woman badly deformed. The dysentery got among them and three more died.

A week later they arrived on the Darling opposite Pooncarie. They were taken across in a boat and poor Lumpy fell out of the boat and was drowned. So out of thirty-three, only twenty reached Pooncarie. The girl who was described as good looking was taken by a squatter and married a boy of her own colour, who was working at the station. There is nothing more to say.

Just two years saw the last of them. With the exception of this one girl, the tribe was extinct. She had one son, and died on giving birth to her second child. And so the Bora took them all. But they are only a few who have suffered by white man's civilisation. Haven't the Aborigines been civilised right down from the first advent of whites to the present day? The same protection continues, even to the half-caste descendants of the white man.

Harry Mitchell told me that the son of the last girl of the Scotia tribe, is still alive and that he is known as Mulga Fred. Others claim that the boy when very young went travelling with a buckjump show and is known as Queensland Harry. I know both those old Aboriginal showmen, both good rough riders and whip crackers, but I don't suppose we will ever know which is the sole survivor of the 'Scotia Blacks'.

Christmas

The plain was filled to the brim of its encircling hills with heat. The vitality of the Federal capital that stretched over the plain in outline still ebbed away daily through the narrow channel of the railway and by the arterial roads to Goulburn and Yass. Everyone who could get leave was going away for Christmas, home to Melbourne or Sydney, or just away from Canberra. Three days before Christmas. Leave had reached saturation point and the staffs of the Government offices were down to the irreducible minimum. While those going were in the majority over those staying the atmosphere had been gay, but now the heat pressed down on the devitalized city where those left felt that they had nothing to hope for this side of Easter. The trickle of visitors from outside was so thin as to make no difference. The hotels provided a barometer of the sinking population. The Canberra, as being the haunt of the privileged emptied first so that by Christmas Day hardly one of its regular patrons was left. Hobart House at the bottom of the scale could still number a dozen or so.

The hotels of Canberra differ one from another in three things only — name, situation and tariff. They follow the pattern upon which the Federal Capital is built and that is hierarchic. They are seven in number beginning with the Canberra and passing down in nice gradations under the names of State capitals to Hobart House between which and the girls' hostel and bachelor quarters there is nothing. It is a nice question whether the similarity of the hotels within and without was due to democratic feeling that insisted on giving to the least of the public servants all the advantages enjoyed by the most highly paid or whether the elimination of differences was a cunning trick to separate the sheep from the goats on financial grounds while cynically depriving them of the cover of preference. It cuts both ways of course. The member of Parliament is forced to spend his substance on the Canberra just as surely as the post-office clerk is forced to declare his degree by living at Hobart House.

Hobart House was quite a pleasant place to live, well run and spacious. Visitors to Canberra who did not know the rules of the game, often chose it. It was a bland looking building in dark brick with two wings at a wide angle between which the sun rose. It was like a benevolent duenna sitting among the harlequin scatter of cottages that housed the married public servants whose salaries ranged them with the inmates of the hotel.

The guests at Hobart House were for the most part young clerks or women who had lifted themselves above the girls' hostel. They spoke of that charming place, Spanish mission with vermilion shutters and little cypress trees in tubs, as if it were Hades. They were mostly teachers and secretaries. The teachers had all gone in the course of nature a week before. Most of the secretaries had escaped in the wakes of their chiefs, more than half of the young men had got away by dint of applying early or had wangled leave at the last moment. One having no leave due to him had got himself sent to Melbourne on official business. He was always a resourceful fellow.

Coming in to luncheon — he called it mess though he had never been in the army — the day before Christmas Eve, Mr Gibbons judged that the company had reached bedrock. He looked disparagingly at them as one looks at remainders but paused in his dignified progress at a table occupied by four young men, to say 'Ah, the indispensables.'

'No, Mr Gibbons,' stout Mr Juliffe answered, 'the mugs.'

Every one laughed. They were filled with the mild good humour of resignation.

Mr Gibbons passed on followed by his wife and daughter. As the oldest inhabitant, Mr Gibbons occupied a strategic table that commanded the whole dining room; for the same reason he felt he had the right to premier service. Even before he was seated the waitress could feel his eyes fasten like fish hooks in her back. His wife began thinking automatically 'I wish that girl would hurry.' Molly crumbled her bread and stared at the water-jug.

Mr Gibbons read the menu through aloud in a rather rich voice, then he considered it and finally delivered his verdict. Mrs Gibbons was always very cursory about her food and was pleasant to Clara to make up.

While luncheon was being brought Mr Gibbons took stock of everyone who was left over the top of his glasses, his dome like forehead thrust forward, his neat grey beard withdrawn into the V of his collar. There were twelve of them and a few visitors who did not count. There were the four young men all wishing no doubt that they could take [off] their coats. Mr Gibbons was against the taking off of coats in public and sat through the worst weather in his little box of an office fully clothed even to a starched shirt front, vainly hoping that his example shamed the others. The pride of a man who has a cold bath in winter was as nothing to his. There was Vera Simpson sprawling her bare arms across the table beside Cliff Somers. She called him her young man and Mr Gibbons supposed they were engaged. He couldn't be spared from his department and she had stayed back to be with him. They did not look very pleased with each other but then they never did. Their courtship of one another had had the harsh metallic quality of Vera's red hair — a laughing squabbling occasionally vindictive affair, with an undercurrent of ardour that without the veil of sentimentality seemed anything but decent to Mr Gibbons. Vera he ignored and Vera did not mind. He knew it would be dangerous to do anything else. For Cliff he felt the hostility he insensibly felt for all young men — people who might still succeed where he had failed. Cliff did not look like a clerk, heavy handed, heavy mouthed, but he would probably go crashing forward with those powerful shoulders and sullen impervious front. There was Lois Ralston, very young still, very fine, very quiet, with no gift for making friends or enemies. The girls' hostel was the place for her, she didn't belong in the freer atmosphere of Hobart House. There was Gaden who sat at her table, a man with a grievance, a terrible bore. Mr Gibbons himself had a grievance but he did not talk about it. It was more than a grievance, it was a mortal hurt, he had not succeeded. He valued position above everything in the world but he had not attained it. When he looked in the glass he found it hard to believe for he was the best imitation of a man of authority it is possible to achieve. He had all the outward and none of the inward marks of success. Some of the happiest moments of his life had been when he was mistaken for a Cabinet Minister. He looked exactly as Cabinet Ministers are expected to look — bland, rich in years, mellow, authoritative, weighty. It was natural to him, he carried through the most intimate and informal moments of his life with superb aplomb. In his bath he behaved as if he were receiving a deputation. But at Hobart House no one of course could be mistaken for a Cabinet Minister because they did not frequent the place. All this magnificence was expended on a very paltry job in the Printing Office. He had, it is true, a minute office to himself where he spun out a fine intricate web of returns that interested no one. It was callously believed in the Department that he had been given this job to keep him quiet and since it did not matter in the least, was given freedom to erect card indexes and elaborate systems to his heart's content. It wouldn't be for long for he was sixty three and would be due to retire in two years. He couldn't understand his failure to rise in the service. Year by year his dignity increased, his sensitiveness to insult increased. He was always imagining affronts, always thinking of his due. Canberra had made him worse. In Melbourne he had been lost in a great population. He had been able to lead his private life apart from his official life and to make of it what he at least felt to be a success. Here he was chained to his job, branded, in prison. There was no society but official society, the Blue Book, that cruel naked record of every public servant's salary, position and age, was in every one's hands. This place put the final screw upon his failure, it exposed his position — an old man long out-distanced by his juniors. Hobart House was bad but he could not cram his pride into one of the little pill box houses that would have been allotted to him. He might have been able to stay at the Perth next in grade above Hobart House, but the margin of tariff between the two hotels paid for the upkeep of his car. Much of his self respect had become bound up in the car so that to give it up would have been another bitter defeat. His wife believed too that he would rather lord it at Hobart House, taking advantage of his years and his long residence than sink into the commonality at the Perth, but then a sediment of bitterness had gathered in her heart and the least breath was sufficient to stir it through her blood.

One of the twelve was still missing, that boisterous young fellow Smith from his own department. A distant banging of wire doors announced his coming then he burst into the room indecently, hot, fatiguingly cheerful. He couldn't wait to reach his seat. 'I say, you fellows,' he called out half across the room. 'What do you think? I've got leave, luck, what?'

The effect was instantaneous. He didn't seem to notice anything but flung himself down in his chair so that a puff of hot air came from him.

'How did you manage it?' asked one of the young men not trying to conceal his bitterness.

'Just wangled it. Soup, Clara. I'll go across to Yass on the service car tonight and pick up the express.'

They hated him. Even the visitors were aware of it and turned their eyes on him in a dull stare. The man and woman in spectacles and their three plain fair children looked at him enquiringly with the last of their intelligence. They had come to Canberra because of its educative value and all the morning in the heat the parents had been conscientiously pointing out objects of interest to their progeny and telling them out of the guide-book how much everything cost. The dyspeptic widow raised her head apprehensively. The motorist who had stopped for luncheon only thought 'what a crew' and thanked God he was not as they.

Smith had done a dreadful thing. He had dispersed their resignation, he had offered the fatal contrast, had dragged them back into the arena to suffer their defeat anew. Old Gibbons turned positively yellow. If it had not been a man from his own department he wouldn't have minded. The young jackanape had influence, he was another of the favoured ones. He had not himself applied for leave but that did not prevent him from being jealous. The company fell apart aimless and scattered like beads when the thread of a necklace has broken.

December 24th

Christmas was a burden to them all. It was like an obvious tune to which one is unable to respond, calling insistently for a response one is unable to give, repeating itself again and again while one suffers the tortures of impotence. The Government Departments paid lip service to Christmas by closing at twelve and everyone was cast out into the heat to choose between waiting for a bus or walking. The means of transport were doing their share to exacerbate the situation. Offices were scattered far apart in the giant plan of the city. The Commission's buses linked them in a loose web. Now that Canberra was nearly empty the timetables were reduced and buses ran or did not run with maddening inconsequence.

Vera and her young man walked across the paddock called Site of the National Museum, their heads bent against the heat. The grass was the colour of dust, smelt of dust and shed its barbed seeds upon them. They walked apart in two wavering lines, exasperation in their hearts. Vera wondered why she had been such an ass as to stay behind to be with Cliff. In this heat love was about as refreshing as flat soda water. It just showed you how stupid it was to be unselfish.

Cliff was resentful. Why had Vera insisted on staying? Since he had to stay in this hole of a place he would have got through it best alone. He would have put his head down to it and hunched himself up in moroseness, suspended animation as it were, so that he could live through the time without exposing himself. But now he supposed Vera would expect him to be pleasant. He was damned if he'd be pleasant to Vera or to any one else.

The house when they reached it offered only a temporary haven. At first it seemed cool and then the tepid twilight of the dining room became as insufferable as the heat of the sun. Hot soup. No one had ever heard of iced consomme apparently, what barbarism! Mr Gibbons noted with displeasure that the cooking showed all those signs of casualness that generally precede a festival when the cook's attention is focussed on the future. He had no sympathy with slackness.

'I don't think we can go out again this afternoon' said the mother of the three children to her husband in a low voice. The children sat in splodges too tired to keep their mouths shut and the sun had burnt their fair skins scarlet across their cheek bones and over the unformed little noses.

'It seems a pity to miss anything and we will only be here two more days.'

'Perhaps we could go up to the Nurseries in the cool of the evening if there is a bus.'

'Yes,' he said brightening, 'we could do that.'

'It would be a pity to miss anything. I mean to say goodness knows when we'll come again so we ought to see everything.'

They were badly off and holidays like this were very rare. They could not help feeling conscientious about not wasting a minute.

The manageress was very busy preparing for Christmas Day. She even meant to decorate the public rooms in the evening. She would do it herself with the help of a friend because of course one couldn't expect extra from the maids. She even felt like apologising to Cook for Christmas, the poor woman felt the heat so. On Christmas Eve, in the middle of her preparations Mrs Forbes was overtaken by a sense of their futility. 'Not one of them cares a straw about Christmas' she thought. 'If only there was one single solitary person to care and be pleased with me I'd enjoy it.' Christmas is a thing you cannot possibly enjoy alone. Mrs Forbes felt lonely all of a sudden. 'It's plain stupid to be going to all this trouble' she told herself. 'Perhaps if I went down to the shops and saw the decorations I would feel better about it.' But it was too far and too hot. 'I'll just do my duty by them. Since it's Christmas, they'll have to have Christmas dinner, even if it's too hot to eat or they'll complain.' The third person plural loomed in all her thoughts. 'They' was to her a single conglomerate guest, who wrestled with her, argued with her, supplicated her continually and to whom she paid a defensive but almost ritualistic tribute.

The dyspeptic widow came to her door and knocked, a little flickering knock. 'It's my water. I always have a cup of hot water an hour after dinner. Doctor's orders, you know. But there's no one in the kitchen so I can't get it.'

'I'll get it for you Mrs Phillips.'

'Oh thank you so much. I didn't want to trouble you. It needn't be boiling you know but it must have boiled.'

Mr Gaden was lying in wait for her. 'Just a minute Mrs Forbes. My room is deuced hot — now the house is half empty couldn't I change over?'

Down the passage Mr Gibbons loomed. They were upon her, the pack was after the white hare.

The afternoon passed away like a sluggish stream of warm water. Evening came. The houses that were still inhabited broke into patches of torrid yellow light. Sprinklers were turned on in the fenceless front gardens and a few gramophones awoke to cry in the night. The darkness brought no surcease from the heat. The night was like a lidless eye. Every one in the unreasonable depths of their hearts expected a miracle and was angry because there was none. The season when people expected to be cheerful would come and go and they would get nothing out of it.

Mrs Phillips made her preparations for bed, arranging all the things she might need in the night on her bedside table, a glass of water, her indigestion tablets, a bottle of citronella, smelling salts, a Bible. She was in no hurry to get into bed. She knew she would not sleep. By next Christmas she would probably be dead, and a good thing too, but she found no real elation in the thought. The bell of the Catholic Church began to ring for midnight Mass. The sound lifted a latch in her mind and she began to remember other Christmasses when the children were young, Stanley and Alma and Winifred, when her husband was alive and they were well off. She had been as happy and secure as anyone in the world. She had known she was happy, she didn't have to reproach herself for not having appreciated the good times while she had them. She had come away to escape Christmas and to relieve her children of the necessity of inviting her to their homes. She knew so well how it would be. Alma wouldn't want her because she would have to have her husband's people and she couldn't, no, she couldn't get on with old Mrs Brown even at Christmas time, and it wouldn't be convenient for Winifred with a young baby and the three other children. Of course Stanley's smart wife wouldn't want poor old mother in the middle of her fashionable Christmas house party. They were good children, they wouldn't dream of letting her stay quietly in the boarding house, they would argue it out among themselves and there might be a little feeling about it, but they were always sweet to her. She had had to pretend that her heart was set on going away for Christmas, that the doctor had suggested it. If only she had a big house and plenty of money and could have had them all to spend Christmas with her, how happy she could have been. Winifred could have rested, she would have got a special nurse for the children, the Browns would have had to find somewhere else to spend their Christmas and she'd have given a party smart enough to satisfy even Stanley's wife. Or if only Maurice hadn't died and left her alone, they could have been happy, just the two of them together, and no one would have worried. They could have remembered other Christmases without pain and talked of old times. Because she had neither husband nor home and very little money, she had lost everything else, even her children. Their very love was not proof against the hard fact of her age and dependence. 'No one has been unkind to me but I am very unhappy because I have nothing of my own,' she thought. She got up and went to her suitcase. She would take one of the powders the doctor had given her for when she could bear her sleeplessness no longer. Tonight she must sleep, draw down a black curtain over the too raw knowledge of her unhappiness.

Mrs Gibbons went to her daughter's room. Molly in a coolie coat was brushing her long dark hair. Only her hair was beautiful but there was too much of it. Done up it looked clumsy. Between the veils of her hair her face looked paler and younger and in her eyes as she brushed there was an intent withdrawn look as if she listened to the faint echo of a tryst with adventure that she had not kept. Molly was thirty.

Mrs Gibbons sat on the edge of the bed. She really had nothing to say. She had wandered in here in her restless seeking after comfort and she knew by Molly's face that she had surprised and interrupted her. Interrupted her in what? There was nothing here. It could only be her thoughts, and what could they be? Since she was here, she had better talk.

'Did Gordon say anything in his letter about motoring up to see us?'

'No. He's giving the children a Christmas tree tonight. They are going to Eleanor's place tomorrow and to the sea side for three weeks. Sounds cosy, doesn't it?'

Molly knew that she knew all this. They were just making conversation as they always did.

'Father is very annoyed because Lin hasn't written or sent. I do think he might have written for Christmas if only to save me from a lecture on the ingratitude of children.'

Molly smiled at her in the glass. 'It's just Father's way, don't take any notice of him. He thinks more of Lincoln than of any of us because Lin always took him with a grain of salt.'

'Don't you?'

Molly shrugged her shoulders. They couldn't talk about him. They never had and they couldn't now.

'Christmas Eve,' said Mrs Gibbons, vaguely fumbling for another point of contact. 'It's a dull Christmas for you, dear.'

'Perhaps I've grown out of Christmas. It really doesn't mean anything to me.'

Mrs Gibbons felt that she too had grown out of Christmas. 'Yes' she said, 'but I can't help wishing it would mean something. It ought to be a sort of emotional clearing house. It would do us so much good if we could all feel something quite obvious and definite, in chorus as it were.'

'There's too much chorus as it is, other people's feelings dragging at you. Christmas seems a little' she paused tying the end of her plait with a tape and pulling it tight, 'messy. I'll be glad when it's over.' She was obviously ready for bed. She slipped off the coolie coat and stood for a moment in her night gown. Her squarish lines were visible through the thin material, the light brittleness of girlhood was quite gone, she was waiting to get into bed.

Mrs Gibbons rose to go. She paused at the door. 'But you used to like Christmas when you were a child, you did have fun, didn't you?' She was ashamed of the appeal in her voice.

'Great fun, I loved it.' But the cool light voice meant nothing but to be kind. 'Good-night, mother.'

Mrs Gibbons stood in the dark passage. She could not bring herself to enter the room she shared with her husband to watch him lay his things in meticulous order for the morning, to listen to remarks she had known by heart for twenty years, to offer him mild wifely answers. Suddenly after thirty five years of patience she could not bear it. Boredom swept her like nausea. She went on to the little built out verandah at the end of the passage and leant against the parapet pressing her bare arms against the rough bricks. She fixed her eyes on a light until it was drowned in tears. A chaotic dumb misery that she knew now had been pursuing her for years rose and overwhelmed her. She stood absolutely still letting it possess her. Desperate longings fluttered in her mind. 'I'll go back to Molly and tell her I'm unhappy. I can't bear it. I'll kneel beside her in the dark with my arms round her and my cheek on hers. We will cry together and melt away my pain. Oh, Molly, Molly, together. She isn't happy. Forgive me Molly, for not having made you happy. I meant to protect you but I didn't succeed. It wasn't protection you wanted was it?' But she didn't move. She had not the courage to put her sudden longing for her daughter to the touch. To go now and talk to her as they never had talked would be too crucial a thing to do. Molly wasn't a child any longer, not even really young. The memory of the mature set lines of her body under the thin nightgown came between them. Molly was just another woman and they had very little in common. Motherhood like Christmas could be outgrown. Would Molly find her love just messy?

She was a little calmer, she could even marvel at this sudden assault of grief and try to isolate its cause. She had found something irreparable waiting for her in the dark passage, the irreparable past waiting for her between her daughter's room and her husband's, accusing her. Something as slow and quiet as a force of nature had ruined her happiness and only now when it was ruined did she know it. Like a map she saw the past spread out, Edwin's vanity, his touchiness, his strictness with the children. She had bent her will to his, flattered him, done all she could to keep things running smoothly in the home. It had been 'Hush, darling, don't disturb father.' 'You mustn't do that when father is at home, it vexes him.' She had shielded them from their father, kept all the good things in her own gift and at the same time fed his vanity, encouraged him to be overbearing. When father and children did come into conflict there was no fund of intimacy to draw on. The children expected misunderstanding and selfishness from him; his mind was focussed on the powers and rights of fatherhood. Always the mother stood between them sacrificing herself to peace. With advancing time old Gibbons grew more vain and overbearing, he became a petty tyrant. The boys were glad to leave home, Molly protected herself in another way. She didn't flatter and wheedle as her mother did — she withdrew into herself to a stronghold where her father could not reach her. She mutilated her life, proofed herself against the endless tedium of his arrogance by a stubborn self sufficiency that cut herself off from others. He scarcely interfered with her, accepted from her as sufficient the worn small change of filial duty, asked very little of her. He wasn't strong. Even his cantankerousness gave way before a determined front. For all these years his wife had been pandering to a man of straw while she lost her children. If she had joined with the children reasonably and cheerfully, and bluffed him out of his foolishness, four of them to one, all would have been well. Instead she had made him a sacred bugbear. Four of them to one and she would have been with the children. She had wrecked them all on a pebble, an error of judgment, a stupid sacrifice. She thought on, brokenly, disjointedly, the flotsam of thirty five years jumbled in her mind. She had read her riddle too late. She had set too high a value on Edwin, taken him too seriously. He wasn't worth it. She felt no immediacy, only when she thought of returning to her room did she feel again the prick of distress. She could not bring herself to return.

The bell of the Catholic Church began to ring for midnight Mass. A shadow emerged from the house and hurried down the road. As it passed a lamp standard Mrs Gibbons recognised Juliffe, the fat young man in the brown suit. His movements were furtive and hasty as if he were ashamed of the sentiment that was taking him to church. Mrs Gibbons stayed where she was until her body ached with fatigue. Exhaustion broke down her disinclination to go to her bedroom. All grief and all pain were swallowed up in the desire to rest. In the dark passage no presence awaited her. She held her breath listening to her husband's quiet breathing and slipped into bed undetected with relief.

Lois Ralston awoke in the night. She had no idea of the time but night was at its zenith. From her bed she could see a great arc of sky with the stars blazing in the moonless night. She lay and stared at them in tranquil amazement. She had never seen stars like this in a night so still and splendid — night of beauty, night of miracles. Her heart was flooded with happiness. Tonight was not like other nights, it was Christmas. All her nineteen Christmasses had been happy, this one would be happy too. Last Christmas she had met Tom, perhaps next Christmas they could be engaged for he would be twenty one. Like shining candles the Christmasses of her life stood before her and behind her. She did not have to watch the miracle of stars. There would be plenty more. She fell asleep.

December 25th
Christmas morning was hot with an ashy smear on the horizon that might mean change. Into the drought stricken fields had come a tinge of purple. The hills that hemmed in the capital were slate blue. The white blocks of Government offices were like incandescent wedding cakes.

Two of the young men set an old gramophone going in a vain effort to disperse the sabbatical air of the day. By ten o'clock dinner had already begun to make itself atmospherically felt. The smell filled Mrs Phillips with foreboding. All the food would be rich and heavy, nothing she could eat and refusing would make her conspicuous.

Clara began to set the tables, singing with a twanging voice. It was a thing that had never happened before. Every one passing the door stopped and peeped through the fly screen.

'The old tree's blossomed,' said Juliffe.

The small tables were put together to make one long one with flowers and fruit down the centre and the special mid-week issue of clean napkins were folded fancifully into lilies, mitres and fans. Gaden looked at the scene with disgust. 'Forcing Christmas down our throats' he thought, and determined not to give up one jot of his gloom.

By eleven o'clock every one had lapsed into quiescence and was waiting consciously or unconsciously for dinner. There was a sudden rush and clatter outside. One of the young men opened a drowsy eye.

'Has the change come?' he asked.

'No, you silly ass, someone has driven up in a motor car. Another Christmas reveller, God help him.'

'Sounds a cheery sort of cove.'

There were flying steps in the corridor.

'Who was it?'

'Couldn't see.'

'Something might have turned up. You never know.' They strolled out in single file, disconsolate cigarettes hanging from disconsolate lips, to look.

When Lois heard the car stop she knew. She stood for one trembling vivid second, then ran to the stairhead, down the stairs and along the corridor. In the entrance hall she ran into a young man with his arms full of parcels. He opened his arms, scattering the floor with a miscellany of objects and caught her to him. It was the fine reckless gesture of the perfect lover.

'Oh, Tom,' she gasped, as the breath left her lungs.

'Isn't it bully, isn't it Merry Christmas?'

Over Tom's shoulder Lois became aware of four young men standing contemplatively in a row.

'Come in here quick.' She half pushed him through the swing doors into the lounge. It was little more than a jungle of arm chairs and a fire place and had at first sight an aspect of utter vacancy.

'It's all right, old thing, it's more than all right.'

'Oh, Tom darling, how did you manage to get here?'

'Sally and I tottered off at dawn. Give me a kiss while I think where I put the ring.'

A head baldish, bearded, rose over the top of an arm chair. Lois's kiss died on her lips.

'Er, won't you come out on the verandah, Tom.'

Outside a blaze of white sunshine struck them like a blow. Inside Mr Gibbons slid down again into his leather chair. People had no right to rush about in this weather as if they owned the place, it was indecent. The room was hotter, they had let in the smell of dinner and had taken some of his energy away with them. He got up and peered through the glass door to see where they'd got to. They had disappeared. The day looked prematurely old, the sky was pallid and vacant, a great vacuum, the earth was blanched with heat, the distant a sullen blue grey. A cloud of dust seemed to be curling the far horizon. It was apocalyptic. His wife came in and moved over to the writing table.

'The little Ralston girl has a visitor. I met them in the passage.'

'Umph,' he answered, relaxing again into the leather chair that had cooled in his brief absence. No office, no mail, no newspaper. He was bored. He was angry because Christmas was not turning out better. He put it all into the exclamation, and drummed maddeningly on the arm of his chair with his hard white fingers.

Mrs Gibbons took no notice. She indulged herself in the minor pleasure of ignoring his mood. The hotel notepaper seemed to be covered with fine grit, her J nib made a phenomenal noise in the quiet room as it scratched on from platitude to platitude. She looked over her shoulder at her husband and found he had dozed off with his mouth open. He looked foolish and impotent. She stared and stared at him. He had taken her in all these years and that was all he was. She would never be bluffed again. It was too late of course, all the harm was done but still she had the satisfaction of being free. She was tired after last night but triumphant too. To feel so vividly she must be still young, younger than he was. He wasn't capable of anything but vanity now. She had a vision of the two young things she had met on the stairs hand in hand. That was being really young. She glanced again at her husband. No, it had never been like that.

Light quick footsteps sounded in the corridor. Mr Gibbons awoke with alacrity. He opened the door and looked out in time to see two figures disappearing into the manageress's office at the end of the corridor and to hear its lock snap. Mrs Forbes smiled at him with satisfied sentiment as she retraced her steps to the kitchen. He retreated with dignity. The smell of roasting came into the room in a great puff. Mr and Mrs Gibbons looked at the clock.

Half an hour later Juliffe sought out Cliff and Vera on their upstairs balcony.

'Did the apparition of the young lovers appear to you?'

'It did,' said Vera, 'it was exactly like the last page of a soppy novel.'

'He came in a yellow single seater, one ear up and one ear down, been in a number of fights but still game. Pally little car. Thought he was Father Christmas at first, you could hardly see him for parcels.'

'You're very newsy, July.'

'I do seem to pick up things don't I? I know all about them.'

'What's he like?'

'Oh, just a grin on legs. His father is something big in Sussex St, rich in butter fat, you know. He and our Lois have been sweet on one another for a year. He is a student gay and yesterday when the results came out he found he had scraped through contrary to all expectations and his old man was so bucked he gave him a handful of money and told him he could go out and get engaged. So out he dashed and bought the ring and a few oddments, leaped into his yellow peril and here he is.'

'All the world loves a lover,' remarked Cliff.

'And we're only young once,' added Vera.

Cliff caught her quick venomous glance and pinched her arm. Juliffe hadn't finished yet and wouldn't go till he had.

'They've appeared to every one,' he said, 'and we're all changed. Better and sweeter, you know. All they wanted was a quiet place to make love in. They even tried a bathroom but Gaden was in there trying to keep cool. At last Forbie let them have her office. They are there now. Well, so long, it's time we washed our handies for dinner.'

Below Clara beat upon the gong, sending a long tentacle of brazen sound down every corridor. Cliff pulled Vera from her lounge. She came limply and let herself fall against him. He kissed her savagely. She was a little devil but he wanted her. Perhaps they were missing something but then they weren't the romantic sort. They'd be sure to fight later on so why not now? Vera returned his kiss with half shut eyes. A slight tremor ran from her body to his.

The dining room seemed dark and was stiflingly hot. Some one said 'It's clouding over.' Mrs Forbes was showing them to their places as if they were guests. Mr Gibbons's eyes moved sharply, suspiciously from side to side. Had she put him at the head of the table? He would refuse to sit anywhere else. Did she intend sitting down with them? 'And will you take the head of the table Mr Gibbons?' He relaxed. The little widow was on his right and Mrs Gibbons on his left. Clara came to them first. He began to feel like the host of the party. The young people were at the far end of the table. He could see the strange young man sitting next to Lois Ralston. By Jove, she was a pretty little piece and he had never noticed it before, something distinguished about her. Every one addressed himself conscientiously to the hot rich soup. A little simmer of laughter began at the end of the table and spread slowly up, the regulars began to talk to the tourists. Steaming plates of roast turkey and fowl were brought in.

'There's no extra charge for this,' the conscientious tourist whispered to his wife.

'That's why it's such a good idea to come away at Christmas,' she murmured back. 'Now Ruby, don't leave any of your nice chicken.' The little girls hid their pleasure in the food under polite stolidity.

A sudden gust of wind rattled sand against the windows. One of the boys jumped up and ran to the windows. 'It's going to rain' he called back. The sky was massed with dark clouds, they roofed in the plain between the hills. The dusty wind piled them up darker and heavier and the space between earth and sky filled with a lurid storm light. Familiar objects were changed to something sinister and strange under that demoniacal sky. A silence fell on the dining room, other guests broke ranks and gathered with the watchers at the window till only a little group at the head of the table was left.

'What is it? What is it?' asked the little girl Ruby, jumping up and down, unable to see till Gaden made room for her at one of the windows, lifting her up to look out.

'It's raining over there.' The edges of the cloud seemed now to touch the earth in a misty curtain.

'I can hear it.'

The windows were thrown open and the wind came in playing havoc with the table decorations. Large slow drops were falling and the twanging harp music of heavy rain coming nearer and nearer filled the room. Faces turned mutely to the hills were blanched in the storm light. Then suddenly the rain was upon them in a thick silver curtain. You could hear the hiss as it fell on earth scorched by months of drought and on the burnt up grass. It settled down into a steady drumming. The diners drifted back to their cold dinners. Already the scent of grateful earth came through the windows and the oppression of the heat was lifted.

The laughter spread along both sides of the table. Mrs Phillips, a pink flush on her cheek, decided to risk some Christmas pudding. Mr Gibbons was telling her about the Christmasses of his youth and she thought him a very pleasant gentleman. It was a long time now since any one had been kind to her without making her feel old. The three little girls came round with boxes of crackers, mutely offering everybody one, then Lois offering her big beribboned box of chocolates and letting every one see her ring. Mrs Forbes came and whispered to Mr Gibbons 'Would he . . . ?' Yes, he would.

In flowing periods he proposed the health of the betrothed couple so happily in their midst. For a moment Tom and Lois did not recognise themselves in the thicket of verbiage, then they stood where they were, hand in hand, blushing, embarrassed and happy. It had become their party.

After the long feast was over no one wanted to do anything but watch the rain. They stood about in groups and looked at the life giving deluge. It brought peace to everyone. They shared the elemental joy of the thirsty ground. Where the landscape had been cruel and bitter in the morning it was blurred and gentle now, the purple brown of the distances had softened to silver brown, the hills were lost in mist, the water running off the baked earth made a happy gurgle.

Towards sunset there was a lull. The clouds broke in the heat to show a long reach of tranquil primrose sky. The air was cool and pure as the petal of a flower. There was a general move towards the open air. Some one said 'Let's get the car and go for a spin.' Juliffe brought round his crazy Ford that his friends usually feared and scorned to ride in but tonight they piled happily in. One of the tourists had a big car and he gladly filled it, the fair little girls sitting in solemn and speechless ecstasy on strange men's knees. Cliff Somers got out his motor bike and Vera having thrust her long legs into breeches established herself on the pillion. Mr Gibbons turned to Molly 'My dear, will you get out the car?' He turned to Mrs Phillips, 'I hope you will honour us.'

Mrs Gibbons looked sharply at her husband. He was proposing to take the holy sacred car out when the roads were flowing with mud and water, and he was giving a stranger a ride! He stood there, puffed up with benevolence, waiting for Molly, making his beau geste. Everyone had been packed in somewhere, they were ready to start. Mrs Forbes came out to see them go. 'They' had had a happy Christmas, she liked to see 'them' happy. Mr Gibbons was coming towards her, he was probably going to spoil it all with a complaint. He said 'We can't leave you behind, Mrs Forbes, after the splendid Christmas you have arranged for us. There is a vacant seat in my car. I would be delighted ...'

The little yellow single seater with Lois and Tom was the first to get away. It took the long straight road towards the hills and the sunset, and the other cars strung out behind it following it into the fading light through the fresh keen air as if they were pursuing happiness.

White Kid Gloves

Sprawled beneath the sky, the blacksmith's shed of corrugated iron, its back broken and rusty, upheld by jarrah beams and posts; one, new red, squared-off, by the wide-open doors. A swamp gum there, silver body under snake-skin bark, peeling in flakes, an old tree, all that remained of scrub where now a country town spread, with small predatory shops and streets wandering off and losing themselves across cleared plains, among undulating hills.

The blacksmith's shop had grown along one side of a by-street. Within, as you came from the street, the dark was taken up by shapes of wood and iron, hung from the roof, crouched in the corners against the walls. Across a space of earth swept clear, the anvil struck a fang, polished, gigantic; behind, the furnace had the glowing embers of a log in the paddocks at night.

Draught horses, rank and steaming, stood against the wall near the door, their massive quarters fronted out. A chestnut in trotting tackle against the side wall slewed oblique eyes, whinnying.

The blacksmith and his men, moving about the floor from furnace to anvil, from anvil to bench behind the furnace, to the working horses, looked up as a woman walked into the smithy leading her horse; a child on his pony beside her.

'Flash dame, staying at Pratten's ... Nanja-miia,' the striker muttered under his breath.

'My hack is tender-footed. He needs shoeing,' Lady Emilia Howard said when the blacksmith went to her.

Men in the smithy saw the boss go to the horse, lift a foot, then stand off, in the head-up eyes-straight way he had talking to strangers. They did not see the irises of his eyes seethe; his face wither and harden.

As he stood before the woman, she looked stronger, physically fitter than he. A well-made creature, unsubdued, moving with assurance, she cut against the light of the doorway in riding breeches, high polished boots, skirted coat and black hat; her son on a rough pony, long gaiters buttoned over his sturdy legs, under tweed coat and cap, was dressed as no one in the smithy had ever seen a youngster dressed for riding before.

She watched the blacksmith lead her horse from the entrance to a peg on the side wall near the chestnut mare. His head moved against the satiny pelt of her hack; the back of his neck flashed to her.

The child looped his pony's reins over a post near the door and ran to the forge.

Anthony Bridges turned to the furnace and anvil again.

'Oh, smith ...'

Anthony swung to the call. He went to the woman and stared into her face again.

'Your name on the door outside attracted me. I'm looking for a friend, Colonel Bridges, whom I knew in Egypt ... some time ago. Perhaps you could tell me where to find him.'

Cranked-up and wooden, Anthony Bridges replied: 'That is my name. But I'm afraid I have not the honour of your friend's acquaintance.'

His voice clanged in the hollow twilight, wandered among dusty machine-parts hung against the roof, derelict harvesters, stump-jumps, six-furrow ploughs and drills, tree-pullers, string-carts newly painted the blue and scarlet of children's toys. The words sounded foreign, difficult to understand in such a place; their easy politeness, formality, giving the lie to what they said.

It had been raining all morning. A shower pelted along the street now, slashing out of sight the small shops crushed together in a row opposite.

Emilia sat down on an empty fruit-case near the doorway.

'We'll take a felucca and drift along the Nile' ... how could he be the same? How could he be the self-contained, quiet man whom everybody deferred to at Divisional Headquarters? 'Must ask Bridges.' 'What does Bridges say?' 'Hear how Bridges cleaned up those wells on the canal?' How often had she heard such things said. Among adventurous, hard-drinking, go-as-you-please men of the Australian regiments, Colonel Anthony Bridges had a reputation for thoroughness and reliability; for knowing to the letter every detail of military regulation and etiquette. The stories against him were all of a weakness for accoutrement, his fury if boots did not shine like polished metal, or there was a speck on his gloves. His gloves ...

Emilia watched the bare rough-haired levers of those arms and blackened claws at work: gripping along flat tongs, lift a horse-shoe, showering sparks from the furnace to anvil, turn and place it for the striker. She had jeered at hands whiter, smoother, more carefully manicured than her own: at white kid gloves they carried and flaunted when her hands were coarse and red with the constant use of disinfectants, her fingernails broken.

The bare, wooden arms and work-grimed hands menaced her as they moved over the anvil, from anvil to furnace and water-butt. She sickened, was furious, insane with rage and disgust to have been the prey of those arms and blackened claws!

Shining stretches of river ... cushions on the floor of the flat-bottomed boat ... drifting ... three-cornered sail, a moth's wing against sea and sky, pale blue ... silk of light, fading, sequined with stars. Dark figure of a boatman in the bow; throb of an Arab drum ... cries of the town, shrill and contentious, dying away ...

Lap-lap of water against the ancient wooden timbers of the felucca ... moving, unconscious of motion, almost ... stars glittering above ... below ... which was sky, which water? So clear, so still the shining ...

Quiet infiltrating, mystery, murmur of the river. Far away a Nubian boatman singing. His melody thrumming you as though you were one of those primitive, curiously intricate

stringed instruments of early Egypt, chelys, nebel, shawm or
sackbut, thrown there on the floor of the flat-bottomed boat
... Gusts and wispish rhythms of wild music beat against the
brain, with glints of tarnished gold, turquoise, colours and
odours of the mummy cases, buried treasure ... Instincts sang;
wraiths of improvisation from ruined temples, wandering
across the desert, stirred, and waved the feathery nerve crests
until body and sense, luminous, dissolved, were drawn into the
centrifugal sun of being and oblivion.

She had not been Lady Emilia Howard in Egypt, but Emily
Howard, a VAD, doing any sort of dirty work, as a favour, in aux-
iliary hospitals. She had worked hard and felt unimportant; infe-
rior to trained and competent women of the nursing service,
admiring them, envying them in the wards; but unable to get on
with them at all off duty, on their excursions, or social junketings.
So that she went about by herself in much the same detached,
self-contained way as Colonel Anthony Bridges. They had found
each other stranded on a solitary expedition beyond the Barrage.
It had been the first of many together.

Emilia had told Colonel Bridges who she was and why she
was nursing: that her husband, Sir Herbert Howard, had been
crippled by a fall from his aeroplane a year or so before the war,
and they had decided she should do war service for both. Emilia
herself had been eager for any work, however menial and ardu-
ous, to escape the futilities women were wasting their lives on in
England. She and Colonel Anthony Bridges had drifted into a
pleasant companionship with a sense of being safe in themselves,
secure from the incalculable undercurrents of sex attraction.
Their pleasant companionship had gone the way of most pleasant
companionships in Egypt.

'Anthony and yet not Anthony!' Emilia had mocked him
from the cushions of a felucca on the Nile; and found herself
daunted by his silence, his immobility.

Emilia, the self-sufficient, 'para-sexual' as she liked to say,
who set her life calmly in the channels she wished to go, had
found herself challenged and forced to lures she despised, to

break the reserve and controls of her Anthony. She had won him with painted lips, perfume behind her ears, eyes uncurtained, so that he might see her smouldering for him. And there had been the breath of Egypt in it all — moonlit stretches of river and desert sand, glittering tinsel of stars in water and sky.

Even after they were lovers, he had remained bound to the tragedy, or memory, which held him in all but the time they were together. He did not speak of himself before, or beyond, this island of existence. Emilia had tried not to peer across his barrier; her pride affronted. She laughed at him, accepting it; her coarse, work-reddened hands; his own hands, elegant, 'ivorene', she said; that she should play Cleopatra for him, a part so out of character for her!

When Anthony's regiment was ordered into Palestine, she expected her feeling for him and their 'romantic episode' to die down; but it did not. It was still there when she returned to England. There were those years in England with Herbert. Tony was born. She had told Herbert of Anthony and Egypt. He knew of them and stood by her; they had been good friends. Of Anthony, Emilia had heard nothing since she left Egypt. She did not know even whether he had survived those last days of hostilities in Palestine. She had always intended to go to Australia some day to look for him; and when Herbert died she took passages for herself and Tony.

Of people on the boat, she inquired for Colonel Anthony Bridges and could hear nothing of him. Then casually, the Prattens, who were returning after a visit to the old country, spoke of a Colonel Bridges near Nanja-miia, their home. Emilia had not asked whether he was married, or anything about him, rather suspecting a wife and family. But what had Anthony's wife and family to do with her? Emilia did not intend that they should concern her, or she them.

Seven years ago — and this was the first time she had seen him since they were in Egypt!

After coming to Nanja-miia she had heard gossip, of course. People who knew him well were not surprised when Colonel

Anthony Bridges went back to his old job after the war. There had been no end of newspaper talk about his brilliant record of service. But he was a wreck when he came home, shot through the back, nerves of the spine injured. Military sinecures were not chasing wounded men just then; and Anthony was not the man to chase them. He made it clear, he preferred independence and his trade, to leading-strings of any sort, although old Arnold Pratten and Wolga people generally declared it was 'a blasted shame so distinguished a soldier should have to go back to blacksmithing for a living after the war.'

His business was a good one. This forge of the old road to the goldfields had been established by Anthony's father before Wolga was a town; and Anthony had two grown sons to carry on the heavy work of the smithy for him.

Anthony looked light for a blacksmith; was lighter and slighter than most blacksmiths; but men who had worked with him boasted how tough he was — all hard sinew and bone, not an ounce of loose flesh on him. His sons did the heaviest work of the forge now; but Anthony Bridges was a demon to work.

He drove himself relentlessly, wielding iron, breaking young horses, training them in a flimsy trotting spider, and spending week-ends away with his dogs, kangarooing. But pain, and the fighting of pain, were on his bare brown face, in his eyes, and the will which glimmered through them. You got the ache of the man as he talked with every gesture of his desperate energy. He worked to lose consciousness of that crack in his back, Anthony explained to somebody once.

The back of his neck flashed to Emilia again as he stooped over the anvil. She knew the back of his neck better than his face; but not the whip-cord across it, nor the worn leather apron cut in the middle to form flaps over his grey trousers and tied round the waist.

Her brain surged and left her clutching the sides of the empty box she was sitting on.

Tony's voice went through the hollow dark of the shed, exclaiming joyously, asking questions, staccato, eager. Noises of the smithy clanged through it, ching, chang, chang. She could hear men's voices, rough, uncertain, rolling about her; see a huge, shapeless figure there, some distance off, beating down with a hammer. Flashed silver fire leap out from him; leapt to the blacksmith, before him. The blacksmith — that man with the ruckled, unfamiliar, familiar face!

Did he know? Did he guess Tony was his son? Would he teach Tony to swing a hammer like that?

Rain clouted the shed; sharp and clear, raindrops spat into the enclosed twilight and against the new, bright grass, stretching up beside the wall. Emilia could see nothing through the wide open doorways for fume of the rain.

A youth, heavy and powerful, with a face of greasy dough, a mat of fairish hair and ghoulish, adolescent eyes, was dragging nails from worn irons on the hoofs of a draught horse, leg and fetlock flounced with hair, held across his thigh. Long, strong young arms swung, and, clutching, he yanked nails out, knocked off crescent irons.

In the half-light about the furnace the smith and another youth were working, heads, arms, shoulders, trunks to the midriff under shirt and leathern apron, against red mist of the fire. The smith lifted a horse-shoe from the dais of the forge, showering red sparks, laid it on the anvil. Huge, inchoate, the figure of the striker opposite him struck at the horseshoe, chang on the shoe, ching on the anvil. The smith turned and moved the shoe for his blow, turned and moved it at the end of his long tongs. Chang, ching, chang-chang, the rhythmic beat and song of the hammer. The hammer flashed, sweeping down, sweeping off, a planet wandering in space, returning to the nebulous, muscular mass of the man, and flying again.

Emilia was fascinated by it, the deft precision of every action; the way dull obstinate metal obeyed these men. The furnace breathed; a horseshoe glowed red and waxen; the smith wrenched it away, and held it to the striker's hammer; plunged the hot iron into a barrel of water so that it hissed and spat, and withdrew it, steaming, purple, sodden.

Again the smith fitted a shoe, red and waxen from the furnace, on the horse's hoof. Smoke rose in yellow gusts. They swept across the smith, clouding him, cutting him in halves, as he crouched over Nanja's leg. Head and shoulders above the gusts of yellow smoke, he bent; crooked across his thigh, the near hind leg of Emilia's hack, fetlock and fetlock joint, black satin-skinned pastern and hoof.

If I could model him like that! Emilia thought. The grace and wisdom in pose and gesture. Every muscle sprung, direct and sure, to run a well-known track. The horse, standing to him at ease, unperturbed; knowledge and sympathy, wisdom and strength, what he got from the man. Arm and forearm, cutting down from the head, dark, indefinite; that line of the blacksmith's shoulder swung over; bold, clear lines flowing and swerving to his movement. If she could fix them, take them away with her!

Men brought other horses to be shod, coming into the smithy in oilskins. They hung their nags against pegs on the opposite wall and stood smoking and talking to the smith.

'How's things, Anthony?'

'Not too bad.'

The smith did not miss a beat of what he was doing, as he talked to them, moving in rhythmic, mechanical fashion, from one detail to another of his work. Emilia saw that he was fitting the shoes for her hack himself. Through the muffled breath of the furnace, the ching, chang, chang of the anvil, regular, measured movement of the smith from the furnace to anvil and water barrel, hanging of the horseshoe on a peg when it was finished, she could hear the men talking.

'Rooin' this week, Colonel? ... Cripes, that's something like! Me and the boys was out last week-end and got a couple of big chaps and a doe. There's not too many about our way now. Brush, of course ... but they're a nuisance. Goin' out like you do with a car's better sport, I reck'n ... Horses give the 'roos too big a start in rough country. Walking with dogs you do better.'

Emilia did not hear what the blacksmith said. She could only hear the men about him, orchardists and dairy-farmers from the hills.

'Had bad luck ... lost a dog, they tell me, Colonel? ... that rough-haired yellow bitch? It's a damn shame. Wouldn't have been so bad if she had been killed hunting, but on the road coming home! The way the motors get along this road, it ought to be stopped, I reck'n. Near had the wheel dragged off of me cart other night, going out ... There's some, of course, likes the rough-haired dogs better than the smooth. I say myself I've seen as good smooth-haired dogs as rough. But she was as good a 'roo dog as I've seen and no mistake.'

Emilia could not see the blacksmith now for the men standing about him; but the ching-chang of the striker's hammer went on. The youth paring horn from the hoofs of the draught horses spoke occasionally in a rough, mild voice; a horse neighed; the place in the half-dark with the rain beating outside smelt like a stable, though ashes and charcoal exhaled a dry, harsh and tangy fragrance; there was wet paint on carts and cart wheels at the back of the shed; and the men's overalls gave off a faint odour of tar.

'Old Pratten was saying they was mad on the dog he got from you to send to India, Colonel. Killed a couple of leopards, and he was wanting to put his dog to your Emilia, and send out some more. Rotten luck to lose a dog like that ...'

The blacksmith too busy to have much to say to them, the farmers gossiped together. Seeing the woman sitting on that box near the door, they asked Dick Bridges who she might be; went to look at the mare in trotting tackle against the wall; stood off inspecting her; and came to yarn to the smith again.

'She's come on fine, Colonel,' one said. 'Couple of months ago you wouldn't have given two bob for her and she couldn't trot twenty yards without breakin'. Giving her a fly Saturday?'

'Any use havin' a quid on her?'

'Reckon she'll just about do it — if she gets a good start.'

'Seen Mick Ralston about, Anthony?' a full-faced, red-headed man inquired, eyeing Emilia with child-like curiosity.

'No. He hasn't been in for a week or so, George. Not since his wife died,' the blacksmith said.

'When he comes in, ask him if he's got any ducks he doesn't want, will you? Ask him to bring them in for me.'

'Heard how old Paul is? Gone wood-carting up Wyalin way! Cripes! And a couple of weeks ago he was supposed to be all-in. What is he? Over eighty — and wood-carting!'

Men swung out of the shed, laughing; rain splashed about them, their wet oilskins shone in the light.

The anger which had overwhelmed Emilia left her. She felt empty, weary, defeated; as if suddenly she were tired after her long journey; after waiting so many years to see this man; as if now there was nothing to wait for, nothing to look forward to, nothing to go further for. As if really she could not be bothered to move again.

Already she was strangely familiar with the place. Talk of the men who had come into the smithy had made her acquainted with it and with Anthony. She knew him better than she had ever known him; better than in Egypt. There he had been the silent man, distant, reserved. They had encountered, no more. She understood how much she wanted to know him. And now that she knew him; had seen him at work like this with rough and blackened hands, what did she think? What did she feel about it?

He was as much in command here as in camp at Mena or Ismalia. There was military order under the roof of this old shed. She took in the horseshoes along the wall, ranged systematically, rows and rows of them, lines of hammers, tongs, chisels. The bellows breathed at his command, she enjoyed the fantasy, indulging it; striker and youth moved as he willed; rods of iron were wrought into horseshoes; horses, men and metal obeyed him. And he had called a dog he loved and was proud of, Emilia!

Unbelievable. But there it was still, inviolable, unutterable, the caring. It had taken a deeper channel since coming here. She seemed to have been a long time listening to the talk of kangaroo dogs and trotters, of old men carting wood; watching men beat iron, shoe horses. Dismayed, Emilia looked in, and out again at herself, sitting on a box beside the door of this blacksmith's shop.

It was a dream she was in, she was sure. If she could move from the door; if she could get out of the shed, away from the shadow of the windowless roof and walls, it would vanish. But, as in dream, she did not seem to be able to move.

She could see Tony playing with two big dogs at the back of the shed. Like heavy greyhounds, they were: the one grey with lighted, green eyes, the other gingery-fawn coloured — kangaroo hounds. Tony's voice, asking questions, reverberated.

Shining stretches of the Nile ... she could always see them when Tony was chattering away like that, and the moth's wing of a felucca against the sky. Lap-lap of water against the felucca. The song of Nubian boatmen assailed her, enervating, beguiling.

She did not know she was singing; that song of the boatmen drifting across her lips, until a cry from the furnace startled her. She could hear the melody then, winging about the shed, coming from her own throat. She looked back. Anthony was standing, anvil and furnace between them, his face wrenched. His eyes plunged into her. He turned and blundered out through the back of the shed.

Staring out into the rain, she was still sitting there on that box, in the doorway, when the youth who had been knocking off old shoes on the draught horses and paring her hack's hoofs, 'cutting his toe-nails' as Tony said, stood before her.

'Mum says would you like a cup of tea? She's just made some,' he said.

He was Anthony's son, Emilia had gathered, a youth with heavy, powerful limbs, sawny, self-conscious, fluff coming down from his ears along his cheeks; but a man's assurance, worn like the leathern apron covering three-quarters of him, over flannel shirt and yellow trousers.

Emilia looked up from his boots as they stayed before her, boots of unblacked leather, huge and pudding-shaped.

'Thank you,' she said, surprised, and not knowing quite what to say.

She rose and followed when he turned away through the back of the smithy, his heavy limbs thrust out before her, barring the machinery piled there; monstrous, inert wheels, rusty grinning teeth. What an inferno! Who was this youth leading her through it? Where were they going? Past benches spread with tools, tongs, tweezers, hammers, twitchers, nails, stilettos, gimlets, ranged along the wall; and horseshoes, hundreds of them, hundreds and hundreds of horseshoes, all shapes and sizes. On the walls of her brain, they were hanging like that, rusty, plum-coloured, silver. New moons of horseshoes, rows and rows of them.

Light from a door in the side of the shed flashed on her, blinding, exhilarating. She went into it, striding, gulping the clear cold air, grateful to see the sky, earth, and grass, all fresh, newly-washed, so pure and tender.

Across a yard strewn with scrap-iron, rusty machine parts and glassy pools of rain-water, a small brick house, white wooden lace round the verandas, watched the smithy. A neat, prosperous-looking house, with a garden of red and yellow flowers, dahlias, marigolds and geraniums.

The woman who met Emilia on the doorstep was like her house and garden. Emilia could see her house and garden in her.

'It's such a cold, miserable morning,' she said, 'and I always make tea for dad and the boys at eleven. When I seen you sitting in the forge I thought you might like a cup.'

'That was kind ...'

But Emilia was consumed with realizing that this was Anthony's wife, this stout, bland little woman with sleek hair, whose skin shone as though it had been polished. Her blouse drew tight over a full bosom and her skirt went down in a black bell over broad hips and thighs. She looked very healthy and good-humoured. Her wide dull mouth held itself with an expression of patience and perpetual smiling; the eyes were mild and complaining over a soft thick nose and ruddy cheeks.

And this was Anthony's life that she gave him, Emilia exclaimed to herself as she went indoors. So neat and tidy-looking, everything. Oiled linoleums everywhere. An enlarged photograph of Anthony in uniform displaced all else in the sitting-room; and there were several smaller pictures of him on the mantelpiece, with other photographs. But how did he live with those panels of pink flamingos and knowing-looking birds in pea-green landscapes?

An old woman seated beside the table, which had a red cloth and a tray with tea-things on it, stared resentfully at the tall woman in man's breeches who came into the room. 'Mother,' Mrs Anthony Bridges said when she spoke to her; and the old woman called Mrs Bridges 'Annie'. 'Gentle Annie,' Anthony would have called his wife, Emilia imagined; and sung 'Little Annie Rooney is my sweetheart' to her when he was courting her, before they were married.

Emilia smiled to think of it. The critical malignity of her interest relaxed. A spasm of affection swayed her towards Mrs Bridges. She realized how kind and conscientious Mrs Anthony Bridges was. What a good wife she had been to Anthony. Honest and industrious, keeping his house in order, bearing him sons, bringing them up to be decent, hard-working lads. They thought the world of 'Mum', it was easy to see. So did Anthony.

Emilia had a sense of obligation to Anthony's wife. She wished to thank her for being so good to Anthony: as if Anthony belonged to her, Emilia, really, but by some accident, shipwreck, or misadventure, in his early life, he had been lost, cast away and fallen into this women's hands! She had been kind; taken care of him. Emilia was grateful.

Amused at the sway of her thinking, Emilia drank her tea, and listened to Mrs Bridges talking. The misery, sense of defeat and failure, which had overcast her in the smithy was gone. She had forgotten it. She was pleased to be exploring Anthony's life like this, the life he had so carefully hidden away from her; enjoyed hearing Anthony's wife talk of him with pride and a slightly puzzled querulousness, as though he were the most troublesome of her children.

'Dad not coming?' she asked her son, who, it was clear, obeyed an unwritten law by not entering the house in those heavy boots.

He shook his head, supping his tea on the veranda.

'Mr Bridges has never been the same man since the war,' Mrs Anthony Bridges babbled politely, with an air of making conversation. 'Since he came home from the war, that is. Not like himself at all, that restless and irritable; flying off into rages at the least thing. They say the war's made many a man like that, nervous and jumpy. Doctor says, all Anthony needs is rest and quiet. Well, the boys could run the business now, but he won't let them. Never happy unless he's going like mad from one thing to another. If it's not in the smithy, it's away with the dogs, kangarooin', or trainin' trotters.'

The old woman stared disapproval of Lady Emilia Howard's crossed legs in their close-fitting gear and polished boots.

'You talk too freely to a stranger, Annie,' she said.

'Don't you like my boots?' Emilia asked, and smiled to the old woman.

Mrs Bridges looked as if her face had been smacked. She was in the habit of talking like this, Emilia realized. It was more from habit than anything else she was chatting. There were those mild, complaining eyes; the mouth held patiently with a smile.

'I suppose we can't help talking of what occupies our minds most. That's it, isn't it, Mrs Bridges?'

'Of course, mother.' Relieved to continue her story, Anthony's wife went on:

'If only he slept well he'd be better. He doesn't sleep; that's the worst of it. Pulled his stretcher onto the veranda, so as not to disturb me. But I hear him walking about half the night, sometimes. He keeps all his military things in that room off the veranda. And the other night, when I got up, what do you think he was doing? Standing at the chest of drawers — all his gloves spread out! Must be a dozen pairs of them, white kid gloves, he used to wear at the war. And he keeps them all folded up in tissue paper like you buy gloves in a shop. Not a spot on any of them. And when I took out a pair to wear to Bertie's wedding, you should have heard him go off! What he wants all them gloves for I don't know. Never wears them now; not from one year's end to another. Just takes them out, has a look at them and puts them away again. Course he used to wear them in Egypt. Mick Ralston was saying the other day: "You'd never've known the Colonel in Egypt, aunty. First time

I ever saw him, there he was, standing outside his tent at head-quarters, talking to some of the big bugs — as big a bug as any of them himself — white kid gloves and all.'"

Emilia had finished her tea and bread and butter. She thanked Mrs Bridges for them; said she was sure her horse would be ready and that her small boy was getting into mischief over there in the smithy. She stood up; her long legs in their buff breeches and polished boots struck across the oiled linoleum; heels clicked on the veranda steps. She went through the lush coxcombery of the little garden, liking it, the small well-ordered brick house with its wooden lace round the veranda, Anthony's wife, and the shrewd, disapproving old woman, feeling indebted to them.

A quite unconscionable happiness took possession of her.

'White kid gloves ... sleepless nights.'

Ching, chang-chang, hammer sang to horseshoe and anvil, as she went into the shed again. Tony ran to her exclaiming eagerly.

The youth who had taken her out through the back of the shed brought her horse shod, treading daintily, hoofs slick and newly-painted black.

'Where is the Colonel?' Emilia asked.

'Dad?' the lad apologised. 'He's gone sick or something. Cleared out a while ago.'

Emilia looked around the hollow dark of the smithy, taking possession of it. 'Tell him — no, never mind, I'll tell him myself.' Merciless and serene her voice flowed. 'We're going to buy Nanja-miia, Pratten's old place, Tony and I. Will you ask your father if he thinks he could find a dog for us ... like the one that was killed ... and perhaps, some day ... take us kangarooing?'

FRANK DALBY DAVISON

Lady with a Scar

Jim Darrell was in the big chair that filled a gap in one corner of the drawing-room, between the china cabinet and the spindly-legged writing-desk. He chose it because its comparative isolation saved him the need of making polite conversation.

It was called the hermit's chair and there were jocular references sometimes to his preference for it. He didn't mind. He could hold his own with them at banter. The fact was, these Sunday night musicales rather bored him, but in matters social, like most men absorbed in serious affairs — he reckoned — he just tagged about amiably after his wife.

At present he was trying to identify the lady with the scar. She wasn't one of the artists. At any rate, when she came into the room he had noticed the absence of a music case. Nice little woman. At the moment of being introduced he had had the feeling of having met those eyes before. Recollection had almost risen to the surface of his mind and then, tantalizingly, had sunk again. It was still there, like a mouse that refuses to come out and be caught. Her eyes were dark; so dark that in the soft lamplight iris and pupil seemed to merge. There was, too, he had noticed at close quarters, the faintest suggestion of a squint. It was so slight that its possessor was probably unaware of it; but, combined with a certain diffidence of manner, it gave her face a touch of fey, of other-worldliness. Very charming — but where had he seen it before?

She had on a pink gown of some soft stuff — he didn't know the names of these things — and silver brocade shoes. She was sitting in the window-seat making herself agreeable to plump old Harrington, who would soon be airing his frayed tenor. Politely agreeable, now he came to notice closely, as if she were not very interested in what Harrington was saying, or had something on her mind. It was to be gathered that she would be politely agreeable to anyone who was not utterly impossible, that it would be part of her duty to her hostess, like her close attention to the music. Nice little figure, uncorseted, and breasts as firm as a girl's. Locks shorn *à la mode*, and the cigarette, by her amateurish handling of it, a concession to sociability.

It was a pity about that scar. She had turned to drop her cigarette ash into a tray and the disfigured side of her face had, for a moment, been presented to him. The scar extended from the corner of her mouth almost to the angle of her jaw. It looked as if it still hurt — smooth and pink with a white pucker or two near the middle. It drew that side of her mouth down a little and gave to that half of her face a fixed expression of horror. He noticed that she didn't smile or laugh; not solemn, grave. Perhaps that scar would turn a smile into a grimace. He felt an accession of pity for her. It must be rather dreadful for a woman to go through life with a mark on her like that. She must frequently be made conscious of it. By nature suspicious of himself, he heard an inward voice inquiring if the measure of his sympathy for her was not also the measure of her womanly charm in his eyes. He acknowledged to himself that there might be something in the suggestion.

She had turned from Harrington, and her eyes caught his. There was recognition — and something else — in her glance. He looked away quickly — conscious of the scar. He would have hated her to think that he had been staring. From the look in her eyes he gathered that she had recognized him from the start.

A singer and her accompanist were taking their places at the piano; Madame Forsster, as she called herself, and that hank of limp seaweed that she trailed around with her.

Darrell took out a cigarette and sat tapping at the end of it down on the arm of his chair. Somewhere, at some time or other, those eyes, as they had done a moment ago, had looked with meaning into his. Damn it, everything about her was like an echo in his mind! Throughout the course of the song and the double encore he racked his mind for some clue to the lady's identity. Several times recollection came almost within grasp of his will, but each time it slipped away again as if it were having fun with him. The effort was wearying, the lack of result exasperating. He lit his cigarette and sat staring before him through a film of smoke. Perhaps if he ceased trying to force it his memory would function as he desired.

It did. The singer had retired amid a flutter of applause. Conversation had been resumed. Jennie Marshall! The name bobbed up like a bright rubber ball rising to the surface of water. It was only by a conscious act of mind that he prevented his head jerking round toward the lady in pink.

His first feeling was of astonishment. Then came delight. Then came a doubt as to whether the strength of the emotion that ran through him was not unworthy of a man in middle life. He'd not seen her since they were school kids. A glance from her eyes, then, had given him a kick like electricity; a smile, singling him out from others of his sex, had lifted him to dizzy levels of exaltation — and the memory of her favour was still gratifying. The inward voice commented that the boy, evidently, was living somewhere still within the man.

She was a little wisp of a thing when last he remembered her. The image of her rose before his inner eye. Heavy, dusty shoes of a country child, long black stockings, much darned, a blue striped dress — galatea, he'd remembered that — a white pinafore and black hair in a pigtail tied with a scrap of blue rag. There had been no scar at that time; at least, not that he could remember.

He stole a glance at the lady in pink and then looked away. His face was a mask, but inwardly he was smiling. The same Jennie Marshall! He had forgotten her in adolescence — that rather churlish abandonment of childish things — and had remembered her often in maturity. She was one of a score of wispy recollections; things that flitted across his mind in moments of mild bodily activity and complete mental relaxation — at such times as when he was shaving, or when he was watering the garden. Faces and incidents that had passed out of his life; his father setting forth for church on a Sunday morning; the swapping of an old tennis ball for some silk-worms' eggs; a referee counting ten above an ex-champion pug; a glimpse of the Seine below Rouen; old what's-his-name, who used to stop people and give them tracts; vagrant gossamer memories, torn from their context, that rose from below the horizon of matters of present importance and drifted like cloudlets across a tranquil sky.

He looked again at the lady who was *née* Jennie Marshall, and again their glances locked for a second. He saw that she read the recognition in his eyes. The seat beside her was vacant. Harrington had gone to the piano. He would go to her. He was in the act of rising when Dorothy Hazlett, their hostess, crossed the room, and took the vacant seat. Later on would do.

Darrell leaned back, his eyes on the pieces of delft that adorned the plate rail. His attention — it would be presumed — was on the singer. Actually it was taken up with an amused and not unsentimental contemplation of the spring of memories released by his recollection of Jennie Marshall.

An afternoon, along the Illawarra coast, so still that the sound of cattle cropping the short grass came like small explosions. A magpie carolling from the top of a dead gum-tree. Shrill cackle of children just let out of a little wooden box of a school. Scuffle of copper-toed boots in the dust of the bridle tracks that ribbed the grass strip, between the metalled edges of the road and the fences. He tried to give remembered faces to the trooping figures, but only two came back, Tommy Carnegie's and Jennie's. A boy in short trousers and a cotton shirt — himself — was keeping pace with the others, walking along the top rail of the fence. His arms were outstretched to aid him in keeping his balance and whenever he teetered his tongue also popped out to his assistance. His attention was equally divided between his feat of equipoise and a little girl — Jennie Marshall — who was walking along with another little girl in the centre of the road. Love affairs were not uncommon at their school, but, if you valued your peace of mind, they were kept covert. Nothing wrong with a fellow walking along the top of a rail fence!

A voice from the ground: 'Haw, haw! Showin' orf in front of Jennie Marshall an' she ain't even botherin' to look at you!'

The rail-walker, to give the lie by inference to this penetrating taunt, held himself together and walked the length of five rails before he jumped to the ground.

Darrell's features didn't move, but his eyes, from between narrowed lids, twinkled at the delft. A fellow had to go through these things!

Three boys loitering at the parting of the ways — the others had, in ones and couples, dispersed down the side tracks that led to their homes. One boy was himself, another Tommy Carnegie, the face of the third was blank. He hung to the others because he was unwilling to turn his back to them. At last he said he must be going, and dawdled away by himself. With a hundred yards behind him — as he had expected — the voices of the other two came after, 'Hoo, hoo! Jennie Ma-a-a-rshall!' They had caught him with the goods.

A fellow survived these things. Half a mile along the track he saw Jennie coming toward him. Of the dutiful sex, she had gone straight home and was now on her way to Lindlays' farm for milk, her billy-can twinkling in the light of the low sun. It was funny how sharp that memory came back to him; roadside clumps of lantana speckled with pink bloom, the stump of an old coral-tree hoisting one green arm. The Lindlay cows had not long been taken to the milking shed; a thin yellowish dust from their passing was still in the air, the smell of it and the breath of the cattle; even the fresh droppings on the track came back to mind. Jennie was within a few yards of him now. There was a tightness in his throat and he was staring straight before him to give the impression that he hadn't noticed her approach. Their eyes met in passing — Jennie's faintly squinny eye, that made you feel that fairy tales might be true.

'Hullo.'

'Hullo.'

That was all. They were past each other. The terrific moment was over, but by merely speaking Jennie had singled him out, had thanked him for the tribute of his acrobatics on the fence. Jubilation! He went on his way, pausing to look back at Jennie, heart leaping when he saw her turn to look back at him, chilled when she didn't look back again; then marching on, slightly delirious with joy, swinging his school-bag over at arm's length.

Memory ended there. Romantically disconcerting to discover that he couldn't recall how his affair with Jennie had ended. He reckoned it must have been at about that time that his parents sold their farm in that district and moved down the South Coast. Fresh scenes and adventures blotted Jennie out.

Harrington had delivered himself of his first song, and in response to applause, to which Darrell lent generous if not particularly appreciative aid, was spreading the score of his second number on the music rest.

Darrell lit another cigarette, crossed his legs and nursed his right ankle in his left hand. It would probably be Dorothy's turn next; that would give him his opportunity. Harrington's accompanist was playing the introductory measures. Darrell took in Jennie Marshall from the corner of his eye. Like a good little guest, she was all attention to the singer, ankles crossed, her hands lying folded in her lap, awaiting Harrington's best efforts. Jennie had made a nice woman of herself. It was a pity about that scar. He wondered how she had come by it.

While Harrington flew gamely at the upper register, Darrell was anticipating his forthcoming interview with the lady in pink.

He must be prepared to slip into indifference — mere casual recollection — in case the lady proved chilly. Not much fear of that, though, if the look of recognition she had given him was anything to go by. Women mostly treasured up the memory of their early conquests, put them away with a sprig of lavender. Susan had, he knew. He'd tell her about this afterwards.

'I've just succeeded in recognizing you,' he imagined herself saying. He had a baritone speaking voice that he was not altogether ashamed of. He must put a little mellowness into it in addressing her.

'Have you?' As he sat down beside her. 'I knew you as soon as I saw you.'

'You were Jennie Marshall?'

'I was.'

'A lot of water has run under the bridge ...' or something like that, would do next; followed by a series of do-you-remembers. These with a touch of jocularity. Then if they found themselves on a quite friendly footing — as he hoped they would — it would be time to bring in:

'You know, I was desperately in love with you in those days.'

She would probably — fibber — begin by disclaiming all knowledge of that — drawing him out artfully. With the perspicacity of her sex in these matters, she had probably known all about his feelings before he realized them himself; perhaps had even put the ideas into his clumsy head.

And what would follow his confession of an old passion? Well, to learn that would give a little real interest to the evening.

The song was finished. Dorothy was crossing the room. Darrell heaved himself out of his chair. He was standing before the lady in pink. He avoided seeing the scar. Mrs Parmenter was her name now.

'May I sit down?'

'If you wish.' Her utterance was clipped.

He sat down, a little taken aback by her lack of cordiality. She had suddenly become frigid. What was wrong? He must say something. He plunged.

'You were Jennie Marshall, weren't you?'

'Yes.' She spoke the word in a hard little whisper, and shot a glance at him that he found hard to interpret. It was like seeing fierceness in the eyes of a doe. What was it? That scar? He wished that he had been able to seat himself on the other side of her. He must go on; say something.

'I remembered you, er — after a little difficulty.'

'Do you remember causing this mark on my face?'

'Eh!' Darrell looked at her in swift surprise, and then looked quickly away again.

He felt the shock an animal must feel in the first few moments after the trap is sprung. He had caused that scar! The feeling of having the results of a fault exhibited for his embarrassment was not new — but it had never been for anything as serious as this. Notwithstanding his own sense of shock, he noticed that she was trembling. She had spoken as if the words were being torn out of her. He wondered what distressing disclosure was about to take place. The drawing-room seemed to have become immeasurably elongated, as if he were seeing the other people under a spotlight, far off.

'Not — not I — ?' he began hesitatingly.

'Yes, you!' She shivered a little. Her hands were working in her lap.

He wondered if there was going to be a hysterical scene. He groped desperately among his recollections. He could recall nothing of the kind. Surely she was playing some ghastly joke on him.

'But it's impossible!'

'But there is the scar!' The words were followed by a gasp; as if his failing to remember was, for her, the final touch of irony. He had carried an untroubled conscience through all the years.

Darrell glanced at the scar, and winced. So that was how she remembered him — in terms of an injury, disfigurement.

He had imagination enough to realize, from the great strain under which she was obviously labouring, that the present scene was not brought about by the mere accident of seeing him. It had an air of being rehearsed, gone over in secrecy, perhaps at odd times through the years, in moments when she was acutely aware of her disfigurement and recalled the circumstances of the injury. Fate had delivered him to her, and she was living up to the bitter role she had imagined for herself.

She glanced at him swiftly, and away. The soft eyes of Jennie Marshall, burning with a pain and anger, a vengefulness that had no part in her nature. Remorse and dread of the explanation to come gripped Darrell. He felt sweat trickling down his body.

'What happened?' he asked. He bared himself for the lash, feeling that the recital might relieve the strain for her, hoping it might reveal some extenuating circumstance for himself.

She went on to tell him. At the beginning her words seemed as if they were being jerked out of her.

'You remember the spotted gum that grew in the lower corner of the school yard?'

'Yes.' He hadn't until she spoke of it. It was strange how it
popped back into mind.

'You were playing there with two other boys. Marbles. I
stopped to watch you. I think you were afraid of being teased by
the others. You said, "Go on, we don't want you around here!"
And you gave me a shove. It knocked me over. I fell against the
fence-post. Somebody had jammed a jagged piece of galvanised
iron into a crack in the grain — probably to put it out of harm's
way — I caught my mouth on it as I went down.'

She stopped there. Darrell saw three boys watching a little
girl in a white pinafore stumbling across the playground — with
her hands to her face. But that was not memory. It was an invol-
untary act of imagination. He couldn't recall the incident.

There was a silence between them. He was trying desperately, but without result, to think of something to say that was not
inadequate, not banal. She got up and left the room. He had a
feeling that she did so partly out of sympathy for him; that she was
running from a situation that she couldn't endure.

He felt sick and dazed. He tried to wrench his mind away
from the matter, temporarily. He had the evening to finish out
among these people. But somehow he couldn't get his mind away
from what he had just been told.

Susan came to him, a little later, and remarked that he didn't
look well. She suggested that they go home. He agreed, after
some hesitation.

While he was standing in the hall, waiting for Susan, who was
getting her wraps, Mrs Parmenter came up to him. She had
recovered herself a little.

'I'm sorry I told you,' she said.

Darrell pulled himself together. 'You couldn't help it,' he
replied. And, after a pause, feeling that something more was
required, 'I deserved to be told.' That wasn't right, either. What
was wanted was something to set her at rest, something more

sympathetic. He added, 'I am glad you did.' She would know that he shared her feelings as far as he could.

In the tram, on the way home, Susan was troublesomely curious about his indisposition.

'Indigestion, perhaps,' he suggested.

Susan wondered audibly whether there was any bismuth in the house, or whether the chemist would mind being knocked up at that hour of the night.

Darrell, dismally watching the distant city lights, wondered if hell contained a daintier torment than stumbling on the forgotten acts of one's life — not the big rogueries you had plotted and successfully brought off in face of a challenging world, but the spontaneous acts that revealed you to yourself, the small mongrel acts that inflicted unguessed injuries on others.

It seemed a weary time before they were at last in bed, Susan reassured, her head snuggled against his shoulder, the light out, and he alone with himself in the darkness. He lay staring up into the darkness that hid the ceiling, a prickle of perspiration coming to his skin each time he thought of that humiliating school-yard scene. He tried to enter imaginatively into Jennie's life, but couldn't penetrate very far. He had so little to go on. The pathetic part was that as she had proceeded with her brief recital the real Jennie had taken the place of the hysterical woman of a minute before. She was just appealing for his sympathetic understanding.

The matter was going to ride his mind for a while. He knew that. He knew also that there would be eventual escape. Work. Life wasn't so relentless but what a man could elude the pursuit of memory. But sometimes, he knew, the memory of Jennie Marshall — the child and the woman — would return to him unexpectedly, catch up with him. At such times as when he was shaving, or when he was watering the garden.

DAL STIVENS

Solemn Mass

During the Et Incarnatus she kept her eyes closed. This was what Goethe meant, she thought, what the philosophers meant; what they sought after. Awe, said Goethe, is the highest thing in man, and if the pure phenomenon awakes awe in him he should be content; here is the limit. He can go no further. This then was awe.

At first the music had been a white light in her mind. Music was sweet wine, she thought. Beethoven and the Missa Solemnis; Goethe and awe. There had been a wild dancing in her mind as of sunlight upon water. But now a silence had come over the music. She sat with her eyes closed and nothing seemed to take place in her mind. A feeling of amazement, of bewilderment, had stolen over her. But this is beautiful, she thought. This was awe; what the philosophers meant; the thing they sought.

Coming out of the Conservatorium the man with her said, 'Well?'

She put her hand on his arm.

'Don't let's go anywhere,' she said. 'Take me home, Ken.'

'Don't you want any supper?'

'I don't feel like it,' she said. 'I don't want any.'

'But you promised.'

She said, 'I know. But I don't want any.'

'I say, Helen,' the man said, 'you are rather unreasonable.'

'Unreasonable?'

'You promised, you know. You said you would go. Why, you wanted to go to that new place. You said you did.'

She said, 'Please, Ken, take me home.'

'Have I done anything?' he said.

'No,' she said, 'you haven't done anything.'

'Have I offended you?'

'No,' she said, 'you haven't offended me. You haven't done anything.'

'I must have. What is it?'

She said, 'You haven't done anything. Please, Ken, get a taxi for me. I can go home on my own.'

'I know I have done something,' the man said. 'What is it?'

'There isn't anything. Don't ask me to explain. I can't explain.'

'You're rather unreasonable, Helen,' he said. 'I can't understand you.'

'You don't have to try,' she said.

The man walked on to the road and hailed a taxi. It drew up alongside them. It had been raining and drops were clinging to the sides of the taxi. Each drop was a tiny lens.

'Please,' she said. 'I can go home all right. Don't you come with me. You have an early night.'

'I don't want an early night,' the man said, loudly.

'All right,' the girl said. 'You don't want an early night. But don't see me home.'

'Listen,' the man said, loudly again. 'What's got into you? Have I done anything?'

'Oh, dear,' the girl said, 'I've said you haven't done anything. You haven't done anything at all. You've been sweet to me.'

He said, 'So you think I've been sweet to you, do you? That is nice.'

'You'd better get in,' the girl said, 'if you are going to go on like that.'

'Well, well,' the man said. 'Isn't that nice? Isn't this a fine evening?'

He got in the taxi and gave an address. The girl sat back in a corner. When the driver put out the light her face seemed to glow faintly in the half darkness. The taxi nosed away from the city and the wet road unwound from the spools of the wheels. Fan-shaped splashes sprang out from under the tyres.

They sat silent.

Presently the man said, 'Is there anything wrong, Helen?'

'Wrong?'

He said, 'I mean, have I annoyed you in any way?'

'Please, please,' the girl said. 'Have we got to go into all that again?'

'No,' he said. 'We don't have to go into that again.'

'There you go, getting sarcastic.'

'My God,' the man said. 'I suppose you'll say next it's all my fault.'

'It isn't anyone's fault.'

When they were walking up the steps to her flat, she said, 'Don't come in to-night, will you Ken?'

'I wouldn't dream of it,' he said.

'There you go again,' she said.

She stopped before the door and opened her bag and found the key. When he tried to kiss her she drew away from him.

'I'm sorry, Ken. Not tonight.'

He said, 'All right. All right.'

'I can't explain,' she said. 'Don't ask me to explain.'

He did not say anything.

She said, 'I'm sorry, Ken. Not to-night. I don't want you to, to-night. I don't want you to kiss me even. Not tonight. That's why I didn't want you to come home with me. Don't ask me to explain.'

She saw him looking at her.

'No,' she said. 'It isn't that. It isn't that at all. I just don't want to. That's all. Please, don't be cross with me.'

'What do you expect me to do?' he said. 'Stand on my head for joy?'

'Oh dear, oh dear,' she said, 'there you go. There you go again.'

'What am I supposed to do?' he said. 'Look pleased?'

Afterwards when he had gone she began to cry softly to herself.

What Else is There?

'If I owned a piece of land as big as this, I'd have a cow,' said Miss Lacey as she fixed the large enamel billy on the gate by means of a length of wire sticking out for the purpose. 'That's what. I'd have a cow.' She leant across the gate dreamily figuring out things about the cow.

The gate was made of wood and was in two parts, fastening in the middle by means of a loose chain. Like most things in the Gerahty *ménage*, to which Miss Lacey was attached as lady-help, it was adaptable because of having been constructed wrongly, and opened both ways, so that if leant upon in the right manner it swung gently to and fro.

Miss Lacey, having darted a glance towards the house to make sure she was not being watched, continued leaning, and swung, and thought of the cow. It was to be an extremely neat cow, nicely patterned in brown and white, with a glossy tail always in the right place and a soulful look in its limpid eyes. One could grow very fond of a cow like that, she thought, seeing herself tripping down to it every morning with a three-cornered stool in one hand and a shining pail in the other, in approved milkmaid fashion.

> 'Now, some may drink to ladies fine,
> With painted cheeks and gowns of silk;
> But we will drink to dai-ry maids,
> In pock-et mugs of rum and milk!'

she hummed, being for the moment a plump wench with abnormally rosy cheeks instead of a sparse spinster dried beyond repair by the rigours of forty-five western summers.

From where she stood she could see across the creek, flowing placidly between its flat, yellow banks, to where the town hunched its tin-roofed houses together. They looked peaceful and amiable in the last light of the day, smoke floating tranquilly upward from their chimneys. At the end of the town nearest to her the convent stood. The cries of children and their laughter drifted from the playing-fields; 'Sunset on the Hills' in seven stages of expertness came from the seven practice-rooms. Blossoming cedar-trees spilt an overwhelming fragrance.

'Six pints of milk a day and where does it go?' demanded Miss Lacey dramatically of the empty air. 'Heavens! I was that ashamed the other day when the Johnsons dropped in and there wasn't any to offer them in their tea. Six pints and gone by tea-time. A family that uses six pints and upwards rightly needs a cow.'

She straightened herself and was about to retrace her steps when a flurry of door-banging and window-closing came to her ears. 'I may as well stay now,' she thought. 'They're all ready at last.' She hollowed her hands about her mouth.

'Ooh-hoo, ooh-hoo,' she called. 'I'm at the big gate putting the billy out. I'll stay and open it. Kathleen, bring my handbag from the sideboard.'

'Come and get it yourself,' yelled a girl's voice ungraciously.

'It's all right dear,' cried Mrs Gerahty. 'I have it.'

Miss Lacey fumbled with the chain, unhooked it, swung the gates wide and secured them with stones. 'That Kathleen,' she said, 'all cheek. I'd like to have spoken to my elders like she does at her age! A whip round my tail would have been all I'd have got. She'll come to a bad end if she can't hold her tongue.'

The dusk was coming quickly. Looking back towards the house she saw its outlines obscured, its flaunted bougainvillea colourless in the grey light. The garage door was flung open, the engine of the car set running; the head-lamps shone out butter-yellow.

'Get in all of you,' yelled Dan Gerahty. 'I'm not waiting all night. Who's it wants to go to this carnival? Not me, anyhow. Carnivals! Pshaw! Where the devil is that Lacey woman?'

'She's at the gate, father.'

'What's she doing there?'

'She's opening it, father.'

'You don't tell me,' he mocked. The car leapt forward and thundered down the track, passing with a rush of air through the gates, jolting across the gutter and jerking to a standstill in the middle of the road. 'Hurry on there,' he roared. 'I've got no time to waste.'

'Oh Dan —' protested Mrs Gerahty.

Miss Lacey pushed the gates to, flung the chain about them and rushed breathlessly to the waiting car.

'That brought her hopping,' cried Dan delightedly. 'See, Minnie. I told you I've got a way with women.' The car slid forward.

'Well don't play your tricks with Miss Lacey,' said his wife placidly.

'I wouldn't fall for any of his tricks,' retorted Miss Lacey spiritedly from the back seat.

'Wouldn't you now?' demanded Dan. 'Wait till one of these fine nights, me lady.'

'Dan,' whispered his wife, 'you embarrass her.'

'She likes it,' he whispered back. 'Strike me, Minnie, but the poor devil's got to have something in her life. She's got a mouth like a codfish and the wateriest green eyes I ever saw. How do you reckon her mouth got like that? Waiting for someone to kiss her, see, and they never did. Now it's stuck that way for good. If I were a woman with —'

'Sssssh,' urged his wife.

'What for?'

'Have you enough room in the back there?' asked Mrs Gerahty loudly.

'No,' answered Kathleen.

'Jenny's sitting on me,' offered Peter.

'There's plenty of room,' said Miss Lacey. 'Mr Gerahty, there's something I'd like to ask you.'

'Go ahead. Don't mind the wife.'

'Don't you think we ought to have a cow?'

'And who's going to milk it?' he asked cautiously.

'Why, I should, Mr Gerahty. You take it now; we get six pints of milk a day —'

'When you're in business in a town like this,' answered Dan heavily, 'it doesn't do any good robbing anyone else of business. Everyone to his own trade is my motto. You've got to look at it this way, Miss Lacey. I buy a cow and start raising my own milk. Good. Then the milkman's got a right to plant all his relations, see?'

'That doesn't follow, Mr Gerahty.'

'Why not? All right. Let's say that we buy a cow. You're looking after it. That right?'

'Yes. Oh, yes.'

'You ever looked after a cow before?'

'Well, not yet. But —'

'Now say that cow blows up. What are you going to do?'

'Oh, Mr Gerahty!'

'Now, say again, it's time the cow had a calf. What are you going to do about it?'

'Perhaps you could —'

'Hell, no. You'll have to do it. You'll have to take it down to Radley's.'

'Oh —'

'Don't worry. The job getting it there will be nothing to the one getting it home.'

'Dan, please —'

'No, I'm a wake-up to cows,' said Dan. 'Saw enough of them when I was a kid. Did I tell you, Miss Lacey —?'

'Dan!' Mrs Gerahty's voice held a note of warning.

'Are we going to this carnival or not?' demanded Kathleen. 'You're driving that slow.'

'Not, as far as I'm concerned,' answered her father. 'I'd rather be sitting on the woodpile with Miss Lacey talking about cows.' But he accelerated and they went more quickly through the town, the wind sharp against their faces. 'No. I guess Hodges can still be the milk people round here and I'll carry on with the undertaking. What I'd like to know is why there can't be a

Saturday night without me being dragged to a carnival. What's everyone so crazy about?'

'It's the war effort,' answered his wife.

'War,' said Dan. 'Always war. Seems to me you can't look round without there's a war. It fair gets my goat. There's many a good person who could have died comfortable in their bed —'

'Can't anyone talk about anything else but people dying?' demanded Kathleen passionately. 'Any more of it and I'll jump into the creek.'

'Don't talk that way,' remonstrated her mother.

'Oh, let the girl talk,' said Daniel cheerfully. 'Let her jump in the creek, too, if she likes. There's not enough water in it to drown a rabbit. What do you reckon's got into her?'

'Too many funerals,' snapped Mrs Gerahty. 'You're mag, mag, mag all the time about this one and that one. I don't see that anyone in your line of business should bring his worries home with him.'

'Why not?' A man's got to talk somewhere. Do we drive right in or park outside?'

'Seeing there's twenty steps leading down from the bridge I guess we park outside as usual.'

'I was forgetting,' said Daniel docilely. He drew to the side of the road and pulled up.

It was dark now, but lights were gay and plentiful in the little park, exposing the stretches of worn-down grasses and banishing shadows from between the trees, flinging tatters of iridescence to dapple the quiet waters of the creek flowing beside it.

'The only time that creek looks any good is when you can't see it,' said Dan, as they went down the stairs from the bridge.

The stairs were steep and rickety and a draught blew through them from underneath the bridge. Miss Lacey felt it curling under her skirt to fold itself clammily above the tops of her stockings. It made her shiver. If all reports were true, Hell itself was not such a sink of iniquity as that shadowed, dank place beneath the bridge. The things that went on there didn't bear being told about.

The smell of dust and the scent of the blossoming cedar-trees were heavy in the air.

'It's a good night for a carnival,' said Mrs Gerahty.

'I like a moon myself,' remarked Miss Lacey.

'Kathleen,' said Dan sharply, 'if you're monkeying around in the dark with those young men of yours, keep your eye out for snakes.'

Kathleen maintained a lofty silence.

'And while I'm about it,' continued her father, 'you just take my tip and keep away from young Brownlow. He's up to no good. That family's all the same. Don't say I don't know; I used to go out with his dad's sister before I met your mother.'

'Talking about the Brownlows,' said his wife imperturbably, 'what did you think of the joint we had last Sunday, Dan?'

'Brownlows have perfect meat,' murmured Miss Lacey.

'Sakes alive, woman!' roared Dan. 'How do you expect me to remember what I had to eat last Sunday? Tomorrow's dinner interests me more.'

'Well —' began Mrs Gerahty eagerly.

'Mother, remember you're out and that the whole world doesn't want to know what we're eating tomorrow,' admonished Kathleen.

'The whole world!' exclaimed Dan. 'Cripes, that's good! I'd like to be young again and think the whole world was listening to me when I spoke. Come to my age you can yell your head off without a soul listening. No one hears any but themselves talk. Do they, Lacey?' He smacked Miss Lacey playfully on what he considered should be her rump. It was so pitifully non-existent it made him want to cry.

'Stop bawling at the top of your voice,' said Kathleen.

'Who?' demanded Dan.

'You.'

'Is that the way to speak to your father? Lord, Minnie, she's so bad-tempered you'd think she was going to have a baby.'

'Dan!'

'Well, I'm not,' said Kathleen. 'But don't let it upset you.'

'Kathleen!' reproved Mrs Gerahty.

'You all make me sick,' muttered Kathleen. 'I've got more to do than to be having babies. It's all *he* ever thinks of — babies, and people dying.'

'What else is there?' asked Dan blithely.

'Why, he'll be imagining Miss Lacey's having one next.'

Miss Lacey gasped.

'There looks to be a good crowd,' said Mrs Gerahty pacifically. 'Dan, if we lose you by any chance we'll be back here at the gate about eleven.'

'All right,' answered Dan absently. 'Now you remember what I said, Kathleen. You do anything you like but don't go making a fool of me by getting landed with a kid. I'm not being made a fool of in this town, see. You've got to be dignified in my line of business.'

'See you later,' said Kathleen shortly and scurried ahead to disappear among the people.

'Dan, you've got no right to talk to the girl like that,' said Mrs Gerahty. 'Kathleen's a good girl. She likes a little fun but she doesn't mean any harm.'

'What do you mean? No harm! A girl of eighteen and don't mean no harm! What the devil's the matter with her? I tell you, Minnie Gerahty, my daughter's as good as any girl round town. A girl comes to eighteen and doesn't mean any harm, why, she ought to be in her grave.'

'There you go again,' said his wife resignedly.

'I guess I'll buzz off,' replied Dan disgustedly. 'You always upset women by talking of graves and babies. They've got to come to both if they're made right, begging your pardon Miss Lacey. You two talk about last Sunday's dinner. So long.'

Miss Lacey sighed with relief.

'Poor Dan,' said his wife. 'He does talk a lot of nonsense. He's always been the same, shouting at the top of his voice about nothing in particular. Jenny! Peter! Now where did those children go?'

'They made off towards the slide,' answered Miss Lacey.

'Oh dear! Do you notice, Miss Lacey, that children never ask can they do anything these days? They just do it. Do you suppose it's the war makes them like that?'

A few pertinent remarks about upbringing rose to Miss Lacey's tongue, but she suppressed them; twenty years at her calling having made her sensible of what a lady-help could or could not say.

The carnival consisted of strings of lights suspended between trees, a hoopla booth, a chocolate wheel, a slippery-slide, a refreshment stall, and the town band drawn up threateningly in the bandstand. Mrs Gerahty and Miss Lacey made towards the refreshment stall. Here the matrons of the town forgathered to talk over the week's doings and rehash old scandals, also to fore-shadow those about to happen. Miss Lacey was not rightly a matron but she'd picked up interesting oddments in her ram-blings and had a sprightly tongue when it got going. She was excluded merely from the intimate birth details.

'Well, here we all are again,' said Mrs Gerahty brightly. 'How's everyone?'

'Fine, thanks. How's yourself?'

The band struck up, splitting the air with sounds. It was some moments before they accustomed themselves to the noise and collected their scattered thoughts. Then they got down to it in earnest. Above them the lights blinked. Further above still the stars were stolid in the dark sky.

Kathleen thrust her arm through that of Mavis Bell and walked her energetically through the gathering crowd. 'He makes me sick; just sick,' she said.

'Who?' asked Mavis. 'Siddie?'

'No, of course not. My father. I've a good mind to run away.'

'Oooh, you wouldn't be game.'

'Wouldn't I? You wait and see.'

'Remember what happened to Mary Hutchins —'

Kathleen stamped her foot irritably. 'Mary Hutchins! I'm not a fool like Mary Hutchins.'

'Fools or not, it's all the same with girls who run away from here. They all come back the same way.'

'But why should they?' stormed Kathleen.

'Dunno why, but they do.'

'It makes me mad. Hopping mad. Gee, what I've got to put up with from that man. I don't think any girl ever had as awful a father as I have.'

'You musn't say that,' said Mavis, shocked. 'He's real good as fathers go. You shouldn't expect much from a father. He doesn't belt you, does he?'

'Let him dare lay his little finger on me —'

'Well, what are you moaning about?'

'You don't know everything. How mother's put up with him for so long I don't know.'

'But she kinda likes him.'

'She must kinda something, or she'd have gone crazy before this. You know what he did the other time? He came home at three o'clock in the morning and crawled in Miss Lacey's window, shouting at the top of his voice. Shakespeare, he said it was. He was dead drunk. He always drags Shakespeare into things when he's drunk. Anyhow, it gave Lacey an awful fright, which, of course, served her right. She needs a few frights, the old devil.'

'Gosh, Kathleen, you're kind of mad with everyone.'

'I guess I am. And I'm mad with mother, too. Next morning, there she is going round sssshing everyone. "Ssssh!" she says, "Ssssh! Your father's got his malaria again. Sssssh!" Malaria! I'd give him malaria!'

Mavis poked her suddenly. 'Who's the soldier with Siddie?'

'Siddie? Where?' asked Kathleen.

'Over there.'

'Ooh-hoo, Sid,' cried Kathleen.

Sid turned, looked about insolently, caught sight of the girls and waved nonchalantly. He turned away again.

Kathleen dropped Mavis's arm, put her hands on her hips, and was about to tell all and sundry what she thought of Siddie Brownlow when he touched his companion on the shoulder, swung about, and came towards them. She clutched at Mavis. 'Gosh,' she thought, 'gosh. Wish he couldn't do this to me. Wish he wouldn't swing his hat from his shoulder like that. I wish they'd take him to a camp a long way off so he couldn't come home on leave. But do you really get a baby for only once? Why can't someone tell me?'

'Hullo, Kathleen. Gee, kid, you get cuter every day. I guess you must be just about grown up. Has your father got a gun? Hullo, Mavis. You two like to meet a pal of mine? Ben Adam.'

'Abou Ben Adam?' demanded Mavis.

'The very one,' cried Siddie delightedly, turning his attention to Mavis. 'This is Mavis, Ben. She used to be the clever girl at school. Top of the class and all that.'

'What about me?' asked Kathleen, pouting.

'Bottom, I reckon,' answered Siddie. 'But your chest started spreading first.'

Kathleen brought up her hand and slapped him smartly across the face.

'Oooh,' gasped Siddie, rubbing the place gingerly. 'Haven't you got a temper?' he said admiringly. 'It's a wonder your hair's not ginger.'

Kathleen tossed her black curls defiantly.

'Let's do something,' suggested Ben.

'Kath and I were just about to go on the slide,' lied Mavis.

'Right. Let's go on the slide,' cried Ben.

'Sure,' said Siddie. 'It'll get us in the mood.'

'I don't feel in the mood for anything,' said Kathleen.

'But you will before we're done,' answered Sid. 'Come along.'

'What's the use of always getting your teeth fixed, when you've just got to die in the end?' demanded Kathleen.

'Hell! What's got into you?' asked Siddie.

'Take no notice,' advised Mavis. 'She's off her noodle.'

'To the slide,' shouted Ben.

They climbed up the steep wooden stairs, one behind the other. The scent of the cedar-blossoms made the air potent so that the stars whirled and the insecure height made them dizzy with a sense of danger. On top of the slide, the attendant placed a large sugar-bag. They linked arms and got on it gingerly; the four of them together, their thighs touching.

'Are you right?'

Scent of cedar, sound of music. They slipped to infinity, flesh touching, wind rushing, landing a bunch of laughter and limbs in the sawdust below.

'Again,' cried Mavis.

'No,' said Kathleen. 'Let's go down to the creek.'

'Good on you, kiddo,' said Sid.

'That's the idea.'

'No!' Mavis was alarmed. 'Kathleen!' She took Kathleen aside. 'It's too early to go yet. It's not safe to go there until it's nearly time for someone to come looking for you.'

'Not safe, hooey,' hooted Kathleen. 'Who wants to be safe?'

'Oh, Kathleen!'

'Come along, girls.'

'Let's go and have a cup of tea,' suggested Mavis brightly.

'Hoi,' shouted the boys together.

Kathleen laughed. 'You remind me of Miss Lacey. She's always after cups of tea.'

'It's all old maids have got,' said Siddie.

'I say,' demanded Ben, 'which girl is mine?'

'I guess I am,' answered Mavis resignedly.

They sauntered towards the creek. The music followed after them, softened by distance. There was the smell of earth and water commingling where the creek hollowed the dark earth of the bank.

'See that tree, there?' said Siddie. 'Nearly drowned myself near it when I was a kid. There's a root going out into the water. I climbed along it and stooped to wash my hands. Next thing I knew I was in the water.'

'And what happened?' asked Mavis.

'I forget. I guess someone fished me out. I'm still here, aren't I?'

'You might as well have been drowned,' said Kathleen. 'You'd have got it over.'

'Got what over?'

'Dying. You can only die once. Once it's over, it's done with.'

'She's all messed up about dying,' said Mavis, sneeringly.

'I'll cure her of that,' answered Siddie. 'Here, kiddo, sit down and talk to your old uncle.'

'As long as you only sit,' said Mavis sharply.

'Oh, you shut up!' cried Kathleen. She sat down suddenly, put up her arms and dragged Sid down beside her. 'I guess I'm crazy tonight.'

'I guess you're lovely.'

She half-sobbed. 'If you don't hurry, I'll walk out there and drown myself,' she whispered.

'Remember, you've brought this on yourself.'

'Kathleen, are you all right?' called Mavis.

'Shut up. Go away.'

'All right. But don't think I'm going to be sympathetic.'

Kathleen half-sobbed, half-screamed.

'Be quiet,' urged Siddie. 'Kathleen! Kathleen! I didn't mean to hurt you, sweetheart. Kathleen, listen. I'll tell you something. I'm frightened of something, too. I don't want to be shot in the stomach; not in the stomach. Kathleen, listen to me, you little devil. Kathleen, darling. Hell, I guess I don't care now if I am or not.'

'Where,' demanded Dan Gerahty, 'is Kathleen?'

'I'm here,' answered Kathleen, materializing from the shadows.

'I haven't had sight or sound of you all night.'

'Just as well for your peace of mind,' retorted Kathleen sweetly.

'Well —' Dan suddenly burst out laughing. 'She's my daughter, all right. I'll allow that, Minnie, she's my daughter. Where's Lacey?'

'I'm here,' said Miss Lacey, meekly.

'Guess what. I've been talking to a fellow from the other side of Maryborough. Funny for a fellow from right the other side of there to get right down here. Just shows what wars can do. Well, this fellow knows of another fellow who's got some cows to sell —'

'Oh, Mr Gerahty!' cried Miss Lacey.

'Oh, Mr Gerahty,' mimicked Dan, and threw his arms about Miss Lacey.

'Dan, Dan!' remonstrated his wife. 'Stop embarrassing the poor girl.'

'It's time she was embarrassed,' said Dan stoutly. 'Besides, she likes it. All women do.'

'Oh, all right,' said Mrs Gerahty resignedly. 'You're not the first man to make a fool of himself shouting about what a woman does or doesn't like. Let me tell you, Dan Gerahty, there's not one man living who knows.'

Murder!

Dr Phantom, the most eligible bachelor between Mallow's Marsh and Hornsby Junction, did not admire women, he did not really care about children, but, since his manners were perfect, being the product of a kind heart, not of the etiquette book, on seeing Miss Juliet McCree (though, being sixteen, she was a mélange of both his abhorrences) balanced on one knee on the highway, her horse's hoof resting on the other knee, he drew up to ask whether he could be of any use?

'My horse is quite lame! The hairpin buckles every time I get it under the stone in his shoe!' Juliet explained, lifting a glowing face. 'How I shall find my way to Mallow's Marsh I can't guess, and dear Grandmama McCree has given me a Charlotte Russe (it has two glasses of Grandpapa's best port in it) to take to the new Rector's wife. Beside, it is St Agnes' day! I have to dress the well.'

'Dress the well?'

'In thanksgiving for the *particularly* good drinking water we have at Mallow's Marsh. It's delicious, really. Last year we dressed all six wells, but this year I have just brought some daffodils and tinsel, and a figure of St Agnes, and I shall do the Rectory well, if they let me.'

Standing up, Juliet gave Dr Phantom the benefit of her lively regard.

'Oh! You are driving your Tilbury,' she exclaimed, enchanted. 'I am so glad to have the chance of seeing it without having measles, mumps, whooping-cough, or scarlatina! I found a four-leafed clover as I was leaving Carefree Farm — you know my Grandparents live there since Grandpapa retired? His son-in-law, my step-papa, bought it and gave it to him!'

'Oh, yes! I'd heard — so generous a gift!'

'When my horse went lame I was afraid the clover was proving a complete failure as a luck-bringer, but no! I do call it a piece
of good fortune to meet you and see your new turnout.'

Leading her horse, Juliet walked round the vehicle.

'An osier-cane body! Gold as a guinea! Japanned wood
wheels! Picked out with yellow! Striped like a wasp, really. A hood
you can hoist up and down!' She felt its supple texture. 'Leather!'

'*Russia* leather!'

'I believe you! And what a picture your new mare is!'

The mare was indeed a wayward beauty.

At one instant she would stand on two elegant legs to look at
the blue, distant Razorbacks, and another she would waver and
tittup sideways, backwards, forwards, perversely seeing in the
hedges or ditches meandering giraffes, elephants, or all that a
horse most dislikes. At the same time she flecked gobbets of foam
from her churned bit, rolled her treacle-soft eyes till the whites
showed red-veined, or pricked her fidgety ears backwards 'in the
most adorable way' as Juliet pointed out.

Dr Phantom was beginning to wonder whether he had
bought the right animal, one which the vendor had promised
'could do everything except wait at table'. He felt, therefore, a little comforted by Juliet's praise of it. This extreme nervousness
might, perhaps, be an endearing trait? He twisted the reins round
a hook on the mirror-bright dashboard, while his groom, his
'Tiger', wearing a neatly belted green uniform and a cockade in
his black top hat, jumped down from his perch hidden behind the
hood, and ran to hold the mare's bridle.

Dismounting briskly, standing beside Juliet on the red spongy
road, Dr Phantom looked with a minimum of enthusiasm at her
unkempt colt, and, having taken a clean duster from the Tilbury,
he lifted the debatable hoof with fastidious care, to pronounce
that no remedy was possible without the aid of a smith.

'I heard that you had put down the Hyde Park,' Juliet said,
still lost in admiration, '*that* was smart enough in all conscience,
but this positively whistles with splendour!'

Indeed, the slim precision of its craftsmanship evoked memories of an ant's waist, or a spider's web or any other such naturally spindly miracle of nature. It was a superbly attenuated vehicle.

Dr Phantom looked complaisant.

'Yes! My partner, Dr Boisragon — it's hard to imagine him as your uncle — coveted my Hyde Park. And you know what he is?'

'Do I not!'

Dr Phantom looked away from her shining regard.

'I found it more restful to let him have it. I got the coach-builder in Parramatta to make me this Tilbury, which needs only one horse and a boy instead of two horses and two men. Directly he saw it — if you please — Dr Boisragon asked me to exchange it for the Hyde Park!'

'Now isn't that just like Uncle Peter! He thinks he has a right to get everything he wants! Not only what he *needs*, don't you know?' She raised her eyes again to eyes that immediately withdrew their gaze. 'He has never spoken to me since that awful day — I was twelve, then — when he accused me of stealing his Red Roman! He told Mama I am a thief and a liar. He thinks no sin too bad for me to commit. But, quite frankly, Dr Phantom, I know, in reality, very little more about sin than Moses did. And in his knowledge of it (judging by the *paucity* of the Ten Commandments) he does not go very far.'

'Don't speak so slightingly of Moses! You shock me.'

'I'm praising him, really, for his innocence of heart. Don't you always feel that he has to eke out his experience, rather — there is so much that he leaves unsaid?'

'Absurd child,' Dr Phantom said to himself, 'she is too thinly clad for this raw spring day! Her grandmama bought that family up on starchy food, hasty-pudding and choke-dog, as Juliet called their 'treats'! Charity child dishes! And as for that flighty, selfish mother of hers — off to Paris with a brand-new husband!' Pity shook his heart! He held out a hand from which he had stripped a pig-skin glove.

'Hop up, child. I'll drop you at Mallow's Marsh.'

The saddle was bestowed under the seat. The horse was turned into Farmer Salter's paddock among the grazing cattle.

Dr Phantom climbed into the driving seat beside Juliet; the Tiger, who had been swinging like a bat from the mare's bridle, let go, and, like the wind, off they flew, the boy having flung himself into his perch as they went.

It was a perfect though astringent morning in early Spring.

The sprouting grass, unbrowned by frost, showed through the mirror-like surface of a thousand puddles in which grey ibis fished — for frogs? Every grazing beast had its chirping retinue of wag-tails. Whitethorn and Traveller's Joy caressed every sliprail. The wide, almost treeless, emerald plain was greedily devoured by a man-eating sun, ardent as a beast of prey.

High above the gay equipage flew a milk white dove.

Looking up, Dr Phantom remembered to have seen just such another bird, flying in a paradise all its own. When was it? He followed the glinting wings, thinking, 'Yes, I was happy, four years ago, when I watched that other white bird! I was standing beside Juliet then, too, in Parramatta High Street. Yes. That was the time! I remember thinking — so I did — that earth is like a pear, that has one perfect moment!' He felt some stirring in his singing heart, he thought again, 'Yes! Life brings moments when one feels superbly happy — for no reason that one knows of!'

He saw, laid out like wax flowers in a glass container, the small symbols of an earlier flame; a pink lawn handkerchief, a regurgitated nectarine (a Red Roman), and he recognised a lost illusion without regret.

He and Juliet, bowling along the shining roadway, were both happy; time had candied (as it does) their griefs.

'I wanted to go to Scutari, in the Crimea, to join Florence Nightingale. She was taking thirty-seven nurses out, and would have welcomed another doctor! I may manage to go, yet, though my partner has so far refused to relax the terms of our agreement. He won't give me a year's furlough.'

'The war with Russia will soon be over.' Juliet attempted consolation.

For some minutes they progressed with a crablike movement along the rutty highway, the mare only sometimes remembering that the earth was her proper element.

'I find,' Juliet remarked, after a thoughtful silence, 'that a group of people in a particular place has a peculiar reality all its own. Away from that place, parted from each other, such people are different. That is why I dread going back to Mallow's Marsh, where once I was so happy.'

'Yes,' Dr Phantom glanced at her serious profile. 'A Curate in your Grandfather's place — that will be sad to see!'

'Do you remember such a group in your own life?'

Dr Phantom was cautious.

'I remember one day, when I was lying with my brothers under a wattle tree in flower — I still see the yellow against the blue sky — and, I remember, that we decided all we were going to do when we grew up — that might be vivid because it's a collective memory — one they remember as well as I do?'

'Life is made up of a succession of such groups.'

'Life is peculiar. Look at the way some people keep on coming into one's life.'

He stooped to look under Juliet's hat brim, but her eyes evaded his.

'Yes, indeed!' She, however, heartily agreed. 'Parties now! People who have never met before — how their destinies get entangled!'

A light spring cart drawn by a handsome dray-horse had been lumbering and jolting towards them for the past quarter of an hour.

'Why!' Juliet, watching it, exclaimed, 'I do believe that is the Rectory cart with old Ruby in the shafts, and that Man Thomas is driving it! We left it for the curate's use!'

To her delight it proved to be none other.

Since in that neighbourhood no-one dreamt of passing without exchanging the time of day (a lost phrase, that), the Tilbury drew up by the side of the road, and got as near to stopping as the mare allowed. Man Thomas very easily chirruped old Ruby into immobility. He and the dray and the mare looked just the same, Juliet radiantly noted. Brass earrings as big as bracelets gleamed through the frizzy hair of Man Thomas's unshorn locks. His beard was Byzantine, certainly, its waves stiff and deep as the furrows of a Babylonian King's. A Mithrydite returning from a lion hunt — some such carved frieze his presence evoked.

And now he came charged with news.

He knew his manners. He asked, first after Juliet's grandparents, her brother, Cook Teresa, and every farm hand and animal at Carefree Farm, with a persevering fidelity. But his hearers, all the same, sensed the bringer of tidings.

'Sims like,' Man Thomas said at last, 'Sims like as Curate has murdered his wife.'

'What!'

'Sims like.'

'Whatever makes you say such a thing?'

'Disappeared, she has.'

'Oh, come!' Dr Phantom was amused. Juliet's delight at meeting such a bizarre friend had touched him, still —

'She's not in Church, she's not in Rectory, she's not in Mallow's Marsh — I'd swear to that.'

'When was she last seen?'

'Saw her myself, I did, the day Curate arrived. I passed her, walking on the road to Fisher's Ghost Crick.'

Man Thomas fanned himself with his hat. 'English, she were.'

'How could you guess that?'

'Too tall, flat chest, big feet, nose like Mr Nosey Parker's, and talking through it like a blackbird, she were. I knows an English-woman when I sees one.'

'Has no one seen her since?'

'First or last. Granny Peachy says she's in the Ottoman. I holds she's in the well. Churchwarden, he asked the Curate right out, 'Where is your wife?' And the Curate laughed. Laughing all the time, that young gentleman is! But I be going for to fetch the police.'

'Are you, and Granny Peachy and the Churchwarden the only people who suspect the Curate of this crime?'

'Mid not have been a crime — '

'Oh?'

'Mid have been a necessity, like.'

Dr Phantom knew dismay. Could he leave Juliet at the scene of so recent a murder? Yet, his patient, he with the ruined stomach — it was the usual complaint hereabouts — beyond Fisher's Ghost Creek, he could not be neglected.

'Yes,' Man Thomas continued with relish, 'whole of Mallow's Marsh knows as he murdered her. If not — where is she? That's what we asks! We've looked under the culverts and bridges, in the ponds and cricks, we've combed every nook! We done it thorough. And all the time, there was His Highness, a-peeping at us from every window in turn — doubled up with laughing. All he does is laugh!'

Man Thomas said 'Hup' to Ruby, who, waking out of a doze, broke into a wilful trot that caused the cart to sway from side to side, and soon carried Man Thomas on his way to the Police Station in Parramatta.

'Grandpapa and Grandmama both like the Curate. Even Grandpapa (a Cambridge man, as you know), said, "for an Oxford man he is an exceptionally harmless type."' Juliet re-tied the ribbons of her hat. 'Would Grandmama have sent me to take a Charlotte Russe to a man capable of murder? *She* would have seen at once if he had been at all eccentric!'

Dr Phantom guided the dancing mare over a bad bit of road.

'Personally I was surprised that she should have sent you so far on such an errand — '

'She meant to console me.'

'Console you?'

'Mama had sent me a present from Paris.'

'Then why "console"?'

Juliet hid her face below her brim.

'She sent me a doll.'

Dr Phantom burst out laughing.

'Grandmama says she must have gone out shopping with some young admirer, and so might have wanted to appear very young! So she sent me a doll, and Donalblain,' her voice faltered, 'a set of corals.'

Dr Phantom stopped laughing.

'Grandmama immediately went off to the dairy and made a Charlotte Russe — a most expensive one! As she stirred and whipped and poured in one valuable ingredient after another, she kept saying, most indignantly, 'A child? Juliet with a doll? Oh, yes, my fine high madam! I'll teach you what kind of child your daughter is!' Dear Grandmama very seldom loses her temper, but when she does — Oh! She's dangerous!'

'Dangerous?'

'She acts!'

'I see.' Dr Phantom remained thoughtful.

Mrs McCree was angry with her daughter-in-law, not for marrying again — apparently she had approved of the marriage — but for sending Juliet a doll — well! That was understandable! But how did the pudding sent to the Curate's wife provide an answer to that?

He had a lively tussle with the mare, who wanted to leap a three-rail fence — on either side of the road, she did not mind which — then he observed, 'If I do not set you down at Mallow's Marsh Vicarage, I may be spoiling some plan of your grandmother's. She is a woman who knows what she is doing. I'll drop you at the gate, and pick you up again on my way home.'

'Frankly,' Juliet laughed, 'I don't believe a word of Man Thomas's story.'

Half an hour later Juliet waved good-bye to Dr Phantom from the Rectory gate, and opening it, walked up the long-familiar path.

'There is the polyanthus — in full flower. There are the clumps of clove pinks. But how bare the windows look. No curtains. And there's no mat at the front door.'

She knocked.

Steps sounded on the bare boards upstairs. It seemed that someone slid down the banisters, then the door opened, and the 'new Curate' (now Rector) stood before her.

He was incredibly fair. His hair was almost flax-white, his complexion pale as milk; his eyes, however, were not an albino's, but as blue as cornflowers.

'My Grandmama, Mrs McCree, has sent you a Charlotte Russe — for your wife.'

He appeared to be convulsed with mirth.

'Impossible!' he laughed, 'Mrs McCree *knows*.'

Absurdly amused, led his visitor into the morning-room, which overlooked the orchard wall, and the well in its patch of long grass shaded by a wattle bush, now in flower. Far off the Picton Hills gnawed at the sky.

There is one thing in this deceitful world that can never be hidden; that is poverty. Even the usual palliatives, soap and water — and sunshine — though they may adorn it, cannot conceal poverty. The Rectory had never looked opulent. It now shrieked of indigence. As Juliet had already noticed, there were no curtains to the windows, no carpets — one chair; the ottoman, she was amused to see, stood by the window. The wallpaper showed faded patches where the two prints, 'The Fair Trespassers', had hung.

Her host sat on the famous ottoman which may or may not have hidden a corpse.

Juliet handed over the pudding in its basin; she sat on the one chair, facing him, as he kept ejaculating, 'Impossible — a pudding for my wife! *She knows*!' He stopped suddenly. 'How old are you?'

'Sixteen.'

'Heartfree?'

'That is one of the questions I never answer.'

Dazed, but hungry, the Curate brought spoons and plates, and together they embarked amicably on the Charlotte Russe, which was delicious, as both agreed, Juliet's protest — 'but surely your wife should have it?' — only provoking further amusement.

Looking around her, Juliet said, in her usual direct fashion, 'An empty house is sad, isn't it? Don't you find it depressing?'

She had forgotten about the missing wife.

'Did your Grandmama tell you to say that?'

Juliet looked astonished.

'No. Why should she?'

'Did she tell you to mention the patter of little feet?'

The young man began laughing again.

'No. Why ever should she?'

'Can you tell me the name of any character in history who died of laughter?'

'St Hilarious?'

'Call me Hillary.'

'My name is Juliet.'

He left the obvious unsaid.

'Tell me,' he asked, 'have you heard that I am accused of murdering my wife?'

'Oh, yes,' Juliet responded, cheerfully.

'Do you belong to the school which says I killed her with a cleaver and hid her in the ottoman? Or to the school that says I threw her down the well?'

'If you are the bloodthirsty type, delighting in slaughter for its own sake, you slew her with an axe, and hid her in the ottoman. If you are one of those tender-hearted people who cannot bear to see others suffer — you threw her in the well.' Juliet gave him a wide smile. 'I do not know you well enough to guess your type.'

'Let me know when you make up your mind.'

'Yes. I suppose you know that Man Thomas has gone for the Police?'

'Man Thomas? Oh. You mean Ahmen Hotop? Or Totmus the Tenth? That one?

Juliet did not often laugh, but a chirrup escaped her.

'He is such a nice man, really.'

'So are they all nice men, all Assyrian assassins.'

'Well. You have been warned.' Juliet rose. 'I shall go and decorate the well. I have always dressed the well on St Agnes' day. I have brought a saint — such a pet — and some paper roses — '

They went out together.

That was how it happened that Dr Boisragon, driving past in the recently bought Hyde Park, saw his niece and, as he considered, a murderer, putting a wreath of roses on the well-head; the well in which he knew the murdered wife to lie; for Granny Peachy had just told him the whole dreadful tale; and the Churchwarden had affirmed it.

'Ho! Ha!'

Dr Boisragon drove in through the stable gate, and leaving his vehicle, stood watching the young people.

By this time the sun was declining westwards, and long level rays caught Juliet's red hair, making it radiant. They shone gaily through the paper roses with which the well, rope and bucket were now garlanded. The light danced through the flowering wattle. Behind her, the Curate, listening to her chatter as he dangled a foot over the well, was so much absorbed that he did not hear the clink and clatter of the Hyde Park.

'Yes, I quite agree,' Juliet was saying with her usual complete unselfconsciousness, 'as you remark, a Curate *is*, perhaps, the most vulnerable form of bachelor. Other men can entrench themselves behind a facade of whiskers, brandy and rank cigars, and feel reasonably safe. But a Curate —— '

Looking up, Juliet saw her Uncle.

He had been to a funeral. His handsome figure was encased in black, crêpe banded his top hat and was looped in a 'weeper' round his right arm. His gloves were black; his cane, ebony. His stern, classical face was set in its usual lines of regret for the sins of others. How familiar Juliet felt with that air of reprobation for erring humanity!

'Once again, you abandoned girl, it is my duty to reprove you! At twelve you were proved to be a thief and a liar. That, I understood, on reflection, to be the outcome of greed! You were a *glutton* — theft and lying only pandered to that vice! I find you now satisfying even baser appetites.'

'I only took my fair share, Uncle Peter,' Juliet said, in a small, nervous voice.

'*Your fair share*! What! You can stand there and admit your trespass — and *justify yourself*!'

Dr Boisragon walked close enough to tower above the shrinking Juliet, who was entirely bewildered, while the Curate, too, was too much astonished to move.

'You can stand there beside your paramour — that murderer — whose poor wife's body is lying, I hear, drowned in that well, which — with what profane intention I cannot guess at — you have actually decorated with the roses and raptures of vice — oh, you Jezebel! Do you mean to tell me that you had only taken '*your fair share*' — your fair share — *of what?*'

'Of Grandmama's pudding,' Juliet answered, trembling. Yet she was mystified — whatever had she done this time?

'Of Grandmama's pudding! It is the first time I have heard such an expression applied to such a sin — Eve's apple — yes! But, Grandmama's pudding! You wicked girl — is that meant for wit?'

Dr Boisragon really did seem quite astounded.

It was at this opportune moment that the Police, led triumphantly by Man Thomas, joined the group.

The two mounted policemen, to show their zeal, jumped the hedge. Magnificently uniformed, with superb mounts, they made a dashing entrance, and leaping from their foam-flecked horses, they stood on either side of the Curate, whom Man Thomas, elated at being 'in time', pointed out to them as 'the murderer'.

The Churchwardens, who had driven over with Dr Boisragon, and had, with Granny Peachy, been lurking in the safety of the stables, now took their places round the well, while all the inhabitants of Mallow's Marsh (six men, three women and twelve children) peered over the orchard wall.

The scene was set.

The sergeant took out his note-book and licked his pencil.

'From hinformation laid,' he began, 'I 'ave to hinform you as you are under suspicion of 'aving murdered your wife. Name?'

'Hilarious.'

Juliet gave her small chirrup.

It affronted everyone more than words can say.

' — Orlando Furioso — '

Again that irrepressible chirp of laughter from Juliet.

The Police were shocked. Even in their unimaginative minds, 'the girl', as they termed Juliet, was assigned to the position of 'the Murderer's paramour'.

'Yes?' the Sergeant again licked his pencil point.

He scorned to ask how Furioso was spelt.

'Surname?'

The Curate stopped laughing and said, soberly, 'As a matter of fact my name is Plumtree, sometime Fellow of Oriol College, Oxford, and Rector designate of this parish. I am the Bishop's nephew.'

Visibly shaken, the Sergeant stuttered, 'Name of late wife — sir — if you please?'

'I have not got a wife.'

' 'Oo is the murdered lady?'

'There is no murdered lady. I cannot think how this absurd story started. Unless one of the maids at Carefree Farm, where I dined with Mrs McCree a week ago, may have overheard, and misunderstood, a conversation I had with Mrs McCree.'

'Better ask Man Thomas.'

Man Thomas in his simple way was a seeker after truth.

He stroked his glossy crenellated beard and pondered.

'Yes, yes,' he murmured, 'it might be so. Yes. It were Abigail at Carefree Farm as told me new Curate had a wife, like, so she did, so she did! And when I sees that Englishwoman in the lane, I thinks, "that's the Curate's wife" — so I did. And when no-one seed the lady to Rectory — well! I draws my own conclusions, like, so I does! Well — 'twere natural to think as Curate had put her away — now, wasn't it? And everyone agrees to it. Churchwarden and Granny Peachy — ' Man Thomas gave a great guffaw of laughter, 'I sees the joke! I sees the joke!' He slapped his tough thighs and laughed till the tears made watercourses down the furrows and channels of his beard, and the Curate, glad to have found a soul mate, laughed, too, while Juliet gave her small chirrups and spurts of gaiety, as sweet to hear as a thrush's song.

At first the Mounted Policemen did not see the fun, but the Rectory cellar being better stocked than the larder, and, Granny Peachy being an adept drawer of penny ale, they soon relaxed over brimming flagons in the kitchen, they, and every man in Mallow's Marsh, and it was a convivial party that broke up over an hour later.

Dr Boisragon, who made no apology to Juliet, drove away alone in his Hyde Park, which somehow looked less magnificent under new ownership, for the horses were not well groomed, and the curtains not pressed, and the wheels unwashed, and Dr Boisragon, upright and unsmiling, caused no hearts to beat faster.

While unbuttoned mirth rang out from the kitchen, Juliet strolled through the orchard with the Curate.

The almond blossom, always the first to flower, was punctual; the next trees to flower in a normal year would be the damsons; they were punctual; every bough appeared to be crystallized.

One apple was out. Six quinces were early. Against all precedent the cherries, usually the last to flower and first to fruit, were ineffably a month too soon.

Though the sun was sinking, and reasonable larks might have felt at liberty to drop down to the chirping tussocks below, they were pouring their full hearts out still, in unpremeditated bliss.

In a stuffy study in England a scientist, about this time, was penning the words '*Propinquity acts as a liberating stimulus to instinct*'. Two young people in the orchard (had they known it) were proving the truth of this axiom. Juliet, growing aware of her Grandmother's outrageous matchmaking (for the pudding was to introduce the Curate to his wife to be), forgave her. Orlando, who had come from a college which managed to exist without women, who had found Mallow's Marsh an anti-climax to his dreams of preferment, grew aware of the meaning of the words of Martin Tupper, the great Oxford poet, about 'twin-souls' and the 'ecstasy of Being'.

It would be premature to say that the young people left the orchard 'engaged'. But by the time the first constellation took up its position north of the Razorbacks (quite unaware that it was a well-known star, and had been much 'written up'), they were certainly in love.

Dr Phantom, calling for Juliet so late that every star was in its appointed place, and an unintelligible moon rode in the zenith, looked once at Juliet's revealing face, and knew the answer to a question he would never put.

It was, however, eleven months later that Mrs McCree wrote the letter that had been simmering in her heart ever since Peronel had sent her children those infantile toys. To write it, she put on her best dress, a lavender silk affair, bustled like Gibraltar and pleated to the limits of perplexity. With a fresh quill pen she wrote, triumphantly,

'My darling Peronel.

By the time you get this, *you will be a grandmother*! Dear little Juliet keeps very well, and Orlando makes a devoted husband. The Bishop has promised to christen the little stranger — I know you will rejoice — ' and so on and so such!

No letter had ever given a prospective great-grandmother greater joy to write, and Mrs McCree drove into Parramatta in her new basket-work Victoria and posted the letter herself. It was a delicious revenge!

The Jumping Jeweller of Lavender Bay

James Pratt broke his breakfast egg with one sharp tap of his knife-blade. Carefully he turned back the top until it hung neatly by the skin, like a lid on the hinge. He sat and blinked his eyes at the soft pink egg-meat and sighed. Mrs Pratt lifted her head from her own egg and narrowed her eyes at her husband. The morning sun made lights on the swimming, milky egg-yolk, and in the lights James Pratt looked to the bottom of his fifteen years with the stout red woman he'd married. He saw, amongst other things, five thousand four hundred and seventy-five breakfast eggs, with hardly one boiled hard to his liking.

'May I remind you that it's five minutes past eight?' said Mrs Pratt. 'You can dream all day when you get to the shop.'

James Pratt reached out with his knife-blade and flicked the top back on the egg, sealing it down with a tap, as though the egg had never been opened.

Mrs Pratt tilted a stout red cheek and her husband leant down and put his lips against it.

In the hall, where his hat hung, a canary hopped in a cage. Mr Pratt took down his hat and, pursing his lips, clicked his tongue at the bird the way one does to a baby.

Lavender Bay has quiet old houses and quiet old gardens and streets that go down steeply to the water. The little old ferries that cross the blue harbour to Circular Quay and the business streets of Sydney are broken in the wind like overworked horses. Sometimes they have to sit still for a while, rolling on the water, until the engines can get their breath back. Halfway down the hill that led from his house Mr Pratt bought a newspaper. At the bottom of the hill he bought ten cigarettes. At the entrance to the jetty he heard the ferry-bell ring. Mr Pratt blinked his eyes and started to hurry. The gangplank was up when he got to the wharf and the ferry was swinging out into the harbour, bubbling foamed water up the piles of the jetty, breathing hard deep breaths in the chest of the engine.

'Damn it,' Mr Pratt said. He hit his newspaper against a railing in useless vexation and felt for his cigarettes with the other hand. And then it happened, just like that, without a moment's warning.

While he stood there, watching the ferry leave, a strange feeling came over Mr Pratt. It mounted up from his ankles like the sting of iced water. It took his breath like the sting of iced water and it squeezed his heart like a hand. Mr Pratt opened his fingers and the newspaper dropped to the ground. Vacantly, he reached up and pulled his hat hard down on his forehead, took three steps backwards, sprang forward and jumped.

There was four feet of water between the wharf and the ferry. Mr Pratt cleared it without any trouble.

In the city arcade where, twenty years before, young James Pratt had started his jewellery business, repairing the watches of the citizenry and selling engagement rings to mute young couples, the steel shutters across the entrance doors of his shop were still locked at eleven in the morning. J. S. Forest next door, Fresh Cut Sandwiches While U Wait, came out from behind his counter and stood wiping his hands on his long white apron. 'Perhaps he's sick,' his wife said, from where the cool white bread slices piled behind her carving knife.

'Why doesn't he phone, then?' J. S. Forest asked. 'If he's sick he telephones, you know that; me and him have had that arrangement fifteen years.'

'You come inside and get this bread buttered,' his wife said.

James Pratt wasn't sick, he was shaken and puzzled and awed. So shaken and so puzzled and so awed, indeed, that he sat on a high stool in the Hotel Victoria and drank brandy at eleven in the morning. For the first time in ages he forgot the jewellery shop and forgot the stout red wife who telephoned every morning with a list of shopping he took home each night.

When he did get to the shop it was five minutes to lunchtime and the furious telephone had stilled its belling. Mr Pratt took off his coat and hung it up and put his arms through the sleeves of his working jacket. He screwed the jeweller's glass into his eye and sat at his work-bench, head bent low in concentration, the barrel of the jeweller's glass aimed at the black felt square tacked on the top of the table. But the watches needing repair, with their owners' names on the little white tickets, hung forgotten in lines on the wall. For a long time Mr Pratt sat there, the magnifying eye of the jeweller's glass minutely examining the black felt square on the table top.

When Mr Pratt got home that night his wife was waiting for him. She swallowed a chocolate when she heard the front door open. It was only half chewed and made her gulp for a moment.

'So!' she said, laying down a copy of the *Women's Weekly*. 'Would it be too much to ask where you were this morning?'

Mr Pratt blinked. 'I had to go out, Thelma,' he said. He thought for a while. 'I'm sorry dear, I had to see my accountant.' He sat down and tapped on his knees with his fingers. He looked about him almost as though the french clock and the floral lounge-suite and the pot plant and the photographs of his wife's parents were unfamiliar furnishings to him.

'You had to go out,' Mrs Pratt said, nodding her heavy red head with satisfaction. 'You had to go out to see your accountant.' She leant forward. 'Then perhaps you'll explain why Mr Forest rang to ask why the shop hadn't been opened ... Why the shop hadn't been opened at half past twelve in the morning. Oh, you liar!' she added. 'You deceitful man, you've been drinking. I can smell it. Drinking while the business goes to ruin.' The stolid furnace of Mrs Pratt's emotions was fairly blazing under the forced draught of her husband's scandalous behaviour. Tears squeezed out of her fat eye-corners.

'Now, now, Thelma,' Mr Pratt said, reaching across with his hand. 'Now Thelma, don't take on, there's nothing to get upset about.'

But Thelma was upset, properly upset, and she wasn't going to be easily placated. 'Don't touch me,' she wailed. 'Take your hands off me.' She pushed herself up off the lounge.

Mr Pratt heard their bedroom door slam. He sat still for a time, looking at the carpet and blinking his eyes. Then he wandered into the hall. The canary hopped about in the cage. Mr Pratt pursed up his mouth and clicked his tongue, 'Pretty birdie,' he said. 'Pretty Dickie.'

There are experiences in marriage uncommunicable between one partner and the other. Anyone who has been married five minutes knows that. On the way down the hill to the ferry next morning Mr Pratt thought with a shudder about how his wife would receive an account of the phenomenon of yesterday morning. The thought was so unnerving that he put it out of his mind and took off his hat to enjoy the sun on his head. The thing itself, however, could not be put from his mind. For the umpteenth time he went over the event again, from the first moment that strange feeling had come over him, the strange feeling which had mounted up from his ankles like the sting of iced water. He counted the memories one by one, cherishing them like the beads of a rosary. Half-way down the hill he bought a newspaper. At the bottom of the hill he bought ten cigarettes. The ferry was waiting when he got to the bottom of the jetty. Mr Pratt stood on the edge of the wharf, blinking his eyes, staring into the water. The ferry-bell rang and still he stood there.

The deckhand who cast off the mooring ropes watched Mr Pratt. He rattled the gangplank by its hand-rail. 'Wakey, wakey!' he shouted. 'Rise and shine or the crows'll eat yer eyes out!'

Mr Pratt started and hurried up the gangplank. The deck-hand slipped the mooring rope and coiled it into a pile. 'Cripes almighty!' he said.

Two days afterwards, Mr Pratt jumped again. He dawdled his way down the hill and when he got to the wharf the ferry was almost five feet out. Mr Pratt felt the ice water mounting up from his ankles. He dropped his newspaper, crouched his shoulders, sprang forward and jumped. And it happened. There could be no doubt about it. It happened, all over again.

Four feet or five feet is no great distance, in terms of a measured jump. Schoolboys jump farther every day, out of youthful high spirits, and nobody remarks on it. Mr Pratt's jump, as a distance negotiated between a departure-point and an arrival-point, was wholly negligible. But that wasn't the point. Mr Pratt had, in fact, jumped out of this world. The convolutions of time and space had got all mixed up that summer on the wharf at Lavender Bay.

When Mr Pratt launched himself on that first fateful morning, he had seemed to see, at some point in his flight from the wharf to the ferry, a completely different plane of existence. It was, according to a record he left in the jeweller's shop, exactly as though he had looked over the edge of a saucer. And what Mr Pratt saw there changed his life like a wave from a wand.

It was a sandy world he saw. Long, rolling barriers of gold-coloured sand with buildings like palaces in rose-coloured marble. Near the edge of the saucer a lake of blue water wound its edges through shrill green trees with yellow-crested canaries hopping in the leaves, bubbling their throats in unearthly music. In that place the breezes were perfumed, and when the leaves stirred on the trees they tintinnabulated like tiny silver bells.

On a mat near the water a yellow-eyed girl lay on one rosy elbow. The curve of her thigh was like the music of ten thousand violins; her lips were half-opened lotus-buds; the richness of her belly was heaped golden grain, and her breasts were like pomegranates and her hips like wine-jars.

Mr Pratt only had the thatch of his thinning brown hair and blinking sad eyes above the edge of the saucer, but the girl saw him. She saw him, the yellow-eyed girl. She stretched herself at Mr Pratt and his heart went off like a cannon. She shook back her yellow hair and slowly, most clearly and distinctly, she crooked a pink finger and called Mr Pratt.

It is not to be wondered at that Mr Pratt went off and drank brandy, that he forgot his arrangement of fifteen years standing to telephone J. S. Forest if he were not coming to business, or that he found it discreet to make up a small lie for Thelma. He had good reason for all of these backslidings.

On the occasion of the second jump undertaken half in the hope of discrediting the first experience and half in the hope of confirming it, the distance jumped from the wharf to the ferry was increased by approximately one foot. On this second jump Mr Pratt got all of his head and part of his shoulders above the edge of the saucer. He was actually able to bend his head inside the rim. The yellow-eyed girl tinkled with laughter and called Mr Pratt more frankly than ever.

For the next four days Mr Pratt jumped every morning. At the bottom of the hill he would wait for the ferry to ring its bell and then race down the jetty and fling himself into the air. At the end of that time he had increased the distance to over six feet and had mounted the saucer as high as his waist.

The jewellery business was already showing the strain of Mr Pratt's preoccupation. His work went downhill at a rate directly related to the length of his jumps. Moreover, people were beginning to talk. On the morning of the sixth jump he noticed in the minute of taking off that the rails of the ferry were lined with the passengers, and he heard through the thudding in his ears their raised chorus voices, 'Come on Pratty, you can do it.' He wanted privacy above everything when he came down on the ferry after seeing that yellow-eyed girl. But the other passengers clustered around and put out their hands to help in his landings and patted his back and asked him if he was jumping for bets.

Life for Mr Pratt, was becoming involved.

In the evening of the morning on which Mr Pratt made his eighth jump, estimated by the ferry deck-hand at seven feet nine and a half inches, Mr Pratt came home late from his business. He had stayed behind working, trying to catch up on the growing lines of ticketed watches hanging broken and silent on the hooks on his walls.

Thelma met him before the front door had closed properly behind him. 'Look at this!' she screamed. 'What are you doing, you brute, shaming me to the world! You're mad, that's what it is, mad like your uncle that's supposed to be in the TB home. He's locked up in the asylum, that's where he is, and you're as mad as he is.'

'Now, Thelma, you shouldn't say things like that,' Mr Pratt said, taking the copy of the newspaper she thrust at him, blinking his sad grey eyes.

'How will I ever show my face outside?' his wife said, bubbling tears into her handkerchief. She lumbered down the hall and Mr Pratt heard the bedroom door slam. It was a familiar punctuation-mark in that house.

On his way through the hall Mr Pratt paused and clicked his tongue at the canary. In the lounge he put on the wireless and settled himself in a chair. He opened the folded newspaper. On the front page there was a three-column photograph of himself in mid air, coat-tails flying, a mad look on his face. The photograph was captioned 'THE JUMPING JEWELLER OF LAVENDER BAY,' and the story made his ears burn.

Mr Pratt sat in his chair thinking, for a long time. Then he got up and made a bed on the couch. He fried eggs and bacon and ate in the kitchen. Last thing before bed he went into the hall where the canary hung in the cage near the hat-stand. He opened the feeding door and put in his hand, wrapping the canary gently in his fingers. He held it up and let it nibble at his lips. 'Sweet dickie,' he said, clicking his tongue. He opened his hand. The canary sat there for a minute turning its head. Then it put out its wings and swooped into the sky, a small free spot of yellow in the moonlight that shone over Lavender Bay.

Mrs Pratt appeared briefly early next morning. She announced that she couldn't bear the shame of living among her neighbours just then, and that she would go to her parents until her husband collected himself.

'I think that would be best, Thelma,' Mr Pratt said.

Mrs Pratt stood thunderstruck, looking at her husband as though she had never seen him before. Then the tears bubbled out again and she ran to the bedroom and the door slammed behind her.

At half past seven the telephone rang. It was a newspaper reporter asking for an interview. Mr Pratt politely declined.

At twenty to eight a photographer rang. Mr Pratt took the telephone off the hook and laid it on the table.

At five past eight he knocked on the bedroom door. 'I'm going now, Thelma,' he said.

'Go away, you go away,' Thelma answered.

Mr Pratt let himself out of the door and walked down the hill. He didn't stop for his paper, he didn't buy his ten cigarettes. Near the jetty he stood in a doorway, looking out over the splintery blue waters of Lavender Bay, blinking his eyes in the sunlight. He heard the ferry-bell ring. He heard the engines pumping. He heard the gangplank being pulled up and still he stood there, blinking.

Mr Pratt smiled. The smile looked funny on his face, it looked as though a mistake had been made, that it didn't really belong there. Then he pulled down his hat, buttoned his coat, and started to run.

Through the gates of the jetty Pratt pelted, down the boards of the jetty he ran, he didn't even see the reporters who awaited his coming, or feel the flash-bulbs in his eyes. The ferry was a good fourteen feet from the wharf by then, and a woman screamed as Pratt came in for the take-off. His feet hit the edge of the wharf with a wallop as he launched himself into the air. Up he went, coat-tail flapping, flash-bulbs popping, up he went with the cheers of the passengers in his ears. His head came over the rim of the saucer and the yellow-eyed girl was still waiting there; up he came, to his waist, to his knees, to his ankles.

Well, they dragged the water of Lavender Bay, but they never found Mr Pratt's body. The photographers cursed in bewilderment as they developed the negatives in their darkrooms. Mr Pratt printed fine on some of the frames, suspended between the sky and the ferry. But on others, with the wharf and ferry clearly etched, he just didn't print at all.

To Margaret

There is a widespread idea, obviously originating in the bulb-growing industry, that all Dutchmen are good gardeners.

Nonsense, of course, and I know of more than one employer who has found it out to his cost. A man isn't necessarily an authority on sheep because he was born in Australia, or on the bagpipes because he hails from Scotland. There is, nevertheless, always the exception that for so many people becomes the rule, and Hans — call him Vandeveer — must have blown new life into the Dutch gardener fallacy wherever his green fingers took him.

Because he *was* Dutch and he *was* a good gardener. One of those inspired craftsmen who are an embarrassment to all other craftsmen who come after them. He was also something of a poet, which may not be particularly interesting, and something of a lover, which is.

It was the only case I ever came across of a gardener falling in love with the boss's daughter, and I learned all about it because I was the one who succeeded him when he got his marching orders as a consequence. I took over only a week after he'd gone, when the garden was still fresh from his talents and the household still reeling under the shock of his romance. I found a glorious garden, an employer still frozen into a bitter mistrust of all gardeners, and a confiding housekeeper who told me that 'Miss Margaret' had cleared out to relations in Bendigo, and that her mother had followed her in an effort to persuade her to return.

But of all this I knew nothing when, at nine o'clock on the first morning, Mr Cameron, master of the house, stopped to speak to me on his way out to the city. He was a barrister, with

145

a future, I'd have guessed, in the Arbitration Court if he kept along with the right political party. A tall, dignified man somewhere below middle age, with a slow deep voice, cold eyes, and a lean handsome face that reminded me of a well-known bust of Julius Caesar.

I was older than him, with a long experience of employers, and I mistrusted him on sight. And even though, as I've said, I knew nothing of what had been going on, there were little things, even in that first brief interview, that made me wonder what I'd stumbled into. I'd been engaged through a nurseryman, and although Cameron therefore had good reason to study me, I thought there was something unnecessarily harsh and judicial in the way his grey eyes looked steadily into mine.

'Good morning, Johnston. I think I have the name right?'

'Yes. Good morning, Mr Cameron.'

He must have had plenty of confidence in his nurseryman, because there followed none of the questions I was expecting. Instead, he made it clear from the beginning that there would be no excuses in the event of difficulties or failures.

'You'll find everything in good order here.'

'It is, Mr Cameron. You must have had a good man.'

'I had.' He spoke with a noticeable dropping of the corners of his lips. 'He was Dutch. He'd had a very good training.'

I waited, hoping to learn if the Dutchman had left voluntarily, but nothing came. His eyes left me for a moment to scan the garden at large.

'I do a lot myself, though. The garden is my hobby.'

He need hardly have told me that. One day a week could never have achieved such an effect. And the place was not only perfectly kept; it was designed with imagination and richly founded. One of those lush, stately gardens that indicate an owner of fastidious tastes and all the means necessary to indulge them. Tall cypress hedges muffled the noises of Hawthorn Road, and of Balaclava Junction only a few hundred yards away. A sense of deep peace, of remoteness and isolation, had seized me the moment I'd stepped inside. There was a lively breeze blowing, but little of it penetrated the garden, and there was a greater twittering of birds than one expects to hear in a big city. I'd already observed many rare trees and shrubs, and several that were new to me. It was springtime, and a wide flagged path leading straight from the gate to the house, arched with roses and other climbing plants, was still dark with winter moss along the sides and littered with the fallen petals of wisteria.

Cameron nodded to indicate a small bed in the lawn not far from where we were standing. An oblong bed with an edging of alyssum just broken through, and the centre all dusted over with finely sifted stable manure as if something had recently been sown there. 'That bed is fully planted. It has linaria in the middle — dwarf Fairy Bouquet. He sowed it just before he left.'

I could see that it hurt every time he referred to the Dutchman.

'When was that, Mr Cameron?' I asked.

'A little over a week ago. You can let me know next Wednesday if there is anything you require. Mrs Briggs, the housekeeper, will give you your money when you finish. You won't meet Mrs Cameron today; she's away just now.' And with that he left me.

I didn't like him. An employer whose garden is his hobby is always a menace, but there was something else to Cameron. He hadn't once smiled. I was looking forward already to the day when I would find it necessary to challenge that Julius Caesar stare.

Mrs Briggs gave me morning tea. She just brought it out to the front porch, called me, and immediately went inside.

But at lunch-time I got the story. I'd decided that, as none of the heads were at home, I might as well eat in pleasant surroundings, so had taken my billy to the porch again. Soon after I'd finished eating she came out quite deliberately and joined me for a yarn. I suspected that the reason why she hadn't talked at ten o'clock was that she wanted plenty of time.

I had already met her, but only for a moment when, at eight o'clock, she'd given me the key of the toolshed at the kitchen door. Her appearance now on the porch bore out the impression she had left with me: a flurried, ageing little woman scared half out of her wits by a difficult household in which she had stayed too long. I knew the type: too near the end of her working days to venture into fresh fields, and still too useful to be thrown onto relations or into an old people's home. I was to find, however, that there were circumstances that made Mrs Briggs a rather special case.

She wore a white apron over a black frock, and had grey hair, a pinched, mousy little face, and hands all puffed and twisted by rheumatism.

She said she had come out to see if I'd like more tea, but when I told her I'd had enough she showed no inclination to go in again. She smiled the kind of smile you get from a person who is naturally pleasant but has little to smile about.

'I know how it is,' she said, looking at my billy as if she'd still like to fill it up. 'A man can drink a lot of tea at twelve o'clock when he's working hard.'

'I've had more than enough, Mrs Briggs.' I saw that she wanted to gossip, and added, just to give her an opening: 'You've got a nice garden here.'

Her eyes followed the path all the way down to the gate. 'Well, it should be. It's always been well looked after.'

The situation didn't seem to be one calling for much subtlety.

'Mr Cameron told me the last man was a Dutchman. What did he leave for?'

'Oh, you know how it is, he just ...' She began to fumble with her apron and gave me a confused glance, obviously torn between a desire to talk and doubt as to whether I was to be trusted. She broke out suddenly: 'Between you and me, gardener, he had to leave. There was a bit of trouble.'

She sat down in an old basket chair facing me and I waited, regarding her with an expression which I hoped was one of sympathetic interest.

'They found out there was something going on between him and the daughter.'

'What!'

One of her poor twisted hands came up in disapproval of my smile. 'Nothing wrong, mind you! I've known Miss Margaret since she was a baby, and a better girl you wouldn't find in all the world. I don't think there was a bit of harm in it. But there you are, Mr Cameron seemed to think there was, and that was the end of it.'

Up till then I'd been visualizing my predecessor as a man at least as old as myself, which was rather more than the age of romance.

'He must have been young, then, Mrs Briggs?'

'Hans? Oh, yes, about twenty, same as Margaret. And a nice fellow he was too. You'd hardly know he was a foreigner to hear him speak, although he never had much to say. Very quiet and polite. He must have come from a good home.'

'Good-looking?'

'He was good-looking all right! I don't wonder at Margaret …' Mrs Briggs hesitated, and gave me another cautious glance. She knew she was talking too much, but couldn't help herself. She was enjoying every minute of it. 'They were only a couple of kids making eyes at each other. I was watching; I'd have known if it was going any further. Margaret couldn't hide anything from me if she tried.'

'There must have been something in it.'

'Oh, Hans was struck on her all right. What I mean is that there was, well, no harm in it. Margaret — '

'Just secretly laughing at him?'

'No. I think she was a bit pleased about it. He had such a nice shy way with him, no liberties. He always managed to be somewhere near the path of a morning when she went out, with a flower for her — she's a chemist in some big Government place. And she'd keep that flower fresh for the best part of a week. Oh, I saw plenty. Just little things, but they all added up. Wednesday mornings she was always up and about a bit earlier, hanging round the dining-room window, peeping to see if Hans was in the garden.'

'Wasn't Mrs Cameron awake to it?'

'Of course she was. But she was like me, she couldn't see any harm in it. And she liked Hans. She got the blame for it, though, like she gets the blame for everything that happens in this house.' Mrs Briggs closed her eyes and lifted up her hands. 'My God, if you could have heard the way Mr Cameron went on! He seemed to tumble to it all of a sudden. He brought an orchid in for Margaret one night — it was a Wednesday — and next morning wanted to know why she was wearing the flower Hans had given her. It was deliberate, the kind of thing he was always up to. Then he went for Mrs Cameron. Told her it would never have happened if she'd been taking proper care of her daughter. As if anything *had* happened! You'd have thought the girl had been led astray. Anyway, there was a fine to-do over it, and the next time Hans came he got the sack. I don't think Mr Cameron was even going to tell him what it was all about. But I told him. I told him as soon as he knocked on the door for the key at eight o'clock. So he was ready. And doesn't the very fact that he started work show that he had nothing to be ashamed of? He was putting in some seed near the gate when Mr Cameron went down at nine o'clock.'

'Cameron waited till nine?'

'You don't know Mr Cameron yet! You wouldn't get him to change his habits, not if the world was on fire. Everything's got to be done exactly the same every day of the year. He'd think he was giving Hans a bigger shock, too, if he went down at his usual time — he's like that. Anyway, it didn't take him long. I was watching out of the window. The pity was I couldn't hear anything. Not that there was much said. Hans was all packed up and on his way out in a matter of minutes. Mr Cameron wouldn't make a scene.'

No, I reflected, not with his gardener.

'And Margaret cleared out?' I asked.

'That very afternoon. She came in about three o'clock when there was only me in the house, and started packing up. I tried to reason with her, but I might as well have talked to that brick wall. It wasn't only Hans, you know. There was trouble twelve months ago over a boy-friend she had. Mr Cameron broke *that* up, and he was no gardener. His father was a doctor.'

'Mr Cameron sounds a difficult man.'

'Difficult? He's a beast!' Really carried away now by her story, Mrs Briggs said this with a vehemence that startled me. 'It's never been a happy home. The wonder is he's ever been able to get anybody to live with him. I'd have left years ago if it hadn't been for Mrs Cameron. I can stand up to him a bit, but he's had her bluffed from the very day they were married. I felt I couldn't leave her with him. The things that woman's had to put up with! D'you know what he does when he really wants to hurt her?'

I shook my head.

'He calls her by her first name. Now then, would you think that was possible?'

'It's a new one to me, Mrs Briggs.'

'Yes, and you'd need to hear it to believe it. Years ago, when he had her in tears over some fiddling little thing she'd done that he didn't like, she complained that he never called her by her first name. And it was true, I never used to hear it from one week's end to another. And ever since then, when he really wants to be nasty, he calls her "Barbara". That's her name, all right, but you just ought to hear the way he says it — as if it was a dirty word. And it isn't as if he had any reason for it, because she's never been anything but a good wife to him. Too good, although he seems to think it's the other way round. I think he's always felt he'd married beneath him. None of her friends were ever good enough for him, they never come near the house now.'

'Whose relations did Margaret go to?'

'Her mother's. That's why he won't do anything about it. He says her home's here if she wants it. It's going to be awful tomorrow if Mrs Cameron comes back without her.'

And that, as I remember it, was the full story. There were a few anecdotes about Cameron, about Mrs Cameron, about Margaret, but nothing that added substantially to the picture I already had. I was more sure than ever that I would not get along with Cameron, but I went back to my work glad that I'd got the job, and full of curiosity over what was going to happen in the next week or two.

It was a pleasant day, that first one, one of those calm lovely spring days that stick in the memory. There was a nice sense of freedom, too, in the fact that Cameron had left me to my own devices, and that no curious eyes were watching me from the windows of the house. During the morning I'd disposed of all routine work such as cutting the lawns and sweeping the paths, and spent most of the afternoon lifting and re-laying a straggled edging of agathea along a wide border facing north. A warm sun played on my shoulders, and the air was full of the invigorating fragrance of spring — stocks and cinerarias and freshly turned earth.

How well it all went with the story of Hans and Margaret! I kept thinking of them both, but it was Hans who had taken the greater hold on me. He was inevitably so much more real than the girl. I'd seen neither of them, but the spirit of the young Dutchman, in the very evidence of his talents, was with me wherever I turned. I had no small pride in my own talents, but that garden humbled me. It troubled me that it was the work not of an old master, but of a young man only on the threshold of experience. It seemed to me that, as far as Hans was concerned anyway, the affair ran deeper than Mrs Briggs suspected. Hans had been speaking to Margaret, not with just a single flower offered every Wednesday as the girl went out to work, but every day, and with a whole garden of flowers. As the afternoon wore away an odd feeling grew on me that I was moving on fairy-tale ground, that I had no right to be there; that, fortuitously, I had become possessed of something to which I had no claim. Where was Hans now? And what were the chances of his ever seeing Margaret again?

On the following Wednesday I met Mrs Cameron. In approaching the house, and just before coming abreast of the gate, it was possible to see into a corner of the garden to the right of the path, and I had a fleeting glimpse of a pale blue dressing-gown alongside the bed where the alyssum and linaria had been planted. Why she should skip when she heard me coming I couldn't understand then, but by the time I'd got off my bicycle, crossed the footpath and opened the gate, she was already heading towards the house.

She evidently decided, though, that I was too close to be ignored, and after a few doubtful paces she stopped, looked backwards, and gave me good morning. She was a woman of medium height, slender, and rather nice-looking in a matronly kind of way. She had a gentle voice and a warm, friendly smile.

My sudden arrival seemed to have embarrassed her, and knowing that some women don't like to be caught in their dressing-gowns by male employees I kept striding out so that I would pass her quickly. She had to stand aside to leave room for the bicycle, and in the brief moment in which I met her eyes I saw nothing of that cold calculating detachment which usually meets the new man. There was something else. Something which I would hesitate to describe as fear but which was certainly anxiety. Something which fitted in significantly with the need for her to stand aside for me — and with Mrs Briggs's story. It was symbolic, as if she recognized in me one more link in a chain of events which she dreaded, but to which she had become resigned.

I saluted her, and returned as courteous a response to her greeting as I could.

She moved her head to indicate that part of the garden she had just left, and made a remark designed merely to fill in the moment I took passing. 'I was admiring the viburnum. It's always very beautiful in the spring.'

Conversation wasn't intended, so I just nodded my approval, commented that the tree was in a particularly good position, and next moment had left her behind.

At the kitchen door, when I went to get the key of the toolshed, I found out why she had scuttled when she heard me coming.

Mrs Briggs came out in a state of suppressed excitement. 'You seen the seed yet, gardener?' she asked in a whisper.

'What seed?'

'Down near the gate.'

'I've seen nothing yet.'

'Go down and have a look at it!'

She thrust the key into my hand and listened to hear if anybody was approaching behind her. 'There's the very devil to pay. That seed Hans put in, it's in Margaret's name — just wait till you see it! I can't talk now, he's on the prowl. I think he's going to get you to dig it in. Don't go down straight away, he'd know I'd been talking to you. He's mad as a hatter. See you later ...'

I was in a hurry to find out what it was all about, but I changed into my overalls, got out some tools, strolled round the garden, and finally came up alongside the bed near the front gate.

And there it was, surely as charming a tribute as ever was paid by a lover to his lady. Thousands of tiny linaria seedlings broken through in the warmth of the past week — *TO MARGARET* painted in letters of vivid green right across the square of rich brown earth.

It was magnificent, a perfect germination. Under the rays of the early morning sun it fairly rippled and glowed. I could have flung out my arms and leapt into the air with sheer excitement. *TO MARGARET*. This was what Mrs Cameron had been looking at as I reached the gate. I, too, just looked and looked and looked. I could feel Hans smiling over my shoulder. The whole story was instantly lifted to a higher level. How beautifully it was conceived, and with what loving care it had been executed! 'I told him as soon as he knocked on the door at eight o'clock,' Mrs Briggs had said. 'He was putting in some seed down near the gate when Mr Cameron went out.'

And Cameron was going to tell me to dig it in!

It would be like being told to strangle a baby or set fire to a church. I realized that I was no longer just a passive spectator; I was going to be involved, whether I liked it or not, and that within a matter of minutes.

It needed only seconds to decide I would be no party to vandalism, but I was still wrestling with the problem of how best to get out of it when, almost on the tick of nine o'clock, Cameron appeared. I was working near the house, and he called out to me from the front steps.

'Ah, Johnston!'

'Good morning, Mr Cameron.'

'One minute, please.'

I began to walk towards him, but he didn't wait for me and was halfway down the path before I caught up with him.

'There's a couple of little jobs I'd like you to do some time during the day.' At a point where a side path led off to the drive at the other side of the hedge he stopped and pointed to a rose branch which had broken loose and was hanging down about head-height. 'You'll find one or two like this. Tie them in, will you?'

I nodded. I had already seen them, and was annoyed that he thought it necessary to tell me what to do with them. Or was this just an idle preliminary?

'The other thing . . .' Stepping onto the lawn he looked down at the tell-tale seed-bed with an expression of hatred. 'I want you to turn this in and replant it.'

'You'd lose anything up to three weeks, Mr Cameron,' I said. 'That alyssum is well forward. It would be past its best when the linaria — '

'I'm aware of that, but we'd still get some kind of a show.' He was already moving away, but I tried again.

'You know, Mr Cameron, in a matter of five or six weeks you wouldn't be able to read that. Once the plants get well up and begin to spread — '

'It's the next five or six weeks that I'm concerned about,' he interrupted coldly. Taking one hand out of his trousers pocket he stabbed towards the bed with a long slender forefinger. 'I don't approve of monkey tricks like that. Ask Mrs Briggs for the seed. I got some more during the week.'

'Very good, Mr Cameron,' I said. I still didn't intend to dig it in, but an overwhelming desire to follow the story for just one more week prevented me from quarrelling with him there and then. Only a few minutes later I was glad of that restraint. I heard the creak of the front door, and Mrs Briggs beckoned me over to the porch.

'The car's gone, hasn't it, gardener?'

'Yes, Mrs Briggs.'

'Talk quietly. She's in her room getting dressed. She's all right, but I don't want her to know I'm talking to you about it. She's coming out to see you about the seed. Did he tell you to dig it in?'

'Yes.'

'You haven't ...'

'No.' I was going to add that I had no intention of doing so when she went on in the same urgent undertone:

'Well, wait till you've seen her. There's going to be trouble over that bed. You should have been here to see the way he went on about it. The things he said to her! I told her afterwards if it had been me I'd have put my hat on and walked straight out and left him. I'm beginning to think there's something wrong with him. She says that if he does touch it she will leave him. But she's said that before.'

'I'm not going to dig it in, Mrs Briggs. But somebody else will. He could do it himself.'

'He will, too. Nothing will stop him now that he knows she wants it. Anyway, she'll be out in a minute.'

'Any news?'

'Margaret won't come home. She's back in town. She's got a new job, but she won't tell her mother either where she's working or where she's living. She rang up yesterday. She says she doesn't want to make any more trouble.'

'And Hans?'

'Not a word. I'd better go in...'

Mrs Cameron came out soon afterwards. She'd made up her face and was wearing a dove-grey dress of some winter-weight material that swung gracefully as she walked. She really was quite attractive, and I guessed immediately from her relaxed manner that Mrs Briggs had said something to her about my attitude to the seed. She came to the point without any manoeuvring.

'Good morning, Mr Johnston. Did Mr Cameron say anything to you about the seed-bed near the front gate?'

'He told me to dig it in, Mrs Cameron.'

I tried to let her see, both by my tone and expression, how I myself felt about the matter. She was watching me carefully, no doubt wondering how much I knew.

'Don't you think it would be a pity?'

'Of course I do, Mrs Cameron. I don't want to touch it.'

'Would you be brave, Mr Johnston, and leave it for another week if I asked you to?' Her smile had quickened, but there was a shakiness in her voice that left me in no doubt as to who was being brave. 'Just to give me time to have another talk with him about it.'

She looked down the garden in the direction of the bed and made a few confused movements of one hand that finished up fingers to lips.

'It's just a bit of — innocent nonsense. Hans shouldn't have done it. But he's gone now. And it will be a nice show if it's left, won't it?'

'It's a perfect sowing, Mrs Cameron,' I assured her professionally, and with plenty of enthusiasm. 'And perfectly timed. It will come in just when the alyssum is at its best.'

'Then do leave it. I'll tell Mr Cameron I asked you to.'

'Thank you, Mrs Cameron. In that case I won't touch it.'

Something of the admiration I felt for her courage, and perhaps of what I knew, must have shown in my face, for she dropped her eyes suddenly and was in a hurry to leave me. Surreptitiously, I watched her walk around the garden, pick a few flowers, linger for a minute or two at the contentious bed, and go into the house. I didn't see her again.

Nor did I see much of Mrs Briggs. I was looking forward to getting all the details, perhaps at lunch-time, but with Mrs Cameron at home I decided to have lunch seated on a case against the sunny garage wall. All I got was a bit of hurried gossip from the old lady when I took my billy to the kitchen door. She told me that things had 'just about come to a head' inside.

'She doesn't tell me everything, you know, gardener, but the night before last I heard her threaten to leave the house herself if he doesn't do something to bring Margaret back. He just laughed at her. He knows she hasn't a penny of her own. I was listening in the hall. 'You're frightening me, Barbara!' he said, and next minute he turned the wireless on full blast. And her sobbing her eyes out on the sofa. It's like a morgue here now. It was only Margaret that made it possible for anybody else to stay in the house with him. Mind you don't let anything slip when you're talking to them.'

'Don't worry about me, Mrs Briggs.'

I had already told her about Mrs Cameron's request not to dig the seed in. 'Anyway, next Wednesday will probably see the end of me here.'

She gave me a troubled look. 'There's not much doubt about that. He's a man that just won't be crossed.'

'I'm not Mrs Cameron!'

'That poor woman! It'll be dreadful tonight when he comes in. He'll go and look at that bed before he puts a foot inside the house. I didn't think she'd dare do it, but it's about time she stood up to him. You'd better go — she's just in the dining-room.'

Throughout the rest of the day that bed of seedlings drew me like a magnet. My work was all at the other end of the garden, but time and again I went down just for the sheer joy of looking at it. It thrilled me that Mrs Cameron had proved to have enough of the woman in her to see in it something peculiarly precious and beautiful. Margaret was her daughter, and there was nothing to indicate that she was anything but mildly amused over Hans's infatuation, but — blessings on her! — she wasn't going to see it dug in like a dead cat. I had no doubt that in the hour or so between my departure and Cameron's homecoming she would be down there, poring over it again as she had been at eight o'clock in the morning, dreaming over it, investing it, perhaps, with all the poetry and colour she herself had ever been denied in that house of tyranny.

I was old enough to know better, but I too had dreams. There was a spell on the place, and as the hours passed it grew on me, with musings that began merely as charming fantasies and ended with an element of tragedy. Everything dies, and I saw Hans's message not only as it was that day, but as it would be tomorrow if Cameron spared it, and the day after, and every day until it burned itself out.

Hans must have known that his love for the girl could never be anything but hopeless, and something out of Thomas Carlyle kept coming back to me, Louis XVI's farewell to Marie Antoinette: 'And thou, dear soul, I shall never, never through all the ages of time, see again.'

What else could Hans have been thinking when he wrote his living message? It was easy to picture his youthful face bent over the friendly soil, his fingers moving swiftly with every bit of skill that was in them.

And here it is. Hans is gone, and Margaret is gone, but the quiet garden is full of their presence, and every day that passes the symbol will grow and grow. The little plants will push out, tumbling over and filling in the spaces between the letters. And as the name itself vanishes something else will take the place of form, and the message will lose nothing in eloquence. There will be colour, all the tender pastel shades of a flower I know well, framed in the deep lilac of alyssum. And to the understanding eye it will never read anything but *TO MARGARET*. And when the hot winds of summer come, and the exhausted plants huddle closer to the earth with every shower of rain, it will still be Hans who is speaking...

I didn't dig it in. But I took what I knew was a long farewell look at it that evening as I passed out by the gate.

On the following Wednesday it was indeed gone.

Even though I was prepared, there was a stab of something keener than disappointment as I stood on the path and looked over at the naked soil within the alyssum. It wasn't merely desolate, it was offensive. A challenge. I could well imagine Cameron observing my arrival from one of the windows: 'that'll teach you!'

To her for whom it was really intended it must have been agony, like having the mutilated body of someone well loved laid at her feet.

I went on up to the house hating Cameron from the bottom of my heart, and ripe for trouble as I'd never been ripe for it before.

At the kitchen all was silent. I had to knock twice before Mrs Briggs came hurrying in from regions beyond. The inner door was open. I couldn't see anything through the fly-wire screen, but her laboured breathing and scuffling footfalls reached me seconds before her urgent 'Sssh, gardener! I'm coming.'

She opened the door as if she were dead scared of being seen talking to me. Her eyes were red and puffed from weeping, and her hand trembled as she gave me the key.

'I don't think you'll want it for long. He's mad about that seed.'

'He dug it in?'

'Sssh! He did it that very night. She's gone.'

'Mrs Cameron?'

'The very next morning, the minute he turned his back. I'll have to get out too, it's like a madhouse. He didn't think she would. It's given him a shock — not so sure of himself — he's walking the floor half the night.' She glanced fearfully over her shoulder. 'We'd better not stand — '

It was a fair indication of the nature of the man that even in those circumstances he still waited until nine o'clock before coming out to face me. I'd made up my mind to 'have a piece of him', as the good Australian phrase goes, and had, therefore, confined my activities to a few minor jobs which could be cleared up at a minute's notice. All these activities were deliberately chosen in the vicinity of the alyssum bed.

I was sweeping up fallen leaves on the path when I heard the front door open and his long firm stride begin to approach. Right to the last second I kept my attention on my work, struggling with a growing excitement.

But the moment I looked at him there was an unexpected reaction. I felt pity. There was the same rigid arrogant stance, the same tight lines around jaw and lips, the same scowling forehead. But something else was missing. Something of last week's icy calm. I'd have known without having been told that he was losing sleep. His eyes were heavy and inexpressibly weary, and instead of the stare of stern accusation I'd been expecting there was doubt, as if he were trying to reconcile something in my appearance with something he'd heard about me — or with something I'd done.

'Good morning, Mr Cameron,' I said carefully.

He was looking past me now at the newly smoothed surface of the alyssum bed. I nodded towards it. 'I've just planted it again.'

I waited, giving him time to decide whether or not we brought Mrs Cameron into it, and to my satisfaction he just grunted. Then I caught the sudden intake of breath, the almost imperceptible squaring of the strong shoulders, the vindictive brightening of the tired eyes. And I realized that he was deliberately disciplining himself, and that any pangs of regret from which he might be suffering would not extend to me. He was as full of fight as I was, and if anything in the nature of compromise or reconciliation within the home was contemplated no mere gardener was going to be a witness of it.

'I suppose you realize,' he said harshly, 'that we've lost a precious week through your failure to carry out my instructions of last Wednesday?'

This is it, I thought. No half-measures, Johnston!

'Then why the hell didn't you sow it yourself? You dug it.'

His head jerked backwards ever so slightly, but he took it precisely as I expected him to. 'I see,' he said quietly, and kept on looking at me for what became an embarrassingly long time. His face twitched as if, of all things, he was going to smile. 'So that's how you feel about the job?' he asked at length.

'That's how I feel about you,' I said.

'All right.' Still with no sign of annoyance, he felt in an inside pocket and took out a wallet. 'Half a day. That's probably more than I'm obliged to give you in the circumstances. You can put away your tools and go home.'

And that was all. Ten minutes later I wheeled my bicycle down the path for the third and last time. Near the gate I paused to look again at the little bed, speckled now with a few fallen white petals of viburnum.

For I also had left a message in flowers: *TO BARBARA.*

PATRICK WHITE

Miss Slattery and her Demon Lover

He stood holding the door just so far. A chain on it too.

'This,' she said, 'is Better Sales Pty Ltd.' Turning to a fresh page. 'Market research,' she explained. 'We want you to help us, and hope, indirectly, to help you.'

She moistened her mouth, easing a threat into an ethical compromise, technique pushed to the point where almost every-one was convinced. Only for herself the page on her pad would glare drearily blank.

Oh dear, do not be difficult, she would have said for choice to some old continental number whose afternoon sleep she had ruined.

'Faht do you vornt?' he asked.

'I want to ask you some questions,' she said.

She could be very patient when paid.

'Kvestions?'

Was he going to close the door?

'Not you. Necessarily. The housewife.'

She looked down the street, a good one, at the end of which the midday sun was waiting to deal her a blow.

'Housevife?'

At last he was slipping the chain.

'Nho! Nho! Nho!'

At least he was not going to grudge her a look.

'No lady?' she asked. 'Of any kind?'

'Nho! Nefer! Nho! I vould not keep any vooman of a permanent description.'

'That is frank,' she answered. 'You don't like them.'

Her stilettos were hurting.

'Oh, I *lihke*! How I *lihke*! Zet is *vhy*!'

'Let us get down to business?' she said, looking at her blank pad. 'Since there is no lady, do you favour Priceless Pearl? Laundry starch. No. Kwik Kreem Breakfast Treat? Well,' she said, 'it's a kind of porridge that doesn't get lumps.'

'Faht is porritch?'

'It is something the Scotch invented. It is, well, just *porridge*, Mr Tibor.'

'Szabo.'

'It is Tibor on the bell.'

'I am Hoongahrian,' he said. 'In Hoongary ze nimes are beck to front. Szabo Tibor. You onderstend?'

He could not enlist too much of himself, as if it were necessary to explain all such matters with passionate physical emphasis.

'Yes,' she said. 'I see. Now.'

He had those short, but white teeth. He was not all that old, rather, he had reached a phase where age becomes elastic. His shoes could have cost him a whole week's pay. Altogether, all over, he was rather suède, brown suède, not above her shoulder. And hips. He had hips!

But the hall looked lovely, behind him, in black and white.

'Vinyl tiles?' Her toe pointed. 'Or lino?'

After all, she was in business.

'Faht? Hoh! Nho! Zet is all from marble.'

'Like in a bank!'

'Yehs.'

'Well, now! Where did you find all that?'

'I brought it. Oh, yehs. I bring everysing. Here zere is nossing. Nossing!'

'Oh, come, Mr Tibor — Szabo — we Australians are not all that uncivilised. Not in 1961.'

'Civilahsed! I vill learn you faht is civilahsed!'

She had never believed intensely in the advantages of knowledge, so that it was too ridiculous to find herself walking through the marble halls of Tibor Szabo Tibor. But so cool. Hearing the door click, she remembered the women they saw into pieces, and leave in railway cloak-rooms, or dispose of in back yards, or simply dump in the Harbour.

There it was, too. For Szabo Tibor had bought a View. Though at that hour of day the water might have been cut out of zinc, or aluminium, which is sharper.

'You have got it good here,' she said.

It was the kind of situation she had thought about, but never quite found herself in, and the strangeness of it made her languid, acting out a part she had seen others play, over life-size.

'Everysing I hef *mosst* be feuhrst class,' Szabo Tibor was explaining. 'Faht is your nime, please?'

'Oh,' she said. 'Slattery. Miss Slattery.'

'Zet is too match. Faht little nime else, please?'

Miss Slattery looked sad.

'I hate to tell you,' she said. 'I was christened Dimity. But my friends,' she added, 'call me Pete.'

'Vitch is veuorse? Faht for a nime is zet? Pete!'

'It is better than going through life with Dimity attached.'

'I vill call you nossing,' Szabo Tibor announced.

Miss Slattery was walking around in someone else's room, with large, unlikely strides, but it made her feel better. The rugs were so easy, and so very white, she realized she hadn't taken her two-piece to the cleaner.

'A nime is not necessasry,' Szabo Tibor was saying. 'Tike off you het, please; it is not necessary neither.'

Miss Slattery did as she was told.

'I am not the hatty type, you know. They have us wear them for business reasons.'

She shook out her hair, to which the bottle had contributed, not altogether successfully, though certain lights gave it a look of its own, she hoped: tawnier, luminous, dappled. There was the separate lock, too, which she had persuaded to hang in the way she wanted.

An Australian girl, he saw. Another Australian girl.

Oh dear, he was older perhaps than she had thought. But cuddly. By instinct she was kind. Only wanted to giggle. At some old teddy bear in suède.

Szabo Tibor said:

'Sit.'

'Funny,' she said, running her hands into the depths of the chair, a habit she always meant to get out of, 'I have never mixed business and pleasure before.'

But Szabo Tibor had brought something very small and sweet, which ran two fiery wires out of her throat and down her nose.

'It is good. Nho?'

'I don't know about *that*' — she coughed — 'Mr Szabo. It's effective, though!'

'In Australien,' Mr Szabo said, and he was kneeling now, 'people call me Tibby.'

'Well! Have you a sense of humour!'

'Yehs! Yehs!' he said, and smiled. '*Witz!*'

When men started kneeling she wanted more than ever to giggle.

But Tibby Szabo was growing sterner.

'In Australien,' he said, 'no *Witz*. Nho! Novair!'

Shaking a forefinger at her. So that she became fascinated. It was so plump, for a finger, banana-coloured, with hackles of little black hairs.

'Do you onderstend?'

'Oh, yes, I understand all right. I am nossing.'

She liked it, too.

'Then faht is it?' asked Tibby Szabo, looking at his finger.

'I am always surprised,' she answered, 'at the part texture plays.'

'Are you intellectual girl?'

'My mind,' she said, re-crossing her legs, 'turned to fudge at puberty. Isn't that delicious?'

'Faht is futch?'

'Oh, dear,' she said, 'you're a whale for knowing. Aren't there the things you just accept?'

She made her lock hang for this old number who wouldn't leave off kneeling by the chair. Not so very old, though. The little gaps between his white teeth left him looking sort of defenceless.

Then Tibby Szabo took her arm, as though it didn't belong to her. The whole thing was pretty peculiar, but not as peculiar as it should have been. He took her arm, as if it were, say, a cob of corn. As if he had been chewing on a cob of corn. She wanted to giggle, and did. Supposing Mum and Wendy had seen! They would have had a real good laugh.

'You have the funniest ways,' she said, 'Tib.'

As Tibby Szabo kept on going up and down her arm. When he started on the shoulder, she said:

'Stoput! What do you think I *am*?'

He heard enough to alter course.

A man's head in your lap somehow always made you feel it was trying to fool itself — it looked so detached, improbable, and ridiculous.

He turned his eyes on then, as if knowing: here is the greatest sucker for eyes. Oh God, nothing ever went deeper than eyes. She was a goner.

'Oh God!' she said, 'I am not like this!'

She was nothing like what she thought she was like. So she learned. She was the trampoline queen. She was an enormous, staggery spider. She was a rubber doll.

'You Austrahlian girls are visout *Temperament*,' Tibby Szabo complained. 'You are all gickle and talk. Passion is not to resist.'

'I just about broke every bone in my body not resisting.' Miss Slattery had to protest.

Her body that continued fluctuating overhead.

'Who ever heard of a glass ceiling!'

'Plenty glass ceiling. Zet is to see vis.'

'Tibby,' she asked, 'this wouldn't be — mink?'

'Yehs. Yehs. Meenk beds are goot for ze body.'

'I'll say!' she said.

She was so relaxed. She was half-dead. When it was possible to lift an arm, the long silken shudders took possession of her skin, and she realised the southerly had come, off the water, in at the window, giving her the goose-flesh.

'We're gunna catch a cold,' she warned, and coughed.

'It is goot.'

'I am glad to know that something is good,' she said, sitting up, destroying the composition in the ceiling. 'This sort of thing is all very well, but are you going to let me love you?'

Rounding on him. This fat and hairy man.

'Lof? Faht execkly do you mean?'

'Oh, Tibby!' she said.

Again he was fixing his eyes on her, extinct by now, but even in their dormancy they made her want to die. Or give. Or was it possible to give and live?

'Go to sleep,' he ordered.

'Oh, Tibby!'

She fell back floppy whimpery but dozed. Once she looked sideways at his death-mask. She looked at the ceiling, too. It was not unlike those atrocity pictures she had always tried to avoid, in the papers, after the War.

It was incredible, but always had been.

By the time Miss Slattery stepped into the street, carrying her business hat, evening had drenched the good address with the mellower light of ripened pears. She trod through it, tilted, stilted, tentative. Her neck was horribly stiff.

After that there was the Providential, for she did not remain with Better Sales Pty Ltd; she was informed that her services would no longer be required. What was it, they asked, had made her so unreliable? She said she had become distracted.

In the circumstances she was fortunate to find the position with the Providential. There, too, she made friends with Phyllis Wimble.

'A Hungarian,' Phyllis said, 'I never met a Hungarian. Sometimes I think I will work through the nationalities like a girl

I knew decided to go through the religions. But gave up at the Occultists.'

'Why?'

'She simply got scared. They buried a man alive, one Saturday afternoon, over at Balmoral.'

When old Huthnance came out of his office.

'Miss Slattery,' he asked, 'where is that Dewhurst policy?'

He was rather a sweetie really.

'Oh yes,' Miss Slattery said. 'I was checking.'

'What is there to check?' Huthnance asked.

'Well,' Miss Slattery said.

And Huthnance smiled. He was still at the smiling stage.

Thursday evenings Miss Slattery kept for Tibby Szabo. She would go there Saturdays too, usually staying over till Sunday, when they would breakfast in the continental style.

There was the Saturday Miss Slattery decided to give Tibby Szabo a treat. Domesticity jacked her up on her heels; she was full of secrecy and little ways.

When Tibby asked:

'Faht is zet?'

'What is what?'

'Zet stench! Zet blue *smoke* you are mecking in my kitchenette. Faht are you prepurring?'

'That is a baked dinner,' Miss Slattery answered. 'A leg of lamb, with pumpkin and two other veg.'

'Lemb?' cried Tibby Szabo. 'Lemb! It stinks. Nefer in Budapest did lemb so much as cross ze doorways.'

And he opened the oven, and tossed the leg into the Harbour.

Miss Slattery cried then, or sat, rather, making her handkerchief into a ball.

Tibby Szabo prepared himself a snack. He had *Paprikawurst*, a breast of cold paprika chicken, paprikas in oil, paprika in cream cheese, and finally, she suspected, paprika.

'Eat!' he advised.

'A tiny crumb would choke me.'

'You are not crying?' he asked through some remains of paprika.

'I was thinking,' she replied.

'So! *Sink*-ing!'

Afterwards he made love to her, and because she had chosen love, she embraced it with a sad abandon, on the mink coverlet, under the glass sky.

Once, certainly, she sat up and said:

'It is all so *carnal*!'

'You use zeese intellectual veuords.'

He had the paprika chicken in his teeth.

There was the telephone, too, with which Miss Slattery had to contend.

'Igen! *Igen*! IGEN!' Tibby Szabo would shout, and bash the receiver on somebody anonymous.

'All this *iggy* stuff!' she said.

It began to get on her nerves.

'Demn idiots!' Tibby Szabo complained.

'How do you make your money, Tib?' Miss Slattery asked, picking at the mink coverlet.

'I am Hoongahrian,' he said. 'It come to me over ze telephown.'

Presently Szabo Tibor announced he was on his way to inspect several properties he owned around the city.

He had given her a key, at least, so that she might come and go.

'And you have had keys cut,' she asked, 'for all these other women, for Monday, Tuesday, Wednesday, and Friday, in all these other flats?'

How he laughed.

'At least a real *Witz*! An Australian *Witz*!' he said on going.

It seemed no time before he returned.

'Faht,' he said, 'you are still here?'

'I am the passive type,' she replied.

Indeed, she was so passive she had practically set in her own flesh beneath that glass conscience of a ceiling. Although a mild evening was ready to soothe, she shivered for her more than nakedness. When she stuck her head out the window, there were the rhinestones of Sydney glittering on the neck of darkness. But it was a splendour she saw could only dissolve.

'You Austrahlian girls,' observed Tibby Szabo, 'ven you are not all gickle, you are all cry.'

'Yes,' she said. 'I know,' she said, 'it makes things difficult. To be Australian.'

And when he popped inside her mouth a kiss like Turkish delight in action, she was less than ever able to take herself in hand.

They drove around in Tibby's Jag. Because naturally Tibby Szabo had a Jag.

'Let us to go Manly,' she said. 'I have got to look at the Pacific Ocean.'

Tibby drove, sometimes in short, disgusted bursts, at others in long, lovely demonstrations of speed, or swooning swirls. His driving was so much the expression of Tibby Szabo himself. He was wearing the little cigar-coloured hat.

'Of course,' said Miss Slattery through her hair, 'I know you well enough to know that Manly is not Balaton.'

'Balaton?'

Tibby jumped a pedestrian crossing.

'Faht do you know about Balaton?'

'I went to school,' she said. 'I saw it on the map. You had to look at *some*thing. And there it was. A gap in the middle of Hungary.'

She never tired of watching his hands. As he drove, the soft, cajoling palms would whiten.

Afterwards when they were drawn up in comfort, inside the sounds of sea and pines, and had bought the paper-bagful of prawns, and the prawn-coloured people were squelching past, Tibby Szabo had to ask:

'Are you trying to spy on me viz all zese kvestions of Balaton?'

'All these questions? One bare mention!'

Prawn-shells tinkle as they hit the asphalt.

'I wouldn't open any drawer, not if I had the key. There's only one secret,' she said, 'I want to know the answer to.'

'But Balaton!'

'So blue. Bluer than anything we've got. So everything,' she said.

The sand-sprinkled people were going up and down. The soles of their feet were inured to it.

Tibby Szabo spat on the asphalt. It smoked.

'It isn't nice,' she said, 'to spit.'

The tips of her fingers tasted of the salt-sweet prawns. The glassy rollers, uncurling on the sand, might have raked a little farther and swallowed her down, if she had not been engulfed already in deeper, glassier caverns.

'Faht is zis secret?' Tibby asked.

'Oh!'

She had to laugh.

'It is us,' she said. 'What does it add up to?'

'Faht it edds up to? I give you a hellofa good time. I pay ze electricity end ze gess. I put you in ze vay of cut-price frocks. You hef arranged sings pretty nice.'

Suddenly too many prawn-shells were clinging to Miss Slattery's fingers.

'That is not what I mean,' she choked. 'When you love someone, I mean. I mean it's sort of difficult to put. When you could put your head in the gas-oven, and damn who's gunna pay the bill.'

Because she did not have the words, she got out her lipstick, and began to persecute her mouth.

Ladies were looking by now into the expensive car. Their glass eyes expressed surprise.

'Lof!' Tibby Szabo laughed. 'Lof is viz ze sahoul!' Then he grew very angry; he could have been throwing his hand away. 'Faht do zay know of lof!' he shouted. 'Here zere is only stike and bodies!'

Then they were looking into each other, each with an expression that suggested they might not arrive beyond a discovery just made.

Miss Slattery lobbed the paper-bag almost into the municipal bin.

'I am sursty,' Tibby complained.

Indeed, salt formed in the corners of his mouth. Could it be that he was going to risk drinking deeper of the dregs?

'This Pacific Ocean,' Miss Slattery said, or cried, 'is all on the same note. Drive us home, Tibby,' she said, 'and make love to me.'

As he released the brake, the prawn-coloured bodies on the asphalt continued to lumber up and down, regardless.

'Listen,' Miss Slattery said, 'a girl friend of Phyllis Wimble's called Apple is giving a party in Woolloomooloo. Saturday night, Phyllis says. It's going to be bohemian.'

Szabo Tibor drew his lower lip.

'Australian-bohemian-proveeenshul. Zere is nossing veuorse zan bohemian-proveeenshul.'

'Try it and see,' Miss Slattery advised, and bitterly added: 'A lot was discovered only by mistake.'

'And faht is zis Epple?'

'She is an oxywelder.'

'A vooman? Faht does she oxyveld?'

'I dunno. Objects and things. Apple is an artist.'

Apple was a big girl in built-up hair and pixie glasses. The night of the party most of her objects had been removed, all except what she said was her major work.

'This is *Hypotenuse of Angst*,' she explained. 'It is considered very powerful.'

And smiled.

'Will you have claret?' Apple asked. 'Or perhaps you prefer Scotch or gin. That will depend on whoever brings it along.'

Apple's party got under way. It was an old house, a large room running in many directions, walls full of Lovely Textures.

'Almost everybody here,' Phyllis Wimble confided, 'is doing something.'

'What have you brought, Phyl?' Miss Slattery asked.

'He is a grazier,' Phyllis said, 'that a nurse I know got tired of.'

'He is all body,' Miss Slattery said, now that she had learnt.

'What do you expect?'

Those who had them were tuning their guitars.

'Those are the Spanish guitarists,' Phyllis explained. 'And these are English teddies off a liner. They are only the atmosphere. It's Apple's friends who are doing things.'

'Looks a bit,' the grazier hinted.

Phyllis shushed him.

'You are hating it, Tib,' Miss Slattery said.

Tibby Szabo drew down his lip.

'I vill get dronk. On Epple's plonk.'

She saw that his teeth were ever so slightly decalcified. She saw that he was a little, fat black man, whom she had loved, and loved still. From habit. Like biting your nails.

I must get out of it, she said. But you didn't, not out of biting your nails, until you forgot; then it was over.

The dancing had begun, and soon the kissing. The twanging of guitars broke the light into splinters. The slurp of claret stained the jokes. The teddies danced. The grazier danced the Spanish dances. His elastic-sides were so authentic. Apple fell upon her bottom.

Not everyone, not yet, had discovered Tibby Szabo was a little, fat, black man, with serrated teeth like a shark's. There was a girl called Felicia who came and sat in Tibby's lap. Though he opened his knees and she shot through, it might not have bothered Miss Slattery if Felicia had stayed.

'They say,' Phyllis Wimble whispered, 'they are all madly queer.'

'Don't you know by now,' Miss Slattery said, 'that everyone is always queer?'

But Phyllis Wimble could turn narky.

'Everyone, we presume, but Tibby Szabo.'

Then Miss Slattery laughed and laughed.

'Tibby Szabo,' she laughed, 'is just about the queerest thing I've met.'

'Faht is zet?' Tibby asked.

'Nossing, darling,' Miss Slattery answered, 'I love you with all my body, and never my soul.'

It was all so *mouvementé*, said one of Apple's friends.

The grazier danced. He danced the Spanish dances. He danced bareheaded, and in his Lesbian hat. He danced in his shirt, and later, without.

'They say,' whispered Phyllis Wimble, 'there are two men locked in the lavatory together. One is a teddy, but they haven't worked out who the other can be.'

'Perhaps he is a social-realist,' Miss Slattery suggested.

She had a pain.

The brick-red grazier produced a stockwhip, too fresh from the shop, too stiff, but it smelled intoxicatingly of leather.

'Oh,' Miss Slattery cried, 'stockwhips are never *made*, they were there in the beginning.'

As the grazier uncoiled his brand-new whip, the lash fell glisteningly. It flicked a corner of her memory, unrolling a sheet of blazing blue, carpets of dust, cattle rubbing and straining past. She could not have kept it out even if she had wanted to. The electric sun beating on her head. The smell of old, sweaty leather had made her drunker than bulk claret.

'Oh, God, I'm gunna burn up!' Miss Slattery protested.

And took off her top.

She was alarmingly smooth, unscathed. Other skins, she knew, withered in the sun. She remembered the scabs on her dad's knuckles.

She had to get up then.

'Give, George!' she commanded. 'You're about the crummiest crack I ever listened to.'

Miss Slattery stood with the stockwhip. Her breasts snoozed. Or contemplated. She could have been awaiting inspiration. So Tibby Szabo noticed, leaning forward to follow to its source the faintest blue, of veins explored on previous expeditions.

Then, suddenly, Miss Slattery cracked, scattering the full room. She filled it with shrieks, disgust, and admiration. The horsehair gadfly stung the air. Miss Slattery cracked an abstract painting off the wall. She cracked a cork out of a bottle.

'Brafo, Petuska!' Tibby Szabo shouted. 'Vas you efer in a tseerkoos?'

He was sitting forward.

'Yeah,' she said, 'a Hungarian one!'

And let the horsehair curl round Tibby's thigh.

He was sitting forward. Tibby Szabo began to sing:

'Csak egy kislány	(Only one little girl
van a világon,	in the world,
az is az én	and she is
drága galambo-o-m!'	my dear little dove!)

He was sitting forward with eyes half-closed, clapping and singing.

> 'Hooray for love,
> it rots you, ...'

Miss Slattery sang.

She cracked a cigarette out of the grazier's lips.

'A jó Isten	(The good God
de nagyon szeret,'	must love me indeed)

sang Tibby Szabo,

'hogy nékem adta	(to have given me
a legszebbik-e-e-et!'	the most beautiful one!)

Then everybody was singing everything they had to sing, guitars disintegrating, for none could compete against the syrup from Tibby Szabo's compulsive violin.

While Miss Slattery cracked. Breasts jumping and frolicking. Her hair was so brittle. Lifted it once again, though, under the tawny sun, hawking dust, drunk on the smell of the tepid canvas water-bags.

Miss Slattery cracked once more, and brought down the sun from out of the sky.

It is not unlikely that the world will end in thunder. From the sound of it, somebody must have overturned *Hypotenuse of Angst*. Professional screamers had begun to scream. The darkness filled with hands.

'Come close, Petuska.'

It was Tibby Szabo.

'I vill screen you,' he promised, and caressed.

When a Large Person appeared with a candle. She was like a scone.

'These studios,' the Large Person announced, 'are let for purposes of creative arts, and the exchange of intellectual ideas. I am not accustomed to louts — and worse,' here she looked at Miss Slattery's upper half, 'wrecking the premises,' she said. 'As there has never been any suspicion that this is a Bad House, I must ask you all to leave.'

So everybody did, for there was the Large Person's husband behind her, looking though he might mean business. Everybody shoved and poured, there was a singing, a crumbling of music on the stairs. There was a hugging and kissing in the street. Somebody had lost his pants. It was raining finely.

Tibby Szabo drove off very quickly, in case a lift might be asked for.

'Put on your top, Petuska,' he advised. 'You will ketch a colt.'

It sounded reasonable. She was bundling elaborately into armholes.

'Waddayaknow!' Miss Slattery said. 'We've come away with the grazier's whip!'

'Hef vee?' Tibby Szabo remarked.

So they drove in Tibby's Jag. They were on a spiral.

'I am so tired,' Miss Slattery admitted.

And again:

'I am awful tired.'

She was staring down at those white rugs in Tibby's flat. The soft, white, serious pile. She was propped on her elbows, knees apart. Must be looking bloody awful.

'Petuska,' he was trying it out, 'will you perhaps do vun more creck of ze whip?'

He could have been addressing a convalescent.

'Oh, but I am tired. I am done,' she said.

'Just vun little vun.'

Then Miss Slattery got real angry.

'You and this goddam lousy whip! I wish I'd never set eyes on either!'

Nor did she bother where she lashed.

'*Ach! Oh! Aÿ-yaÿ-yaÿ! Petuska!*'

Miss Slattery cracked.

'What are the people gunna say when they hear you holler like that?

As she cracked, and slashed.

'*Aÿ!* It is none of ze people's business. *Pouff! Yaÿ-yaÿ-yaÿ-yaÿ!*' Tibby Szabo cried. 'Just vun little vun more!'

And when at last she toppled, he covered her very tenderly where she lay.

'Did anyone ever want you to put on boots?'

'What ever for?' asked Phyllis Wimble.

But Miss Slattery found she had fetched the wrong file.

'Ah, dear,' she said, resuming. 'It's time I thought about a change,' she said. 'I'm feeling sort of tired.'

'Hair looks dead,' said Phyllis Wimble. 'That is always the danger signal.'

'Try a new rinse.'

'A nice strawberry.'

Miss Slattery, whose habit had been to keep Thursday evening for Tibby Szabo, could not bear to any more. Saturdays she still went, but at night, for the nights were less spiteful than the days.

'Vair vas you, Petuska, Sursday evening?' Tibby Szabo had begun to ask.

'I sat at home and watched the telly.'

'Zen I vill install ze telly for here!'

'Ah,' she said, 'the telly is something that requires the maximum of concentration.'

'Are you changing, Petuska?' Tibby asked.

'Everything is changing,' Miss Slattery said. 'It is an axiom of nature.'

She laughed rather short.

'That,' she said, 'is something I think I learned at school. Same time as Balaton.'

It was dreadful, really, for everyone concerned, for Tibby Szabo had begun to ring the Providential. With urgent communications for a friend. Would she envisage Tuesday, Vensday, Friday?

However impersonally she might handle the instrument, that old Huthnance would come in and catch her on the phone. Miss Slattery saw that Huthnance and she had almost reached the point of no return.

'No,' she replied. 'Not Thursday. Or any other day but what was agreed. Saturday, I said.'

She slammed it down.

So Miss Slattery would drag through the moist evenings. In which the scarlet hibiscus had furled. No more trumpets. Her hair hung dank, as she trailed through the acid, yellow light, towards the good address at which her lover lived.

'I am developing a muscle,' she caught herself saying, and looked round to see if anyone had heard.

It was the same night that Tibby Szabo cried out from the bottom of the pit:

'Vhy em I condemned to soffer?'

Stretched on mink, Miss Slattery lay, idly flicking at her varnished toes. Without looking at the view, she knew the rhinestones of Sydney had never glittered so heartlessly.

'Faht for do you *torture* me?'

'But that is what you wanted,' she said.

Flicking. Listless.

'Petuska, I vill gif you *any*sink!'

'Nossing,' she said. 'I am going,' she said.

'*Gowing*? Ven vee are so suited to each ozzer!'

Miss Slattery flicked.

'I am sick,' she said, 'I am sick of cutting a rug out of your fat Hungarian behind.'

The horsehair slithered and glistened between her toes.

'But faht vill you do visout me?'

'I am going to find myself a thin Australian.'

Tibby was on his knees again.

'I am gunna get married,' Miss Slattery said, 'and have a washing-machine.'

'*Yaÿ-yaÿ-yaÿ! Petuska!*'

Then Miss Slattery took a look at Tibby's eyes, and rediscovered a suppliant poodle, seen at the window of an empty house, at dusk. She had never been very doggy, though.

'Are you ze Defel perheps?' cried Tibby Szabo.

'We Australians are not all that unnatural,' she said.

And hated herself, just a little.

As for Tibby Szabo, he was licking the back of her hand.

'Vee vill make a finenshul arrangement. Pretty substenshul.'

'No go!' Miss Slattery said.

But that is preciesly what she did. She got up and pitched the grazier's stockwhip out of the window, and when she had put on her clothes, and licked her lips once or twice, and shuffled her hair together — she went.

JUDITH WRIGHT

The Nature of Love

Villers-Bret (call it that) was a decayed soldier-settlement from
the First World War; by 1938 few of the farms still existed. Some
had been taken up into others more prosperous, some had gone
back to bush, their tottering gates propped back, seedling eucalypts growing over their entrances. On one of the last remaining
apple-orchards, tucked away under the shadow of Mount
Jameson, I had discovered the Schwarzkopfs.

They had not been there long; less than a year. We seldom
went out towards Mount Jameson; it was at the back of our place,
and Villers-Bret was at the end of a dying road. But one hot day
in November, someone had dropped a match on the other side of
the mountain ('those careless idiots over on Spencer's Creek'). It
was dry, and windy from the north-west, and the grass and low
scrub on the flanks of the mountain were sapless as kindling.
When the fire appeared over the spur, the wind was already blowing blackened leaves and ash in our direction.

The fact that the Schwarzkopfs' farm also lay in its path was,
for us, incidental. Their cleared flats were the best place to fight
it, since the creek was accessible and a break could be burned
back there, in the windless shelter of the mountain. My father, my
sister Helen and I galloped there over the short-cut through our
back paddocks, that had once led to Villers-Bret's store, when
that was still in existence.

When we reached the farm, a man was standing on the
verandah of the four-roomed house, coughing and gripping the
rail with one hand, a hand with what seemed, for a farmer, curiously long white fingers. My father shouted at him, gave him one
glance as he replied, and went on along the creek. 'New here,' he

explained to us tolerantly; 'these blasted migrants don't know enough to keep themselves alive.'

At the fence, however, we found Lisa. She was standing beside three old kerosene-tins of water that she had carried from the creek, and a pile of wet bags, and she was waiting for the fire to reach her. It was perhaps a quarter of a mile off and burning well, and she would not have had a chance against it.

At first she refused to let my father light the grass to burn a break, thinking that he was merely abetting the intentions of the fire. I had to explain things to her while Helen and my father did the work.

She listened carefully and nodded. 'I see now. It is very good of you to come to save us.' As I knew that our corn-cultivation two miles down the creek was in fact our first consideration, and our stock and fences the second, I was then ashamed. She set to work and helped with the break, and by the end of the afternoon we had turned the fire into the swamp country where it could burn itself out without doing more damage.

However, incidentally to saving our corn and fences, we had saved the hundred old apple-trees on the Schwarzkopfs' farm, the six cows that Lisa milked, the old horse that she guided in front of the single-furrow plough, and the little cultivation where she grew potatoes and pumpkins. These things had kept the Schwarzkopfs in food and supplied mending-cotton and skeins of wool, with which Lisa criss-crossed their clothes until they had become little more than web-work of the neatest convent darning.

Accordingly she took us back to the house and fed us with apple-strudel from the earliest windfalls, chokingly sour, and thick cream and coffee, while Eric talked to my father and played host. I saw her large eyes shadowed by her cheekbones, as she moved about above the kerosene-lamp on the table, and her capable hands from which she had scrubbed the charcoal with a worn old floor-scrubbing brush on the tankstand outside, and fell in love on the spot.

Not with Eric, though he was the beauty of the pair; but with Lisa. It is necessary, at seventeen, to be in love, but there was no one my own age to be in love with. I was filling in time at home, waiting to be allowed to take a job somewhere in the city (seventeen was considered too young for a girl to leave home), and meanwhile teaching my young sister while the boys were away at boarding-school. Helen, of course, fell in love with Eric; I could see her across the table, watching his pale wax-clear profile, presented with a slight upward tilt of the jawbone and sidelong glance. He had a tumble of hair and moustache as glossy as a horse-chestnut, and a way of playing a few bars of something on the old propped-up piano they had brought with them (a scrap of *Träumerei*, a snatch of Wagner), that was obviously meant to ensnare.

My instinct, however, I see as I look back, was right. There was no profit in Eric; but to love Lisa was to receive. And I was hungry; at seventeen one is always hungry, to be taught, to be admired, to be loved.

Lisa's broad cheeks, her tilted anxiously-smiling eyes, her wide hard hands and the dragged-back hair in a madonna-bun on her nape, all proclaimed that she had no time to waste on herself. Unlike Eric, all she did was thorough and complete; she left no corners unswept, her cows were thoroughly stripped, her cow-shed cleaned, her pumpkins and potatoes weeded. And when, on my Sunday-afternoon visits, after the dishes had been washed and put away and the coffee drunk, she finally sat down to her piano, she would square her elbows, draw a breath, and without pausing or looking up would plunge into, through, right to the end of a Bach fugue, a Franck prelude — something, anything, earnest, methodical and somehow noble.

If that had been all, perhaps I would not have sat so long to listen; but Lisa always had something more than one expected of her, still to be given, and before long the piano would change its song and the lightest and most delicate notes would come pouring from it as smoothly as though Mozart himself had been playing.

Eric, who never finished anything, would lie round for a while listening, ordering 'Play the E minor rondo, Lisa,' but would get up after a while and stroll off somewhere, to eat apples or whittle wood. As for me, I had not enough of Lisa to waste it, and would sit on the cane chair that had lost all but two canes in the back, and watch her and her hands.

Those hands could do anything: milk a cow, scrub a room, sew that exquisite convent-sewing (she had darned my shirt so that my mother exclaimed at it), pour out Mozart or cut noodles with perfect accuracy from the big sheet of paste they had just rolled into mathematical evenness. I received so much at those hands, during the time I knew them, that it was no wonder I poured my unspeaking love towards them whenever I watched.

'Well, Alice,' Eric would say wickedly, tossing his shimmering hair, 'I hope we'll see you next Sunday. Poor Lisa, she never sees anyone, you know, except you — I don't mean to say that you aren't anyone — and of course me. But I don't count. Do I, Lisa?' And without looking at her (they seldom seemed to look at each other), he would pick up her hand and kiss it, lingeringly, directing the gesture at my jealousy, not at Lisa's smile.

Eric was well aware of me, and naturally did not like my imperviousness to his beauty. Every foolishness I let slip was picked up, whittled to sharpness and at last, perhaps weeks later, lodged exactly in some sensitive part. Unpractised in the rivalry of love, I could not return these pricks, and looking back I think it served me right.

As to how the Schwarzkopfs had come to Villers-Bret, why they had bought the little dying farm from old John Perkins (who always referred to them as 'the Huns', having been one of the original soldier-settlers there), I never asked. Simply, they were there, and in being there served the purpose of my seventeen-year-old heart, which in its pursuit of experience and relationship was in reality as cold as a frog's though I did not know it. I watched Lisa with the devotion of a dog watching a bone, and listened to her playing, and saw and heard nothing at all.

My mother and father, however, were much more interested in these questions than they were in Eric and Lisa themselves. It was said the Schwarzkopfs had come from South Australia — lots of Germans down there — and had brought with them enough money to buy the farm, tied in a spotted handkerchief in the bottom of a suitcase. This was so scandalous that my mother refused to believe it. Money belonged in banks or in cheques, and to carry it round naked, as it were, was like parading the street in one's underwear.

'Some people will say anything. It's just because they *look* a bit out of the common. But it's certainly a queer place to come to — those Continentals generally stick together. Don't they ever tell you anything, Alice? Goodness knows you've been over there enough lately to have their whole life-histories.'

'I don't ask,' I said, immediately making a virtue of this. 'I don't ask because it's their business. I hate all this country-town inquisitiveness.'

'Hm; more likely you never thought of it for yourself. Well, they can't have been here long, good as their English is. I notice it's her job to do the work outside, ploughing and milking and all, and that's regular peasant-style German for you.'

'She only does it because she's stronger than Eric. He's been ill.' Secretly I criticised her for doing so much for Eric, and putting up with his shiftiness over work; but I did not want anyone else intruding into that secret world which contained Lisa, and thus worked by its own laws. In fact, I wanted Lisa to myself.

By this time, Lisa was teaching me music, as well as giving me her friendship and kindness, and her Sundays — the only day, I now believe, she had for anything except hard work. When I reached the farmhouse it was always clean, the dinner cooked ready, even if it was only potato-cakes and cheese and noodles. Eric would loll at the table, eat half-complainingly, sneer sweetly at the presents I had brought for Lisa. Certainly they must have seemed to him, and perhaps to her, almost mockingly useless — a home-made lavender-bag, a hand-embroidered handkerchief, a pot of jam — and the Schwarzkopfs were not getting richer.

Winter set in hard and cold, and the westerlies began early. Dry cold air poured over the landscape and searched through the thickest clothes like snow-water; the cows cropping dry scraps of grass grew as bony as clothes-racks under their staring coats. My mother began to worry about the Schwarzkopfs, and sent joints of meat from the Friday killing over with me most Sundays. As far as I could see, it was all the meat they ever ate.

Once, Lisa was out when I came; she had gone far up the mountainside, and came home staggering under a sheaf of grass she had cut herself with an old scythe. It was mostly blady-grass, and very dry, and when she put it in front of her favourite cow Gretel, Gretel took no notice. She was lying near the bails, not far from her calving, and very weak.

'She will not eat,' Lisa said. She bent over the cow for a moment, then stood up and folded her arms. 'Eric wants to kill her, for meat.'

'I've brought you over some mutton,' I said. 'that'll be better than killing poor old Gretel. You may be able to save the calf.'

'There is no milk. The other cows are almost dry. It is better for the calf not to live at all — I suppose.'

'But you can't kill a cow near calving,' I said. 'She may have a heifer — and then if the weather changes, and it rains, you might keep them both.'

'The weather will not change,' Lisa said. 'I feel there is much worse to come. But no, I am not dreaming of letting Eric kill her. If she dies, she must die in her own way, not in his. I will not have her killed.'

It was not the first time I had suspected a note of hostility, almost of spitefulness, in her tone when she spoke of Eric; but this time it was unmistakable. There was also another note, of woe almost, that must have slipped in unawares because of her physical tiredness. She might perhaps have been asking for an ear into which to tell a story; appealing for a friend.

I am ashamed to remember how quickly I withdrew. Behind the high-cheekboned Madonna into whom I had turned her, a real Lisa suddenly looked out, a face grimacing in pain, a wry mouth that might suddenly call for help, or demand some acknowledgment in me of a common humanity. I had nothing to give such a woman, though from her hands I had taken a great deal. Instead, I pulled from my saddle-bag the parcel of meat my mother had sent over, and gave it to her with a few light self-protective phrases. Lisa looked at it for a moment in silence before she thanked me.

Inside the house Eric had lighted a big fire; the stove was hot and the kettle singing. We had mutton chops and baked pumpkin and coffee. Eric was very gay, flushed with the heat of the fire and the dry air, his eyes sparkling. The warmth melted me towards both of them; we seemed to sit in fellowship heightened by the angry sound of the wind outside.

'Just for once, Lisa,' Eric said suddenly, 'a bottle of the white wine, do you think? This is good food, and good meat requires wine. We have been cold all day, and now we are nearly warm again; let us celebrate Alice's kind present and our good fortune.'

Lisa nodded and opened the cupboard. I could not help noticing how little was in it — the other half of the pumpkin, a few potatoes, a pound or two of flour, a tin of treacle. There were two bottles lying on their sides on the bottom shelf, and she brought out one and opened it.

Though I was seventeen, I had never tasted wine, which my mother regarded as faintly sinful, my father, probably, as cissy, since he came from Scotland and drank whisky when he drank at all. I thought of refusing, but in the end took the thick glass that Eric filled for me.

'This is the first meat we have had for days,' said Lisa cheerfully, confirming what I had suspected. 'It is a pity Eric is such a bad shot. He missed a rabbit on Wednesday and we were very anxious for that rabbit.'

Eric threw another big log on the fire. 'Lisa is only rude; she cannot shoot at all. And my hands were frozen to the rifle. I thought Australia was always warm and sunny, Alice; the world is always destroying my illusions.'

He laughed and talked, Lisa answered more cheerfully than usual, and I took sip after sip of wine and felt the heat of the fire making my face burn and my eyes sting. I began to feel myself truly out in the world at last, in Eric's sophisticated company, for he was talking of things I had no more than heard of: of the ski-runs of Tirol, of the Rhine running under ice, of vineyards and vintages, of the famous wine-makers of the hills near Bonn, of castles and islands. Leaning intimately on the table, we began to sing, first in English, then Lisa began a German song and went to the piano, and Eric joined in. The bottle was empty and I was half-asleep. I put my head on my arms and listened to their voices which mingled lightly and sweetly, and tears came into my eyes at the beauty and worth of life and Lisa, and the beauty and worth-lessness of Eric. I fell asleep, warm and melancholy, to the sound of their singing.

When I woke, however, I felt I had been awakened by some-thing unpleasant, though I did not know what. They had stopped singing. Eric stood at the window, hands in his pockets, staring out at the bare flats and the trees struggling with the wind. Lisa was playing, stubbornly and rather heavily, a Bach fugue.

'I must go,' I said, 'the pony will be getting cold and it's dark so early now. I'm sorry I went to sleep and missed the singing.'

Lisa closed the piano and got up. 'Please thank your mother for us, Alice, for the good meat.'

'Yes,' Eric said, 'please thank your father too. It is lucky for us we have such kind rich neighbours.'

'We're not rich,' I began, but thinking of how much less rich the Schwarzkopfs were, I was silent. I determined to come over as soon as I could and bring them something more — a cake, some preserves, whatever I could beg from mother.

Lisa looked at Eric with her head bent forward dangerously, but said nothing. She came with me to the yard, where the pony was tied, and together we examined Gretel the cow. She lay there as before. I knew that a really weak cow will lie sometimes for days, unable to give birth, but I did not say so. I helped Lisa to tie an old rug made of sacks around her as well as we could, and rode home in the half-dark.

Next day, Helen had a bad cold, and was made to stay in bed and miss her lessons. I was free, and went with my father riding round the paddocks, looking for weak cattle to be moved into the nearer paddocks, where they could be given a little extra hay.

After two days, Helen's cold was no better, and we had still one paddock to go through. It was the far paddock, bordering the short-cut to Villers-Bret.

'I'll look through them tomorrow,' I told my father; 'it won't take long.' I would go to the Schwarzkopfs afterwards and take Lisa a plum-cake.

I had asked my mother about this, and she had promised it rather reluctantly. 'You're getting too involved with those people, Alice.'

'Pooh,' I said, 'involved! It's just that they're having a hard time of it. I can't take music-lessons without paying something for it.'

There was a gate from the paddock on to the old road, so I packed the cake in a sugar-bag on the saddle, and rode straight out there in the morning. There was a lot of timber left in the paddock, which made it hard to muster, but left the cattle plenty of shelter from the wind. I quartered it systematically, but found few cattle; evidently they were huddled in the little hollow hear the road gate, above which a curving ridge ran, hiding the valley except from its crest. When I reached the top of this ridge, I could see into the hollow as if it were an amphitheatre. In this amphitheatre a very strange scene was taking place.

The cattle I was looking for were there all right, and a small mob of sheep as well — my father's best weaners. The cattle were staring, heads all one way, as cattle will at anyone unexpected. The direction of their gaze led me to the unlikely figure of Eric, dressed in a tweed knickerbocker shooting outfit, and hidden from the road by a clump of trees. He had dropped to one knee, and was just steadying his gun on his mark, which was one of our fattest wethers, feeding a little way from the mob.

It was like a sudden gush of cold water, making me gasp, yet react very fast. I could not possibly let him shoot; nor could I withdraw, for in a moment or two he would look up and see me clearly on the ridgetop, not a hundred yards from him. In any case, I was righteously enraged, remembering the cake in the sugar-bag balanced on the pommel of my saddle; and I felt a strong sense of property in those wethers, which I had known since they were lambs.

I tried to shout something, choked, and cleared my throat. However, Eric heard me, and with a violent start looked up. I had no way out but to ride over.

'Out shooting?' I decided to say carelessly. But the words refused to come. Eric must have known from my expression that I had clearly understood the scene. To my complete stupefaction he now raised the rifle again, but this time pointed it at me.

This was absurd. It was reasonable enough for people to steal a sheep occasionally; I had never found anyone doing it before, but I knew it often happened. But nobody threatened other people with rifles — that was behaviour quite outside reality. I had been strictly brought up, and I knew that you did not allow the business end of your gun to point at anyone, even if you knew perfectly well it wasn't loaded. Accordingly, I did not believe it was happening, which must have made me appear brave and in charge of myself, when in fact I was not so at all.

'Put that thing down, Eric,' I shouted; 'you'll get into trouble handling a gun in that silly way.'

Eric, however, had clearly lost his head. Pale and sweating, he in turn shouted at me. 'You will tell no one of this, Alice. Nobody at all. Promise, or I will shoot. Swear you will tell nobody.'

I saw with purely practical alarm that his hands were shaking violently. 'You point that thing at the ground,' I ordered.

Slowly Eric lowered the gun. 'I know you will be sensible, Alice. I was going to shoot a sheep — I admit it. It was for Lisa. She is hungry and she needs good food. We have no money, and Lisa is going to have a baby. You understand?'

'A baby — Lisa?' I quite forgot about the gun.

'You understand? A man must kill for his wife and child.' Eric sounded so pompous that I began to laugh. He looked at me with real dislike.

I found all sorts of considerations balancing themselves in my mind. 'All right,' I said at last, 'I won't say anything — that is, if you leave our sheep alone. And other people's too, I added, thinking of the Simmondses nearby, and their ewes in lamb. 'I'll bring Lisa what I can, and you can practise shooting rabbits — there are more than enough of those to keep you going. As a matter of fact, there's a cake in this bag for her now. You can take it home with you. I won't say anything.'

'Particularly not to Lisa? She wished nobody to know ...'

I was wondering if Lisa had any idea where Eric was. It was the first treacherous thought I had had about her, and before I could stop it another came, which was that we had not counted those sheep for some time. 'I'm mustering these sheep,' I said falsely, 'and my father will be wondering where they are if I don't hurry. You'd better get on home.'

I went round the sheep and took them up the ridge, while Eric walked back, dragging the gun and holding the cake-tin, and looking, in his knickerbockers, extremely foolish and out of place. This pleased me. However, when I had counted the sheep and found that none were missing, I began to remember the round black hole in the rifle-barrel, and how decidedly it had been directed at me. I thought my mother had been right in saying that I was becoming too involved with 'those people'.

So on Sunday, instead of going over for my music-lesson, I cut out a dress, and pretended I was too interested in getting it tacked and fitted, to want to go out anywhere. That would have lasted all the afternoon, except that by three o'clock I heard voices in the garden, and looking out saw Lisa talking to my mother.

When I went out, rather reluctantly, I thought she seemed shy with me. No, she would not stay for a cup of tea; she was late in getting home and the cows must be milked; she had only come out for a walk and to thank us for the cake; Eric would come home and wonder where she was. I had never heard her talk like this, with a shrill edge and uneasily, and my mother too looked at her thoughtfully.

'Did you really walk all the way?' I said. It was a good six miles across country.

'I had a lift, with Mrs Carter; she was to town going. But I wanted to walk, it is good exercise.' It was not like Lisa to invert her sentences, either; and I thought this was no time for her to need more exercise, when she worked all day in any case.

'Of course you mustn't walk home,' my mother said. My father had taken the old utility truck, our only vehicle, over to the bottom paddock dam, where the cattle were beginning to bog as they came in to drink, and corduroy had to be laid. It would be a long dirty job, and he would not be back before dark.

'I'll catch Helen's pony and my own,' I said, 'and we'll ride home, and I'll lead the pony back.' She protested earnestly, but I was already on my way to the horse-paddock. Besides, I was curious to know why she had come.

She was not at all a good rider, but once in the saddle she stayed there like a sack of flour.

'But you should not have done it. I would have enjoyed the walk, and the cows have so little milk now that the milking is soon over.'

'What happened to Gretel?' I said.

'She died a few days ago. The calf was born dead, too.' Lisa looked at me sideways. 'Eric was angry. He said I should not have kept him from killing her; she would have made good meat, but it was spoiled.'

'Oh?' I said, but the subject seemed rather dangerous. I changed it. 'I'm glad the cake arrived safely.'

'It was for that I came to thank your mother — and for all the other things, of course. I did not expect to see you.'

'Why not? I was coming over today, but I had a dress to make …'

'We cannot expect you to come every week. Eric was lucky, meeting you on the road that day. He tells me it was quite an accident.'

'Well, yes.' I felt my face going hot and a giggle coming, at the word, but I choked it down into a cough. 'I thought he had better take the cake. I was — out mustering sheep.'

Lisa had turned half round and was watching me, and her face too was burning. 'And — did you have much to say to each other?'

I examined this for a moment, since the way it was spoken seemed to hint a trap. How much did she know?

'No, we just said hello. He was out shooting, but he — hadn't shot anything when I saw him.'

'You are sure you did not intend to meet him?' She was jerking nervously at the pony's mouth, and he began to prop and sweat.

'Don't do that, Lisa, it's bad for his mouth.' This was awful. I was now certain that she knew or guessed what he had been doing. 'No, indeed, I didn't know he was there. If I had, I mightn't have — well, you know I never can find much to say to Eric.'

'Oh, no, you never say much. But you look at him. I have seen you.'

I was struck as if by lightning; turning round to look at her, I found myself breathing through a wide-open mouth. My image of Lisa and of the world cracked across and rearranged itself drastically. Was that why she had come over that afternoon? Had she wanted to see if I was out — with Eric?

'Lisa,' I cried, 'you're completely wrong. If I've come to see you, it's only been for — for you.' She laughed sharply. I began again. 'Look, Eric did tell me one thing, and — and it pleased me a lot. About — about the child.'

She let out a small cry; her eyes turned black and her face white. I had evidently not helped the situation.

'I'm sorry, I forgot — he told me not to tell you I knew.' I stammered on, for she was crying now, large incredulous tears. 'But why don't you want people to know? I think it's lovely — I'm so glad you're having a baby.'

Lisa dropped her head and began to plait her fingers in Robin's mane, but she had stopped crying, with a gasp. She rode on in silence.

'He told you that I was to have a baby,' she said at last. 'You are sure of that?' I nodded, deep in distress.

'It was a lie. Now you must tell me. He would not have told you a lie unless he had some purpose. What had you — what had he done?'

My throat swelled with panic and I said nothing. She pulled up the pony and dropped the reins altogether, crying out, 'Alice! What had he done?'

I could see no way out, and I got off my pony. While we sat together on a log, and the ponies cropped dry grass in the cold wind, I told her how we had met.

She thought it over for a while, and then she began to laugh. I laughed too, since there wasn't anything else to do.

'You have told me,' she said at last, when she had stopped laughing and so had I. 'Now I can tell you. I owe you that, since all the while I had suspected you and you were only being kind.'

'I wasn't!' I exclaimed. 'I came — I come because I want to. I come for you, because you're so — good to me.'

'Now you are being kind again. You won't have to bother any more, because we're going away.'

Wind stung in my eyes and my lips were cold.

'When? It will take a long time to sell that farm.'

'We won't trouble. We can borrow enough money to go back where we came, and there's the piano. But first I must tell you.' She took a long lock of her hair, that had come out of her bun, in both hands, and quite calmly began to pull it. Some of it came out. I watched in horror.

'Eric is German; I am Swiss. Eric is married, but not to me — I think not to me. No, wait. He married his cousin, a Jewess. He too is Jewish, partly Jewish.' She pronounced it Yewish, so that for a moment I did not understand what she was saying. 'They had a baby.'

I winced at this.

'We had known Eric for years, for my father keeps a hotel in Geneva and Eric was a traveller, you know, a commercial traveller, in German wines. One day he knocked at the door; he asked could he stay for a little, there was trouble. We knew what it must be.'

'Hitler,' I mumbled.

'He stayed awhile; then we told him, if he could get his wife and the baby out, we would take care of them, because the news from Germany was bad. He went. When he came back, he was crying and weeping; we could get nothing from him. I was sorry for him. Eric is good at crying ...'

'But surely ...'

'No, wait. Then he told me his wife was dead, the baby dead. He was afraid for himself. Would I marry him and we would go away together? I was very sorry for him; I married him in Geneva. My father had cousins out here; he gave us a little money, and we came out to Australia. We got work in the vineyards, with my people.' She paused for a while.

'Then came out another man, a man who knew Eric. When he saw Eric in the vineyard, he said to my people, what are you doing with this man? He has betrayed his wife into a concentration camp, and his own child, and to save his own life, and he ran away and left them.'

My breath stopped as at the climax of a horror-picture.

'We went away from there next day, with our money, and found this farm because it was cheap. Eric says none of that is true, all is lies. But Eric too tells lies. Who am I to believe? Eric is a coward, I have found that out too. Perhaps he would even have killed you — I don't know. But the child? No, no!' she exclaimed, forgetting me altogether and twisting her hand in her hair with an extraordinary gesture. 'He could never have done that to the child!'

We sat there for a long time, not moving.

'Now we are going back,' she said. 'I have known for a long time that we must go back. We will try to find them. Perhaps they are not dead.' She untied Robin's reins from the fence and gave them to me. 'I can accept no more of anybody's kindness. I shall walk home and tell Eric we are going. You must take the horses back; look, almost is the sunset.'

'Please ride him the rest of the way, Lisa,' I begged, 'it's another three miles and it's so cold. I should never have told you. I can't forgive myself.'

'Goodbye, Alice. I am sorry I did not trust your kindness, and I have told you such things. You must forget them.' She slipped under the fence to take the short way home.

I followed her beseechingly, stammering about the pony. The tears on my cheeks were cold as snails.

She took my hand through the barbed wire, and turned away. I watched her set off, then turn back again.

'Do you know what is the worst of all, Alice? It is my wickedness. I hope they are dead — both dead.'

She walked away through the thin trees, the tress of hair blowing and her bun coming out of its pins.

After a while I rode home again. I felt as though I had climbed some very steep cliff, following painfully after Lisa, but from the top I could now perceive something of the nature of love. It was the last thing she gave me, and I did not see her again. That was in July, 1939.

Street Idyll

Jenny was going to the hairdresser down the hill. Everything was in order, gloves, bag, key in purse, milk bottles to take down, fires out, time to go.

At the last, she held up the magnifying mirror to her face, checked in the bathroom mirror, wardrobe mirror for skirt, shoes. She knew she would see him somewhere on the hill.

She came neatly downstairs, not to fall on the old ragged matting in the smeary brown hall. Up the street, fresh and bright: rosebush, white patch on stone fence, don't stare at it, it resembles a face; curtains in basement opposite, sort of crochet grid; flagged yard, hello to red-haired cleaner, garage to let: and so to the corner where the big church is and the red pillarbox where she posted so many letters.

Beside it, a seat for old people for sunny days. Once, even she and Gill had sat there. A wedding for a neighbour's daughter; her tears dried, her throes past, the future assured. They were not invited, but they were glad; women, men, girls, craning like pigeons at the church gate, confetti like pigeon food.

Jenny and Gill liked to look at weddings; marriage was in their minds. They had nothing but good to say of marriage. It was the best state for men and women; there was a calm and thrilling joy, there was forgiveness, solace, peace, certain home and country, without passport, rent book, marching, petitions.

Otherwise, Jenny would not have sat on a bench; she had a horror of it, as a proof of old age, impotence, neglect.

True, she thought, if some old person actually was sitting there, it is sad to have to creep out of a back room, unloved by relatives, or a sole chamber, a bedsitter in one of the old buildings down this street.

It was, in a way, a very good place, in the air at the top of the hill, with traffic going ten ways, the schoolchildren from the council high school and three private schools up and down, the respectable girls two by two for church, from that school; what? The Rasputin? The Razumovsky? Voronoff? Impossible. Some Russian name.

Name of Royal family?

The people saw children in the lunch hour heading for the wine shop at the corner, which also served as a tuck-shop, ice-cream, peanuts, chocbars; the women toiling home with shopping trolleys, dog people walking dogs, the greyhound, hairless dachs, longhair fox, ancient alsatian, small white peke, cherished mongrels.

Yes, old lonely people liked the noise, dust, oil; they liked the hundred children, fifteen dogs — it reminded them of another earlier life perhaps. Loquacious, silent, self-muttering, frozen in bitterness, terribly ridged, valleyed with age; what were their relatives — loving, rude, sullen, venomous?

They were people who knew they did not count except when they showed up at the post office for their pensions or at the polling station.

Jenny softened her heart. Gill liked to sit on park benches and talk to people. He liked everyone. Once or twice she had met him there; in the park and he told what people said, or what the children had done, dangerous things or naughty things. 'The woman did not answer, she seemed offended; we had not been introduced, this is England.' Gill believed everyone was his equal and had a soul as sunny as his; he hoped others were like that.

Such ideas would flit through her head in an instant as she passed the bench by the letterbox. Now, she was round the horse-shoe bend of the churchyard and she started downhill, searching in the far distance for Gill who might now be visible among the shopping crowds.

She stared carefully, not only to see him at the first moment possible, but to see him make the crossing, for it was a death spot, a traffic black spot down there, where three streets met, not to mention the station yard, hotel parking lot and parade. Gill was shortsighted.

Gill had beautiful eyes, hazel with a bluish rim, and, in fact, his father had dark blue eyes. Gill said blue in a peculiar manner, 'Blew' to rhyme with dew, and she teased him, saying: 'And twitched his mantle blew.' He laughed and was hurt. Though perhaps, who knows, that was the way Milton said it?

When they played *Cymbeline* at Newcastle-upon-Tyne in 'the Doric', as they say up there, in Northumbrian; Cymbelline, Cloten, Guiderius, Arviragus, even Philario and Iachimo spoke Northumbrian — the program notes said that this was closer to the language in Shakespeare's ear than anything you will hear at the Old Vic or on the BBC.

Iachimo, Lachimo, yes. Was that where she got the name for one of the two large glossy photos of Gill she had, one sober, one glad, and which she called *Tristan Lachrimo* and *Baron Lachlaches*, which pleased Gill?

There was Gill, a short square peg in a quadrilateral situation, streets, footpaths, flagged courtyards, low block buildings, trudging along.

She could see him and knew that soon he would mark her out, coming down the hill with no one about. What is more, he knew her height and lope, which he called a stride. 'You think I stride?' 'You do stride.' She reined in her steps, but on the hill you had to take long steps, go fast. He was looking about now, crossing; he could not see her yet — five hundred yards and more.

Just where would they meet? It was always exciting; her heart beat a little faster. Not too soon — spin it out! Now he was across, looking left and right and over.

He began to pass the real estate agent's, the little alley, the dress-shop, the bingo parlor, once a cinema where they had seen foreign films; now he was at the auctioneer's.

Now they were close, they did not look any more. She glanced to one side — the house converted to business premises, with neglected lawn and low bushes where someone threw away his or her gin bottles.

Now his big dark eyes were on her; she looked away. They met, their faces lighting up. Why were their eyes for a moment on the ground? So that passersby would not see the rapturous, intimate smiles which they felt irrepressibly forming behind their cheeks right up to their ears. They halted, fastened their eyes on each other.

This had all happened before. Sometimes, a passerby, a pillowy, hatless woman, in a print dress with parcels, a nice thinning elderly man in a hat, climbing the hill with his washing, had hesitated in surprise, almost as if they feared an incident.

This square-cut, dark man, and this tall fair woman who came to a stop suddenly, and, without greeting began to murmur — they were not alike, they looked like strangers to each other; and they had never lost this look; reared in different countries, different traditions.

They stood there, not knowing what to say, for there is nothing to express the emotion that brought them together the first time and now brought them together.

She described arcs with the toes of her shoes — her best shoes; for she had known she was going to meet him; he looked around, filling in time, as a cat or bird does.

Then they looked at each other flatface, smiled and she said: 'I saw you when you were passing Sainsbury's.' 'I saw you too, way up the hill.' 'You know my look.' He corrected her: 'It was your walk, your Australian walk.' 'It's true, I saw an Australian in Tottenham Court Road the other day; it was his walk.'

There was a pause, because the last words were only to fill a pause. There was nothing to say, but they could not break the web which had already grown between them, a quick-weaving, thick-netting web, which occurred always, in speech, in silence; but was more embarrassing in silence, because so felt.

It tugged like the moon at waters, sucked like a drain, had already grown part of them like barnacles on rocks, difficult to get away from; nothing fatal in it. They stood quiet, embarrassed, unable to move away; their thoughts going 'Er-er-er-.'

'Well,' then a slight smile, a grin, too, 'All right — ' 'I won't be long.' 'OK.' Each takes a step to pass, hesitates. The tissue is dissolving, but strands hang on; they take another step and turn, 'Goodbye.' 'Goodbye.'

They wave. They really hesitate to quit each other. It would be better to turn and go up the hill with him, than to go on to the hairdresser; it seems a pointless, vapid business; but to go up with Gill at this moment when he knows she is expected elsewhere would be impossible, an extraordinary weakness, and inconceivable swoon of personality. There is danger in such disorder.

Elle garde son secret, elle le garde.

'I'll be home by twelve,' says Jenny. 'I'll be waiting for you,' says Gill.

For the fact is, though this took place every time they met, this leaning forward to meet, this painless suffering of separation, Jenny and Gill were husband and wife and had spent nearly forty years together.

Jenny and Gill are no longer there; someone has hacked to pieces the bench for the old people; there are small changes; but very often I now meet on the hill another couple, he short, handsome, with his fair hair bleached by age, she bleached too, but once very pretty; and they have one motion, in harmony, and predetermined, like figures on a town clock famous for its colouring and carving; and by the air they carry with them, and the look of gold, I know that is how they feel, also.

A, B, C, D, E, F, G, H, I, J, K, L, M, N, O, P, Q, R, S, T, U, V, W, X, Y, Z.

I select from these letters, pressing my fingers down. The letter (or an image of it) appears on the sheet of paper. It signifies little or nothing, I have to add more. Other letters are placed alongside until a 'word' is formed. And it is not always the word WORD.

The word matches either my memory of its appearance, or a picture of the object the word denotes. TREE: I see the shape of a tree at mid-distance, and green.

I am writing a story.

Here, the trouble begins.

The word 'dog', as William James pointed out, does not bite; and my story begins with a weeping woman. She sat at the kitchen table one afternoon and wept uncontrollably. How can words, particularly 'wept uncontrollably', convey her sadness (her self-pity)? Philosophers other than myself have discussed the inadequacy of words. 'Woman' covers women of every shape and size, whereas the one I have in mind is red-haired, has soft arms, plain face, high-heeled shoes with shining straps.

And she was weeping.

Her name, let us say, is Kathy Pridham.

For the past two years she has worked as a librarian for the British Council in Karachi. She, of all the British community there, was one of the few who took the trouble to learn Urdu, the local language. She could speak it, not read it: those calligraphic loops and dots meant nothing to her, except that 'it was a language'. Speaking it was enough. The local staff at the Council, shopkeepers, and even the cream of Karachi society (who cultivated European manners), felt that she knew them as they themselves did.

At this point, consider the word 'Karachi'. Not having been there myself I see clusters of white-cube buildings with the edge of a port to the left, a general slowness, a shaded verandah-ed suburb for the Burra-sahibs. Perhaps, eventually, boredom — or disgust with noises and smells not understood. Kathy, who was at first lonely and disturbed, quickly settled in. She became fully occupied and happy; insofar as that word has any meaning. There was a surplus of men in Karachi: young English bachelors sent out from head office, and pale appraising types who work at the embassies; but the ones who fell over themselves to be near her were Pakistanis. They were young and lazy. With her they were ardent and gay.

Already the words Kathy and Karachi are becoming inextricably linked.

It was not long before she too was rolling her head in slow motion during conversations, and clicking her tongue, as they did, to signify 'no'. Her bungalow in the European quarter with its lawn, verandah, two archaic servants, became a sort of *salon*, especially at the Sunday lunches where Kathy reigned, supervising, flitting from one group to the next. Those afternoons never seemed to end. No one wanted to leave. Sometimes she had musicians perform. And there was always plenty of liquor (imported), with wide dishes of hot food. Kathy spoke instantly and volubly on the country's problems, its complicated politics, yet in London if she had an opinion she had rarely expressed it.

When Kathy thought of London she often saw 'London' — the six letters arranged in recognizable order. Then parts of an endless construction appeared, much of it badly blurred. There was the thick stone. Concentrating, she could recall a familiar bus stop, the interior of a building where she had last worked. Her street invariably appeared, strangely dead. Some men in overcoats. It was all so far away she sometimes thought it existed only when she was there. Her best friends had been two women, one a school teacher, the other married to a taciturn engineer. With them she went to Scotland for holidays, to the concerts at Albert Hall. Karachi was different. The word stands for something else.

The woman weeping at the kitchen table is Kathy Pridham. It is somewhere in London (there are virtually no kitchen tables in Karachi).

After a year or so Kathy noticed at a party a man standing apart from the others, watching her. His face was bony and fierce, and he had a thin moustache. Kathy, of course, turned away, yet at the same time tilted her chin and began acting over-earnest in conversation. For she pictured her appearance: seeing it (she thought) from his eyes.

She noticed him at other parties, and at one where she knew the host well enough, casually asked, 'Tell me. Who is that over there?'

They both looked at the man watching her.

'If you mean him, that's Syed Masood. Not your cup of tea, Kathy. What you would call a wild man.' The host was a successful journalist and drew in on his cigarette. 'Perhaps he is our best painter. I don't know; I have my doubts.'

Kathy lowered her eyes, confused.

When she looked up, the man called Syed Masood had gone.

Over the next few days, she went to the galleries around town and asked to see the paintings of Syed Masood. She was interested in local arts and crafts, and had decided that if she saw something of his she liked she would buy it. These gallery owners threw up their hands. 'He has released nothing for two years now. What has got into him I don't know.'

Somehow this made Kathy smile.

Ten or eleven days pass — in words that take only seconds to put down, even less to absorb (the discrepancy between Time and Language). It is one of her Sunday lunches. Kathy is only half-listening to conversations and when she breaks into laughter it is a fraction too loud. She has invited this man Masood and has one eye on the door. He arrives late. Perhaps he too is nervous.

Their opening conversation (aural) went something like this (visual).

'Do come in. I don't think we've met. My name is Kathy Pridham.'

'Why do you mix with these shits?' he replied, looking around the room.

Just then an alarm wristlet watch on one of the young men began ringing. Everyone laughed, slapping each other, except Masood.

'I'll get you something,' said Kathy quietly. 'You're probably hungry.'

She felt hot and awkward, although now that they were together he seemed to take no notice of her. Several of the European men came over, but Masood didn't say much and they drifted back. She watched him eat and drink: the bones of his face working.

He finally turned to her. 'You come from — where?'

'London.'

'Then why have you come here?'

She told him.

'And these?' he asked, meaning the crowd reclining on cushions.

'My friends. They're people I've met here.'

Suddenly she felt like crying.

But he took her by the shoulders. 'What is this?' You speak Urdu? And not at all bad? Say something more, please.'

Before she could think of anything he said in a voice that disturbed her, 'You are something extraordinary.' He was so close she could feel his breath. 'Do you know that? Of course. But do you know how extraordinary? Let me tell you something,

although another man might put it differently. It begins here' —
for a second one of his many hands touched her breasts; Kathy
jumped — 'and it *emanates*. Your volume fills the room. Certainly!
So you are quite vast, but beautiful.'

Then he added, watching her, 'If you see what I mean.'

He was standing close to her, but when he spoke again she
saw him grinning. 'Now repeat what I have just said in Urdu.'

He made her laugh.

Here — now — an interruption. While considering the
change in Kathy's personality I remember an incident from last
Thursday, the 12th. This is an intrusion but from 'real life'. The
words in the following paragraph reconstruct the event as
remembered. As accurately as possible, of course.

A beggar came up to me in a Soho bar and asked (a hoarse
whisper) if I wished to see photographs of funerals. I immediately pictured a rectangular hole, sky, men and women in coats.
Without waiting for my reply he fished out from an inside
pocket the wad of photographs, postcard size, each one of a
burial. They were dog-eared and he had dirty fingernails. 'Did
you know these dead people?' He shook his head. 'Not even
their names?' He shook his head. 'That one,' he said, not taking
his eyes off the photographs, 'was dug yesterday. That one, in
1969.' There was little difference. Both showed men and
women standing around a dark rectangle, perplexed. I felt a
sharp tap on my wrist. The beggar had his hand out. Yes, I gave
him a shilling. The barman spoke: 'Odd way to earn a living.
He's been doing that for

Kathy soon saw Masood again. He arrived one night with his
shirt hanging out while she was entertaining the senior British
Council representative, Mr L., and his wife. They were a cautious
experienced pair, years in the service, yet Mrs L. began talking
loudly and hastily, a sign of indignation, when Masood sat away
from the table, silently watching them. Mr L. cleared his throat
several times — another sign. It was a hot night with both ceiling
fans hardly altering the sedentary air. Masood suddenly spoke to
Kathy in his own language. She nodded and poured him another

coffee. Mrs L caught her husband's eye, and when they left shortly afterwards, Kathy and Masood leaned back and laughed.

'You can spell my name in four different ways,' Masood declared in the morning, 'but I am still the one person! Ah,' he said laughing, 'I am in a good mood. This is an auspicious day.'

'I have to go to work,' said Kathy.

'Look up "auspicious" when you get to the library. See what it says in one of your English dictionaries.'

She bent over to fit her brassiere. Her body was marmoreal, the opposite to his: bony and nervy.

'Instead of thinking of me during the day,' he went on, 'think of an exclamation mark! It amounts to the same thing. I would see you, I think, as a colour. Yes, I think more than likely pink, or something soft like yellow.'

'You can talk,' said Kathy laughing.

But she liked hearing him talk. Perhaps there'll be further examples of why she enjoyed hearing him talk.

That night Masood took her to his studio. It was in the inner part of the city where Europeans rarely ventured, and as Masood strode ahead Kathy avoided, but not always successfully, the stares of women in doorways, the fingers of beggars, and rows of sleeping bodies. She noticed how some men deliberately dawdled or bumped into her; striding ahead, Masood seemed to enjoy having her there. In an alleyway he unbolted a power-blue door as a curious crowd gathered. He suddenly clapped his hands to move them. Then Kathy was inside: a fluorescent room, dirty white-washed walls. In the corner was a wooden bed called a 'charpoy', some clothes over a chair. There were brushes in jars, and tins of paint.

'Syed, are these your pictures?'

'Leave them,' he said sharply. 'Come here. I would like to see you.'

Through the door she could feel the crowd in the alleyway. She was perspiring still and now he was undoing her blouse.

'Syed, let's go?'

He stepped back.

'What is the matter? The natives are too dirty tonight. Is that it? Yes, the walls; the disgusting size of the place. All this stench. It must be affecting your nostrils? Rub your nose in it. Lie in my shit and muck. If you wait around you might see a rat. You could dirty your Mem-sahib's hands for a change.' Then he kicked his foot through one of the canvases by the door. 'The pretty paintings you came to see.'

As she began crying she wondered why. (He was only a person who used certain words.)

I will continue with further words.

Kathy made room for Masood in her house, in her bed as well as the spare room which she made his studio. Her friends noticed a change. At work, they heard the pronoun 'we' constantly. She told them of parties they went to, the trips they planned to take, how she supervised his meals; she even confessed (laughing) he snored and possessed a violent temper. At parties, she took to sitting on the floor. She began wearing 'kurtas' instead of 'blouses', 'lungis' rather than 'dresses', even though with her large body she looked clumsy. To the Europeans she somehow became, or seemed, untidy. They no longer understood her, and so they felt sorry for her. It was about then that Kathy's luncheon parties stopped, and she and Masood, who were always together, went out less frequently. Most people saw Masood behind this — he had never disguised his contempt for her friends — but others connected it with an incident at the office. Kathy arrived one morning wearing a sari and was told by the Chief Librarian it was inappropriate; she couldn't serve at the counter wearing that. Then Mr L. himself, rapidly consulting his wife, spoke to her. He spelt out the *British* Council's function in Karachi, underlining the word British. 'Kathy, are you happy?' he suddenly asked. Like others, he was concerned. He wanted to say, 'Do you know what you are doing?' 'Oh, yes,' Kathy replied. 'With this chap, I mean,' he said, waving his hand. And Kathy left the room.

People's distrust of Masood seemed to centre around his unconventional appearance and (perhaps more than anything) his rude silences. Nobody could say they knew him, although just about everybody said he drank too much. Stories began circulating. 'A surly bugger,' he was called behind his back. That was common now. There were times when he cursed Kathy in public. Strange, though, the wives and other women were more ready to accept the affair. There was something about Masood, his face and manner. And they recognized the tenacity with which Kathy kept living with him. They understood her quick defence of him, often silent but always there, even when she came late to work, puff-eyed from crying and once, her cheek bruised.

Here, the life of Kathy draws rapidly to a close.

It was now obvious to everyone that Masood was drinking too much. At the few parties they attended he usually made a scene of some sort; and Kathy would take him home. Think of swear words. She was arriving late for work and missed whole days. Then she disappeared for a week. They had argued one night and Kathy screamed at him to leave. He replied by hitting her across the mouth. She moved into a cheap hotel, but within the week he found her. 'Syed spent all day, every day, looking for me,' was how she later put it. 'He needs someone.' When she was reprimanded for her disappearance and general conduct, she burst into tears.

In London, the woman with elbows on the table is Kathy Pridham. She has unwrapped a parcel from Karachi. Imagine: coarse screwed-up paper and string lie on the table. Masood has sent a self-portrait, oil on canvas, quite a striking resemblance. His vanity, pride and troubles are enormous. His face, leaning against the tea-pot, stares across at Kathy weeping.

She cannot help thinking of him; of his appearance.

Words. These marks on paper, and so on.

PETER CAREY

He Found Her in Late Summer

1.

He found her in the later summer when the river ran two inches
deep across glistening gravel beds and lay resting in black pools in
which big old trout lay quietly in the cool water away from the
heat of the sun. Occasionally a young rainbow might break the
surface in the middle of the day, but the old fish did no such thing,
either being too well fed and sleepy or, as the fisherman would
believe, too old and wise to venture out at such a time.

Silky oaks grew along the banks and blackberries, dense
and tangled, their fruit long gone into Dermott's pies, claimed
by birds, or simply rotted into the soil, vigorously reclaimed
the well-trodden path which wound beside fallen logs, large
rocks, and through fecund gullies where tree ferns sent out
tender new fronds as soft and vulnerable as the underbellies of
exotic moths.

In one such gully a fallen tree had revealed a cave inside a
rocky bank. It was by no means an ideal cave. A spring ran continually along its floor. Great fistfuls of red clay fell frequently and
in the heat of the day mosquitoes sheltered there in their swarm-
ing thousands.

Three stalks of bracken outside its dirty mouth had been broken and the sign of this intrusion made him lower his hessian bag
of hissing crayfish and quietly peer inside.

It was there he found her, wild and mud-caked, her hair tangled, her fair skin scratched and festered and spotted with
infected insect bites. She was no more than twenty years old.

For a long time they regarded each other quietly. He squatted on his heels and slapped at the mosquitoes that settled on his long, wiry brown legs. She, her eyes swollen, fed them without complaint.

He rolled down the sleeves of his plaid shirt and adjusted his worn grey hat. He pulled up his odd grey socks and shifted his weight.

She tugged at her dress.

At last he held out his hand in the way that one holds out a hand to a shy child, a gentle invitation that may be accepted or rejected.

Only when the hand was lowered did she hold hers out. It was small and white, a city hand with the last vestiges of red nail polish still in evidence. He took the hand and pulled her gently to her feet, but before a moment had passed she had collapsed limply onto the muddy floor.

Dermott adjusted his hat.

'I'm going to have to pick you up,' he said. It was, in a way, a question, and he waited for a moment before doing as he'd said. Then, in one grunting movement, he put her on his shoulders. He picked up the bag of crayfish and set off down the river, wading carefully, choosing this way home to save his passenger from the blackberry thorns which guarded the path along the banks.

Neither spoke to the other, but occasionally the girl clenched his shoulder tightly when they came to a rapid or when a snake, sleeping lightly on a hot rock, slipped silkily into the water as they approached.

Dermott carried his burden with pleasure yet he did not dwell on the reason for her presence in the cave nor attempt to invent theories for her being so many hundred miles from a town. For all of these things would be dealt with later and to speculate on them would have seemed to him a waste of time.

As he waded the river and skirted the shallow edges of the pools he enjoyed his familiarity with it, and remembered the time twenty years ago when it was as strange to him as it must be to his silent guest. Then, with the old inspector, he had done his apprenticeship as his mother had wished him to, read books, learned to identify two hundred different dragonflies, studied the life cycle of the trout, and most particularly the habits of the old black crayfish which were to be his alone to collect. It was an intensive education for such a simple job, and he often reflected in later years that it may not have been, in an official sense, compulsory, but rather a private whim of the old inspector who had loved this river with a fierce protectiveness.

The examination had been a casual affair, a day trek in late spring from where the old Chinese diggings lay in soft mossy neglect to the big falls five miles up river, yet at the end of it he had successfully identified some two hundred trees, thirty insects, three snakes, and described to the old inspector's satisfaction the ancient history of the rocks in the high cliffs that towered above them.

It was only much later, after a child had died, a wife had left and floods had carried away most of his past, that he realized exactly what the old man had given him: riches more precious than he could ever have dreamed of. He had been taught to know the river with the quiet confident joy of a lover who knows every inch of his beloved's skin, every hair, every look, whether it denoted the extremes of rage and passion or the quieter more subtle moods that lie between.

Which is not to suggest that he was never lonely or that the isolation did not oppress him at times, but there were few days in which he did not extract some joy from life, whether the joys be as light as the clear web of a dragonfly or as turbulent as the sun on the fast water below Three Day Falls.

The winters were the hardest times, for the river was brown and swollen then and crayfish were not to be had. Then he occupied himself with a little tin mining and with building in stone. His house, as the years progressed, developed a unique and eccentric character, its grey walls jutting out from the hillside, dropping down, spiralling up. And if few walls were quite vertical, few steps exactly level, it caused him no concern. Winter after winter he added more rooms, not from any need for extra space, but simply because he enjoyed doing it. Had ten visitors descended on him there would have been a room for each one, but there were few visitors and the rooms gave shelter to spiders and the occasional snake which feasted on mice before departing.

Once a gypsy had stayed during a period of illness and repaid his host with a moth-eaten rug of Asiatic origin. Other items of furniture were also gifts. An armchair with its stuffing hanging out had been left by a dour fisheries inspector who had carried it eighty miles on top of his Land Rover, knowing no other way to express his affection for this man on the river with his long silences and simple ways.

Books also were in evidence, and there was an odd assortment. Amongst them was a book on the nature of vampires, the complete works of Dickens, a manual for a motor car that now lay rusting in a ravine, and a science fiction novel entitled *Venus in a Half-Shell*. He had not, as yet, read any of them although he occasionally picked one up and looked at it, thinking that one day he would feast on the knowledge contained within. It would never have occurred to him that the contents of these books might reflect different levels of truth or reality.

'Nearly home,' he said. They had left the river and passed through the high bracken of Stockman's Flat. He trudged in squelching boots along the rutted jeep track that led to the house. He was hot now, and tired. 'Soon be there,' he said, and in a moment he had carried her through the thick walls of his house and gently lowered her down into the old armchair.

She huddled into the armchair while he filled a big saucepan with water and opened the draught on the stained yellow wood stove.

'Now,' he said, 'we'll fix you up.'

From the armchair the girl heard the words and was not frightened.

2.

There was about him a sense of pain long past, a slight limp of the emotions. His grey eyes had the bitter sweet quality of a man who has grasped sorrow and carries it with him, neither indignant at its weight nor ignorant of its value. So if his long body was hard and sinewy, if his hair was cut brutally short, there was also a ministering gentleness that the girl saw easily and understood.

He brought warm water in a big bowl to her chair and with it two towels that might once, long ago, have been white.

'Now,' he said, 'one of us is going to wash you.'

He had large drooping eyelids and a shy smile. He shifted awkwardly from one water-logged boot to the other. When she didn't move he put the towels on the arm of the chair and the bowl of water on the flagstone floor. 'Don't worry about getting water on the floor,' he said.

She heard him squelch out of the room and, in a moment, imagined she heard a floor being swept elsewhere in the house. Outside the odd collection of windows she could see the tops of trees and below, somewhere, she heard the sound of the river. She picked up a grey towel and went to sleep.

3.

The tin roof was supported by the trunks of felled trees. The stone walls were painted white, veiled here and there by the webs of spiders and dotted with the bodies of dead flies. In one corner was a bed made from rough logs, its lumpy mattress supported by three thicknesses of hessian. A tree brushed its flowers against the window and left its red petals, as fine and delicate as spider legs, caught in the webs that adorned the glass.

She lay naked on the bed and let him wash her.

Only when he came in embarrassed indecision to the vulva did she gently push his hand away.

When the washing was over he took a pair of tweezers, strangely precise and surgical, and removed what thorns and splinters he found in her fair skin. He bathed her cuts in very hot water, clearing away the yellow centres of red infections, and dressed each one with a black ointment from a small white jar which bore the legend, 'For Man or Beast'.

He denied himself any pleasure he might have felt in touching her naked body, for that would have seemed wrong to him. When the wounds were all dressed he gave her an old-fashioned collarless shirt to wear for a nightdress and tucked her into bed. Only then did he allow himself the indulgence of thinking her pretty, seeing behind the cuts and swellings, the puffed eyelids, the tangled fair hair, a woman he might well have wished to invent.

She went to sleep almost immediately, her forehead marked with a frown.

He tiptoed noisily from the room and busied himself tidying up the kitchen in a haphazard fashion. But even while he worried over such problems as where to put a blackened saucepan his face broke continually into a grin. 'Well,' he said, 'wonders will never cease.'

When dinner came he presented her with two rainbow trout and a bowl of potatoes.

4.

It would be two days before she decided to talk and he passed these much as he would normally have, collecting the crayfish both morning and afternoon, gardening before lunch, fishing before dinner. Yet now he carried with him a new treasure, a warm white egg which he stored in some quiet dry part of his mind as he worked his way down the rows of tomato plants, removing the small green grubs with his fingers, he smiled more often than he would have done otherwise.

When a shadow passed over the tangled garden and he looked up to admire the soft drift of a small white cloud, he did not look less long than he would have normally but there was another thing which danced around his joy, an aura of a brighter, different colour.

Yet he was, through force of habit, frugal with his emotions, and he did not dwell on the arrival of the girl. In fact the new entry into his life often slipped his mind completely or was squeezed out by his concentration on the job at hand. But then, without warning, it would pop up again and then he would smile. 'Fancy that,' he'd say. Or: 'Well I never.'

The girl seemed to prefer staying in the house, sometimes reading, often sleeping with one of Dermott's neglected books clutched to her chest. The swellings were subsiding, revealing a rather dreamy face with a wide, sad mouth and slightly sleepy blue eyes. A haze of melancholy surrounded her. When she walked it was with the quiet distraction of a sleep-walker. When she sat, her slow eyes followed Dermott's progress as he moved to and fro across the room, carrying hot water from the fire to the grimy porcelain sink, washing a couple of dishes, or one knife or two forks, stewing peaches from the tree in the garden, brewing a herb tea with a slightly bitter flavour, sweeping the big flagstone floor while he spread dirt from his hob-nailed boots behind him, cleaning four bright-eyed trout, feeding the tame magpie that wandered in and out through the sunlit patch in the back door.

He whistled a lot. They were old-fashioned optimistic songs, written before she was born.

When, finally, she spoke, it was to talk about the sweeping.

'You're bringing more dirt in than you're sweeping out.'

He did not look surprised that she had spoken but he noted the softness of her voice and hoarded it away with delight. He considered the floor, scratching his bristly head and rubbing his hand over his newly shaven chin. 'You're quite correct,' he said. He sat on the long wooden bench beneath the windows and began to take off his boots, intending to continue the job in stockinged feet.

'Here,' she said, 'give it to me.'

He gave her the broom. A woman's touch, he smiled, never having heard of women's liberation.

5.

That night at dinner she told him her story, leaning intently over the table and talking very softly.

It was beyond his experience, involving drugs, men who had abused her, manipulated her, and finally wished to kill her. He was too overwhelmed by it to really absorb it. He sat at the table absently cleaning a dirty fork with the table cloth. 'Fancy that,' he would say. Or: 'You're better off now.' And again: 'You're better off without them, that's all.'

From the frequency of these comments she judged that he wished her to be quiet, but really they were produced by his feeling of inadequacy in the face of such a strange story. He was like a peasant faced with a foreigner who speaks with a strange accent, too overcome to recognize the language as his own.

What he did absorb was that Anna had been treated badly by the world and was, in some way, wounded because of it.

'You'll get better here' he said, 'You've come to the right place.'

He smiled at her, a little shyly, she thought. For a brief instant she felt as safe and comfortable as she had ever been in her life and then fear and suspicion, her old friends, claimed her once more. Her skin prickled and the wind in the trees outside sounded forlorn and lonely.

She sat beside the kerosene lamp surrounded by shadows. That the light shone through her curling fair hair, that Dermott was almost unbearably happy, she was completely unaware.

6.

Weeks passed and the first chill of autumn lay along the river. Dermott slowly realized that Anna's recovery would not be as fast as he had imagined, for her lips remained sad and the sleepy eyes remained lustreless and defeated.

He brought things for her to marvel at: a stone, a dried-out frog, a beetle with a jewel-like shell, but she did not welcome the interruptions and did not try to hide her lack of interest so he stood there with the jewel in his hand feeling rather stupid.

He tried to interest her in the river, to give to her the pleasure the old inspector had given him, but she stood timidly on the bank wearing a dress she had made from an old sheet, staring anxiously at the ground around her small flat feet.

He stood in the water wearing only baggy khaki shorts and a battered pair of tennis shoes. She thought he looked like an old war photo.

'Nothing's going to bite you,' he said, 'You can stand in the water.'

'No,' she shook her head.

'I'll teach you how to catch crays.'

'No.'

'That's a silky oak.'

She didn't even look where he pointed. 'You go. I'll stay here.'

He looked up at the sky with his hands on his hips. 'If I go now I'll be away for two hours.'

'You go,' she insisted. The sheet dress made her look as sad as a little girl at bedtime.

'You'll be lonely. I'll be thinking that you're lonely,' he explained, 'so it won't be no fun. Won't you be lonely?'

She didn't say no. She said, 'You go.'

And he went, finally, taking that unsaid no with him, aware that his absence was causing her pain. He was distracted and cast badly. When a swarm of caddis flies hatched over a still dark pool he did not stay to cast there but pushed on home with the catch he had: two small rainbows. He had killed them without speaking to them.

He found her trying to split firewood, frowning and breathing hard.

'You're holding the axe wrong,' he said, not unkindly.

'Well how should I hold it then?'

She stood back with her hands on her hips. He showed her how to do it, trying to ignore the anger that buzzed around her.

'That's what I was doing,' she said.

He retired to tend the garden and she thought he was angry with her for intruding into his territory. She did not know that his mother had been what they called 'a woman stockman' who was famous for her toughness and self-reliance. When she saw him watching her she thought it was with disapproval. He was keeping an anxious eye on her, worried that she was about to chop a toe off.

7.

'Come with me.'

'No, you go.'

That is how it went, how it continued to go. A little litany.

'Come, I'll teach you.'

'I'm happy here.'

'When I get back you'll be unhappy.'

Over and over, a pebble being washed to and fro in a rocky hole.

'I can't enjoy myself when you're unhappy.'

'I'm fine.'

And so on, until when he waded off downstream he carried her unhappiness with him and a foggy film lay between him and the river.

The pattern of his days altered and he in no way regretted the change. Like water taking the easiest course down a hillside, he moved towards those things which seemed most likely to minimise her pain. He helped her on projects which she deemed to be important, the most pressing of which seemed to be the long grass which grew around the back of the house. They denuded the wild vegetable garden of its dominant weed. He had never cared before and had let it grow beside the tomatoes, between the broad leaves of the pumpkin, and left it where it would shade the late lettuce.

As he worked beside her it did not occur to him that he was, in fact, less happy than he had been, that his worry about her happiness had become the dominant factor of his life, clouding his days and nagging at him in the night like a sore tooth. Yet even if it had occurred to him, the way she extended her hand to him one evening and brought him silently to her bed with a soft smile on her lips, would have seemed to him a joy more complex and delightful than any of those he had so easily abandoned.

He worked now solely to bring her happiness. And if he spent many days in shared melancholy with her there were also rewards of no small magnitude: a smile, like a silver spirit breaking the water, the warmth of her warm white body beside him each morning.

He gave himself totally to her restoration and in so doing became enslaved by her. Had he been less of an optimist he would have abandoned the project as hopeless.

And the treatment was difficult, for she was naked and vulnerable, not only to him, to the world, but to all manner of diseases which arrived, each in their turn, to lay her low. In moments of new-found bitterness he reflected that these diseases were invited in and made welcome, evidence of the world's cruelty to her, but these thoughts, alien to his nature and shocking for even being thought, were banished and put away where he could not see them.

She lay in his bed pale with fever. He picked lad's love, thyme, garlic and comfrey and ministered to her with anxious concern.

'There,' he said, 'that should make you better.'

'Do you love me, Dermott?' she asked, holding his dry dusty hand in her damp one. They made a little mud between them.

He was surprised to hear the word. It had not been in his mind, and he had to think for a while about love and the different things he understood by it.

'Yes,' he said at last, 'I do.'

He felt then that he could carry her wounded soul from one end of the earth to the other. He was bursting with love.

8.

As he spent more and more time dwelling with her unhappiness he came to convince himself that he was the source of much of her pain. It was by far the most optimistic explanation, for he could do nothing to alter her past even if he had been able to understand it. So he came to develop a self-critical cast of mind, finding fault with himself for being stubborn, silent, set in his ways, preferring to do a thing the way he always had rather than the way she wished.

Eager to provide her with companionship he spent less and less time on the river, collecting the crays just once, early in the morning while she slept. In this way he lost many but this no longer seemed so important.

When she picked up a book to read in the afternoons he did likewise, hoping to learn things that he might share with her. He felt himself unlettered and ignorant. When he read he followed the lines of words with his broken-nailed finger and sometimes he caught her watching his lips moving and he felt ashamed. He discovered things to wonder at in every line and he often put his book down to consider the things he had found out. He would have liked to ask Anna many things about what he read but he imagined that she found his questions naive and irritating and did not like to be interrupted. So he passed over words he did not understand and marvelled in confused isolation at the mysteries he found within each page.

The True Nature of Vampires had been written long ago by a certain A. A. Dickson, a man having no great distinction in the world of the occult, whose only real claim to public attention had been involved with extracting twenty thousand pounds from lonely old women. Needless to say none of this was mentioned in the book.

Dermott, sitting uncomfortably on a hard wooden bench looked like a farmer at a stock sale. He learned that vampirism does not necessarily involve the sucking of blood from the victim (although this often is the case) but rather the withdrawal of vital energy, leaving the victim listless, without drive, prey to grey periods of intense boredom.

On page ten he read, 'The case of Thomas Deason, a farmer in New Hampshire provides a classic example. In the spring of 1882 he befriended a young woman who claimed to have been beaten and abandoned by her husband. Deason, known to be of an amiable disposition, took the woman into his home as a housekeeper. Soon the groom and farm workers noticed a change in Deason: he became listless and they remarked on the 'grey pallor of his skin'. The groom, who was a student of such matters, immediately suspected vampirism and using rituals similar to those described in the Dion Fortune episode, drove the woman from the house. It was, however, too late to save Deason who had already become a Vampire himself. He was apprehended in a tavern in 1883 and brought to trial. After his conviction and execution there was still trouble in the area and it was only after a stake was driven through the heart of his exhumed corpse in 1884 that things returned to normal in the area.'

One night, when making love, Anna bit him passionately on the neck. He leapt from her with a cry and stood shivering beside the bed in the darkness.

Suspicion and fear entered him like worms, and a slow anger began to spread through him like a poison, nurtured and encouraged each day by further doses of A. A. Dickson's musty book. His mind was filled with stories involving marble slabs, bodies that did not decompose, pistol wounds and dark figures fleeing across moonlit lawns.

His eyes took on a haunted quality and he was forever starting and jumping when she entered the room. As he moved deeper and deeper into the book his acknowledgment of his own unhappiness became unreserved. He felt that he had been tricked. He saw that Anna had taken from him his joy in the river, turned the tasks he had enjoyed into chores to be endured.

He began to withdraw from her, spending more and more time by himself on the river, his mind turning in circles, unable to think what to do. He moved into another bed and no longer slept with her. She did not ask him why. This was certain proof to him that she already knew.

Yet his listlessness, his boredom, his terrible lethargy did not decrease, but rather intensified.

When the jeep arrived to pick up the crayfish its driver was staggered to see the haunted look in Dermott's eyes and when he went back to town he told his superiors that there was some funny business with a woman down at Enoch's Point. The superiors, not having seen the look in Dermott's eyes, smiled and clucked their tongues and said to each other: 'That Dermott, the sly old bugger.'

9.

He had nightmares and cried in his sleep. He dreamed he had made a silver stake and driven it through her heart. He dreamed that she cried and begged him not to, that he wept too, but that he did it anyway driven by steel wings of fear. He shrieked aloud in his sleep and caused the subject of his dreams to lie in silent terror in her bed, staring into the blackness with wide open eyes.

He thought of running away, of leaving the river and finding a new life somewhere else, and this is almost certainly what he would have done had he not, returning from a brooding afternoon beside the river, discovered the following note: 'Dear Dermott, I am leaving because you do not like me anymore and I know that I am making you unhappy. I love you. Thank you for looking after me when I was sick. I hate to see you unhappy and I know it is me that is doing it.' It was signed: 'With all the love in my heart, Anna.'

The words cut through him like a knife, slicing away the grey webs he had spun around himself. In that moment he recognized only the truth of what she wrote and he knew he had been duped, not by her, but by a book.

It was evening when he found her, sitting on the bank of a small creek some three miles up the jeep track. He said nothing, but held out his hand. They walked back to the river in darkness.

He did not doubt that she was a vampire, but he had seen something that A. A. Dickson with his marble tombs and wooden stakes had never seen: that a vampire feels pain, loneliness and love. If vampires fed on other people, he reflected, that was the nature of life: that one creature drew nourishment and strength from another.

When he took her to his bed and embraced her soft white body he was without fear, a strong animal with a heavy udder.

The Letters

I'm going to get out the letters.

'I'd rather you didn't.'

And why not? I want to show you what you were once. What you were when we lived together. Before power and marriage etc made your personality into a social technique, unitl it hides its face behind a flashed-on smile. You've become a shimmer of courteous responses. I watch you on TV. And with me you've become a grunt. Because your personality couldn't survive your oh-so-model life.

'I said not to get out those letters.'

All those things you do at Home you've told me about to make me suffer. Do you know what they are? Elusions.

'What word is that?'

Elusions. What you do is not hobbies. They're ways of evading the eyes and faces of people. To avoid the need to truly react. I see it all now. Because I study only you. The paradox of politics. It is at the very heart of life but, for those who pursue it, it is a way of escaping life. I see it all now. It's all structured reaction. You and your coins and cannons. That's interesting. Your two prized collections of coins and cannons. Money and guns. I hadn't seen that before. When you come here, though, you drop the shimmer of courteous responses and become a grunting stasis, but at least that's real. That's animal.

'Your vocabulary is overreaching.'

Not quite a person. A grunting stasis. But that's real. I'm the last remaining person on earth who knows you. And who can sometimes find you. Your Wife doesn't know you. I can tell. The only time your muscles fall loose is when you are here. Is here,

here with me! For those moments when I undress you, bring you to erection, when you lie naked, just another man, and when you moan and moan and cry out and murmur and cry and come — those noises show me that there is a writhing person in there. And my only moment of power. Oh, but then — zip — you're gone again and each piece of clothing goes back on — hey presto — the Man of Affairs. Herr Cabinet Minister.

'Don't prattle.'

I will. I will read out from the letters. Look at the letters, hundreds, now so nicely bound. Will you one day have a government person, or one of those heavies, come around and destroy them? Or me. Why do you permit me to have them? I suppose because there is no way of them being linked to you. How many pages you once effused — over me. Look.

'You're becoming hysterical. Take them away. Take them away from my face.'

I will read: '... On that drive to Canberra you acted so impulsively, so impishly ... did you realise that it was the first time that you didn't have to be coaxed? Or bribed or forced? Although you had always wanted to do it, once you were made to do it, it was not until that day in the car that you initiated it. You had until then, I suppose, liked the game of feeling that it was against your will, your nature, or whatever. You enjoyed playing the stubborn, sullen boy. It was from then on, from that day of that drive, that you were a different person, a special person with a special destiny and aware of it. Which I had of course known, and had of course known you would one day be made to realise ...'

And I thought it meant at the time that I had 'fallen in love' with you. But for you it meant that I was ready for anything that you required. That I was in a new phase. But at least your letters, if they were not 'love' letters, were effusive and you were fascinated by me and you used words to me. At least there were words then, including words about yourself.

Let me recall the 'drive to Canberra'. That evocative memory. It was your election campaign. We were driving through the electorate. I was fifteen. No. I was probably fourteen. Had I even done the School Certificate? I had been released from school after one of your 'notes' had arrived at the Headmaster's office and I was told that there was a government car waiting for me. The faces of my friends staring down from the school windows. I'd pack my things knowing that I would be whisked away to some hotel, to be fucked into a daze. And later, sometimes, to be used by your 'associates'. Made drunk. And the drugs, oh yes, the muscle relaxants. Or no — sitting around in hotel rooms while you talked to people about things I didn't understand. That is what I remember most. You talking to foreign people. I remember once hitting on the idea of filing my nails in front of them. I think I wanted to embarrass you, it seemed an outrageous thing for a schoolboy to do and you said coolly, 'Yes, your nails could do with some attention — we don't like grubby boys,' and those in the room all laughed knowingly. I went from the room flushed and confused, close to tears, but you didn't come after me. I came back later and they had gone and I cried in bed with you in the submission of utter lost confusion.

Anyhow. The drive to Canberra. We were driving fast. I moved over to sit hard against you, remember? I put my hand lovingly up to your neck and my fingers into your hair. I did it because I now felt 'in love' with you. Do you remember what you said? You said that I was too close, there'd be cars coming up behind us and you'd be recognised and lose votes. I said that you could possibly gain votes from homosexuals. You were amused by my using the word 'homosexual' and said that it was the first time you'd heard me say it. I blushed, but you made me say it again, although I didn't want to. You made me say that I was a homosexual, but I resisted saying it. And then I said it, turning weakly to you and taking your hand, putting it to my lips and saying it through your fingers and my kiss. 'Oh yes, I am, I am homosexual.'

'You have an unhealthy memory.'

And you smiled — at the time I thought you smiled because I pleased you, but I think now you smiled because of private thoughts — and you said that I was a 'special class' of homosexual. But there in the car then I undid your fly and went down on you, into that fundamental smell of urine and the lingering odour, almost imperceptible, of excreta (but it was there), down over your penis and through the imported underwear which you got for us, before you married — does she buy that dreadful underwear you wear now, or do you wear it to identify with the normal folk? — and I licked the head of your penis through the silk and it oozed its juice making the silk transparent and I worked my mouth and the silk on your penis head while we drove at 100 mph through the wheat country and the hot, dry sun. You spread your legs to give yourself. Moaning, on and on at 100 mph in that Rover car you had then. I smelled the hot leather of the upholstery. The ever-so-slight smell of petrol fumes. The slight dry-cleaning fluid smell of groin. I gobbled and stimulated you, taking your balls up into my mouth, my tongue working you around and around, playing up and down, and then a finger fully in your anus. And then you came into my mouth pulse after pulse, the semen dominating and wiping out all the other senses, although they came back, one by one, the texture of the silk first.

'Your memory is unhealthy.'

Remember, I took from you your semen and then lay there, my face in your lap. I remember plainly, while I had my head buried down there and you were coming into me, I remember thinking — is he ever going to stop. Is he ever going to stop? Is this possible, what have I done? I was very young.

'Don't go on — stop now.'

When you finally finished, I sat up, wiped my mouth on a tissue, wiped you, and did up your fly, and we drove into town across the bridge. Within half an hour you were adressing a meeting and shaking hands with the mayor and his wife.

I remember you sending me to a newspaper office in the town to book space, or something, for your campaign advertisements, and a nosey old editor with an eye-shade asking me if I were your 'son' or a campaign worker or what. I said, 'Aide de camp.'

I though that rather good at the time until you told me back at the motel that I had mispronounced it.

Those early campaigns were the only time, though, that you've taken me into your politcal life, even if I were only some-one in the car, unexplained.

Excepting, of course, the Camden days, and they were hardly political. Those house parties. The old men and senators, or whatever, feeling me, talking about me being 'pretty', and you saying to me after, 'Just keep smiling at them, let them do what they want.' You were so torn then — you couldn't do without my body then, but you felt that sometimes it did your career good for me to pleasure the Old Men of the Tribe. You were anxious though, the only time I could truly say you felt anxious about me, that I might become someone else's boy, but yet you had to risk it, had to prostitute me. And then you got where you wanted and put me into this, this 'town house' — is that what we call this? And it has come to this — me locked here, virtually, visited by, God what is he called? An accountant? He never lays a finger on me. More's the pity.

Why doesn't she dress you with some style? You're both rich. You used to wear such beautiful clothing, but why drip-dry shirts — why? They are for travelling. Tell her, tell her they're for when you can't have laundry done. And for Chinese waiters.

'You are not to mention her.'

Yes. We won't bring her into it. She's sacred. Miss Sacred Heart Country Party Whore 1955.

'Stop!'

And you came back from the meeting in town to the motel and came to my room giggling. You never giggle now. Aren't Herr Cabinet Ministers allowed to giggle? I was sitting up in the motel eating chocolates and listening to country and western music and you thanked me for washing out your underwear. But then you giggled and said that the mayor had followed our car into town and overtaken us near the bridge. You had said hastily to the mayor that I was a 'nephew'. 'Nephew?' said the mayor. 'No, you were alone in the car. There was no one else in the car when I overtook.'

'You involved me in risks.'

So you locked me away. No, we could go back to those days without the risks. I am older now. I would be a good private secretary. I've told you this so often. But, of course, I don't hold the same charm.

'You have your place.'

My head between your legs.

'I don't think, really, that you need more whisky. Put it down.'

How I wish you were always around to tell me to stop, to tell me what to do. I was reading some woman and she says that's what it is all about — 'extinguishing the consciousness'. Obliterating the personality. I understand my state. I relish it.

'Theoretical books are bad for you.'

Don't worry, this is not about the liberation movements. That's not my liberation. I know that. I know now that my liberation is to be found in the opposite direction. The liberation through obeisance.

'Mmmmm.'

For instance, I could cut your initials in my arm. I could do that to show you what I mean.

'Don't talk like that. I've had to stop you talking about that sort of thing before.'

What about when you had that doctor friend of yours inject me with some drug which made me helpless and warm and open and you had me, when I was fourteen, you and then those other two men. For hours. I was so dazed I couldn't work out what was happening to my body. You were training it somehow to behave in some sort of way you wanted, and you broke me so that I couldn't behave any other way.

'Oh shut up.'

All right. But I will cut your initials in my arm.

'Stop that.'

He shouted at me, but I went to the bathroom and found a razor blade and came back to him.

He sat there. I knelt before him, I was still in the satin jocks and satin smock that he liked me to wear, and I stretched out my bare arm.

'If you must' he said, a change of voice, he was switching now, turning on to it, participating.

You should brand me.

'It would be safer to have you tattooed.'

Yes. I'd like that too.

'Go on — cut yourself. Cut my name in your arm.'

He really wanted me to cut myself.

I cut. I did it. I cut one letter. The blood came out in a string of globules. I baulked at the second letter. I would have done it but I was stopped, the effort required to mutilate one's skin, especially when the skin is perfect, as mine was, unblemished young skin, the effort was exhausting.

'The other letter — go on,' he said, 'cut the other letter.'

The bastard.

Bastard.

I closed my eyes, opened them, and cut the loop of the next letter and then dropped the blade, I stared at the blood on my arm and then licked it, licked both the wounds, and then needed to sit.

I felt faint, and then his arms were about me, the world moved, unsteadily.

He pulled me to him. I had earned it.

'You stupid boy,' he said. I sunk to my knees.

He had an erection. He had an erection and I felt it through the silk of his pyjamas. I kissed his penis through the pyjamas and I was back then in the car with the hot leather, I hugged him around his thighs.

He led me over to the bedroom and pushed me down on the bed lifting the smock, pulling down the satin to bare my arse.

My face went down on to my bleeding arm and I tasted again my own steely blood as I felt him move himself into me, as I arched my buttocks to take him. He came, ejaculating into me, almost as soon as he entered, and the throb and the thrust of the penis were so distinctly felt that it was as if they were drawn with pen and nib and ink on my nervous system, the hot sperm bursting against the sensitive lining of my anus.

When he'd had his way, he rolled off and said, 'You should put sand into the wound — to permanently scar yourself.'

I told him that I would do that. If I had been able to move, I would have done something like that. I was held to the bed by a heavy blanket of sensual pain. I was centred.

I will do that, I told him, I will.

I put my head against him and cried.

He then said something, something humorous, maybe tender, he said, 'They are the most obscene letters I have received,' and he put his fingernail on the blood-smeared intials and traced them, hurting me, tracing them with his sharp fingernail.

He then asked me to come to the bathroom, he had to go, he wanted me to wash him.

I said that I would after I had put something on the wounds.

He said that could wait.

BEVERLEY FARMER

Snake

We are not told anywhere, are we, that winters in the Garden of Eden were not cold? The olive and the lemon ripen in winter and it could not be Paradise without them. Lemon and olive, sour and bitter, my mother would say: they suit you, Manya. Mama misjudges me.

I think as winter comes, why huddle here in three warm rooms? Why not go to Athens, say, and see Aunt Sophia? My dear old Aunt Sophia. Walk up to the Acropolis again. Order coffee and sit and watch the hollow city brim with a violet glow, and the lights and stars shine out. Sit on the cold stones of the theatre, high above its golden statuary, where I saw Euripides performed, Aeschylus. Or even go to Crete. It's sunny there. But I feel anxious away from here now.

Three years ago I went away. Mama and I went to the village in Macedonia when her sister Vasso died. As always when the ferry casts off in the crescent harbour of Mytilene I felt lost, speechless with dread. The Thessaloniki ferry passes between Turkey and Molyvo in the strait. I see Molyvo in the distance, its blue citadel. I never rest — those weeks in the frozen village, my God! — until we pass it again. So I might stay and see my olives through the press instead.

Aunt Vasso's own sons hadn't come down from Germany. Uncle Manoli, a dour man at any time, hardly spoke. After the funeral we were snowbound for silent weeks. I remember the full cheese-cloths hung high on black branches of the grapevine over his front door, their icicles of whey pointed down like teats. A wolf off the mountains howled at night. We cooked what we found: macaroni, rice, icy potatoes and onions, eggs, my aunt's

tomato paste and preserved pig from a crock deep in snow on the
window sill. There was milk. We made cheese day by day and
stored it in its crock in brine, weighed down with flat river stones.
At night — from three o'clock, I remember, it was night —
Mama and I huddled by the sooty *somba* roaring with apple wood
until we succumbed in the stuffy dim yellow room to stupor and
sleep. My uncle kept a horse and goats in the barn. An Arctic winter of darkness they lived through, shivering and crusted with
excrement. He came home to milk the goats — we boiled the
milk — and then sat in the *kafeneion*, glowing with ouzo, silent.
The river froze. I had been there before, but in summer. Thank
God I need never go again.

I keep busy all day in the garden, and at night I read. I paint a
little and my work sells in town. It is not dull, just peaceful, in
Paradise. And our green Lesbos is not like other islands. Lesbos was
rich in art and poetry when Athens was a village and Thessaloniki
still under the sea. They are as natural to Lesbos as her olive trees
are, and we who love them are not thought eccentric here.

Still, I am thought eccentric. I am over forty and have never
married. Mama has stopped her wailing over me and her tireless
matchmaking. No man would have me now. Even Mitso the Idiot,
who tried to rape me at a wedding once, would scowl and snarl at
the thought now. As a girl I had no money, only beauty. That has
gone. My dowry was my olive trees and the garden. Lemon trees
grow here, pear and quince and apricot, peach and almond. We
have red hens and a vegetable patch. This little house too would
have become mine on my marriage, though my mother was left
nothing else, as that is the custom here. Then my daughter's in her
turn. I think Mama would be upset if I did marry. Not because of
the house — she would stay here, of course — but because we
make a good couple, she and I, whatever she says. We get on.

The first few times we saw Louka and my cousin Dimitra in
company Mama worried, sighed, watched to see how I was taking
it. I have never told her the whole story. She guesses that, perhaps.
Perhaps she even forgets now that I was engaged to Louka. She
forgets my daughter. She fusses over them when they visit. She

spoils their boys with sweets. It gives me no pleasure to see Louka. No pain either.

———

I was twenty when Louka came back from his army service to work in his father's restaurant in Molyvo. I was staying with my cousins there — Dimitra was still a schoolgirl — in their stone house at the base of the Genoese fortress, the citadel on the hilltop. In the whitewashed sun of the chapel next door striped cats lay sleeping. We could see from three windows the stone arm of the port curled round its fishing boats.

Louka had always flirted. Now he came to the house so often, and singled me out so persistently and so respectfully, that we knew he was serious. His mother called on my aunt to discuss the match. My cousins were thrilled. My aunt asked me what I thought. Yes, I said. The priest in his gold brocade came. We exchanged rings and were engaged.

It's hard to believe now what a passion I had for Louka.

He was beautiful, though, I remember, his hair so heavy and black when he let it grow, and his athlete's body dark brown and golden. After the rush in the restaurant he would sit with the tourists joking in scraps of their languages and put on music to teach them to dance the *sirto*, the *tsamiko*. The *zeïmbekiko* he danced by himself, his head sunk between his shoulders like a sated tomcat. He glanced at the women. Enthralled with Louka, they all clapped in time. There was ouzo, but most drank wine, yellow *retsina* from the barrel with its faint rankness of urine, of salt: as if the men treading it, unwilling to stop, let urine and sweat slip down their thighs into the must ...

On still nights I could hear the *bouzoukia*. I lay awake. When the music stopped, the restaurant was closed, Louka could come and whisper at my shutters. Shutters in Molyvo are solid, not slatted. I was a good girl, and shy. I wouldn't open them. '*Den m'agapas?*' he would growl, his voice thick.

'You know I love you.'

'Then let me see you.'

'I mustn't. I can't.'

'Come on, Manya, open the shutters, I just want to see you, just for a moment. Manya!'

'No. Go home, please, Louka, *please*. They'll *hear*.'

Some of those nights — or mornings, by then — he must have had Valerie with him.

––––––––––

She was not a typical tourist. Not one of the Europeans who descend in hordes to loll on the pebble beach oiling their bones or hire donkeys and ride giggling across the headland to bathe naked at the sandy beach and the hot spring. She was staying with some Australians who lived all the year round in Molyvo. But she looked like them. She smoked and drank and slept with men. She was tall and brown with lank yellow hair and a cat's pale eyes. Her nose and shoulders were thin, red under the freckles. What would a man like Louka want with her? So when friends warned me, I scoffed. Laughing, I accused Louka, but in fun. He tried to laugh.

'Don't look so guilty,' I teased.

Shifting and shuffling, he lit another cigarette and pleaded not guilty. I said I would call witnesses. I laughed as I scored this point but Louka leapt up.

'All right then,' he said. 'So it's true. So what?'

'You're in love with *her*?'

'Valerie? Don't be stupid.'

'Then — *why*?'

'Look.' *He* would not look. He breathed smoke in and coughed. 'I'm in love with you. You know I am. These others, they're whores.' These? How many? 'They won't leave you alone. I'm only flesh and blood, Manya, for God's sake!'

'But, if you loved me, you couldn't —'

'Don't be such a baby!' He thrust his face close. To kiss me, I thought, and drew back. But no, it was twisted with feelings I could not read, of hatred, of desperation.

'*Afti me gamaei*.' She — makes love to me (so to speak). He bared his teeth to say it. Then he walked out.

––––––––––

I found Valerie sipping her morning coffee alone by the balustrade of a *kafeneion*, her eyes half-closed against the dazzle of the strait. She had no idea who I was. I sat at her table. 'Manya,' I said, pointing to myself.

'*Ego* Valerie,' she smiled.

'Louka,' I said, showing my gold ring and not smiling. She frowned. Her nose had peeled and her brows and lashes were white like cat's whiskers. She had a pocket dictionary. She looked in it and asked in broken Greek if I was Louka's wife. Not yet, I said, we were engaged, and found the word for her. She looked wise.

'Hmmm. *To paliopaido*,' she grinned. The bad boy. She shivered and picked up her towel. '*Thalassa*, Manya?' she said. '*Ela, pame?*' She really thought I'd go to the beach with her. She shrugged, grinned and flapped away down the steps. I was too amazed at the cheek of her to smack her face. I had expected to.

———

Louka, grown fat and bald, deceives Dimitra with tourists in summer — more deftly now, I hope — and with other men's wives in winter. Everyone knows. She will never leave him, though, nor he her. There are children, two boys: the elder a solemn bookworm, the younger a darling, a sparkling boy, and the children I do envy Dimitra. Nothing else. Sour grapes, Mama would say. No. Dimitra, each time she catches Louka out, attacks the woman. I, with my small experience, had more sense. She sobs and shrieks. She spat at one in the restaurant, pulled another one's hair. Louka takes her home and humbly swears that she's his one true love. He's lucky he married Dimitra.

At the theatre once I saw *Agamemnon*. He had led grown men to the slaughter for another man's whore and for gold. So he was returning a hero to Clytemnestra, with his slave girl in tow. I have often dreamt since of her net and axe in the stone bath and Agamemnon quietly like a great fish pumping his blood through the water. She had a right to do it. He deserved death. Never for infidelity; she was unfaithful too. Death for their daughter's death. He led her into the trap at Aulis. I would strike the blow too, in Clytemnestra's place.

But not in Medea's. One summer night at a stone theatre cut into a hill among pines, the sky clear, the sea like milk, Medea writhed and growled for us and stabbed her little boys. For this she was raised in a god's gilt chariot and sat, the moon rising behind her, and gloated. Dimitra was there. It's whispered in the family that she holds this threat over Louka's head, should he dare to leave her …

When my Sophoula died Louka, I suspect, was relieved. He had never seen her. 'Who says I'm its father, anyway?' I'm told that he said. I prayed for Louka's death. I screamed to God for justice, of all things. I was mad for some time. I'm sane now and no longer pray or believe. I keep the fasts. I go to church with Mama. I eat the bread sopped in wine from the priest's chalice. God doesn't lift a finger.

Lesbos is close to Turkey. I have seen from the ferry people walking in the streets of Baba in Turkey as we passed between Baba and Molyvo in the strait. Our barracks and theirs are crowded with troops. The beaches are mined. We live in dread of another war. They do too. They love children, as we do. I believe that there is one thing that might save the world from destruction: our love of children. This is stronger than hate, or nothing is. This hope, or no hope.

————

Louka, when I next saw him after our quarrel, was at his most easy and charming, full of anecdotes about life in the army that convulsed my aunt and cousins. I was on edge, I remember. I had come to my decision. After the preserves and the coffee I stood and announced that Louka and I had arranged to meet friends at the restaurant. He looked stunned. Outside he asked me where we were going. 'Don't ask me yet,' I said. It was a sultry afternoon, the whole town sleeping. I led him to the gullies past the olive grove where couples went. We lay on the dry grass.

'Now look. Manya, darling —'
'Take me,' I said quickly. 'Make me yours.'
'Do you mean it?'
'Yes. I want you. Take me now.'
He put his arms around me.

'Manya, not here. Not now.'

'Why not?' I cried despairingly. 'What's wrong with you?'

I didn't mean it the way he took it.

He pulled his shirt off, only his shirt. In the heat his body was rank and shone like varnished wood. The hair had stuck in curls round his dark nipples. He grasped me. Our teeth clashed and I shut my eyes. Tugging under my skirt, he lay on me and forced in hard and split my legs open. The pain, my God! I clung as he thudded on me. When he rolled away there was a sucking noise. He found a drop of blood and flicked it off.

'Louka?' I was close to tears.

'I hurt you. I'm sorry.'

'It's all right. I love you.' *S'agapo. S'agapo.*

Sighing, he lit a cigarette. Then abruptly he was on his feet. 'Cover yourself,' he hissed, and four boys, local children I think, burst on us there. They exploded into joyful whinnies and ran jostling and prodding to the beach.

'*Gamo to,*' Louka swore.

That was the first and the last time in my life, let the gossips say what they like. It was two whole days after it before I saw Louka. I spent them in bed pretending to be ill, but really ill, in a torment of shame and bewilderment. There was no one I could tell it to.

When he came at dawn and whispered at my window I — well, wasn't I his now? — I flung open the shutters. Appalled, Louka gazed up, swaying on the blue cobbles, Valerie clutched to him with one arm. She struggled free when she saw me, hissed furious words at him and clattered down the steps. I slammed the shutters. For a while Louka pleaded — those hoarse endearments of his — as if nothing had happened. Finally he stumbled away.

———

I didn't see Louka again for years. I left Molyvo abruptly to come here. I went for long walks alone and brooded. A broken engagement was shame enough to account for my misery, and Mama didn't pry. By autumn I knew I had to tell her. She wanted to hide me away with relatives — 'for your sake, Manya' — but I couldn't have borne to leave here.

I saw Valerie again that winter (winter, but the morning heat was heavy, very still and dusty, more like summer) at an umbrella-shaded table on the waterfront, reading. Drops of sweat glazed her red nose, her forehead and the sunbleached hairs of her upper lip. She looked up.

'Hey! Hey, Manya!'

I swung away, but she ran up behind me.

'Manya! *Tha piies kafe, kale?*'

Why not? I would have coffee. Her Greek sounded better. I nodded my ironic approval and she grinned, leading me back. The coffee ordered, we were silent, facing a sea that heaved and glittered at us. We made laborious small talk, what little we could. When the coffees and iced water came, she flicked through the little dictionary she still had and asked when the wedding was to be. 'Wedding?' I was as red as she was. Did she think me such a fool?'

'Louka *s'agapo*,' she said. Louka I love you? She saw my face and tried again, pointing at me. Louka *s'agapo* Manya.' She meant that Louka loved me.

'*Agapaei*,' I corrected. 'Yes? How nice.'

The coffee was strong and sweet and I drank the whole glass of water. In the thick sunlight her brown legs glistened with white hairs. Many Greek women are as brown as Valerie — I am white all over like cream cheese — but our body hair is dark. Some try to be rid of it; I never have. Those white-furred legs of hers Louka had opened. Did he still? I wondered, but only dully. I was weary.

'Manya *agapaei* Louka? she was persisting. I showed her my hand with its gold ring gone. 'Ah,' and she gazed with real regret. The Athens ferry had docked further along the quay and crowds with bags and boxes were hurrying there. She tipped small change on the table, picked up her bags — on one, I remember, swimming flippers flapped like an upturned seal — and jumped up.

'Manya, I must go, forgive me.' We say that when we go: she meant nothing more by it. '*Addio*.' Kissing me on both cheeks, wishing me luck. I felt too dazed and ill to speak. She looked back once in the surge of people to wave. I thought she gaped: perhaps she had just seen my swollen belly.

———————

I had my baby in Athens and would not give her up. Aunt Sophia, our old Communist warhorse, was godmother and gave her own name when my mother refused. When I was well enough I brought Sophoula back here. For the evening *volta*, when families parade, I wheeled her along the quay in front of everyone. I suckled her a whole year. She walked at the age of one and swam at two. Before she had all her baby teeth she died of leukemia. I never saw a child to match Sophoula. Dying, she said 'Mama, where are you?' I was there holding her. I have worn black since that day.

It was God's judgment on my sin, people nodded. So may their sins be judged.

———————

In this room my child and I slept: here I laid her out and waited with her for her burial. I often sit, as I sat then, at the south window and watch the sun, the moon, then the sun again. Having lived here all my life, I need its smell of paint, its floor of striped rugs, its dark points where at night the lamp will lay a gold hand on a cracked water-jug, three red stripes, a window sill.

Here in this room I painted Souphoula naked in her coffin, among pears and apples and grapes, a bunch of blue grapes in her hand. I drew in every detail of her: the ringed nipples, each crease and nail of her fingers and toes, the lips folded between her legs, her curled ears, her eyebrows with the mole under the left one. Had I been roasting the body on a spit my mother's horror would hardly have been greater, although, afraid of her mad daughter, she let me have my way.

'The pears are rotting,' was all she said. So they were, even before Souphoula was. 'Let the poor child have flowers.'

'It's not flowers that matter,' I seem to recall saying. 'It's the fruit that matters ——'

'Is this what you will do to me as well?'

'—— and death is the seed inside it!'

'What will become of us, Manya?' And she refused to sit up with me. I left her to receive the few mourners who came. My mother loves her visitors. I let no one in to see the child: my mother placated them. I sat alone with the candles and kept watch as Souphoula stiffened and then was limp again and her face changed. At first I talked to her. Then I brushed and plaited her hair. In daylight I painted her as she had become. Then I dressed and covered her for the last time.

I have nearly all the paintings that I did when I was mad: all interiors with figures, as these were. Mostly they were self-portraits, mostly nude. The rooms in them are full of the whiteness that snow reflects, or moonlight; and so are the bodies. I have never shown or sold these. I can only look at them myself from time to time. I know they are here against the wall, as the dead are in the earth. I know without looking.

I still paint myself nude. I have one on the easel now. It shows the blue branchings of my veins, the shadow of bones within, the slackness of my throat and breasts and swinging thighs — all my white meat run to fat, its tufts and wrinkles and moles. It shows everything. Still, it lacks what *those* had. My best work is in landscapes these days: watercolours done in precise detail. The parapets, yellow and violet-grey, of the fortress. Hills and their trees. The leaning figures in black of old women who mind goats. Children with shaved heads of brown and black velvet. Birds and insects and snakes. Old men lapped in shadow at the tables of *kafeneia*, sea light wandering on them as they drowse, these long afternoons.

––––––––

Dimitra came to see me before she married Louka. I was fond of her when she was little, though I had not seen her since. I would never have tolerated such questions otherwise.

'I know you were engaged to Louka once. My mother —'

'What would your mother know?'

'I don't know.' She had trouble finding words. 'She doesn't know I'm here. She won't talk about you.'

'Good.'

'I've always thought of you as my big sister, Manya.'

'Have you? Why? We never see each other.'

'I always have. I wanted to be like you. Were you — in love with Louka?' Her jaw was trembling. 'Did he — why did you go away?'

'Pride. Ask *my* mother.'

'It's just that I — am I making a mistake? Should I really marry him?' At this point she hid her face in my shoulder. She was warm to hold. I stroked her plait of hair.

'Well, but you love him, don't you? You want to.'

'But will we be happy?'

'Sometimes. Why not?' She gazed with wet eyes. 'I hope you will,' I said. This was my pride speaking. 'Look,' I said then, and turned one of the nude self-portraits that I never show around to show her. 'It's beautiful.' She blushed and looked away. 'But you should have asked me first.'

'It's not you, Dimitroula.' She looked amazed. In fact it was exactly like her but for the eyes. Hers were, and are, like brown glass; mine, like green. 'Look at the eyes,' I said.

'Yes. But, Manya, even so —' She was white now.

'I did it years ago. How strange life is! If I painted the eyes brown I could give this to you. As an engagement present.'

'No. She shuddered. 'Oh, don't. No.'

At a friend's wedding once, when Louka and Dimitra were showing off their first baby, Louka clinked his glass on mine, leaned over and wondered in a hoarse whisper how I had stayed so beautiful. He said I was his one true love. He was, as usual, drunk. 'Darling,' he mumbled. 'Do you still love me a little?'

'To *our* child,' I said, and clinked his glass with mine, smiling even more sweetly. 'She should have been ten this year.'

He went back to his seat next to Dimitra.

Our garden is a few kilometres out along the flat coast on a lagoon full of seaweed and sandbanks. I hardly ever leave it now except to shop in Mytilene once a week. I love the crammed old shops that smell of roasting coffee, anchovies and cumin and olive oil. Skeins of late grapes flow there, withering, fermenting. At a waterfront table I sip my coffee, knee-deep in shopping bags. At twilight the harbour water is still. Darkness frills the images of boats at anchor and of sharp-winged gulls. Boys lolling on the edge fish among lights and stars.

I visit my old art teacher shivering in her frayed villa, its tiles all tufts and nests, its windows cracked by a giant magnolia that is her pride. Excrement from empty swallows' nests trails down her walls inside and out. She is sitting for me. Children jeer at her gate and scramble to safety. 'Mad old Maria,' they shrill. Her eyes water. She turns off the table lamp to hide the tears. Maria is my name, of course: Manya, Maria. Is this how I will end, I wonder? A palsied crone mocked by children — I who love children?

My mother fears arthritis and angina. She fears death. Last year the village secretary wrote that they had found Uncle Manoli, her sister's widower, dead in the snow one morning. Mama was full of such grief, so many tears! 'Well, you have a hard heart, Manya,' she said. 'You won't even shed tears for me.' But what was old Manoli to Mama? No. It was just — Death.

Our life is calm. My companion, apart from Mama, is a cat patterned in black and white like a penguin. He lies breathing on a velvet sofa with his pink paws in the air. He is a shining seal; an owl when his black eyes shrink to gold plate with one black split from top to bottom and his blink is stern; a fanged snake when he yawns. He is everything in one, but his name is Fidaki, Little Snake. As a girl I once tried, from a sense of duty, to kill a snake I found writhing on my path. I threw rocks and silently the snake dodged, jerking and scraping, its gold eyes wild. All my rocks missed. Ashamed, I stood back and let it slide into a field of maize, its tongue touching ahead of it bronze clods of clay.

Maybe snakes hunt in our own garden, but if so I've never seen one. Fidaki himself hunts, but he is belled, the birds tease him. Mama said that Little Snake was no name for a cat. I said that the Garden could do without Adam and Eve, but must have its snake.

'Well, so it has. You are its snake,' she smiled. 'Yes you are, Manya! Its fallen angel.' Smiling, but I could see she meant it.

Stan and Mary, Mary and Stan

Both the Rossmores were worried about Stan but said nothing of their fears to each other.

He was soon to return to university in Sydney after the mid-winter holidays, and was not saying a word about it. Mrs Rossmore kept checking his room to see if he had done anything with the books he had emptied from his case and put on his table when he came home. Exams would be in a few months after he got back. She had put a lamp there for him, but even it had not been moved to a new position and she was sure he had not lit it. She saw a light through his window passing (unnecessarily) along the veranda but knew it to be a candle by which he was reading a detective story.

'Where's Stan?' Mr Rossmore asked one night by the sitting room fire after tea.

'In his room with his books,' Mrs Rossmore answered. This was not a lie, and it would not be necessary to mention it to Father O'Malley at confession.

Next day Mr Rossmore, coming up behind Stan's straight young back in the corn paddock, asked if he was all set to go back on the coach out of Cobargo on the Monday, a week away. (Even Rossmore acknowledged it a foolish question. What other way was there to go?)

Stan's shoulders wriggled and Mr Rossmore supposed he ducked his head, for he saw briefly a little more of Stan's sunburned neck. Inwardly he rebuked himself. He was paying good money for Stan's education; Stan wasn't taking it on himself to decide his future! He was going back alright. If his mother knew of any doubts there would be a nice old upheaval! And what would he say to Frank and Harry, his brothers with lesser properties and average children (very average). My son the doctor. Dr Stan Rossmore. Dr Rossmore. It had been his mother's dream since they found him reading at four years of age. Too clever for farming by far.

Eric, the younger son, could have two years at agricultural college if he did well enough with the Marist Brothers in Goulburn where he was a boarder. Stan was the brain. What was going on inside that head, covered with tight ginger coloured curls? Not with Eric's dark good looks, but with a freckled face with pale blue eyes that seemed to be strained, as if they did not see as well as stronger coloured ones. Mr Rossmore had to stride out to keep up with him, and when they reached their horses, tied to the old pear tree at the corner of the paddock, Stan swung onto his and Mr Rossmore had a job disguising an enormous effort to keep up. Stan manoeuvred his horse onto the single track up the last gully, galloping ahead and making it appear like a courteous gesture allowing his father a clear path. I'm a wake up, Bert said to himself, seeing the chestnut's rump bounding away between the line of poplars. Stan had to stop, though, when he was through the big gate and wait for Mr Rossmore to pass through. (A well mannered boy, I'll say that for him.) When the gate was closed there was only a short canter to the house, and too late to start anything up.

And at dinner there was Jessie coming in and out all the time and Rene in charge of things as always. She kept an eye on their plates and talked about Cobargo events, giving them more importance than they warranted. There was a ball soon in the School of Arts, the annual Catholic ball, which everyone worthy of a place in the sect and over the age of fifteen would attend.

Mary, Gordon and Tom Jussep usually went.

This year, a fortnight after the death of Mrs Jussep, they would be in a period of mourning.

Everyone thought of this. 'Will the Jusseps be going?' Madge asked. Ah, here was something to cheer Mrs Rossmore, with most of her mind on Stan, eating his stewed steak and cauliflower and with an expression she could not read. Stan was allowed two dances with Mary Jussep aside of those in the progressive ones. This was only polite and Mrs Rossmore would have insisted, but she didn't need to, for few could fail to notice the eagerness of Stan when he bent over Mary, sitting on the bench against the wall, and the way her hand sprung out to go into his. She would stand quickly, but not without grace, and put her wrap (not warm enough for a cold June night) and shabby little bag on the seat, keeping her eyes away from those next to her who were looking hard for anything serious in this. Mrs Rossmore usually saw as well, for she was out of the supper room by this time and ready to take her place on the floor with Bert, despite his irritating habit of pumping her arm up and down as if it were a well handle.

The Jusseps would be missing from the ball, thank goodness, (only because it freed her of certain worries).

'Of course they won't be going!' Mrs Rossmore said, frowning on Madge, who had a cheekful of mashed potato. She laid her knife and fork evenly on her plate and stared until Madge, swirling the potato around a few times, finally swallowed it, ducking her head and turning red with the effort. Stan's very pale lashes batted his freckles a couple of times. 'The Jusseps I'm sure would know better than that!' Mrs Rossmore murmured.

No more was said until they were up to the pudding.

Then Mrs Rossmore said Eric might go this year.

'It would be something for Jim,' she said. Jim was Eric's school friend with whom he was spending the first part of the holidays on a property outside Goulburn. Jim would spend the last part at the Rossmores'. Madge was excited at the prospect. They were yet to meet Jim, and Madge was wishing she could see Patty and share speculation with her on what he would be like.

Stan thought of the School of Arts without Mary. The decorations drooped, the music sounded tinny and hollow, and the sandwiches tasted dry. He might not go. Mrs Rossmore read something of this in his face. Ever since he was a little boy his freckles had stood out when he was about to do or say something of a rebellious nature. No, she wouldn't press the point, just go ahead and air his suit and iron his best shirt and hang them in a conspicuous place on the day of the ball the following Friday.

'Mrs Jussep won't be cooking for the ball this year,' Madge said. Her cakes had been among the most professional of those from all the Cobargo cooks. Mrs Rossmore felt cheered by the loss of rivalry and despondent at the loss of the cakes. She rose quite abruptly and began clearing the table as if she should start at once creating extra time for the added workload. Jessie, hearing the rattle of plates, hurried in worrying that she was at fault.

Mr Rossmore was displeased. He had wanted Madge to go off and play and he and Stan and Rene to engage in intimate conversation about Stan's next half year at university. But Stan was on his feet too and, shocking them further, announced he would ride to the sharefarm and ask Joe Jussep if there was anything he could do to help.

'Me too! Me too!' Madge cried, abandoning all parental ruling in her wild desire to see her friend. She stood, such a pathetic and eager figure in her wrinkled stockings and short wincyette dress, now pulled down and wrapped around her knees and held there in her excitement. Stan forgot his own worries and looked tenderly on her.

'Let her come,' he said. 'She can ride behind me.' Madge began to race off after an ecstatic bound in the air, then had to stop and turn to her mother for direction. She was fearful of what she might see on her mother's face.

But Mrs Rossmore, with a swift glance at Bert, could find no grounds for objection. It would not be wise to cross Stan at this stage. She had a pair of little sausage lips that were parted when she had a glitter of concern in her eyes. This is how her eyes were now.

Then she lowered them and dropped the little stack of bread and butter plates onto the tray Jessie held. 'Put on your warm skirt then,' she said, 'and your blue coat.' (It was her second best.)

Madge flashed a triumphant look to Jessie, she couldn't help it, unwise as well she knew. She went off straight of back, suddenly sedate as if about to prepare for a formal and dignified occasion. Stan went off to put the saddle back on Larry and Mr Rossmore, suddenly deciding he did not want a conversation with Mrs Rossmore, took his tobacco and went to look at the new peach and apricot trees bearing for the first time this spring.

Mrs Rossmore was left to Jessie. To Jessie's surprise she took a tea towel and stood beside the draining board with Jessie at the sink, nervous that she might not be as thorough as she should under this unaccustomed scrutiny. They both heard the thud of Larry's hoofs die away and Jessie, with an odd air of satisfaction, wrung out the dishcloth to give the kitchen table its best wipe down in a week.

'There they go!' she said.

There they go! thought Mrs Rossmore, her throat thick, her shaking hands hanging up the tea towel. She went rapidly out, her back telling Jessie she was not returning. Jessie gaped after her. Well, I must say that didn't last long. I needn't have been so fussy after all. She gathered up the saucepans from the back of the stove where she put them to dry thoroughly, something Mrs Rossmore had been trying to get her to do since she came six months ago. She took off her apron and hung it behind the pantry door and went off to her bedroom to get on with her fancywork until four o'clock. She was happy about Madge. Do the little thing good, she said to herself, climbing into her unmade bed and reaching for the wicker basket that held her tea cloth and cottons. She decided not to go on with the pansies in satin stitch, but to have a change and do some stem stitch on stems and leaves. She bit off the first thread from a silky skein, a lovely moss green, with a feeling of excitement.

Madge had a similar feeling sitting behind Stan on Larry, bouncing along the cart wheel tracks towards Jusseps. She lay her face in the curve of his back. Like a little gully, she thought, the tiniest gully in the world, rubbing her cheek there to make sure there was a ridge. 'You alright there?' Stan said with his face turned just enough for her to see his pinkish cheek and the freckles. She had freckles too and her hair was a little darker than his and not as curly. She hated both. Patty Jussep's hair was like a beautiful creamy silk table runner thrown over her head. Madge admired it, especially when it swung out then settled back exactly as it was before. Her straight fringe did the same.

'Let me,' Madge would say, giving it an unnecessary smoothing down when she and Patty were reading at playtime under the school pines, and Patty had both hands pushing the fringe up from her forehead.

Most of Cobargo favoured curly hair, which made Patty something of an oddity. 'Absolutely the straightest hair I've ever seen. Absolutely,' a Cobargo matron said.

'Draw a line, straight as Patty Jussep's hair,' a big rough Thompson boy hissed to his equally rough classmate in school.

'One day she'll be mistaken for a haystack and come to school with half a head where a sickle got her,' the classmate hissed back.

Madge wanted to tell Sister Joan on them, but Patty's scarlet cheeks and drowned blue eyes made her decide she wouldn't, and spare her friend the humiliation of hearing the words repeated.

In sight of the Jusseps' house, Stan and Madge saw Patty in the yard, her hair showing out like a white handkerchief on a dark bush.

'You'd know that hair anywhere,' Stan said. It was different the way he said it. Acceptable. Madge placed a small but passionate kiss in the hollow of his back.

She slid off Larry's back and stood quite close to Patty, barely able to believe it was real. Mary came down the back steps and crossed to them. Stan had no hat to remove, but nodded to Mary over Larry's neck, his fair chin bobbing in the thick, dark brown mane as if he had suddenly sprouted a beard. Mary smiled her big wide smile over her splendid teeth at the sight, and the two girls looked with joy on Stan and Mary's delight in each other.

'Come somewhere with me,' Patty whispered, as if Stan and Mary should be left alone. Patty turned towards the house holding Madge's hand in one of hers, with the other across her mouth in acute embarrassment. She was taking Madge into their shabby, untidy old place after the grand Rossmore house! Where would she take her? To the kitchen, where Joyce was washing the dinner things in slapdash fashion, anxious to be done and Malcolm and Bernie were wiping up, it being their turn to do it? If Patty had been visiting the Rossmores, she would most likely have been taken to Madge's room, kept neat by Jessie, the bed beautifully made and the latest holy pictures displayed on the chest of drawers or bedside table, Madge having told her this is where she put them. Patty felt great shame that hers could only be tucked into the frame of a picture of the Sacred Heart on the bedroom wall. She always thought the face of Jesus took on a wistful look when this happened, as if He were losing credibility. Patty shared the room with Joyce and Nina, she and Nina in a double bed and Joyce in a single one. They were made, but the dressing table would be littered and the one chair piled with clothes, even shoes, not with a cushion on a lovely slant as she imagined Madge's bedroom chair. She knew what she would do. Take Madge to the good room! Mary had washed the quilt after Mrs Jussep's feet marked it when she had died there. Madge would know she didn't sleep there, but there would be no need to mention this, and they could sit on the two chairs, and Patty, although it would be difficult, could avoid looking at the bed.

But reaching the sitting room, Patty saw the door of the good room was closed, not wide open as it always used to be, showing off the brass bed and the big hooked rug and the lamp with the pale pink base and pearly white chimney her mother would never allow anyone to light.

'We'll sit here,' Patty said, taking one half of the cane seat in the sitting room, pleased with the nicely plumped cushions, though wondering if Madge thought the patchwork terribly old fashioned. Madge saw the picture.

'Exactly the same as ours!' she cried, writhing her hands on her lap, fighting to control her excitement.

'Is it? Is it too? Is it truly?' Patty said, fearful that Madge's generous heart might be making this up.

'It is,' Madge said solemnly. 'Cross my heart and hope to die. It is the very, very same.'

They both glanced at the closed door at the word 'die'.

Madge spread her pleated skirt with downcast eyes and Patty
did the best she could with an old serge tunic handed down from
Joyce, worn now over a grey jumper, skimpy and badly matted
with constant washing. Patty wondered it if could be improved
with a belt, if she could find one. Madge, pink of face with her
freckles turned a rusty brown, looked pointedly to the doorway
leading to the veranda, keeping the door of the good room well
out of her vision. She wanted to know Patty's feelings about her
mother and those of all the others. Were they still crying on and
off? Everything looked normal, except that Mrs Jussep was missing. Madge had never seen Mary smile so wide. It was terrible not
to know, but she couldn't ask.

'I should have brought my jacks,' she said, now looking at the
rug in front of the fireplace. More shame invaded Patty. Her jacks
were in a bad way, two of the five with sharp edges liable to cut
you when you came to the part of the game where you picked
them up from between spread fingers.

'I've thought of something!' Madge said getting to her feet.
'We'll go to the creek and get us a set!'

Find smooth round stones just right for jacks, in the creek
bed with Madge? Nothing could be better! They would slip away
before Joyce saw them, for she considered herself in charge of the
house now and might find something for Patty to do, humiliating
as it would be with Madge there.

'Come on!' she cried, hand out. They took the way that lost
sight of the house almost at once, plunging down an embank-
ment to the cartwheel tracks that ran from the cowbails and
dairy to the main road. Crossing the tracks they tore down the
slope so steep you had to run, you were liable to tip over at any
other pace. Patty led the way, sure of her footing through a
spreading blackberry bush, hopping from rock to rock, around
which the bush rambled, and looking back to see that Madge was
following. They scrambled onto a log fallen across the creek and
together jumped onto a dry patch of the creek bed. Madge was
in charge now, digging with her shoe into a crusty edge of stones
bordering a shallow water hole, picking up and pocketing any

that were likely jacks. Patty with no pockets had to hold hers in a bulging hand.

'Let's spread them out somewhere and pick a set,' Madge said. They found a place, a patch of short grass, a new growth which had sprung up under a low growing wattle defying winter. They had to break the ends of several branches to fit underneath and sit, one on either side of the patch, a small soft green rug spread by nature for the very purpose of a game of jacks. This discovery shone simultaneously in the eyes of Madge and Patty.

'You go first,' Patty said, remembering Madge was the guest.

The eyes of the two of them following the flight of the first stone thrown upwards caught sight of two figures on a grassy slope on the opposite side of the creek, a couple of hundred yards away.

It was Stan and Mary sitting in the sun with Larry and Mary's grey, named Jock, behind them, reins trailing on the ground.

'Oh, look,' breathed Madge. 'Can they see us, do you think?'

The two of them slid deeper under the wattle. The feathery fronds tickled their faces but they got a good view of the reclining figures, with the sun behind making a red brown fire of Mary's hair and a lighter one of Stan's.

'They can't see us,' Patty breathed.

'What are they saying, I wonder?' said Madge. 'Oh, I wish we could hear!'

Stan was telling Mary he didn't intend going back to university. He hated the course, lectures were agony. He wanted to be a farmer, not a doctor. He slid down on the grass, and curved an arm over his head as if he were in bed and getting ready for sleep. Madge and Patty watched fascinated, half expecting Mary to slip down too and fit herself into the hollow of his body. But she put her hands farther back behind her, both supporting her and pinning down the reins of Larry and Jock, who were starting to fidget.

'I'm supposed to feel nerves with my fingers,' Stan said, 'real nerves. I can feel nothing.' Mary saw his hands smallish, with short fingers twitching in the agony he felt at their uselessness. She wanted to take hold of one of them but was embarrassed about her own hands. She never seemed able to wash them clean of milk after stripping cows twice a day. A sticky substance lingered between her fingers despite the thorough scrubbings. When she went to dances her pleasure in the dance was spoiled by wondering all the time if her partner was offended by her hands. She formed the habit of jamming her fingers together, causing the young Cobargo men, several with an eye on Mary, to want to inspect her hand to see if she had something wedged there.

So now, much as she wanted to, she couldn't take Stan's hand, just rub one of hers on the grass between them. Through half-closed eyes Stan was admiring her long fingers and clean nails cut level with her finger tips, for he hated the new fashion of long nails on women and hoped it never reached Cobargo.

Stan, with his eyes on Mary's hand, said she was the first he had told about his plan for abandoning his medical course. When she turned the hand over he took hold of it and she began to squeeze the fingers together, but he threaded his fingers between hers, so dry and cool she was filled with envy and mortification. Gradually she loosened the fingers, and when she freed her hand and clasped both around her knees, he left his lying on the grass almost as if it didn't belong to him. His eyes were nearly shut. Was he crying? Mary felt tears prick at her own eyes. She began thinking of her mother. Stan would open his eyes and take her hand in a moment and say he was sorry Mrs Jussep had died. He did not go to the funeral, so he hadn't yet spoken to her of it. Mary moved throwing her long nearly straight hair down her back. Stan put a hand out and twisted a fistful, without opening his eyes.

'You have the loveliest hair of any I've ever seen,' he said.

'I couldn't have,' Mary said, although believing him. 'All those girls you see in Sydney!'

'There's some in the course,' Stan said. 'One has this great awful moustache.'

Mary with her lovely smile was grateful for the moustache.

Stan put out a hand and touched her waist. He kept his eyes shut.

'I have to tell her, Mary,' he said. 'My mother.'

Mary went stiff. His mother. Mrs Rossmore with those lips she hardly ever put together. She looked briefly and swiftly on Stan and saw his lips were folded back, showing a gold filling between his two front teeth. Tom needed to go to the dentist. Mrs Jussep, just before she died, had been trying to arrange for the two of them to go to Bega and have some fillings done, staying overnight with a married cousin. Mary's face warmed. She had started to think of Stan at home all the time. With him at the dances and tennis matches. Stan and Mary, Mary and Stan. Stan Rossmore and Mary Jussep, Mrs Stan Rossmore, Mary Rossmore.

Stan opened his eyes and saw the deep pink of her cheek. 'Mary!' he said. 'How will I tell her?'

Mary saw her own mother, her face like grey mud in a creek bed long dried up, her hair a different grey, the face dead, the hair still with life there. Looking over the paddocks, some pale chocolate squares ready for spring planting, Mary found it hard to believe all this was still here and her mother gone. She jumped up rather quickly and put both arms over Jock's neck to climb on. When she was turning Jock she saw Stan mounting Larry with a sulky face.

'They're going,' Madge breathed to Patty. 'Where?'

'Somewhere to kiss passionately,' Patty breathed back. Madge tore a piece of bark from the tree and chewed it, then scrubbed her mouth free of the black and bitter taste.

'We might find some gum to chew,' Patty said, for the wattles often oozed a thick, pale substance encased in a crust that had to be picked with a sharp fingernail to release the gum, which was neither sweet nor savoury like a flavourless honey. Madge shook her head and scrambled into the clear, as if dismissing gum chewing as something belonging to a childish past. Her small face was tense, her chin up; she was striding away ahead of Patty who had to run to keep up. She put out a hand and took hold of the hem of Madge's coat.

'What will your mother and father say, do you think?' Patty said.

Madge dropped her head and slowed down. 'She mustn't know.' she said.

'If there is a wedding she'll have to know,' Patty said. Madge shook her head quite violently. She had a vision of her mother's little sausage lips parted and her eyes quite wild.

'Madge!' Patty cried urgently, for Madge was hurrying again along the creek bank and Patty had the terrible feeling she was hurrying out of her life as well. They crossed the creek on the log and up the hill, Madge sure of her footing now, Patty following, unsure of everything, most of all Madge.

'Will you tell your mother?' Patty asked, aware that it was a foolish question, for Madge had already answered more or less.

Then suddenly Patty stood still, holding out her arms to balance herself. In a moment she collapsed to the ground folding her legs under her and clinging to the tops of tussocks. Madge looked back and sat too, then slid down near her.

'I know,' she said. 'Your mother.' Patty lifted the hem of her tunic and scrubbed her face, only caring a little that she had no handkerchief.

Madge bowed her head until it touched her knees around which her arms were wrapped.

'Don't cry,' she said to Patty's neck, which was like the rim of a frail white china cup above her collar.

Patty cried on. Madge put a hand to her back running the tips of her fingers down the tunic. Then Patty flung herself around and lay her head against Madge's coat, one button cutting into her forehead and another scraping her chin.

This is how they were for a minute or so, like two abandoned puppies, separated from a pack of wilder, stronger dogs and uncertain whether to take up the struggle to rejoin them.

Then Madge called out 'Look!' and Patty lifted her head and there two or three hills away were Stan and Mary bringing the cows home for the afternoon milking. Stan was behind the herd and Mary on the lower side. Madge and Patty watched, urging them with their small beating hearts to swing their horses and come together. But Stan moved Larry around to the higher side, and Mary turned Jock to ride where Stan had been. Stan then urged Larry into a trot until well clear of the herd and several yards in front. The pummelling hearts of Madge and Patty said they had quarrelled. Perhaps not. Stan stood in the stirrups and flung an arm across his head in a large wave. Mary did not wave back. His back was to her so it would be a wasted effort.

Oh, gallop up to him, gallop up to him, cried Patty's heart. But if Mary had any such thoughts, the black cow Helen took charge of them, and decided then to break away and with her silly canter make for the clump of quince trees. Mary sent Jock flying after her.

'Quick!' Madge said, scrambling to her feet and pulling her away up the slope. 'Stan is going! He might go without me!'

Patty reached the cartwheel tracks first and helped hoist Madge up by the shoulders of her coat. Madge wriggled the coat back into position again and flew ahead. 'Stan might forget me!' she cried.

They saw him talking to Mr Jussep near the back gate to the house. Madge, as if still in fear of being left behind, ran faster, throwing her arms over her head like a swimmer.

Stan pulled her up onto Larry and she was crushed behind him, closing her eyes in her small glowing face as if the visit had now reached a peak of perfection. Mr Jussep stook back courteously to acknowledge the departure and Madge, when Larry moved off, flapped an arm in Patty's direction.

They rode in silence until within sight of the Rossmores' house. Madge freed her mouth from against Stan's warm and quivering back.

'Will you marry Mary Jussep?' she asked.

Stan kicked Larry into a canter and Madge needed to put her face back and cling tighter.

'I'm marrying no one!' Stan threw over his shoulder.

Madge saw behind her shut eyes Mrs Rossmore's little sausage lips come together and her eyelids fall.

It was like a window closing suddenly on a celebration inside a room, for fear some of the jubilation might escape.

A Clear Conscience

Let the screech-owls screech and the moralists snap and yap at my heels — I am unmoved. I am not to blame.

My innocence, however, is not the issue. My only reason for retelling the tale is to establish the truth of what happened once and for all. My aim, in a word, is lucidity, above all lucidity. As if by vapours from some putrid swamp, the truth has become so clouded by fabrication and false report that the facts of the case have all but disappeared from view.

Our first meeting is etched clearly in my memory. It was at brunch at the Foleys, one Sunday in April. Brunch was served on a green tray in the courtyard, green being more a summer luncheon colour I should have thought, but the Foleys have never been sticklers for detail. The warm, crusty croissants were a comfort, the coffee a mild Colombian roast, and high up above in the crown of the umbrella tree there were honeybirds creating havoc. The womenfolk were still pottering in the kitchen, I remember, and Roy Foley was being faintly disagreeable, sniffing around the main point of the conversation (my script), hesitating to lunge. 'Yes, I like it, Roger, I like it very much,' he kept saying, toying with the Swiss marmalade with those long, unaccountably tanned fingers of his. 'Yes, I do like it, Roger, and God knows I get very little I do like coming across my desk these days.' He really talks like that — 'coming across my desk'. 'But I'm wondering about the audience appeal side of it ...' Here he trailed off. And at that very instant she wandered out through the French doors into the courtyard.

She headed towards us with the air of a child looking for a lost ball, not exactly disregarding us, but preoccupied with something else. In a yellow tracksuit. Of course, the Russians and Germans have written a lot of high-sounding rubbish about 'love at first sight' (so-called), describing in tedious, overblown detail how it strikes its victims like a cobra, like cholera or a bolt of lightning. Well, no aurora borealis lit up the sky for me, I assure you, and indeed I find that whole nineteenth century dramatisation of a simple first frisson morbid and totally unconvincing. The yellow struck me, I admit, and the cold, sad, cat's eyes, but that's all.

'Ah, Louise, Louise, this is Roger, a friend of ours — or perhaps you met last — er — Saturday, was it?' Roy was dithering. Louise circled slowly and sat down. Roy rambled on a bit, trying to light on a suitable topic for three people who didn't care about each other to exchange views on. He failed. Louise, I knew, was his sister-in-law. Our wives bustled out with more coffee, pumpernickel and cheese and swept Louise up in a gust of sisterly good humour. Borne aloft briefly on their bonhomie, she smiled and chatted for a few moments and then seemed to sink again, eddying downwards in a slow spiral of despondency.

I was beginning to be intrigued. Just pinpricks of quickened interest, mind you, nothing of consequence. I drew her out. She wrote. Oh? What? Plays. Oh, really? Anything I'd have seen? Probably not. Try me. And so on. Her tense stillness was engaging. Did it suggest she was disconcertingly close or immeasurably far away? My wife, meanwhile, was darting in and out of the conversation like a wasp — 'Pass the cheese', 'Isn't it *hot*?', 'And where are you living?' (Not 'do you live', I noticed.) Like all rudderless women my wife is forever getting her bearings. Despite her peevish forays, however, Louise and I forged a delicate link. When the others wandered off to the far end of the courtyard to admire Roy's bromeliads, I caught her eye across the table strewn with coffee-cups and croissant flakes and suggested we meet again before too long and talk about her latest script — after all, I was an old hand. She wasn't averse to the idea and even smiled, I thought, perhaps a little kittenishly. As we drove home, I was aware of a pleasant yellowish blur at the edges of my mind.

_____

On reading my description of our first meeting, I must say, in the interests of absolute lucidity, that the description is, in certain details, somewhat impressionistic. In fact, to be absolutely candid, it's largely nonsense. And, again, I mainly blame the Germans and the Russians: they've made it quite impossible for us to grasp *the thing in itself* any more, stripped of all the verbal dross and metaphysical flimflam. I mean, 'Colombian roast', 'first frisson', 'slow spiral of despondency' — God alone knows where I dredged all that up from. Not that the versions concocted by my wife, or Roy's, bear any closer relation to the truth — far from it. According to one of my wife's more hysterical accounts, for instance, I set the whole thing up expressly to humiliate her in front of our friends and it was nothing but a cynical, ruthless attempt to murder our marriage, while Roy's wife, not to be upstaged, claimed for months that Roy had engineered the whole thing to humiliate *her*. Why would he bother? Women are born spinners of tales, as a rule with themselves as the central character.

No, that's all a lot of hogwash and the unadorned facts are these: technically, I first met Louise quite by chance, improbably as it may sound, at an ABC staff party in the company of a poet wearing a beard and a Hawaiian shirt, and I found her attractive and not, I thought at the time, disinclined to pursue the dialogue we had established. So I asked Roy Foley, who was hovering, to invite us both to lunch some time. So he did. And quite frankly, I was captivated. There is nothing more seductive than utter vulnerability sprinkled with the grit of self-respect. Claws concealed by silky paws.

We did meet again, of course, after the Foleys' lunch, and discussed her play over Viennese cakes and smoky tea in a smart, colour-coordinated cafe with bland pastel prints on the walls, near Taylor Square. What drew me on? I think her restrained playfulness, the grace and tenderness of the pale hands reaching across the table to fondle petals, napkins, even the fragile handle of my teacup, together with the feline watchfulness of her black-edged eyes, as hard, and soft, as amber beads. I tracked her through the maze of her playscript, pruning here and nurturing there, and when we emerged at the other end, relaxed, relieved and stimulated, I thought of home, my wife, my blinkered Trotskyite daughter and my son, his mind askew with tarot cards and natural living, and knew, with a quiver of certainty and a sudden dry stickiness on the roof of my mouth, that I was about to commit adultery.

I was not 'in love'. I emphasise this point because befuddling notions such as this have needlessly confused the issue all along. At night, when the children were out at their futile meetings about solidarity with Bolivian miners and herbal cures for stomach cancer, my wife would be forever whining at me: 'Are you in love with someone else? You're in love with someone else.' How tiresome it was and ultimately meaningless. What is it supposed to mean, this phrase 'in love'? What specific sensations does it refer to in the real world, if any, and, if any, why not name them?

I have been open and frank about my attitude to these questions since adolescence. I have consistently maintained that concepts such as 'commitment', 'responsibility' and 'fidelity' are not so much outmoded as meaningless, and meaningless in the most direct sense: these words do not refer to anything identifiable in the real world. What *is* identifiable is that I entered into a contract of cohabitation and mutual consideration with my wife. Why such a contract should exclude emotional involvement and occasional copulation with other persons has never been clear to me and I have never, or almost never, subscribed to that view of it. However, as I explained to Louise right at the start, or as near the start as practicable, the validity of the contract itself was always permanent as far as I was concerned. My wife is a mean-spirited, snappish creature, and my children are bizarre and in the thrall of ideologies which are stultifying and alien to me, yet on the whole the arrangement works well enough. I see no reason to terminate it. But it includes, as far as I am concerned, the possibility of my indulging myself emotionally and diverting myself sexually with other people from time to time. I'm not talking about *ménages à trois*, swinging couples or asking my wife to entertain my mistress at morning tea or any of that modern claptrap. I don't claim to be in the avant-garde, I merely claim to be civilised. I had thought Louise understood that from the outset.

The winter drew us together. There were picnics in Centennial Park, surrounded by mallee-hens, Italian children and mohair rugs; there were dinners at cosy French restaurants and takeaway Chinese on Sundays; we even hired a car once and drove down to Gerringong to sit on the huge white sweep of beach, high up where the tussock-grass starts, and watch the milky green surf batter the sand; and there were evenings at home in her tiny lamp-lit flat, eating curry with a fork and discussing her play, which by then was in production and not going smoothly. I noticed, naturally, the growing insistence that we arrange our next meeting for a specific place and time; I noted, too, the unobtrusive ways she wove the fringes of our separate lives together, and couldn't help being struck by the little surge of excitement that always came over her when we met. But I always thought she understood my terms.

Looking back, I think perhaps Louise mistook the trappings of passion for passion itself. She misread my responses. The simple fact is that she invited a sort of gentle savagery on my part, and enjoyed it, and was so abundantly easy to pleasure. Certain lips may purse with distaste at such intimate details, but I must record for the sake of complete lucidity that when she made love to me, eyes closed, awash with pleasure, mewing, arching and scratching, I found it, for banal chemical reasons, infinitely arousing. It inflamed me, engorged me. But it wasn't passion. (I honestly believe, with hindsight, that I've only felt real passion twice: once for my wife, when we were young and it just welled up inside me, spontaneously like hunger or nausea, because everything about her — her legs sheathed in stockings, her pale fingers, her baby-talk, her rhythmic walk, the way she put spectacles on to read a book, her yawns, her shoulder-blades, everything, everything,

everything was utterly beautiful; the second time it was for a waiter in a spaghetti-house near Taylor Square, it lasted three weeks and was a total mystery to both of us. It was not passion I felt for Louise.)

At some level, it now transpires, Louise and I were writing our lives into vastly different scripts. Oddly enough, it was Roy who first alerted me to it, in his heavy-footed way. We'd met entirely by chance at the Stag near Taylor Square (and not, as Roy would later have it, in the foyer of the Academy Cinema — Roy is too precious by half about his reputation, there is nothing remotely *louche* about the Stag). I'd looked to one side after ordering a drink, picking out faces and profiles in the reddish gloom, and my eyes had connected with Roy's. There he was, one elbow on the bar in the classic pose. He'd been grinning at me (but to himself) for some minutes, it would seem. It was probably not his first drink he was clutching.

'And how's the gay Lothario?' he asked abruptly.

Various ripostes came to mind, but I heard myself answer rather feebly: 'And what's that supposed to mean?'

'It's supposed to mean,' he said with a fixed grin, 'that I gather you've been seeing rather a lot of my sister-in-law lately.' It was entirely unlike Roy to be so direct. He was obviously squiffy, not to say sozzled.

'That's what you gather, is it?' I said, looking straight ahead at myself in the mirror behind the bar.

'Yes, it is. It's what everyone gathers.' He sidled closer. 'Look, Roger, you may not think it's any of my business but —' I kept staring at myself in the mirror. In the red light my skin had an oddly greenish tinge to it. 'But —' he said again, fumbling for the *mot juste*, 'I think I should warn you that you may be getting in deeper than you think.' This was more like Roy Foley.

'Say what you mean, Roy, for God's sake.'

'Well, Louise is pretty wound up about what you're doing to her — I mean, she's been around at our place every second night, crying her eyes out, I mean, she's really upset, she doesn't know what the hell's going on.'

'Well, for a start, she's in a mess with her play, the director's totally screwed it up, no wonder she's at screaming point. If anything, I thought I was giving her quite a lot of support at a critical time.' Even in his inebriated state Roy was not impressed. His grin had faded.

'That's not the problem, mate.' *Mate*? 'The problem's you. Of course, you're sitting pretty. Best of both worlds and all that. Louise is at breaking point. You'd better sort it out pretty quickly.'

There's a pause while I stretch out my hand, take my glass, drink two mouthfuls and put my glass back on the counter. In the mirror our faces are etched with green. I shift my weight to the other foot.

'Roy, you're right — it isn't any of your business,' I say. Roy downs his drink, lightly tongues his lips, wheels and walks out. All style and no substance. Commonplace.

The above is a verbatim report of the conversation. Roy's little embellishments to the effect that I denied all involvement with Louise and was in fact in the company at the time of the treacherous director himself, Colin Crewe, is just so much humbug. How does this sort of garbage ever gain credence? I did indeed bump into Colin in the men's room as I was about to leave, but that's all there was to it.

I then did what everyone would do in the circumstances: I went straight home to my wife. I wondered vaguely as I watched her move about the house switching lights on and off, wrapping and unwrapping things and answering the telephone, if she had any inkling of what was afoot, but rather thought not. Not, I might warn the snarling moralists, that there was in all this the slightest element of deceit on my part. *Au contraire*: my wife and I have a civilised understanding that neither of us will conceal information about extramarital adventures from the other *if such information is requested*. I might add that in twenty years of marriage my wife has never confessed to any extramarital affairs, so either she has not kept her side of the bargain or her fantasy-life is so impoverished it simply doesn't run to such escapades.

There was, therefore, no question of deceit. I want that matter cleared up once and for all. In fact, it is against all such mind-muddying relativistic concepts as 'deceit' and 'honesty' that I am embattled. I stand for truth — more than that, I stand for *the* truth about any given situation. Religion and a lot of addle-brained Germans have, of course, concocted between them a lot of narcotic fantasies about 'spiritual truths', 'moral purity' and so on, and the Russians haven't helped, either. Nor, as the case of my son makes perfectly plain, have all these muddleheaded gurus currently befuddling the minds of the young. It is, as I say, precisely against this kind of muddying and befuddling of the mind and its rational processes that I take up the cudgels. I throw down the gauntlet to the irrational and mysterious, to soothsaying, spiritualism and psychic powers, to astral travel, auras and arcane philosophies, to inner truths and insipid Christliness, to voodoo and visitors from outer space, vegetarianism and Madame Blavatsky; I spit on your mullahs and Marxists, your Mormons and Maoists, your faith-healers and fateful signs, on Dostoevsky and Dylan, on Pascal and Pope John Paul — humbug, that's what it all is, inane gibberish and fatuous humbug!

I explained all this to Louise the next time I saw her. What I urgently wanted her to grasp was that, whatever she might choose to do with the characters in her play, however she might wish to manipulate them and label them ('wicked roué', 'hardly-done-by wife', 'grasping capitalist', 'innocent dupe' and so on — the usual), she must not do that to me in real life. I won't be written into anyone's script. I refuse point-blank to be cast as an irresponsible lover or deceitful husband, I utterly reject all attempts to categorise me as a selfish fence-sitter, amoral lecher, pusillanimous Don Juan. The facts are, as I pointed out to Louise at the time, that we had an arrangement which provided for regular meetings to our mutual satisfaction and nothing more. It wasn't a melodrama we were acting out, but life itself. (She seemed distracted, disconsolate, disconnected. Did I sense disdain?) I tried then, adroitly, as I thought, with the sole aim of sparing her feelings, to turn the conversation to her play. She tossed her hair out of her eyes (we were sitting uncomfortably at her kitchen table), became absorbed in her fingernails and refused to communicate. I knew, of course, that rehearsals were going badly — the cretinous Colin Crewe had totally misread her script and he flew into a rage, flailing his arms, at the merest suggestion that the writer's opinion on what he was doing might count for something — but I thought that with some skilful manoeuvring I might induce her to change tracks. I failed. So embedded was she in her own blank misery, so trapped inside the role of victim, that nothing apart from her misery had any claim on her attention. I went into the other room and watched a British comedy on television. Then, *faute de mieux*, went home. I will not tolerate people who, while in full possession of their faculties, dive head first into a sea of misery and then thrash about screaming for help. Self-immolation is the supreme idiocy.

That night, for the first time since we'd met, I felt a minute but identifiable bolt of elation as her door clicked shut behind me. This was not a good sign.

As long as man looks at the world around him through the prism of poetry he'll get nowhere. I fell to contemplating this truth as I sat on my balcony later that evening and looked out across the city — sleek slabs of lighted glass and masonry, thrusting up into the mindless, almost starless Sydney sky. I gazed up at it. *La grandeur de l'homme est grande en ce qu'il se connaît misérable. Un arbre ne se connaît pas misérable.* 'Man's greatness lies in knowing himself to be miserable. A tree does not know itself to be miserable.' Well, no, it wouldn't do, of course, because it's a tree. What mystical mumbo-jumbo! Poetry, not a *pensée*! No, the vault of heaven provoked no *angoisse* in me, because, unlike Pascal at Port-Royal three hundred years before, I knew exactly what it was. Man 'a thinking reed', *les dieux infinis* — pretty words concealing ignorance. Poeticise ignorance and it becomes a 'truth' — a petty conjuring trick, no more. As I keep telling my son, entangled in his karma and dharma and to kwong dai, there is no mystery, only the still unknown. Of course, his head is so stuffed with marijuana and magical mantras that he just stares at me glassily and says I should seek the Godhead within me. I really think all this rabbit-food is having a bad effect on his brain.

I wish, on reflection, that I had made all this plainer to Louise while I had the chance.

The climax came the night her play opened, and the denouement was swift to follow. This fact has, naturally, been played down by those intent on turning the whole affair into a tragedy with Louise in the role of an unquenched Phaedra. It was not a tragedy, nor was it a melodrama, with me playing the part of green-eyed villain. It was purely and simply an arrangement which was misunderstood by one party and went wrong. It was a night of inky blackness in mid-July, a night for succubi and unclean spirits, and at the Phoenix Theatre they were out in force. Inside the grubby foyer, hung with posters proclaiming past disasters and littered with polystyrene cups, all was oddly hushed. Little huddles of people in greys and browns stood around in the cold, dragging out conversations they couldn't remember beginning. The bell rang and the grey-brown knots untied themselves and drifted towards the stairs. Louise came in swiftly from the street looking distraught and sealed off. She barely nodded as she headed for the stairs. I felt empty. When the lights had dimmed, I scuttled up the stairs and into a seat near the exit. There were a few rasping coughs and a spotlight pierced the blackness. It had begun.

The disaster was total. The play teetered for ten minutes on the brink, while the audience congealed into a heavy mass of indifference, and then plummeted. I cringed. The air was brittle with anxiety. Interval became a hysterical attempt to put a bright face on it. 'Odd, very odd', 'I'm not sure I'm quite *into* it yet', 'The lighting's absolutely marvellous — who did it again?' 'I can't quite see where it's headed yet — it's certainly unusual ...' Eyes flick around the foyer, seeking escape. Over near the door I espy the *Herald* critic perusing his programme with distaste. Louise has fled into the lane outside. Roy wisely spends the interval in the men's washroom.

After the second half, which in mortification on Louise's behalf I have virtually wiped from my mind, I also fled. As I darted out the door I caught sight of Roy laughing loudly in the emptiness of the foyer as he passed a white wine to the *Herald* critic. Louise was nowhere to be seen. I slipped out into the blackness of the lane and headed for the Stag. I needed to collect my thoughts. In the bar I stared morosely into the glittering black mirror behind the bottles and tried to focus on what had to be done. I arrived at Louise's rather late feeling decidedly unsettled. And for some strange, no doubt physiological, reason, pitiless.

Louise was in a pitiful state. In fact, she was lying groggy and wretched on the floor of the sitting-room, with a lamp still burning in one corner and the room bathed in pale green light from the lampshade. I made black coffee in silence in the kitchen. She drank it without saying a word. Then it started.

'Well, what a fiasco,' she murmured.

'Yes.'

'I wish I were dead.'

'Don't be silly.' I sat down on the floor beside her. She leant back against the armchair under the lamp. 'Anyway, it wasn't your fault, Louise. Colin wrecked it.' I looked out at the multicoloured sky, pulsating with neons. There was, of course, no moon. I had nothing much to say.

'It's not just that.' Here we go.

'What is it?'

'Don't you know?' Drawn, bedraggled, haggard.

I snorted. Why did I snort? A mystery of the organism. I hadn't meant to. The effect was galvanising.

'Well, let me tell you, Roger.' She struggled up into a sitting position. 'I really *loved* you — did you know that?' I winced. How I hate that word! Jesus loves you, your mother loves you, you love your dog, your wife, rhubarb pie — what in God's name does it mean? I wonder if there's a tribe of people somewhere who have no word for it but instead say what they mean. Then she let fly with a long, ill-considered tirade about my supposed selfishness, my callous indifference to others (her), my refusal to consider her wants and needs, my insistence on playing the game according to my rules, my lack of feeling, my arbitrary sexual behaviour —there's no need to document it word for word, the script can be heard on late-night television any night of the week. 'I feel so cheated,' she said finally, lapsing into moody silence. Her face coloured appealingly.

'I don't know what you expected from me, Louise,' I said after a measured pause. 'I had no idea you felt so strongly. You knew right from the start — there was never any question about it — that what we had was all I wanted. I never asked you for any sort of commitment. And I don't see why we can't continue like that.' What could have been clearer and more to the point than that?

'Because it's not what *I* want, that's why. Feelings aren't like a dried flower arrangement you just stick in a vase and stand back and admire, you know. They grow. I'm involved. I want more. I can't stand the way you go back to your wife at eleven-thirty. I hate your wife. You don't seem to like her very much yourself.' She was very agitated, hence the non sequiturs.

'Look, you're overwrought, what with what happened tonight and everything. Why don't we talk about this some other time when you're feeling calmer?' For some reason this seemed to make her even more agitated. 'Of course I'm bloody overwrought!' she said — well, yelled, actually. 'I've been crushed utterly. I thought I had a lover and I've got a gentleman caller, I thought I had a love affair and I've got an arrangement, I thought I had a play and I've got ... nothing. I've got nothing.'

There was a strained pause and then soft sobs. My mind hovered beneath the peeling ceiling, curling around the jagged flakes of paint, jabbing at the yellowing corners. Down on the carpet Louise was sobbing. I couldn't come down.

'I feel so empty,' she said.

'Do you want me to go?'

'Do what you like.'

'I'll go.' We sat there, hunched against the settee, for what must have been another half an hour in total silence. Even the sky outside quietened into an inky blue. The refrigerator hummed, a clock ticked, and Louise gulped and dabbed and became silent.

Finally she stirred. 'I think I'll have a bath.' That's all she said. Softly, simply. She made to get up.

'Let me run it for you,' I said and made for the bathroom. As I turned on the taps and watched the steaming water gush out, I suddenly felt strong again, and free, almost exhilarated. 'I'll go and leave you to your bath,' I said with a small smile I knew I was copying from television. 'Have a good sleep and I'll call you tomorrow.' She got up. 'Bye, then,' she said and went into the bathroom. The door clicked softly shut. Once I was outside, I now know, she got into the bath, slit her wrists and died in a sea of warm blood.

Those, then, are the facts. As is evident, I trust, to all but the most prejudiced observer, the culprit in this most unfortunate affair, if it is necessary to identify one, is poetry — in the broadest sense. By this I mean that it was the demonic urge to write herself into an ornamented story, to observe genre in every detail of her own life, that was to blame for Louise's untimely end. Now, I am not naive enough to think that this can be altogether avoided. It's just that the truly cultivated man, the truly free man, must choose with taste from a range of narratives. Louise tried to write me into a romance of the kind you buy at airport kiosks. That was her mistake. These perceptions will, I know, be well beyond the purview of the Mr and Mrs Foleys of this world. I need not expatiate on *their* interpretation of events — the misjudged, malicious twaddle they've been peddling as their version bears eloquent testimony to the doltish level of their thinking.

My aim has been to set the record straight, not self-justification, to cast the light of reason on a confused series of events, not to apportion blame. All the same, I hope my main point is apparent enough: my conscience is clear.

Enough Rope

Every now and then an energy builds up in me and I know that it's time to visit Michael. Quite suddenly everything, the set of rooms I move through, the seesaw glare and darkness as I pass outside and in, the glint of the dam down on the boundary, becomes the background to a dream.

I rush the boys off to the school-bus and throw my packed bag into the car. Ian just watches me. But we've finished seeding and I haven't visited my mother for a long time.

At the first roadhouse in the metropolitan area I ring Michael at the school where he is teaching.

'Oh hello,' he says. I can hear the faint, endless barracking of children in a playground. 'Tonight? Yes, fine, see you then.' He could be making an appointment with an anxious parent.

I always arrive rather windswept on Michael's doorstep. This is a tradition. It is not windy on the quiet streets of Lakeside Estate where Michael has lived since his marriage. But he used to live on the top floor of a block of flats with a cosmopolitan's-eye view of Perth. In those days, when the boys were very young, I was always late. I would stand for a moment in the cold tunnels of city air and study the careful schoolteacher script of *M. Makevis* beside the door.

I still wear an air of haste and escape now, dodging among the hanging baskets on Michael's discreet front porch. It is a form of apology. I juggle with my bottles in their damp paper sleeves — beer, wine or champagne, I try to vary them so as not to look too predictable.

'Bon soir', says Michael, while his door-chimes are still pealing. This greeting is again a tradition. Years ago at teachers' college, we liked to season our exchanges with 'adieu' and 'merci bien' and 'c'est pas mal tu sais'. Unlike the French however, we do not kiss on meeting. It leaves, has always left, a tiny gap, during which Michael takes my bottles into the kitchen and I try to decide where to sit.

There is something deliberate about Michael's clatter in the kitchen.

'Is Lauren home?' I call across the bar.

'She's rehearsing.' He brings in our drinks. 'She's got a recital next week.'

She wasn't home the last time I visited either.

'Your house is looking great', I say, though in this dimmed light I can't notice any change. Couches seem to grow out of the pale carpet. The smoky glass of the coffee table is still unsmudged and bare. It stretches between us, shin to shin. His are crossed, in pale jeans.

'We finished the music room last week.' He puts down his drink. 'Would you like to have a look?'

For the first time he leads me into the private part of his house. An old sensation of conspiracy unfolds as I follow him down a corridor. We used to stifle laughter in my mother's kitchen once, making coffee late at night. Something about the canisters' diminuendo from big FLOUR to little TEA ...

'... but the view'll improve when the trees have grown', he is saying. We are crossing a little courtyard. I glimpse a plastic washing basket, an upturned mop, ordinary domesticity. 'She always hated me listening when she practised.' He smiles at this over his shoulder as he unlocks the door.

The music room smells new, of pine and cement. Lauren's baby grand stands sleek and black in the middle of the room. There is an old couch under a bare window. Michael stays by the door.

'I bet Lauren's in here all the time', I say, opening the piano.

'Not a great deal yet.' His hand is on the light switch, ready to go. 'She's very involved with this Bach group. Out nearly every night. Though she's got a friend, a flautist, who comes over in the day sometimes to play duets.'

He locks the door again as we go out.

'How are the boys?'

This is better. We are on sure ground here. For Michael this is no routine enquiry. They are restless, I say, and too rough with each other at the moment. Ian says they need pulling into line. My voice is hesitant. I think they're bored at school.

Michael nods. He starts talking about his class. The theme this term is the planets: the space-ship they're building is becoming more complex than he can always understand. It incorporates the school computer. The boys in his class are working really well together since they started this project.

I say I do not think Miss MacPherson at the Yardoo Primary goes in for the space age. 'I wish *you* taught the boys.' I think I say this every time I see him. And he just gives the same half smile and goes on talking. Of course. Even as a student Michael had his own ideas. I listened, but ended up going with the stream: *don't let the little bastards get you down.*

I think about the time I brought the boys here to see Michael. As usual we were staying with my mother.

'You certainly have your hands full', my mother always says.

Michael had taped the World Cup soccer final ready for them on his video. He showed them how to make a milkshake.

'Wow this place is like that TV commercial', I heard them tell him in the kitchen. They swivelled on his barstools and tried their jokes on him.

'Can we go to Michael's?' they still ask me when we're driving to the city.

Michael is still talking. This year he has been posted to a school in a wealthy middle-class area. The kids are great — Michael always says this about his classes, they're *his* kids now — but there are different sorts of problems. Some of the parents push their children, ask Michael when he'll be giving the class real work to do.

'Have I told you this already?'

'No no, go on.' I can watch him as I used to when he talked. In winter his face is so pale it's almost luminous. 'Milkface': that's what the kids called him when he first came to Australia. He stood on the edge of the playground in the shorts made by his mother and saw that no one else wore shorts below the knee. He told me that once.

'Things are changing', he is saying. 'I think the children are the only ones who can keep up.' Now he's cupped his palm and balanced his empty glass on it. 'But you have to trust them, you have to let them go a bit ...' He flicks his glass with the other hand and strikes a precarious note.

Michael and Lauren have no children. This has never surprised me although they've been married for some years. Perhaps it's because I always think of Lauren as being very young. She must be in her late twenties now, but the last time I saw her she was as thin and childlike as ever. She has a little flat white face, with eyes and nose and mouth crowded together, and a bush of crinkly brown hair springing back from her forehead.

I couldn't say that I really know Lauren. When Michael wrote to tell me he was married, I arrived at the new house with champagne and a wedding present. Michael met me juggling a glass of dissolving disprin. Lauren had a headache, she was going to bed. She sat in a dressing-gown on the arm of his chair while he opened the present.

'Thanks very much', she said as she got up to leave.

She was very gifted, Michael explained in a low voice. Her mother had pushed her, practice six hours a day, no friends, talent quests, frilly dresses. It was amazing she still wanted to play at all. She was very strong really, knew what she wanted. He was helping her work towards that.

Yes, I'd said then, looking around me. Lakeside Estate. Full-page, colour supplement, *Where your dreams become realities*. We drank a toast to his marriage, smiling but not finding much to say.

I've never told Michael about the time I saw him and Lauren at the lake. We were down for the Show, I'd taken the boys there to let off steam. They disappeared, I sat in the car to look at people. It was a wet and windy Sunday afternoon.

Some sort of a club, or an office on picnic, was playing a rather bossy game of cricket with an outfield of girlfriends slouching among the eskies. I saw them suddenly, weaving their way through the players. Their familiarity, Michael's leather jacket, Lauren's hunched shoulders and blowing woolly hair, materialised for me as if I'd been expecting them.

I saw Lauren break away, veer towards the lake, stand looking down with her hands in the pockets of her parka. Michael followed, said something to her, set off towards the kiosk. He walked right near my car on his way back to her. I saw that he was holding two icecreams. His head was bent and he had a little smile on his face. You've got your hands full, Michael, I caught myself thinking.

Tonight Michael and I are shifting fast from second gear into third. We haven't got this far past the rituals for a long time. Michael's given up on getting drinks for us from his bar. He's put a flagon of wine and the whisky bottle on the table between us. Through it I discover an aquarium view of my blind stockinged feet.

Better make this my last, I think into my wine. Or second last. But already I'm feeling that gathering of cheer that means it could be too late for limits. Recently I've been rather pushing the limits, all around the district. *You* certainly enjoyed yourself, people tell me later. The end of every social occasion has been a blank. When I come to, I'm alone in a quietly throbbing car. Ian is outside, opening our gate in the moonlight. He gets back in the car, I shut my eyes, the car lurches forward, then throbs to itself again. I open my eyes. Ian is closing the gate. Limits.

I don't want Michael to know this. I don't want him to have to escort me reeling to the car. Or worse. Throwing up into his native garden. There's a lot I don't want him to know about me. My triviality. My laziness. How much I weigh. Our relationship, as I've often told myself, is characterised by a beautiful restraint.

Although tonight Michael himself is not holding back, I notice. As he leans forward to pour himself another whisky, a strand of hair falls across his forehead. He leaves it there. He rips open a packet of peanuts and makes an avalanche of them into a bowl. Both of us ladle up peanuts and munch in an absent-minded way.

'You know Michael', I say, 'there isn't one sign of Lauren in this room'.

He looks at me.

'Ah yes.' My remark hangs between us. 'Ah yes. My waiting room.'

'Oh I don't mean ...'

'My waiting room. Where I *wait*.' There's that little smile again that creases up his eyes.

'Lauren's rehearsing ...'

'Ah yes.' I don't recognise the new cut of his tone. It goes with the smile. '*And* Lauren cannot drive. Therefore the flautist must give her a lift. The Polish flautist.'

This time I say nothing.

'And I wait.' He says this to me as if I might accuse him of something.

Michael and I can't sit and face each other any more. Michael has wandered off somewhere. But first he's put on some soft jazz, as if to keep me company.

I'm sorry, I say across this room where I don't belong. I've never known what Michael wanted of me. Even if that meant keeping away.

What now? I lean back, shut my eyes, waiting. But my centre of gravity seems to have moved to my left ear. I slide my cheek down into the rough surface of Michael's couch. With one eye I survey a tweed horizon. I see the colours of the native garden growing across this suburban block. Grey sand laps the feet of a raw brown fence. Dull green nursery saplings shake their name-tags beside gravel paths. He says their names to himself as he passes. One day they will wave a private shelter around his house, her music room.

How do I know about waiting?

Once Michael and I sat in a cafe, saying goodbye. We had both just graduated. Michael was leaving for Europe the next day. I didn't know where I was going.

It was January, but it had been a day of freak tropical rain. Cars swished by outside in a luxuriant greenish twilight. The jukebox was playing bouzouki music, the cafe-owner smiled at us. We'd often sat here, it was one of the few places in this city with any atmosphere, we said. But this time Michael kept checking his watch. He showed me his ticket and stowed it away again with careful fingers.

'I'd better get you home. I'd better get myself home. My last night and all that.' He smiled at me for our old shared bondage. I did not respond. Our widowed mothers sat on opposite sides of the city. His mother wore black, served sweet black coffee in tiny cups, spoke in another language. But about the same things, Michael said. Probed and warned, chased up lineages. We had been encircled. But he was getting away.

I couldn't look at him. This new, harder presence, no longer attending me, was suddenly proof of its own value. I felt him at the edge of my shoulder, at the tips of my fingers, at arm's length where I had been so careful to keep him. Quiet, pale Michael Makevis.

'Wait!' I said outside the cafe. I was scrabbling in strange desperation for my sunglasses. It had stopped raining, the footpath glared, the air was again thin and bright.

The hallway at home was stuffy.

'That you love?' I chose not to answer. I could still hear his car at the end of our road.

'Let-ter!' She must be lying down because of the heat … There was a manila envelope waiting for me under the jardiniere. OHMS. My posting had come. Grades 3 and 4, Yardoo Primary.

It is raining now, steady winter rain beating on the hollow of Michael's house. The sound has been creeping up on me ever since the music died. The button glows red on the stereo. Salt dribbles from the empty peanut packet onto the glass table. No Michael.

I leap up from the couch, and hobbling on my numbed left foot as if I'm tethered, open the front door. My car still sits askew on the verge, its wheels streaked with wet country dust. The air is very cold. Stamping my foot to life, I shut the door.

I move swiftly now through every room of Michael's house, opening and closing doors, snapping lights on and off. The rooms are smaller than you think back here. I note in passing an intense disorder. Unmade beds in two rooms. I move on. It is not until I come to the end of the corridor that I know he must be in the music room.

I don't switch on the light. He is sitting on the couch under the window. I go across to him.

He says: 'It's worse when it rains. It's like the whole planet's poisoned.'

Back in the house a phone starts ringing. Lauren? My mother? It doesn't matter. I am moving quite by instinct now.

TIM HERBERT

Pumpkin Max

Guttersnipes and starbursts were often on Benny's mind. An aversion to any kind of middle ground. Meantime, his lover Joseph had his own routine to perform; one that kept him ribbing and hissing for much of the morning and getting Benny in a fluster.

'We are all of us lying in the gutter; but some of us are looking at the stars.'

'Such a tired old cliché, Benny,' said Joseph, goading him further with a moonstruck stare.

Benny knew he was innocent. That he had only just discovered the glittering quotation.

'Do you know whose lines you're pilfering?' asked Joseph.

Lingering by the window, copper sunbeams glowed in warm silhouettes through the eucalypts. Benny was ready to try and answer — Poe maybe, then changed his mind to Oscar Wilde. No, it didn't matter. The glow was so enticing.

'Think I'll go out for a while.'

Joseph said nothing. Slippery and smug, thought Benny, for the disdain followed him right out the door.

'And so easy to intimidate.' That was the snarl from Joseph. Certain enough.

At times Benny was clumsy and vulnerable. Overreacting like a snail in close company, he had been brushed with salt and was smarting.

Benny followed the glistening sandstone wall of the Barracks. The soldier in the drab khaki grinned under his slouch hat. On the bus Benny skipped frames between Joseph and the soldier. There was no mistaking it. Life with Joseph was constricting. The Paddo python queen who valued relationships for the crush of intellectual advantage. Benny figured if he stayed there much longer his lover might swallow him whole.

Benny Morrison had not always lived in Sydney. Dad and his Illawarra milking Shorthorns still relished lush pastures at Jamberoo, while Old Dan Morrison coped much better with his bulls than with a son who reckoned he was gay. No, he could not believe it, and neither could teenage Benny when he first encountered the golden mile. Here on Oxford Street he quickly aligned himself to the body sensuous. The granite handshakes of home gave way to timorous fingers of curiosity. Penetration. Those farmers' mouths were parched and hollow. Sydney proffered him love — sultry breath, tongues of fire and the celebration of 'coming out'.

The traders down at Paddy's Market were finishing up. Loading onto the fruit trucks made almost combustible in the afternoon heat, Benny focussed on a swarthy pair of colossi. They were hauling up sacks of pumpkins. Sweat erupted on vexed biceps. A pulse under worn blue overalls. The desire for an exotic fruit: a papaya, custard apple, maybe a sweet yellow babaco had been forgotten. Benny's mind was in reverie to the rhythms of male action.

Dreams bristled when the truck's horn glared and Benny caught the driver's eyes in the rear-vision mirror. 'Perhaps he's been watching me just as long,' he mused, but fantasy revived, evaporated soon when the man tossed himself from the cabin and strode towards him.

Benny was usually shy and always paranoid. The wide grimace on the driver's face seemed a portent of some grim irony. He cantered off, side-stepping broken crates and a path festooned with rotten cabbages.

Through a crack in the warehouse wall Benny re-emerged into the dusty sunlight. It was isolated on this side of the market. Big stacks of rusted storage bins and a wizened Chinese woman fossicking in the gutter. He turned the other way. The taut arms of the driver found him and pushed his body against the wall.

Tropical fruit was unappetising. It seemed almost passé. Benny thought of massy, tubered leeks and pumpkins. Max had a body like that. Smooth, hard buttocks like the perfect sections of a Queensland blue, its firm ribbing unyielding of the dark orange heart. But his own heart had complied. Behind the drums where he lay bare-chested, imperious fingers running over his tan belly and whispering pleasure when Max squeezed him. Benny's joy was maintained, as deep in his pocket he fingered the slip of his new love's address. He would call him Pumpkin Max.

Joseph found out on Wednesday. There really wasn't much to go on. The slip bearing Max's identity had remained in Benny's trousers, but something else escaped. Obsession makes one careless and it hung out like a lurid diorama. Joseph offered his soft, damp hands: a gesture of empathy, perhaps of remorse, for he wanted to communicate without patronising his youthful companion.

Once again the dial on the telephone was spinning into oblivion. Behind the door, Joseph listened to the stale chords of frustration. Max's telephone was impregnable. Benny's fingers cracked the receiver down.

It was Joseph's moment to appear. To be debonair and scathing like at the dinner party when Benny shrivelled up amongst his straight friends: 'Oh we are both homosexual. Didn't you know?' And then he reconsidered. Benny was traumatised. That was enough satisfaction. Joseph wanted his lover to absorb the echoes of himself; to face the consequences of an affirmative sexuality and not to be hounded by the iron shadows of a spurious straightness. To resist the ghouls he needed a thicker skin. Even a vacant obsession would lead to fortitude eventually.

On another day Benny stood outside a terrace. An impeccable blend of sky blue and lemon in an Ultimo lane. A pealing of door chimes rivalled the distant roar of juggernauts along Harris Street, while in the postbox a *Reader's Digest* brochure for Max Slotwinsky confirmed that Benny's passionate letters had found their mark. But while his efforts may have been fruitless, he had not yet despaired. A palpable ideal is its own preservation, as within Benny's mind another existence could be defined — a robust and electric presence, beyond the fluff of the Paddington ghetto. This love was raw and unfathomable. He sat beside Max's door.

At two in the morning his eyes were turgid with grit from the intermittent gusts of a hot westerly wind. Benny had few vivid memories of a long and banal evening; the stolid citizen from Neighbourhood Watch, a drunkard's caterwaul at a 'slope-head' intimidator, and some blood-sporting skinheads: 'Beat 'em on the raps, beat 'em on the raps with baseball bats, Oi Oi.' At last it was Saturday. Market day. He caught a taxi home.

Benny figured Joseph would harass him. He stole into the downstairs bedroom. At ten a.m. and with a tentative 'Hello,' Benny faced a bare-bottomed man in his kitchen. His smile agitated Benny: 'Who are you?' The wanton look faded, replaced with the square grin and hard grip of a Messianic fundamentalist.

'My name's Ti, that's T-I. Joseph's upstairs and you're Benny?'

Benny allowed his hand to slip. 'Are they all the details you have on me?'

Ti laughed and reached for a tea towel. 'Sorry about the strip-tease.'

Benny had brightened up. This blond boy was handsome, winsome, yet Benny felt no jealousy. He also seemed a lot smarter than he looked, with the extra bonus of being refreshingly indiscreet, Benny was given a spontaneous account of the night's events. Joseph had broken taboo: entered the forbidden zone of the Midnight Shift, charging his nostrils with half a phial of amyl and thrusting his frame with Ti in a five hour marathon of techno-funk. Benny was incredulous. It was hilarious. He wanted to wake Joseph and interrogate him, but it was like rescuing an ant from a honey jar.

Had Joseph wanted Benny to follow his lead and perform the unexpected, he would have been disappointed. Then again, there was only pessimism in Benny's anticipation of his encounter at the market. He could depend on Max to ignore him until closing time.

After a month, his antics had become pedestrian. Every time Max had responded almost identically to his first feverish pursuit. Benny felt he had become a kind of degraded barrel girl. The nook among the storage bins being Max's personal boudoir; the only acceptable outlet for a sexuality removed from love. Benny had figured this all out in logical progression, logic that is dull and unashamedly predictable and which Benny had spurned up to now. Two days later he was tossing it off yet again, shocked by Max phoning for the very first time. His sensuous voice gave lustre to Benny's dry stone offerings. Benny asked him over.

Benny found Joseph strangely good humoured. Ti even offered to fix dinner, though Benny knew they were trying to placate him. After all, Ti's moving into the spare room the day before was just a ruse. They were fucking each other when he was not at home. There was no anger. Pumpkin Max was still the priority.

He arrived in cerise singlet, glossy arm muscles locked around a carton of beer. Joseph could win a few points on style, but Max won out on athleticism. Conversation shuffled from terrace renovation, through politics and onto vegetables. Max could be docile and often missed Joseph's innuendo.

'Yes, we do do a good trade in cucumbers,' Max replied.

At other times Max defied expectations. Approving of multiculturalism, land rights, feminism, it did not fit into a working class sensibility. Ti bamboozled Joseph for his 'bourgeois insularity', while Benny felt a great release to spot Joseph in such a demeanour — all coiled up and deflated at meeting an intellectual match in Ti.

Ti's enthusiasm for Max might have also sparked some latent jealousy in Joseph, bringing on a fiery reaction. But though words failed him, his self-control did not and Benny was impressed that the plates of vindaloo had stayed on the table.

Benny's opinion of Joseph had certainly turned around since Ti's arrival. There was now more substance in his ardour, while that customary cynicism had been well diluted. Or perhaps Benny's love of Max had redeemed the now sometime boyfriend. Certainly Joseph was happy with Ti and even acted as his benefactor, for though the new boy may have been bright, he was also unemployed and needed Joseph's money to augment his stained glass dabblings. And Joseph had faith. He liked his bedroom radiating like the Folies Bergères, decked out as it was in rainbow panels of lead-light. Benny liked it as well. They were a flashy trio instead of a dull couple.

'You settled your head athwart my hips and gently turned over upon me. And parted the shirt from my bosom-bone, and plunged your tongue to my barestript heart.'

'That's nice. I like that.'

'It's Walt Whitman.'

'Australian?' . . . 'No, American.'

'Gay?' . . . 'Uh huh.'

They embraced in a dark doorway. Having slipped out to buy more beer, Max carried Benny along. Benny did not approve of the detour (there were garbage bins in the lane), but he stood in the rubbish overspill to hear Max's confession: 'You know that I love you Benny.' He undid his belt.

Benny bought beer in the saloon as Max wandered to the men's room. Benny was glad he had resisted. There was euphoria in his desire for Max and the power from resistance was some ego compensation. Benny had fine-tuned their reception. Instant gratification had been removed, with a rich promise of lovemaking on Max's bed.

Benny waited ten minutes with the brown bagged bottles of beer.

'The bastard's slinked off!'

Benny did not undereast, though he understood his perversity in following. In the taxi he observed Max folding into the shadows on Darlinghurst Road. The city's most notorious beat loomed. Benny stood in the doorway, enticed and then terrified at entering. Someone groaned in a cubicle. He moved away. Leaning behind a Moreton Bay fig, inhaling the wet musk of bark and diverting his mind from a screaming heart.

'Max was a liar. Max did the beats. Max loved him.' It was hard to focus.

Five minutes in an Oxford Street bar and Max's arms were draped around a pimply, red-headed teenager. Benny felt even more humiliated, until Max noticed him. Sex was facile, love is pain. It was not profound. Just an insight into Max's gesture, prompting him to go all the way. It was only a glance but enough to transmit the joy of the chase. Benny could have heard him say: 'Be my fanatic and I'll love you.' He found another taxi and soon was back in Ultimo.

There was a hose curled up on the landing of Max's house. He would turn on the tap and thrust the high pressure nozzle under the door. It was madness and he grinned. The front bedroom awash as he fondled the hard red cap and foresaw the spurting jets of water. He saw an irony too. His sex denied as everything about Max was sexual. His logic surprised him.

Max entered the lane with the red-headed boy. Benny squatted in the gutter at the darkest end. He viewed the cerise singlet and green pants as part of the disguise: the man was half lorikeet, half taipan. They breezed inside.

Benny had finally remembered. 'Lying. All of us lying in the gutter.' It was Oscar Wilde. Caught on love's dunghill. If he had matches Benny would purge himself with fire. There was still the hose.

He listened to Max, screeching and hissing lust. Behind the muslin curtains the two men danced in passionate silhouettes. He knocked hard, called his name and tapped on the glass. The shadows stayed. Benny had always hated being ignored. The nozzle cracked the glass easily. Benny felt like a riot squad breaking up an unruly demonstration.

There was no enjoyment in having Max's big arms around him. To be held up by a body slimy with sweat and water was more repellent, he told himself. Max was explaining, but Benny saw himself as a player in a crazy burlesque. Out on the street, the neighbours watched the wet man Max, his hard cock feebly disguised under a hand towel. Then there was the red-headed boy sprinting down the lane, hugging clothes to his nakedness. And now Pumpkin Max was trying to explain.

'You know that I love you.'

Benny was looking at the stars and laughing.

THEA ASTLEY

Getting There

That winter the frangipani in the convent gardens lost all their leaves before June. There were mornings of slashing frost and then the pallid blue of the high sky. At night the world was gritty with moonlight. By midday patches of sun, warm as sawdust and as golden, sprawled against the chapel walls near the tennis courts and the rear garden trellis where the passion vines grew.

Her best friend whispered, serious behind the covers of *A Winter's Tale*, 'I don't think I can stand it much longer. It's all right for you.'

'Stand what?'

'This place. This *place*.'

Connie felt guilty but relieved for herself. She was a five-day boarder. At the beginning of each term Uncle Harry used to drive her and Will down to Reeftown from Swiper's Creek along the new coast road, and in Reeftown she would wait for the train up to the tablelands while Will vanished behind the doors of his own boarding school. For the first year Uncle Harry made surprise midterm visits as well to each of them on the pretext of bringing a little joy into their lives, but his real reason was an excuse to get away from Clytie and saunter off to the disorderly houses in Sunbird Street, coasting the shores of the goodtime girls.

Clytie suspected. Then she knew. She arranged for the children to spend weekends at her sister's home in Reeftown and returns to Swiper's were limited to term holidays.

'Every weekend?' Sister Perpetua considered this as lingeringly as if it were some cosmic decision on morals. 'It will upset your routine and ours. Does your aunt want to do this?'

Surely her aunt wouldn't want to do this! The mere suggestion spilled its outrageousness all over the glassy linoleum,
splashed across framed Sacred Hearts, Holy Families, nuns on
mission fields.

'I don't know, Sister.'

'It's a training in selfishness. The other girls are not permit-
ted to be so self-indulgent. Of course, I realise yours is a rather
special case, your dear parents being dead. But still.'

'It's Uncle Harry,' Connie explained, her eyes suitably lowered. 'He's not very well.'

'Is he not?' Sister Perpetua looked hard at the closed face
across the desk. 'Frankly, I cannot see the relevance but I suppose
your aunt has her reasons. I could consider this only as long as
these — these interruptions — do not interfere with your
schoolwork, your obligations to school activities and so on. Do
you understand?'

'Yes, Sister.'

'What do you understand?'

Giggle. Shame. The laughter spluttered out uncontrollably.
Then she lowered her head and began a little weep. Three terms
had taught her the usefulness of mollification.

Every Friday, avoiding stocking-mending followed by basketball practice, the slow rattle-trip over the tablelands, the walk in
the eight o'clock dark with Will who met her at the station,
through streets smelling of sea and the despair of the unemployed, to the waterfront. How describe the intensity and ampli-
tude of those Saturday mornings when, her brother hauled back
to school for football practice, Connie, the hated uniform dangling crooked in the wardrobe, pulled on her best summer frock
and sauntered into town to nose along the musty shelves of the
School of Arts; to trail later with unsuitable reading matter to a
patch of grass along the front under the figs, still snuffling from
library dust but prepared to drown in words and ultramarine.

Saturday. All Saturday. Limitless.

At night they slept in sagging veranda beds listening to the sea
while the mosquito netting twisted in the wind through the

wooden louvres. In the dark she and Will threw words to each other softly across the splintered boards.

There she goes, every Saturday, walking through an older Connie's dreams, strollling the waterfront, taking deep breaths of mangrove stink and salt and the personal odours of the town. Her eyes gulped in as much. Blacks slept beneath trees, women shoved their shopping home in recycled prams, carts dragged up side roads, tethered horses dropped dung pads, men propped up pub verandas and sometimes a car rattled past through a halo of dust. By nine the heat clawed at flesh. Horses went limp in sulky shafts and the morning shoppers headed for the purple shadows of awnings. It was then that Connie turned her back on the sea and, facing the high ranges where the convent hid itself in memory and trees, walked a block to the School of Arts, up the stairs and into the long book-filled room with the deep verandas off it from which, again, the bay, the sizzling blue, the hyphen of an island.

The world caught her by the throat.

Every Saturday morning.

She would run lightly with some electric urge up the stairs, hand patting rail, patting rail, the satin polish of the wood slipping under her fingers. She ran into expectancy.

Every Saturday morning.

And every Saturday morning, as if he expected her, or they expected each other, he would be there.

She had noticed him the very first Saturday.

She had looked up from the magazine rack where she was selecting something for Aunt Tess and had become conscious of a large broad-brimmed hat dipping over a deepness — was it brownness? — of eyes, of skin. Was it a sombreness of mouth? There was a morose attaction. He was forty or fifty, she judged, some vast age her years could not guess at, but the thickset and gloomily pervasive stance filled her with unanalysable fear and delight. There was a heavy and clumsily curved imprecision of body, and the more unmoving he stood, the more the nature of this force reached out to her.

And then the two of them, the only borrowers in the long dust-scented room, revolved from rack to rack, shelf to shelf, baiting each other with occasional unsmiling glances of pure gravity in a kind of slow ballet.

It made her sharply aware of her own face and body, of the nakedness of arms and legs, of the slim unformed quality of bone and flesh, and she could sense, across musty histories of the region, the rows of local memoirs, the shelves of classic and popular fiction and piles of damp-mould newspapers, his own grave interest.

Every Saturday.

Silence. The books. Silence. The slow pavane. The desk-clerk writing quietly, uninterested, at the far end of the room. Just the two of them. And then she would look up, suddenly solemn in the juvenile section (*Remember, I am only a schoolgirl!*), hand paused on a tattered spine, turning, her shoulders describing an unhurried arc of the most impure innocence, to find that he was watching.

Sometimes she took a book out to one of the deck chairs on the veranda, and, sitting there confronted by unread pages and the sea, felt his presence in the room behind. Once he came out to the veranda as well and looking at her, looking at her, sat in a chair one away. Then she became too frightened to look across at him though she sensed a spiritual branding taking place. As she walked home later with the books she grabbed up without choice, her excitement shook her and persisted throughout the tumid morning.

There was no one to tell. She did not want to tell. The words she tossed Will in the dark told nothing. It was as if for that briefest of longest hours every Saturday morning, she executed a privately adult mime.

So it went on through May and June. The expectation, the steady exchange of glances, the agreeable sensation of delight and terror. Something prevented her smiling. Was she too frightened to smile? A smile could be the ultimate disclosure of her self. She was not yet ready to smile. On two occasions when other borrowers came early to the library, she noticed that he went directly to the veranda and sat there reading, severed from her by the page, and she would choose her books quickly and leave with a sense of something unfinished.

That winter, too, she developed chilblains on every finger.

At night in the dormitory, the envelope of heat beneath the blankets made them itch unbearably and she scratched and tore at the inflamed flesh until the skin burst and ripped like a rag and her hands became banded with scab and pus.

She couldn't conceal them during class and after a week Sister Boniface turned from the blackboard in the middle of an algebra demonstration and said curtly, 'Do something about those fingers, will you, Constance? Doesn't your aunt know? They're quite disgusting.'

Humiliation came easily at convents. It was good, someone must believe, for the soul. Passion, resentment, the beginnings of diffident cries of protest, even overt anger, would meet a contemptuous 'Control yourself.' Contemptuous? Not quite that. Distaste, perhaps. A sort of well-bred fury and disgust that one could be so — well, so human. Control yourself. They all lived by that dictum. At porridge time, at bread-and-butter time, at stew time, in class and out, in chapel, in study, at prayers, tennis, basketball. *Constance*, a voice would ring out over the bitter grass at the edge of the courts, *don't throw your body about like that. Show some control!* The other girls playing had stared at her as if she were committing an obscene physical display. She felt she had perpetrated a loathsome impurity. Her bottom? Had she shown her bottom? Her breasts? Had they bounced? They were barely there. Had she flashed her gangling thirteen-year-old legs with the sensual motions of a stripper? Had she? She knew about strippers. Her best friend had seen a film in Brisbane and the black-and-white frames recalled in the darkened dormitory still shot guiltily across her mind.

For the rest of that game her services flopped down the court like patted dough lumps. She minced to return balls with her knees jammed together. Should she even part her feet? (*May I walk, Sister Boniface? May I have permission to walk, to part my legs so I may get from here to there?*) She was resentful. Her efforts to avoid immodesty and display the utmost control became tinged with the ironic. For one silly week, she flattened her gently erupting breasts with a broad ribbon band tied under her school blouse lest they offend.

Do something, Constance, about your legs, your breasts, your disgusting, disgusting fingers.

After the last class that afternoon, she excused herself from sport, taking delight in displaying the suppurating reasons to Sister Regulus, and went back to her desk in the classroom where she kept a tin Aunt Clytie had packed with an elementary first aid kit: gauze, cotton wool, a pair of nail scissors, iodine and sticking plaster.

From the chapel came the voices of the school choir practising a Latin Mass. *Agnus dei*, they sang in four heavenly parts, *qui tollis peccata mundi, miserere nobis*. What was the Latin for chilblains, she wondered. And began to giggle. Lamb of God who takest away the chilblains of the world, have mercy on us.

The gauze unrolled across the desk. Through the open doors of the school hall she saw the frostbitten lawns roll to the treeline; above the trees soared a cutting blue. She snipped off a length of bandage and began wrapping the worst of her fingers.

Dona nobis pacem, sang the choir.

It was harder binding her right hand. She felt like a juggler. *Sanctus, sanctus, sanctus*, the choir intoned. Angelic. Angelic. Cut off in mid-polyphony by the pistol crack of ruler on harmonium top and a cry of musical affront from Sister Alphonse, a cry that rang down the chapel corridor, across the winter trees and into the hall. Holding one bifurcate bandage end between her teeth, Connie looped and tugged the other with her free hand. Twist, tug, knot. Furiously she sang, but softly, *qui tollis all chilblains mundi*, over and over. The choir had commenced singing again with the demanded delicacy, and the *attacca* and diminuendo of the repeated syllables brought tears to her eyes.

She started on her thumb.

Then a greyness darkened the already greying air of the hall and a swish of robes, a rattle of beads, particular warnings she carried long into adulthood, sounded behind her.

Angrily Connie kept wrapping, refusing to acknowledge the sounds.

Sister Perpetua's voice spun silkily over her shoulder.

'Well, Constance? Well? Look at me child, when I address you. What are you doing?'

Sister Perpetua stood with her head to one side, angled to match her smile.

Connie held out the still unbandaged fingers. They looked disgusting, just as she had been told.

'Wrapping my fingers.'

'Wrapping? Your fingers?'

The gentle educated voice quivered with disbelief.

'Can't you endure a little pain?'

'Sister Boniface told me to wrap them.'

Sister Perpetua picked at the rosary dangling from her belt, let it slide easily between her fingers, then rattled prayers like pebbles. 'You're soft,' she said. 'Soft. Already we indulge you. Think of Christ on the Cross.'

Connie looked up. Fold upon fold of choral music wrapped round her as the choir spent its adolescent energies on a *jubilate*. The injustice of those words. Rejoice! Rejoice!

'Christ cured the sick,' she argued, stung by inequity. 'You taught us that.' She could feel a shaking in her chest, her heart thumping at her daring, and watching Perpetua's calm mad face, she became terrified at her blurted words. The nun's features seemed to do a little dance. It was as if they had all microscopically changed position.

Sister Perpetua leaned back from her, took a step away and supported her rage on a desk.

'You put yourself above Christ,' she gasped. 'You put yourself above the Church. You interpret!'

Connie could not reply to these charges. They bore the monolith horror from remembered studies of the Inquisitionary

Courts. Grand heresy became a nimbus, the dark around the body.

A blob of yellow matter disengaged itself from the right thumb and plopped to the floor. Her eyes followed it. Sister Perpetua's mouth twisted briefly and from outside the hall a bell rang the end of another division in the day.

'Self self self,' the voice was going on, through the bell's clangor, through the distant noises of feet surging from the chapel and voices that would shortly find them here. 'You think only of yourself. A truly self-involved young woman with no capacity for endurance, for submission to the divine will.' Sister Perpetua thought about the divine will for a few seconds. Her eyes rolled up reverently as if seeking and her lids closed. Connie was embarrassed at witnessing this private ecstasy. 'If it's God will you have chilblains, then it is His will. Do you understand me? And it is your part to endure, to offer them up as an act of submission to that divine will, to one who did so much for you' — her voice cracked at this point — 'He laid down His life.'

The classroom had filled with girls whose voices fluttered into silence as they saw the stage set, the persecutor, the victim. Faces, horrified, delighted, curious, became smug with there-but-for-the-grace-of-God looks. Sister Perpetua ignored them. The extras tiptoed virtuously around the two to their desks, took out textbooks, and bent their heads in frightful assiduity.

Ready for catharsis.

Sister Perpetua stretched her moment of silence to breaking point like an old stager, on, on, on, so that her final words would crack like rocks.

'May God forgive you,' she said, spacing each word monstrously, 'for your unpardonable selfishness. You will come to a sticky end.'

Her hand began to shake wooden prayers from her waist once more. She held her head so far sideways as she examined her victim, she created a problem in balance.

'You're mad,' Connie replied loudly and flatly.

Did she say it?

She hoped she had said it. She wishes she could have. No, she will remember long afterwards, she didn't say it.

The cold air following the opening doors at the end of the hall blew between their voices, carried between the two of them other voices and laughter from the playing fields, the rapturous indifference of latecomers to study, and a smell of drying leaves.

Perhaps she had dropped her eyes submissively, hidden her disfigured hands behind her back while the bandages unwound slowly and she agreed humbly from her shrunken and humiliated self, 'Yes, Sister, yes.'

She saw Sister Perpetua swing away to the senior section of the study block while she stood there, tears of anger and mortification swelling in her eyes but not running over. She sat down and under cover of her desk lid examined her hands and her hatred. Then, slowly and systematically, she proceeded to bandage the last sores.

Her solitariness was underscored by furtive glances. There were smells of sandshoes and sports-smocks, of chillling sweat and the breathy stifled energy of the latecomers. She stared at her Latin grammar and thought of nothing at all. *Nihil nihil nihil*. Automatically she copied a vocabulary list into a notebook, saying the words *nihil nihil nihil* over and over while her mind fled for refuge to the grounds outside, sped over the lawns to the wrought-iron gates and banged them behind, fled down through the hilly township to the railway station, and clattered off along the track through smudged sunsets to the coast, the old house on the front, the sea-bitten veranda, to Tess and Will and Saturday morning.

Next Saturday, she decided. Next Saturday.

He would be there and her private world would become the real one. The convent would shrink like a pip.

Her best friend was nudging her, her hand sticky with caramel.

The gesture was too late. She refused the nudge, rejected the sticky hand, wouldn't look across. *Prohibeo*, she wrote, dutifully and resentfully concentrating, *prohibere, prohibui, prohibitum*.

Next Saturday.

He would be there, the link to otherness, his eyes assessing across the long dusty room.

She knew this and she nourished half-formed notions of mouths and hands and Rochester-like passions springing to life between the dead and dying volumes on walls and tables.

As she wrote she shuddered at the peril of it for she knew what she would do this time.

Then she laid down her pen and touched her burning fingers together beneath the desk. She closed her eyes and saw Saturday behind her lids, ignoring the whispered urgencies of her friend. Too late, she thought. Too late. Beyond this stuffy room she was interesting. Was loved. And she knew what she would do, unsure of what her action might produce, but committing herself to it.

She would absorb his sombre eyes totally. She would float on their desperate lakes until she was beyond reach of shore, beyond.

She would open her lips and smile.

Yes. Turning from whatever book-clutter had trapped her, at that salient moment, moving slowly, immeasurably slowly, she would look into him fully at last.

She would smile.

What the Soul Wants

Was it my fault? I lit the candle. I only wanted to look at him. The sky outside was white with stars, and there were enough windows, but I lit the candle and for a moment I saw, I saw, I saw. The candle tilted, a molten drop his his shoulder, he woke with a jolt. He wasn't angry. He looked at me. I blew out the candle, but it was too late. He got out of the bed. I stood in the garden. He was already gone. The air was still. Not a leaf moved. The dry grass seemed not to receive but to emit the starlight.

I can't go looking for him. I can't go after him. I can't write to him. He doesn't exist. The days pass and as the days pass the blood and body leak out of the idea of him, as the days pass and pass. Little by little he becomes a ghost, no more than a thought, grey and insubstantial. He has never existed. He is a figment. I invented him.

Philip is always leaving. He packs a small bag. He would never use a cliché like *travelling light*. The first thing Philip does when he arrives in a new town is rent a post box. Philip can sit still.

Philip never talks about a ship, or a boat, but I know he's come across water, because his cheeks carry that coldness that comes only from a water wind.

I do the work. Joyfully and with love I serve him.

Philip never uses the word love.

I wait for his letter. But when it comes I do not recognise his handwriting. I hold the envelope and examine the strange, blurred postmark, and I say: 'Now who can this be from?' Sometimes, unless I look at the signature first, I get halfway down the first page before I realise it is the letter I have been waiting for. The letter you want, the letter you long for, will not come today, and when it does, even if it contains the very words you need, you will be sad, you will be disappoointed, you will still be hungry.

Philip never calls me by my name. He must know a lot of women. Sometimes when he comes back from where he's been he absent-mindedly calls me *baby*. Even that I don't mind. It doesn't matter how many women he knows. Not a single one of them is exactly like me.

I wait so long to hear from him that cobwebs grow in my letterbox.

I write a little masterpiece to Philip. What am I doing when I read my own letter over and over? I am searching for his exact response to it. I am trying to surprise myself with something I know by heart. A fruitless enterprise: I am trying to *be him*, at the moment when he reads my letter, but because I don't know where he is, he never will, and just as well, for it is much too perfect. Why can't I write the letters that ignorant people write, desperate letters, full of crossings-out, without margins, set too high on the page, letters that emit dumb sobs?

Philip is beautiful. But he is not always recognisable at first glance. Often at first glance he looks ugly: cramped and twisted, dark-faced, closed-minded.

Philip breaks women's hearts; or rather, women break their hearts over Philip, women who aren't ready for him, women who are still looking for somebody to blame for everything, women who have lost him long ago and can't find him again.

Philip takes me to hear a requiem. He wants to hear a choir. He wants a choir to drown him. The choir twitters, glides, chatters, draws breath in unison, but the hall is too large for drowning and the music is over before it can be filled. Philip leaves disappointed. He dinks me through the dark streets on his bike. I crouch on the bar inside the curve of his torso. I can feel his heart beating with the work of it: carrying me, balancing me, bearing me, as if he were the pregnant one and I the baby. We pass two fountains in the dark: one whispers, the other shouts.

Philip speaks of suicide, of how it is done. I say: 'I'd jump off a building.' He says: 'Would you jump off a bridge?' I say: 'No — oh, no! I'd hate to hit water.' He says: 'But you wouldn't mind hitting concrete.' I say, with a foolish laugh: 'I never think of landing.' 'Neither do I,' says Philip; 'only of taking off.'

In a villa I wake in darkness thicker than night. I stumble panting along the walls of the rooms, feeling with my palms for an opening, a slot, a handle, a way out to air. I come to a metal catch, cold; I twist, I shove, and part of the wall gives way and bursts outwards into the end of an afternoon — but a heavy pot of flowers crashes off the sill, my fault, plummets three storeys to gravel and wedges itself there in two sickened halves. A woman's voice cries from another window: *Feliiiipe!*; three syllables thrown out like a rope towards a valley where darkness already clusters in foliage.

Philip is both here and not here. All the time.

Philip says: 'But that's not *logical*. Can't you *see* that?' I say: 'It's not that I'm *against* logic. It's just that I don't really know what it *is*.' I don't 'know' things the way he does. Things I have been obliged to 'know' in this way soon leave me. He knows everything that could be included under Subjects, and I know everything else. The things I know have no headings, rubrics, categories. 'What did she say to you?' asks Philip; 'what did you say to her?' I try to make a report, but there is no answer.

Philip stays away for a very long time. I have learnt that there is no point in complaining. He would come if he could; if he wanted to.

Philip drives me across the river on a Friday afternoon. Outside the central railway station the traffic comes to a standstill. We roll up the windows against the exhaust fumes. He does not turn the music down, the whole car vibrates to it, I feel the shuddering wherever my skin touches metal. He is telling me about a terrible place, about the things that happen there, the punishments, they never end, ice, fire, devourings and the kicking of heads. A place exists where people do these things to each other. His torso is so thin inside his baggy grey clothes that he might be a skeleton sitting beside me, his hands loosely resting on the steering wheel, his thighs like sticks, his large feet tapping among the pedals. What he is saying fills me with terror and disgust. I have to turn my face away and pretend to watch people passing. A paroxysm starts under my ribs. If this car does not move in one minute I will have to open the door and vomit onto the bitumen. But I listen, I listen, I do not tell him to stop.

Did I send him there, to where he's gone? Was there an obligation or did he go willingly? Did we agree that he would go and I would stay behind? Was it his turn? Should I have gone in his place? Did he shoulder it? Did he leave without a word?

Imagine a man, imagine a man who is always about to arrive, to come back, to turn up, to materialise, always about to visit, to lob, to come home, to show, to wander in from another city, another country, another landscape, from behind the desert, from the stony rises, from that wavering out there, from the indigo between the islands, from elsewhere, from the place without a name, from the opposite direction, from every direction at once. The house is square: it has enough windows: each room has several. She can look out to the north, to the east, to the south, to the west, to all the minor directions in between, she can lean out, stand at the sill, press her mouth to the glass, shoot a glance in passing. She can run from window to window, opening, adjusting. Imagine the waiting. Imagine the seeing of the house through the eyes of the awaited one. The preparations: the binding of the head in scarves, the wrapping of the torso in aprons, the pulling on of gloves, the throwing open of rooms, the thrashing of carpets, the discovery of coins behind cushions, the tearing up and shaking of rags, the bending of elbow and knee, the slop of water in buckets, the whine of small motors. Think of the slow pulse of anxiety as each hair-cut reaches its zenith and declines; the regular renewal of reading matter, the emptying of foulness from vases, the shedding and harvesting of blood, the growth, the trimming of nails, their sharpening; the puffing up and subsiding of quilts, the over-heave of mattresses, the shifting arrangements of table and bed to catch the seasonal angle of light. The fluctuations of readiness. The high fine breathy note of readiness.

The phone rings. I pick it up. It has many extensions in the square house, as many as there are windows, and a woman is on each one — my friends, my sisters, my daughters, my mother — all of them laughing and shouting and crying out my name. I know the caller is Philip, I know the tenor of his breathing, but he is waiting for the girlish clamour to die down before he speaks.

The sun is shining. It is 11 o'clock in the morning. I am wearing a long black coat buttoned up to the neck. I am singing to myself. I am picking my way. It is a courtyard, broken, high in an abandoned building, a central high courtyard, broken, high above the street, once a roof garden, neglected now, dry and stalkless. Have I once lived in this tower? Slept, woken? Climbed the wooden stairs, passed slots of rooms where people dreamed, giggled, groaned, rubbed their torn skin and wounded elbow-crooks, cried out unanswered, subsided in foul sheets? Have I pushed open a trapdoor, a manhole, burst on to the roof, breathed clean air, looked west, looked east? Have I waited here? There is a man in the courtyard, leaning in a doorway. I stand still. He is looking down, he is rolling a cigarette. He raises the cigarette to lick it closed, and sees me standing on the tiles. He says nothing. He licks the paper and seals the cigarette. He is propped in the sunny doorway, one leg straight, the other bent so he can brace his foot against the closed door behind him. His thigh in cheap trousers is a fleshless bone. He nods. He smiles. His back teeth are broken. The unbroken ones are rotting pegs, green-furred. He lights the cigarette. He slips his hand into the inner pocket of his jacket and holds it out to me, closed. I step towards him on the smashed tiles. He puts into my hand an object that feels hard, like plastic or glass. It ought to be warm from his pocket, from his skin, but it is cold. It feels oval, the size of my palm. I flatten my hand out to look. It is a mirror, cheap, pink, the sort that little girls have in little girls' handbags. The glass is cracked, and smeared with blood. I turn it over and examine it carefully. Already I feel the warmth of my hand take away its chill. He says: 'What will you do with the mirror?' I say: 'Look at myself in it.' He smokes, I look at him, I look and look, I need to see him, I feel the small spasms my eyes make as they focus on this part of him, then that. He stands bearing the beam of my scrutiny, sometimes returning it, sometimes looking away. I say: 'Philip. Where have you been?' He closes his eyes, and opens them. He says: 'Where I've been you wouldn't want to go. Where I've been they take everything you've got and give nothing back.' His thinness, his brokenness: it is terrible. I can't help myself. I step right up to him; but he laughs, and holds me away. 'Not now,' he says. 'Not yet. I'm not ready. You always rush me.' I fall back, I let my arms drop. He laughs again, showing his splintered teeth, his swollen gums. 'You really want me, don't you,' he says. I am ashamed, I hang my head: is it that obvious? There is dried blood on his T-shirt, a thick gout of it, over his ribs, low down on his right side. He smokes his cigarette and watches me. He says: 'Is there anything here to drink?' I say: 'There's nothing here. The water was cut off long ago. Everybody's left. No gas. No power.' He smiles. He says: 'Doesn't matter. I'm only passing through. I have to go back.' I am no use to him. I have nothing to give him, nothing he wants. He says: 'Will you come and see me? Will you visit me?' I say: 'I don't know where it is. Can you tell me where? I'm not much good with maps. How will I find the way?' He shrugs, he drops the butt and treads on it. He says: 'Don't worry about it. I'll be in touch. Wait for me.' The tattoos on his knuckles have blurred and feathered, as if his skin had been soaked in water. If he doesn't write to me it's not because he doesn't want to. Where he's been they've never heard of letters. Where he's been they break your teeth and feed you on stones. The parts of him I saw in candlelight he keeps covered now. Are there scars? Is there a wound? Some questions you do not ask. Where he's been they don't have paper, cameras, vegetables, blinds. Where he's been, the windows are carved out of rock; the air outside them is rock. Where he's been you can die of darkness. Where he's been is where nobody expects to have to go. You don't ask questions about where he's been. You look at the body. It trembles. It sweats. It bleeds. You keep your mouth shut. You see the body, and you work it out.

Crested Pigeons

Miraculously observant and acute though it was, the American satellite arching through bright vacancies of space miles above the Sydney Botanical Gardens one sunlit lunchtime could not detect the crested pigeons bobbing on the smooth grass. Not even a prodigy of modern technology like the American satellite could glimpse the crested pigeons. It easily spotted the colour-fully clad joggers; and the lean, serious runners loping the long paths in their silky briefs and singlets; and sunbathing office-girls; and lovers blending together on benches and in shady cor-ners; and children swinging, sliding and seesawing; and a picnicking couple looking sombre on either side of their tartan rug and spread-out lunch. It even saw the iron fence which con-tained them all inside the Botanical Gardens and, beyond that, the glittering inlets of the harbour; and the ocean surrounding them and then the sprawling land on which they all floated together and finally the svelte curve of the world which, like the satellite, hurtled through pre-ordained space. But it missed the crested pigeons, their curious topknots dipping and darting as they pecked. It was something to do with their subtle colouring against the confusion of grass, trees and sky, a sort of evanescence when they flew …

If the satellite could not hear sounds, then that meant it did not pick up the scuff and pad of feet, the laughter of children, the rhythmic groan of unoiled swings and seesaws. And not the loud, sad squeak of the crested pigeons' wings, nor the picnicking man when he said, 'What about the children?' nor, for that matter, his companion when she replied:

— I don't know. I — I just don't know. None of it will be easy.

He repeated 'easy' and laughed, but without humour. A small tic started near the corner of his mouth on the left side and he brushed at it as if it were a fly. But it continued, a quiver, every now and then. He looked at her, seeming about to speak, but said nothing. She stared down at the grass where it met the tasselled edges of the tartan rug. Perspiration glittered on her forehead. Between them, their almost untouched sandwiches and salad dried imperceptibly in the sun and the Riesling warmed in their glasses and in the slim green bottle.

— If you weren't so — so *mean* with words, if you'd just talk ...

He said it gently, encouraging.

— You have such faith in words. You think they fix everything, pin every problem down, where it can be got at ...

— Well, I can't read your mind. All I know is what you tell me. If only you *would* tell me.

A group of girls further down the grass slope suddenly began to giggle uncontrollably as a very fat jogger, purple in the face and bulging out of his shorts and singlet, laboured past them along the path.

The man said, 'He'll be a big lad when he fills out,' and the woman looked up, not smiling but with a slight softening of her eyes as she squinted in the glare.

— You always say that about fat people.

— Am I so predictable?

— Yes, of course you are. So am I. People who've lived together for twenty years *are* predictable. To each other, anyway.

— Yet I didn't predict this?

— No.

Some small children were stalking the crested pigeons. They would creep slowly nearer and nearer, exploding with suppressed laughter, swopping loud, sibilant whispers, until at the last moment they would pounce. And the crested pigeons would lift, wings squeaking, outlines blurring in a rush of feathers, only to drop again a few yards away, pecking and bobbing imperturbably.

—— Should I have?

—— Perhaps. I don't know.

—— Do you know why? Why you're leaving, I mean?

—— It's not someone else, if that's what you're getting round to.

—— I wasn't *getting round* to anything. I just want to know what …

She dropped her gaze, looking as if she might cry. They sat for a long time in silence, staring at the leisurely life of the park, the groupings and wanderings and reclinings among the benign intrusions of trees, shrubs, garden beds. Subtly the light changed, shadows shifted. Panting children, cheeks glowing with their exertions, drifted slowly back to the temporary havens their mothers had made with rugs, prams, Eskys and sunshades.

At last, the man spoke:

—— I just want to know what's gone wrong. That's all.

—— It's not as simple as that. Not just *something gone wrong*.

—— Why is it you can't ever say to me now 'I love you'? You can't, can you?

—— No.

—— It's because you don't. Obviously, that's why. If you can't say it, then obviously ——

—— Don't start proving things to me. *Please*, don't do it. You'll get to your QED as usual, but it won't have anything to do with what I'm feeling.

—— Quite a speech for someone who ——

A little girl darted straight between them leaping their rug, escaping some parental commotion nearby. As if obeying a silent signal, people were standing, brushing themselves down, stretching, gathering litter, cajoling children. A group of workmen arrived in a trailer pulled by a tractor, and began unloading chainsaws, axes and ropes. Runners and joggers, spread all over the place earlier, were now flowing into long ragged queues, whorling into patterns like iron filings, heading for the main gates.

The woman stood up.

—— We'd better go. The boys will be home soon and …

The sudden stutter of a chainsaw drowned out the rest of her words. Soon, whole branches were dropping from the large eucalypts where the gardeners were pruning.

In the middle of the emptying expanses of lawn, where the lunchers and lovers and runners had so recently been, a small boy was chasing the crested pigeons. Disturbed by his joyous sprints, they rose and settled, rose and settled until suddenly, as if exasperated by his tireless persistence, they swept with a sighing and squeaking of wings beyond the tops of the trees. As the flock ascended, the man was saying: 'But we've resolved nothing. We can't talk at home and — we've got nowhere.'

The crested pigeons dipped and looped and went on rising. Quite quickly they became almost invisible — something to do with their colouring, the confusion of background tones and shapes, their blurred outlines when they flew. From up there, the small boy who had tormented them looked like a petulant doll as he slumped in frustration to the ground. And the man and the woman gathering up their picnic, looking smaller and smaller — only the odd word bridging the widening gap: *understand*; *years*; *reasons*; *children* . . .

SUSAN HAMPTON

The Lobster Queen

I don't know what I thought of her then. I know that the details don't matter. It could have been any two women, a thirty-year-old, a fourteen-year-old, falling in love, on a wharf anywhere in the world. Chinese women, for instance. They were very cold. They held each other through their coats, on the wharf.

The older one always woke early and had her first cup of tea by five-thirty. She had ironed a hanky and put it in the pocket of the coat she loaned the girl. On the wharf later the girl put her hand in the pocket. It was still warm.

It may have been a year after when the girl's father found a letter she had hidden in a sock. She had forgotten writing it. Later she realises there are forgotten areas all through her history, spread like fishing nets over the landscape, nets which turn to clouds so areas of nothingness occur. The empty territory of the psyche. In this country the body blurs sideways from the shock of what the nothing must contain.

We are not the same women we were. Everything has changed. When I looked back I could remember some things about the girl. I know there are major blur areas. At this point the details do matter.

In summer they began to fish from a rusted wreck at the end of the breakwater. It was dangerous to walk on, especially in the half-light before sunrise. They were usually the only ones there. At low tide they walked to the bottom of the ship and fished for yellowtail swimming in the hold. The girl said she was tempted to dive in, the water was so green. Her friend said, 'Don't be crazy, there's sharks.'

The woman stood up and rigged her rod with a live yellow-tail and cast into the sea. When she caught her first tailor, she filleted it and used that to bait both lines. 'Tailor eat tailor,' she said to the girl, casting again in one smooth action.

Every movement the woman made, the girl copied her. At first she cast so wildly the hook swung behind her and caught her trousers. They were laughing into each other's faces, in a light nor'-easter wind.

'Here,' the woman said, and she took the hook out. Then slowly she turned the girl around and kissed her on the mouth.

'Do it properly,' the girl said. 'You know what I mean. Kiss me properly.'

The deck of the *Adolf*, wrecked in 1907 on top of six other ships, swayed beneath her. She held the woman for balance, and breathed in her breath. She tasted of sea wind and being outside and early light.

The woman looked at her for a long time, at first with a hot longing, then sadly, and then, with a kind of line across her face she bent to pick up her rod and demonstrated the cast. The girl watched each movement, the tanned fingers releasing the reel clip, the slow backward arch of the back, the forward movement as she cast out so far the sinker was a tiny plop, invisible. The arms straight, strong, exactly in the direction where she wanted the bait to land. She did all this without speaking, then squatted and lit a cigarette.

Waiting for the schools of tailor to come in was like all waiting, a suspension, a positive quietness of the body, the tingling edge of any part of her body knowing it would leap at a movement of the line.

'How will I know,' the girl asked, 'whether it's waves moving the line, or a fish?'

'Your fingers will become sensitive,' the woman said, showing her how to rest the line on the tip of her index finger, teaching her when to wind in a bit, when to let it out.

When the first tailor hit the line they stood and braced themselves, the sensation of a fish was so definite after all, and for twenty minutes they were reeling them in, shining and white, taking them by the gills and unhooking them, casting again. Sometimes they forgot to rebait the hook, everything went so fast, and they caught fish anyway, by the fin, by the gills, because the school was so thick.

After the catch, fifteen or twenty fish at that time of year, they squatted to clean them. The girl watched the woman's fingers fly, scales lifting to the air like sequins, the knife expertly opening the belly, guts being flicked into the sea, the carving of fillets, never a mistake, the roe sacs of pregnant ones, blood on the fingers, sometimes the birds collecting, surrounding them.

The woman let down a bucket on a rope and hauled up water from the hold. They washed the fish. Squatting either side of the bucket they stared at each other, the girl's green eyes soaking blue from the woman's, till the woman leaned back and put her hands to her face. She breathed in, looking through her fingers at the girl, and smiled, shaking her head slightly, wry. At this time the girl knew what the gesture meant, without knowing why.

There would be more waiting at the house. Waiting was a part of everything that happened. The girl waited on the step, or on the chair near the door, while the woman made tea in an aluminium pot.

Sometimes she disappeared to do other things and the girl didn't know where she was. Sounds would tell her — the dog barking at a man who came in asking for a haircut, water running, a bath being run.

'Get in,' the woman said to the girl, 'I'll come later and wash your back.'

In the car, on the lounge watching TV, she held her hand out to the girl. At sundown she opened a bottle of beer and began to cook for the men. She walked the girl home at night. Before they came to the gate she took the girl's head in her hands, holding her face she kissed her once, not 'properly', but breathing in, holding the breath.

In winter the girl stayed in the kids' room once or twice, when the kids were away. In the bed they opened mouths, necks, arms, bellies, but there were places the girl could not touch her, these were her frozen zones, this was what she told the girl. Something is wrong, but nothing is ever explained. Later the girl will write the letter and hide it, unable to post it in case the opening of questions closes everything that has happened. She will hide it in a sock, and forget it. It will not exist.

At certain times of the year they went up the river in a long rowboat the women hired from Mr Lindstrom, the dwarf. He lived in a small house he'd built himself opposite the mangrove flats, and kept bait in two long freezers. A wooden ladder leaned against each freezer, and sometimes the dwarf sat on one of these ladders while his customers worked out where they would fish, and what bait would be needed. He would recommend one thing or another depending on the wind and the tide. There was a windsock in his front yard and a hand-painted notice saying PIPPIES. CHICKEN GUTT. WORMS. PRAWNS. YELLOWTAIL.

It was early winter and there was frost on his lawn. The girl stopped at the small door and looked back at the marks their sandshoes had left in the frost. They bought the packets of bait and he followed them across the road to the river. The woman thanked him and headed out along the jetty. He stood there watching her movements, the darting of a cormorant behind her, smoke from the industries across the river, then ripples in the mudflats beneath them.

'This is not a rewarding liaison,' the dwarf said flatly. The wispy curls on his large head shook themselves in the river breeze. He was standing on the bank, and the girl had stepped down onto the jetty, so they were looking directly at each other. The girl noticed his eyes had kind lines around them.

'I've asked her to go away with me,' the girl said.

The dwarf looked out at the rowing boat, where the woman was storing the tackle bag, the buckets, the picnic.

'She won't go away. She had no family when she came here.'

'I don't think she's happy.'

'Who is happy? Tell me this. She will never take the children away.'

The girl turned to look. The early light had turned the river pink. In the boat the woman sat quietly waiting.

'You must find someone else to love,' the dwarf said.

'It's too late.'

'You will never get to know her.'

'Maybe not. It doesn't stop the love.'

'No.'

'Does everyone know about us?'

'They have guessed. In the town they call you "the boys". They won't say anything.'

'There's nothing to say.'

'No.' The dwarf took her thin hand in his pudgy one and held it softly. His white hairs lifted and settled again on his head. 'Tell her to take you up into Fullerton Cove,' he said, 'to the whiting hole. She knows where it is.'

They have lit a fire on the beach, and cooked a schnapper for lunch. The woman turns to sit facing the sea and lights a cigarette. She smokes it without saying anything. The girl considers how these two years have happened. She is sixteen and nothing has changed, there are no explanations.

Her fingers are not as sensitive as the woman's. She has learnt to tell the difference between the way a tailor and a bream take the hook, how a flathead is exciting, sudden, and swims hard, how a crab will suck and so on. She has learnt the woman's language, which she will forget later, but now seeing a man further down the beach dragging a fish on a rope and bending, rising, putting worms in the tin on his waist she says, 'Must be whiting about.' The woman nods.

The woman has not much use for words. Most of her talk is saved for the dog, and the girl has learnt that a mood can be judged by this. If the woman is happy with the girl she will speak to the dog with such affection and endearments the girl is sure it's for her.

'You darling thing. Look at those beautiful eyes. Come here now and let me cuddle you, gorgeous thing you are. What a girl!'

At other times the dog sits under the table, waiting, till the woman says 'I don't want to SPEAK to you.' None of her moods seem to be related to anything, as far as the girl can see.

On the beach the woman put her cigarette out and said, 'My mother was a good swimmer.' There was a long silence.

'She was in the state team, before she had me. They said' (she looked down towards the wreck, towards the city) 'they didn't know who my father was. I think he was rich, but he never came near her again after I was born, except once when I was in the Home.'

The girl considered this information carefully. It was the longest speech the woman had made in the time she had known her.

'Why were you in the Home?' the girl asked.

'My mother died when I was one,' the woman said.

Suddenly she had lost her straight back, she seemed smaller than before. The girl wanted to take her in her arms.

Could she be reached out for? She was staring straight out to sea. The girl moved and sat in front of her. Now they had locked vision. The woman's eyes had turned into wells reflecting the sea, the fine lines radiating to the edge of the iris seemed painted there like markings on a lizard. She kept her eyes focused on the girl and made slight movements of her head from side to side. Eventually she looked away and lit two cigarettes. She passed one to the girl.

The girl smoked the cigarette because it tasted like the kiss. How many thousands of cigarettes she smoked later because of the memory of the kiss.

The girl realised she was on some sort of path. The way was not clear, but there was a fellow traveller. Later the path would be crowded with women but the girl was not to know this. When she looked ahead now she saw two solitary figures, parting and coming together again, but always parting.

She thought about the woman's mother. The woman could not let herself be held, by a friend, by a *child*, whom she now turned to abruptly — 'I want you to swim,' she said. 'Go and get in the water.'

The girl put down the schnapper bone she was sucking on and walked towards the water. There was a boat in the distance, too far away to see her clearly. She took off her jeans and jumper and stood naked for a while, breathing, telling her body not to feel the cold. She bent to a low dive and stroked out to the first wave, which went over her like a tunnel. Underwater she opened her eyes and saw how green it was, a yellow green light like columns of buildings in other civilisations, then the discrete grains of sand, each one with its edges and vertices. She breast-stroked along the bottom, holding her breath as long as she could — almost a minute — and then came up to face the horizon, gasping slowly so it wouldn't show, and continued out beyond the waves. There was *The Lobster Queen*, the boat her friend was never allowed to go on because it belonged to her husband, and women were thought to be bad luck on fishing boats.

The girl could see the husband and his deckhand moving about, shaking fish from the net. The men didn't look up.

She turned and arrowed back to the waves. Ahead of the breakers, she trod water and began to take deep breaths. When the wave was three lengths behind her she began to swim fast. The wave collected her like a giant hand and she ducked her head and held her arms straight out in front, fingers stretched. Then slowly she brought her arms back to her sides and came in fast on the beach, head first. The wave eddied and she stood up, an aviator, elated, the saltbush in the distance dancing, each leaf an oiled sparkling green.

'Don't you ever do that again,' the woman said. 'You had me frightened half to death, staying under so long.'

The girl bent and nuzzled her face into the dog's neck, nuzzling and pretending to bite, then she dug her fingers in near the dog's tail and brought them backwards through the fur to the neck, growling and the dog growled with her.

Late in the afternoon they went back to the beach for another throw. Squinting, the girl could make out cars on the breakwater and people fishing off the wreck. Then the woman had something on her line and reeled in fast.

'Huh, I thought it was a bloody fish, the way you pulled it in,' the girl said. She stood looking down at a heap of tangled line on the hook.

'No, no. We can use this,' the woman said. She had a hook in her mouth and the sun was shining on her eyebrows and teeth, on her straight nose. Her disappointed face.

The girl helped her undo the line, feeding the end through tangles, then holding it as the woman got progressively further away while unknotting it. Talking to herself about breaking-strain and bream. Then she came back and showed the girl how to tie it on to another line so it would be long enough.

'This is a blood knot, will you remember how to do it?'

'Yes.'

'Will you remember how to do it when I'm dead?'

'Yes.'

At seven o'clock the sheet of wet sand was streaked in pink and orange from the setting sun. The woman stood, a hand in her cardigan pocket, nudging at the sand with a toe. 'Remember when we used to dig out pippies with our feet? Bucketfuls.' The girl caught up with her and said, 'Come on, let's walk.' They went through wave edges and past an old man worming. He had a smelly piece of mullet tied on a string, and was dragging it across the sand after each wave receded. Every so often he bent down and pulled a long worm out of the sand, and dropped it in a tin tied to his belt. His rod was standing upright in the sand further along. 'Must be whiting about,' the girl said. The woman grunted.

That night they went to the hotel and sat in the lounge bar with the other women. They played the jukebox and drank beer till late.

When the girl went to the toilet the woman followed her in and stood with her back to the door watching the girl pee. When the girl finished, the woman pushed her gently to the side wall and put her arms on the wall and brought her face close and kissed her on the mouth. Through the wall the girl could hear 'Put your sweet lips a little closer to the phone, Let's pretend that we're together, all alone' and in her mouth she could her the woman humming the same song against her tongue and her teeth. Then the woman sat and peed, while the girl watched.

'You go out first,' the woman said.

It was the first time the girl had been drunk, and she realised how many times she had seen the woman drunk and not recognised it. She also thought, as they were driving home, she could top the woman's drink up at night — that helping her get drunk would make things happen. Half the night she lay awake thinking about this, it was a moral decision she could make. Her body told her to do it. Her mind said no; her mind won.

In the morning when the girl came into the yard amongst the half-made lobster pots, fish traps, string nets, bits of planking, oil drums, she saw the woman on the step cleaning out her tackle bag. With a minimum of words, and slowing the action of her hands so the girl could follow, she showed her rigs for different fish, when to use a trace, a swivel, and what size sinkers were needed. Then she took the reels off and squatted and showed the girl how they worked, and how to clean and oil them.

'This is an egg-beater,' she said, 'and this is what the ratchet's for. This is an Alvey reel, or a sidecast. It's better for the beach.'

The girl looked at this one — it was the classic type you saw in books with people fishing, a plain reel, made of bakelilte like the old radios.

'I'll get one of these one day,' the girl said.

The woman looked at her and said, 'You'd be better with an egg-beater.'

The girl ignored this. She would get what she wanted. It would never be just a matter of fishing.

Later the woman took her to the shed and showed her the sinker moulds, and pieces of lead they'd collected at the tip, or from people's roofs. They weighed the lead in their hands like butter. For some time they stood in the green light at the bench where her husband's cousin made their sinkers. 'My cousin,' she called him, but the girl knew he was her husband's cousin. It was the tall man who came to have his hair cut in the kitchen.

The woman was in a good mood that morning. She talked quietly about the tides and times of year and what fish liked to eat.

She talked about the different shapes of the insides of fish, she said that mullet could only be netted or jagged because they wouldn't take a hook, and how they had a black lining to their gut.

'Groper do this,' she said, squatting on the lawn near her tomato beds, opening and closing her mouth as she brought her head closer to the girl, who leaned in, her hair brushed by a sheet on the washing line. The woman sat back, grinning, and said 'Now that's enough.'

'How is your boyfriend,' she said, after a long time. 'Do you have a boyfriend at work? What about the man who came into the restaurant?'

'I want *you*,' the girl said. 'Now.'

'Now, now,' the woman said, and went to fill the copper at the end of the shed. In the middle of the day her husband would come home. The shed had low windows at the back which let in the greenish light. Standing there watching, the girl realised that although the woman said she didn't have any love left for her husband, although they rarely spoke and then only to abuse each other, the abuse was the form their passion now took, it was their way of staying together, and the truth was the woman liked to do things for him — but only when he wasn't home. These things were done at certain times of the day — washing his overalls, filling the copper, ironing the shirts he wore to the club in the afternoons. The ironing lay on the floor in neat piles near her tools — the saw, hammer, chisels, brushes — things she needed to fix the house.

He kept his tools separate in the shed, where he spent most of his time when he wasn't on the boat. He had a kettle and tea-things in the shed, where his friends visited him. He had a fridge there, and bales of wire and a cocky in a cage. When he came home he would stand in his overalls, wreathed in steam over the copper boiling his lobsters. Then he would take the catch to the co-op, come home and have a bath, put on his ironed shirt and go to the club and get drunk. He did this every day. At night he came home at ten, took his tea out of the oven and ate it alone, grumbling, while she watched the late news. They didn't do anything together except sleep in the same bed. Once the girl had sneaked into their bedroom. There were little piles of clothes everywhere, and the racing pages from the paper. The girl thought that maybe they had a flutter together now and then, but she would never know this. It was the permanent mystery of adults who seemed to choose not to be happy. They could not give up the things they had because the things were known and clear and warm. If they were warm with abuse it was just another kind of heat.

The girl could see that the man was jealous of her, and that he didn't know what to do about it. Sometimes as she passed the shed he growled at her, which was his way of saying hello, and she would smile and ask how he was, but usually he pretended she wasn't there. He listened to the races on his little radio.

Sometimes the kids tried to talk to him, but he would tell them to get out of his way, he said he was worried they'd get a hook in their foot, or put their hands in his copper of lobsters.

The girl thought he might be uncomfortable because the boy looked like a girl, and the girl looked like a boy, but she never knew. Her own father was not good at speaking to children. So the man seemed normal, but more so. She tried not to think about him. Once he asked if she would like a naughty and she said no and thanked him, and went away with her throat burning.

She had forgotten writing the letter to the woman, and not sending it. Who are we, what are we doing? she had asked. Why is this so strong? Where are the others? She had obviously hidden it in the sock. Her father was waving it in the air and speaking crudely, in his insulted state, and then he hit her once, hard, on the face. When she became conscious she was lying on the bed. He was continuing with his sentences.

Later her father went to visit her friend, trying three hotels and then the house. He told the woman he'd ring up the market where she worked and explain to them just what kind of person she was. He advised her never to touch his daughter again.

Ten years later the girl found out this had happened. She had rung her sister and the sister said 'Just like when Dad —' and the story came out.

'When did this happen?' she said, 'this visit of Dad's — when I was sixteen? What — seventeen? When I was at the restaurant?'

'Look,' her sister said. 'I thought you knew. Didn't anyone tell you?'

'No, nothing,' she said.

'Well look. I think you were sixteen. I used to lie for you, say you'd gone to another friend's place. You were seeing her for two years, three years — were you doing it? You never said.'

'I don't know. Not exactly. Not completely.'

The phone call left her in shock for days. In the kitchen looking at her quince tree through a small pane of blue glass she understood why she'd hated her father. Or why the hate was as strong as the love. Before, her rage had been blind. Her father's face appeared and she bared her teeth.

So many years later, it became clear why the woman had suddenly turned cold towards her. When she visited, the woman would hardly acknowledge she was there. There was no news about which cousin had sunk someone's boat because that bloke had stolen lobsters from his traps. No affectionate talk to the dog who now sat on the girl's lap, or beside her on the step, as if to console her. There were the visits and there was silence. The woman never sent her away, and never said why she had changed. When the girl asked if something was wrong, the woman shrugged, and got up to make more tea.

Sometimes there were strange fish in the sink.

'What's this you've caught?' the girl said. She leaned over, smelling it.

'Trevally,' the woman said.

'What did you catch it with?'

'Beach worms,' the woman said, talking for a while about the habits of trevally.

When the girl tried to talk about things other than fishing, personal things, the woman was silent or changed the subject. She moved her lips around without opening her mouth. She shrugged a lot, and looked out the back door. She always had her hand on the brown dog beside her.

They sat looking at the husband's nets drying on stumps on the back lawn. The husband was watching his lobsters cook, and turning his head to the side now and then to say something to his cocky. He had found the cocky caught in wire on the riverbank, injured, and brought it home and nursed it for months. Sometimes he put the cocky on his shoulder, and fed it with cheese.

The woman made the girl tomatoes on toast and tea with milk and sugar. Then she opened the fridge and took out a lobster she'd taken from her husband's catch the day before.

'Come here,' she said, beckoning with the lobster's feelers. At the bench she showed the girl how to open the lobster, laying it on its back and making a neat cut down the centre of the tail up to the head, and opening the shell away. Now she took a round segment from near the tail and held it to the girl's mouth.

The flesh was moist silk against her tongue. It was as though every sweet flathead fillet she'd ever eaten was a preparation for this craving in the mouth. They set to and devoured the lot, grasping legs and cracking them open and sucking out the flesh. They ate the lobster's brain. They up-ended the shell and drank the juice. Then they wrapped what was left and put it in the bin out of sight.

When they sat down again, the woman's face seemed to set in its lines till she looked like a statue. Sometimes this had happened at night, when she was tired. She sat very still, without speaking.

The dog came in and put its paws on the girl's lap, and looked into her face. Its eyes were a deep gold flecked with brown like a river stone seen through water. Eventually the woman said, 'Maybe you ought to get a boyfriend. Don't you think?'

'If you want me to,' the girl said.

A Bottle of Tears

While Rita was waiting in the corridor outside the doctor's office the door opened and the doctor himself came out, shepherding a tall, thin man on whose face there was a look of intense concentration.

The doctor recognised her and said, rather irritably, 'Are you next? Go in,' so she went into the little room and stood looking aimlessly about at the desk, the examination couch, the lighted screen on which a chest x-ray was hanging, her mind quite occupied by the question of whether or not she should sit down, when the doctor came back and hurried across to the screen, exclaiming, 'It isn't yours!'

'I wasn't loooking,' she answered, 'so it doesn't matter.'

He put his hand on the frame of the x-ray, meaning to remove it, but it drew his gaze again and he looked at it with pain and anger, muttering, 'I wouldn't want to see that in your chest, never,' unconsciously revealing his affection and giving her the impersonal joy one feels at the sight of a fragile-looking plant growing in conditions that bear witness to the toughness of the species. He was indiscreet, she perceived, because he was concentrating so much on the x-ray that he wasn't quite aware of her presence.

With an effort he put it away and, setting Rita's in its place, he produced a complete change of atmosphere, like an Elizabethan scene-shifter.

'Why don't you stop wasting my time?' he asked, pretending severity in order to subdue a smile of joy which would have been really excessive.

'As good as that?'

'Couldn't be much better.'

He opened a book and began to ask routine questions more seriously, and Rita gave the expected answers, but when their eyes met they both smiled, and as Rita was walking to the door her feet performed an irrepressible dance step. She looked back smiling at the doctor, who said, 'No silliness, now.'

'Everything in moderation, even silliness,' she answered, and closed the door behind her.

Outside the weather was splendid, with warm sunshine and a small wind playing in the street. A wonderful day for a walk, she thought, and set off to walk down Oxford Street to Foy's, meaning to drink a cup of coffee on the piazza and look at the park. On her way she paused outside the second-hand shop to smile over a framed panel of looking-glass decorated with a painted white swan, green reeds and a pink waterlily, and decided with surprise that it was pretty.

Suddenly, the money she had saved during months of austerity began to run in her veins and she went in to ask its price. Inside, on a table covered with dusty china ornaments, she found a narrow silver vase and bought that too. She promised to call for the panel and left, quite unrepentant, carrying the vase and planning the redecoration of her room: a dark floor — get rid of that dirty old carpet and polish the boards, she thought, drawing on her energy as freely as on her bank account — no whatnot, no epergne, no jokes except the glass panel, a Lalique swan on the mantel and a white rug with some pink and some green in it. She walked on, planning happily, without noticing her progress, until the laughter of children on the piazza reminded her that the schools were on holiday.

There were only half a dozen children after all, darting about and laughing with upward glances. Then she saw the bubbles, puffed out of a pipe masked with flowers high on the shopfront. The breeze was juggling them and letting them fall, and a little girl who had caught one opened her hand and looked into it with a painless cry of disappointment.

One bubble — how bright it was in the sunlight, outlined sharply with blue and purple — performed a slow descending dance and drifted past a young woman at one of the tables, who let it go and turned smiling to speak to her companion in a language Rita didn't recognise. This was a moment of poetry, a compound of the sunlight and the greenery that framed the woman's head, the foreign voice at home and at ease and the memory of an old map of the Terra Australis that had always prompted her imagination; and she thought, they are the real inhabitants, the migrants, the first since great-grandfather.

How did that thought bring Matt so close beside her that his absence was really a shock? Almost, she had turned to speak to him. It was one of those strange moments when one feels that a previous experience is repeating itself, but she had never been here with Matt. Of course, of course, the woman at the zoo.

Rita sat at the table drinking her coffee, seeing again the tall fair woman in the checked topcoat, standing at the top of a rise, looking down at the basinful of blue water flagged with white sails, saying 'Wunderschön' with quiet satisfaction. It was then that Matt had been standing beside her.

There is something about that trick of the mind, fusing past and present, that moves the heart extraordinarily. Is it oneself one greets with such sadness and astonishment? Rita drank her coffee thoughtfully, gazing at the park but after all without seeing it. Only the stream of traffic that flowed past the park, with the weaving of movement and the flashing of sunlight complicating its surface, drew her gaze and entered her thoughts. When she had drunk her coffee, she went inside to the telephone and rang Matt's office.

When he came to the phone, she said uncertainly, 'Matt? This is Rita.'

The silence that followed was just what she expected, for the underground river of malice ran so far beneath the surface in Matt that he could never be nasty at will; but she was frightened by it for all that, feeling that nothing she knew of Matt was of any value and that at the other end of the line there was an unknown, unlimited power to harm her.

'I don't see much point in this.' Matt was angry, but only Matt, after all.

'I changed my mind, that's all. You don't have to change yours on that account, of course,' she added in a false and arrogant tone that dismayed her. 'I just thought I'd tell you, that's all.' She waited, exposed to the abominable black receiver, feeling tired all at once, thinking that it would be a relief if the blow fell now. How easy it would be not to love at all!

'You really mean it?' Matt's voice was full of reverence, not for her nor for love, but for good luck, which he respected as other men respect money and fame. It was true that Fate was strict with him, and his wit, his kindness and his good looks were slightly tarnished by an amiable resignation.

'Is it all right?' With joy and relief, Rita began to laugh.

'Where are you?'

'I'm in town, at Foy's.'

'I can get the afternoon off.'

'I can't believe that. I'm sure this is just the day you have to work back.'

'No fooling, this is my day. Can you stay where you are? Half an hour, not much more anyhow.'

'All right. I can do some shopping and meet you on the terrace.' She was inclined to laugh at Matt, the scientist ruled by the stars (ruled by every bloody thing, kid; the stars and science, prenatal influences, economic laws, the boss and what have you), but there did seem to be some magic about the day which allowed her to repair so quickly that moment of loss and isolation.

Upstairs in the dress department she found a green and gold dress that seemed to be made for her, and when she tried it on she considered her reflection in the fitting-room glass, that reflection of a reflection one never sees otherwise, the profile of a stranger about to walk away, and was astonished as usual by its beauty.

She had been a plain girl and had become a beauty unexpectedly when she grew up, and the only thing in her face that she recognised as her own was the mark of her inward anxiety, which remained like the ghost of a frown when her face was in repose and gave her a gentle, sympathetic expression. Today for the first time she could accept her good looks without uneasiness as an accidental glory like the weather and the new dress, having discovered transience as the flaw in everything that made it her own. Matt, too, she thought —remembering the urgency of his question, 'Can you stay where you are?' — wanting that one moment kept for him till he came; having just embarked on the current, she thought, of course I can't, and felt wise, experienced and full of courage.

But, as Matt was walking up the steps towards her, she felt quite deformed by nervousness, marooned in a nightmare on a stage to play a part she didn't know and feeling that everything she said to him from now on would be a desperate guess.

She looked at him for a cue, but he took her parcels in silence, looking happy but remote, and his happiness weighed her down with responsibility as if he had given her something fragile to carry.

'New dress,' she said as she handed over the big box. He grinned and took a slip of paper from his pocket, saying, 'Lottery ticket.' He was nervous too, and their laughter sounded forced.

They didn't talk much until they had closed the door of Matt's room behind them and begun to make love readily and without grace, like awkward swimmers getting into water where there is no danger. Rita said then, 'I had the experience of losing you suddenly. It was one of those moments, you know, that you seem to have lived through before, and I thought you were with me for a minute. It wasn't that I found I couldn't live without you, you see — it's so easy to begin to falsify things' —

'Is that what you're afraid of?'

'Oh, the things I'm afraid of,' she was shaking her head, 'they're too ridiculous to mention. Missing the train, losing the key, not understanding the directions, not hearing what the man says. You could overcome any one of them but there are too many.' Her face was bright and heavy with embarrassment, and Matt, quite startled, said, 'Nothing to be ashamed of.'

'What you're ashamed of is just the thing you are. You'll cover it up even with something worse.' She was silent for a moment, then she added, 'Gulliver tied down with threads.'

'What's that?'

'Gulliver tied down with threads, that's what I am.'

Matt didn't quite follow but he was glad to see her beauty restored.

'You know, Matt, I think I could change, perhaps, but I couldn't bear to have it expected of me.'

'I suppose I can stand you as you are.' He added, 'What you don't see is that happiness is pretty commonplace really. Anyone can have it, even people like you and me.'

This was said without irony and Rita could find no word for it except politeness, but it extended the meaning of the word.

'There's nothing new, is there? About being lovers, I mean. It's all in the past, like a graph that's been plotted already.'

'What was I trying to tell you?'

'And now I know.'

Matt said, 'Let's go out to dinner tonight. Somewhere really good, where we can dance. I'll ring up and book a table.'

'Somewhere with a view of the harbour. I could wear my new dress. You know, I never knew what those places were for, before.'

'Some people eat there regularly.'

'Very nice of them, too, to dress up and dance divinely and eat lobster thermidor on our account.'

'Probably they don't look at it like that.'

'Probably not.' Rita was smiling. She had always felt most alone in crowds and in public places, and now she was thinking that she would never really belong to a crowd again.

It was a wonderful evening, and in the elegant restaurant they did not seem out of place. 'Nothing went wrong,' Rita said when they were back in Matt's room, 'but if anything had, it wouldn't have mattered, and that will always be the main part of love for me. All the talk about what love is,' she added, yawning, very slightly drunk, 'I can tell you what it isn't. It isn't an abstraction. I love you has meaning, but the word love has no meaning; it's a participle, particle, something or other.'

'Grammar, for God's sake,' Matt said, laughing and putting his arms around her.

They fell asleep so close together that Matt woke up, hours later when the room was beginning to grow lighter in the dawn, because her sobs were shaking his chest like a grief of his own.

He whispered, 'Old girl, what's the matter?' but she shook her head and went on crying.

When she tried to speak, the man at the clinic appeared on the surface of the storm like flotsam and was drowned again.

'What man?'

He thought he heard the word 'dying', or was it the end of a sob followed by a brief sigh? No; she said coherently then, 'It's a man I saw at the clinic today, a man who's dying.'

For Christ's sake, he thought angrily, why bring that up now? He said, 'How do you know he was dying? Nobody would tell you a thing like that.' But he knew it in spite of himself, for the conviction that had been in the man's eyes and the doctor's voice was in Rita's crying too.

'An accident.' The word was cast up broken. She said again, 'An accident. I connected a face with an x-ray. Something the doctor said.'

There will always be someone dying somewhere, he thought, astonished at this simple device for destroying happiness, and his memory returned to him something it had kept intact, Rita saying in a queer, affected voice, 'I don't think I'm capable of happiness.' At the time he had shouted. 'What damned sickening nonsense,' but after all it was the queerness of truth, a deepsea fish hauled to the surface.

'If you'd seen his face ——,' Rita sat up to look for a handkerchief, and in the twilight he saw a relationship of chin and shoulder that was like the first glimpse of the person one is going to love. Oh, well, he had promised to love her as she was, and now he knew what that meant.

'It seems terrible that I didn't think of him all day,' she said, still wiping away tears. 'It was such a wonderful day.'

'Your crying won't help him, kid.'

'No. I know. If I put my tears in a bottle and sent them to him, it would be nothing, a bottle of salt water. He'd look at it and wonder what the hell. What else is pity, anyhow? If I knew him, if I knew what to say to him better than anyone else, it would all be the same to him. Not because he's dying but for what he is now, cut off.' She took his hand, saying, 'Matt?'

'Yes, my darling?'

'I've been an absolute fool, haven't I?'

As he realised what she meant, his love extended to include the dying man, who was not, after all, an intruder.

JIMMY PIKE

Mirnmirt

When single woman likes a man, she draws this story in the mud with a stick. When woman talks about man, talks about love, she draws this story.

When someone talks, or a man sees that story, then he goes to the woman. Then they talk marriage. Mirnmirt is the marriage law.

When man has finished the law, done everything, he can marry. He has got to learn everything. There are two laws. One for the young boy, takes several months. One for the full man, takes five or six years.

When man come back from bush after manhood, woman waiting. They have a big feast and make man and woman red with clay.

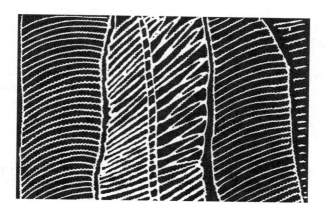

The Red Pearl

It's the dark thing he feels for her: it makes him watch her face in astonishment. Hair scraped back, its whiteness is like a candle over the washbasin, over which she bends with her pots of paint, with her pig bristle brushes and the jars of lard and pigment she balances on the palm of her hand. Her face is pale and shiny. Hair falls in dark curls on her shoulders and neck. The curve of her cheek is what he watches, that moon curve, and then she turns and her features are sickle sharp. Like the teeth with which she bites him. With which she delicately lifts his skin, so small the bit of skin she lifts that he can hardly feel it. It is the nip of an insect felt only in the swelling after it's gone. That is when he feels her: when she is gone.

In the evening the sailor wakes in a fading bar of sunlight, in a room no longer swelling with the sounds, the sudden rushes of the night. He has slept a whole day. The sailor sprawls voluptuous on sheets by no means clean or of any particular colour. The room is filled with subtle smells. With the narrow bed on which he lies, and shoes and strings of beads, discarded clothing on the floor. The sailor's lover is a poor housekeeper. Everywhere he looks is dust, half-empty glasses, plates crusted with the leavings of meals. Her room is a nest of things that shift and sparkle in the light. By the sailor's head are bauble-studded brushes tangled with her hairs. By his feet, the gilt-trimmed masks and fans of painted chickenskin that she flicks and furls with deft movements of her wrist. Across his belly, her colourful scarves nesting twisted like snakes.

The sailor stretches languid, he's a land sailor, long enough landed so that he misses neither the pitch nor surge of the sea. He's a good enough sailor, a singer of songs if he's asked nicely, a speaker of many languages, although roughly, and a teller of tales garnered from the vast Orient: from circuitous travels on ships that have taken him from the brothels and bars of Madagascar to the towns and cityports that edge the Sulawesi Sea. His smooth face belies these many talents and travels, his cherubic countenance the target of maternal grandames who plant kisses on his cheeks and thrust inquisitive fingers into his shirt to pat at his shoulderblades in search of furtively sprouting wings.

In certain rough nightclubs the sailor has been known to shock his worldly audience into silence with his sordid tales of horror and depravity. It's not the tales that rob one of speech so much as the gentle mouth from which these tales issue, and the widely-spaced eyes and boyish frame of the one who tells them; the one who, later, might sometimes be persuaded to leap onto a table in a flurry of movement the eye can hardly follow, to twist and spin and stamp with primeval fervour and gestures that are wickedly lewd. At such gatherings a hush soon fills the dimly-lit room. The enthusiastic clapping that at first accompanies the sailor's dance dies quickly away, and even those actions that occur unwittingly, a shift of the buttocks here, the flicker of an eyelid there, a burst of unwarranted laughter — all these are suspended as he whirls ever faster above them with his lips stretching fiendishly and the light throwing shadows so it seems that his feet strike sparks against the table and his hair stands out in glowing ends and his fingernails curl crookedly, and his eyes widen into pits to suck and swallow everyone whole. But the sailor stops, exhausted, throwing himself into a nearby chair and then everyone is murmuring, clapping, cheering, sipping drinks and so on. The sailor's hair is sweat-plastered to his forehead, some rough-faced woman is smacking her lips against him, and his cheeks are flushed with delight.

The sailor sprawls voluptuous with the stories in his head, and yawns. It's early yet. Soon enough, he will rise. He'll smooth back his hair and eyebrows and pick among the clothes on the floor for the baggy shirt and pants he favours. He'll pull on his pointed shoes and set his cap at a jaunty angle. Already the evening sounds have been replaced with night sounds, with the shouts of hawkers and spruikers and the callgirl banter that floats through the window in shrieks and whistles like the cries of startled birds. The lover's room is in the attic of the Shanghai Bar, is throbbing with the cooling machines in its basement and the paddings and rustlings of the women who sweep, mop and scrub at its dingy interior in hopes of approximating the management's promise of a 'World Class Beautiful Hostess Lounge And Bar'. The heavy bass beat of the resident band, warming up for the night's performance, seeps up through the floor.

In all of the cities the sailor has been to there has always been a Shanghai Bar. That name, like the names Surabaya, Alexandria and Xanadu, conjures up visions of other, more decadent worlds. Exotic realms given wholly to the sophisticated articulation of Pleasure: places of feasting, romantic interludes, adventure; where the settings are always rich and there is singing and dancing, and birds of paradise, macaws and other wild beasts which roam freely and feed from one's hand — in short, all the projections of the Paradise that is to be found neither in the first-named Shanghai nor in the here-and-now of the ones who seek and seek to replicate it. The sailor knows only too well the pleasure of such names. The bar above which he now lies, that shabby counterfeit of the other Shanghai, with its Chinese lanterns, its dragons coiling around pillars clutching precious red pearls, its gold and green booths and bargirls squeezed into sheaths of artificial silk that pinch at their throats, breasts and hips in a way that is mercilessly sexy — all these vibrate beneath him with the promise of *transposition*: of anonymity, abandonment, delirium, dream.

Often men come here to dream. The sailor sits with them in the vinyl booths below, in the smoky limbo of their sundry desires, clinking glasses, swapping jokes and tales and raucous bursts of laughter. The passing Asiatic bargirls are the essence of such dreams, the place tinkles with their chatter as they lean against an arm here, a shoulder there, bending to offer their lips for sucking or biting and their cleavages for the thrusting of tips. It's not them, though, that the men have come to see. The Shanghai Bar, famous for its bargirls, is even more famous for its numerous acts: its singers who are also magicians, pulling sparrows out of ears and flies; its dancers who are acrobats and contortionists, twisting their limbs into bawdy knots; its strippers who eat fire and blow smoke rings from their cunts. The audience votes for the acts by tossing money or rubbish onto the stage, arguments rage between tables. The sailor alone is unmoved. He laughs or jeers with the rest while keeping his coins and empty glasses, his nutshells and cigarette butts. Only one act leaves him silent: expectant as the hour approaches, as the sequin-coated emcee climbs the platform to announce the final act of the evening. *She.*

It's a dark thing he feels for her: only when it's dark can he see her clearly. The night is her element, it flows through the window in lazy spirals, it creaks through the crevices in the floor and walls and weeps through the ceiling to fold like some majestic beast at her feet.

'Dance for me,' the sailor whispers.

If she's in the mood she'll comply. She'll trace languid circles on the dusty floor, her arms will rise and her back arch delicately, and she'll bend her body this way and that, and throw her head back to look at him with unblinking eyes. It seems every part of her moves of its own volition. She, the sum of these parts, is that, and nothing more. Like him, she'll curiously watch the shapes her hands make, curving like the heads of exotic birds. Like his, her eyes will be drawn to the swaying of her own hips, to the rhythmic stretching and spreading of her thighs. The scent that coils from her skin will seduce her. When she agrees to dance, the sailor lies mesmerised.

More often, she'll not hear him. She'll blend mixing powders and scented oils at the washbasin, rubbing these into her skin, or she'll end the dance half-heartedly, crumpling to the floor to smile at him, but not tenderly. At times like these the sailor rises, he slides from the bed in a single movement as if pulled on strings. These times he's reminded of when he first saw her. Then too, she smiled unkindly, and he rose from his seat, amidst clappings and hootings he crossed the space between them, in an instant it seemed, to stand before her, to be stroked and straddled, to be devoured. How poignant are the rites of anthropophagy in the play-acting of new lovers: 'Eat me,' the sailor begged, his flesh a plum in the lover's mouth, a red-centred heart to drip down her chin as she bit into him. She licked him with relish, with strokes that oozed and burned.

These times, like that very first time, the sailor slides to where she is lying, in an instant he is standing beside her and she is regarding his feet. 'Dance,' the lover murmurs to these feet, and they do. The sailor dances, it is that quicksilver dance of twists and jumps that leaves the watcher breathless. Fixed by a pivot that is her eyes, he, not unlike puppets on sticks whose arms and legs jerk rapidly in all directions when a string on their backs is pulled, is staked in front of her, his body rigid, his limbs flying. The sailor moves ever faster. He can't help it, it's a trick he learnt on his travels, a way to fool the human eye. And it seems to him now that there really are sparks under his feet, which hiss and splutter and burn. The sailor is hot, is pinned like a moth in the glare of her gaze, the sailor is on fire, his throat exquisitely dry. His body is licked with flames and his hair beginning to smoulder. And the sailor tears at his clothes, he rips off his shirt and pants, his steaming underclothes and crackling shoes, until he writhes naked before her. Until she blinks, and he falls to the floor. The sailor lies gulping mouthfuls of precious cool air, he is nothing but this gulping mouth, nothing but ears straining for the slither of her body as she slides wilfully towards him.

These days the sailor doesn't dream. He lies in the frenzied neon of the lights that whirl in through the window, idly watching the shadows they trace and tussle on the walls. The street is decked for celebrating, streamers hang from buildings, trees are strung with coloured lights. Now and then the sailor jerks fully awake, he bolts upright, he is shot with the sounds of firecrackers set off by urchins, animals shrieking from gunpowder pellets popping their tails. The street that houses the Shanghai Bar is a street of perpetual movement, excitement, a carnival of senses, as it is advertised, where no one knows what hour it is, what time of month or year, except that it's always festival time. The sailor lies indifferent, his face pensive, his features cast of stone it seems, he lies so still, so faintly smiling.

The sailor knows the value of his smiles, his lips which are expertly curved for charming and disarming, for pleasing pawnbrokers and otherwise tenacious landladies who pile up his plate at the sight of his hollow cheeks and the hungry looks he gives them, and later trade credit for his time. The sailor's been called a ladies' man, but it's not the ladies he is partial to, neither is it seraphic schoolgirls, nor maidens who are whisked by watchful parents out of his way. It's the shrews with spirit that the sailor likes, the women who sleep in the daytime and screech and rip at his face when he leaves them, as he inevitably does. The faded courtesans are his favourites, whose bodies dimple loose and mottled in his arms, and also the girls who sway in sad circles with their eyes closed, their limbs wraith-like, their skins that sag against him already purpling with decay.

It's dancers like the lover this sailor goes for: the ones who shimmer darkly, whose faces are pallid like certain funereal flowers and whose scents, like them, are also thick and sweet and clinging. The one whose body is pale and limpid, who is carved with birthmarks, with knobs and hollows to be discovered haphazardly, to be nuzzled and licked at like extra lips and teats. How the sailor goes for her! This one who swings her legs apart in lazy arcs, and snakes and swivels, and searches the audience for his eye. And after that time the sailor first sees her, he lives for the Shanghai Bar. He lives with the winks and nudges, the slaps of echoing laughter that make him the butt of jokes and the hasty, veiled warnings that are whispered when the lover isn't near. After first seeing her the sailor can't help it, he has to wait for her, he waits, and he pays to wait in her room, to sit and to sip and suck at her: to hang about her like an insect, to curl around her like an eel.

The sailor curls contented, he's a complacent enough sailor, he doesn't even know the lover's name. She will not tell him. 'Call me Bintang Tenggara,' she says. 'Call me Rockin' Rosie. Call me Red Pearl.' These are the names of ships that occasionally dock at the harbour, also the favourite names of the unused ferries that nudge alongside them, housing squatters who patch holes in the decrepit hulls, and keep fowls and pigeons, and swap gossip while shitting and pissing into the sea. In these parts names are precious, to be guarded from baleful spirits, and strangers and spies. The lover doesn't listen when he tells her his name. She calls him: say-loh, which said in her language means 'To die.' He calls her: lover, sweetheart, bintang, rosie, pearl.

Mostly she does not call him, it is he who calls, who leans forward to sing to her, and stroke her, who cleans and carries and reads from the local papers the stories she likes to hear. The lover likes especially the ones with photos, the ones of choppings and murders, of black magic cults dumping mutilated corpses in alleys, as well as the gangfights, and the stories of enterprising men who make slavegirls of demons by sticking nails into their necks. She stares for long moments at the wistful-looking lovers who've tied themselves together and gulped poisons or plunged into the sea. The sailor likes her taste for tragedy. He searches for stories daily, he cuts them out and sticks them above her bed.

Other times he bustles about the room, he's a sailor not without skills, he can wield a frypan and boil water, juggle spoons and swing his sailor's knife in showy circles, chopping the tender chunks of meat she likes. Towards midnight, the lover will run up the stairs from the bar, she will run with sweat and the sharp smells of her body, and she'll be hungry, she'll be ravenous. She will pace the room in fits and starts, scolding him for being slow. The sailor will feed her with hearts, gizzards and raw liver for energy, he'll scoop these from their soggy packages, he'll hold them to her mouth and stroke her graceful neck as she closes her eyes, as she leans to swallow them whole. Housewifely, the sailor will hover over her as she squats by the stove in the corner, picking at the sizzling meats before they're done. And if he's too slow, or if she's too hungry, she won't wait any longer, she'll rant and hiss her displeasure, she'll slam out the door.

Now the night is well advanced but still the sailor lies, his feet occasionally twitching, his body heavy with his breaths and sighs. How the sailor sighs with pleasure! He aches with it, it rumbles in his bones. Soon enough, he will slip from the sheet that folds hot and sticky over him, he'll flex his body and curl back his toes. Soon he will rise to cross the room to the washbasin where he'll stare into the mirror and grimace and hawk and spit. He'll shiver as he splashes water onto his face and arms and he'll prowl about the room then, he'll peer into the lover's cupboards and boxes, he'll rifle through her things. The sailor loves her junkshop of things. He will breathe the acrid camphor that puffs from her costumes, he'll finger her gossamers and satins, smoothing wrinkles, spitting and rubbing at buckles to make them shine. Boxes line the lover's room, from floor to ceiling they perch in ragged piles. The lover is a hoarder, is a keeper of garments she no longer wears, of props that are broken and trinkets that crumble at the touch of his hand. Some trunks are so heavy the sailor can hardly lift them, others are caked with mould and musty smells. Some boxes rattle in his hands, and when he rips them open, they make him cough and splutter, they make him curse and kick at the dusty piles they empty, the mounds of rags and threads and mouldering bones.

The sailor stretches languid, he's a sailor grown idle, grown soft from too much lounging and hardly a sight of the sea. Perhaps he'll wait for the lover to enter. This time each night she will enter. She will fling the door open and stride towards him with scold-

ings and impatient clicks of her tongue. Already dressed for per-
forming, in her feathers and sequins, in the straps that crisscross
her body in peekaboo slices of breast and belly, of hips and
smoothly oiled crotch: already dressed and ready, the lover will
hurry him. She'll push and pull at him until he rises. She'll tug at
his hands and feet, thrusting them into shirtsleeves or pants' legs
while he pretends to be dozy, to be head-lolling and heavy like an
infant in her arms.

The lover will deal with him patiently. She'll duck his flailing
limbs and support his head against the jangling beads and baubles
on her chest, and when the sailor nuzzles her, when he paws at
that glittering armour to tug and squeeze at her breasts, she'll let
him. She'll let him pull her straps askew and lick at her nipples,
first one, then the other, and she'll watch impassively as he snuf-
fles and sucks. The lover will turn him gently, she will prise his
arms away, she will bare the nape of her neck, and rub his face
there. She'll rub his lips to her neckbone, to the calcified knob
that stiffens and quivers as he licks, and she'll sag and sigh, they
will grasp each other and tremble and sigh.

Finally, the lover will push him away. With a jab of a long
fingernail, she'll pierce the skin on one of her breasts and
squeeze between two deliberate fingers, a single, glistening red
pearl. The smell of her drives the sailor crazy. He'll thrash
against her, he'll lick his lips and whimper in a way that will
make her smile. That will make her grasp him by the hair and
pull him ever closer, ever more slowly towards her until he is
there, until his lips are open, and the pearl is in his mouth. The
sailor will swallow: he'll be transposed. For a moment he'll see
through the lover's eyes, smell through her nostrils, watch his
own quivering body cradled in her arms. The sailor will shiver
with fright and ecstasy. In that single moment he will think he
knows her perfectly.

When he has quietened, the lover will finish dressing him.
He's in no state to care about what he wears, but she'll dress him
immaculately. She likes him to be beautiful when he's seen. She
likes him to be beautiful when he's watching her. The lover will

smooth his hair with oils and darken his eyebrows, and dip into her jars of creams and jellies to liven his face, redden his lips. Then she'll slip on his shoes, his shiny sailor shoes, and she'll guide him through the door and down the rickety stairs to the seat by the stage that is saved especially for him. There the sailor will sit surrounded by the clappings and hootings of the Shanghai Bar, by the men who spread their thighs under the tables, tossing dollar bills to a bargirl so she'll sit with her hand in their pants, whispering the prices of delights to be found upstairs once the show is over, or before, if they're eager. The sailor will sit pensive amidst all this revelry, he'll sit hardly moving, staring at the stageboards through the dancers' legs and the acrobats' tumblings: waiting for *her* to appear.

At some point in this sailor's career, in his luscious careering, he will wake to wonder just why and how and where he's been: he's a canny sailor, he has tarried in these parts long enough to appreciate the value and workings of its dreams. The brooding mountains that ring this particular harbour city give it its aura of perpetual anxiety, caught as it is between those jagged peaks so like the crusty claws of the dragons which are said to spawn there, and that ever-encroaching other, the swirling, spirit-infested sea. It's no wonder this city's inhabitants hang suspended in the vortex of their various dreads and desires — balanced, as they are, not on one edge, but two. Insecurely nestled in the crevice between such clashing forces, the city that houses the Shanghai Bar exists in a state of an infinitely heightened sensibility: of fevers, visions, sensual and religious ecstasies, miracle cures. Here, cracks in the pavement are never stepped on for fear of tempting fate. Children and old men alike walk in staccato jumps and skips. Here, honeymooners trail in blissful unawareness through the streets and when they leave, leave trailing behind them the phantoms of their furies, their never-to-be-forgotten honeymoon fucks. Sorcerers and wisewomen trade briskly at the marketplace alongside pirate-tape vendors and boys who sell car parts for a song. Here, demons and other shadowy creatures share streetbeats with racketeers and petty criminals and, like them, have to be appeased.

In certain moods the sailor is given to musing: he lies wakeful, watchful in the shadows of bed and window, boxes and curtains, the assorted debris of this lover's room. Her smells intoxicate him, sometimes it seems he cannot breathe. At times like these the sailor slips into an unwelcome stupor, he tosses and turns, he is filled with indecipherable whisperings, apparitions that are enigmatic and crude. He'll see the old sweeper who tweaked his ear as he passed, pulling him to her stooped level, and lower, to peer at the piles of bones and maggoty remains of rats and geckos in the corridors. 'Eh, sailor!' she winked broadly. 'We got a cat here. A big cat, eh!' The sailor will hear the low laughs and the constant eggings and urgings of the other men to try it, to pull it, to try it, to pull it, to try — The sailor will toss and turn.

He will watch as the lover slips from her costumes, as she sheds her wig and eyelashes, discards her rings and bangles, her fake nails and necklaces to stand naked at the mirror, dipping and rubbing and smoothing and squeezing at her face, her arms, her skin. Sometimes she will make the sailor stare: these times her face is shadowed, is ringed with shadow, and it seems to him that her features rearrange themselves, her eyes glint darkly, her face collapses. She becomes entirely different, entirely new. But then the lover will smooth on her oils and the sailor will blink, and she'll be beside him, touching him all too familiarly, and they'll be tumbling and twisting on her narrow bed, and the sailor will be flying, he'll be soaring, he'll hardly be hearing those echoes that have lodged in his head to pull it, to try it, to pull it, to try it, to pull — and perhaps the sailor will.

He licks and suckles at her favourite knob, he puts his teeth to it, and gnashes and grips and pulls. And like those improbable nightmares that are intimately detailed by this sailor and his companions in their bawdy storytellings at the Shanghai Bar, this one, coming to ridiculous life before his very eyes, will seem all too familiar, will ring all too true. The knob will loosen in the lover's neck. It will loosen with reluctant, sucking sounds, like a plug violently pulled from its plughole, it will come loose in his hand. And the lover will shrivel, she will shrink to hag hair and bones, she will shriek, will rise shrieking to the ceiling to grin and hiss and show her claws. The nail from her neck will be heavy and bloody in the sailor's hand. He will lie transfixed.

Quick as lightning then, the lover swoops to pluck that nail from his trembling fingers, she will swoop to snap it in half and to smile unpleasantly, to slip one half back into the gap in her neck. So to assume her former shape. Just as quickly, before he can duck or squeal, she thrusts the other into his. Imagine the sailor's surprise at being so deftly tricked and coupled. So instantly transformed: his vision expanded, the rush of the lover's blood a delicious roar in his ears. Imagine the sailor's terror. His joy. Now the lover will seem closer than ever before, or rather, it will be he who is close. And she will laugh, her laugh will tinkle like newly-smashed glass. The lover will laugh uproariously. She will hold her sides, and point, and fling up her arms and push back her tangled hair. The sailor will show his teeth. 'Eat me,' the lover will murmur, presenting her bared throat, her breasts. And perhaps the sailor will.

The sailor sprawls voluptuous with the pictures in his head. The night is old now, is dragging drearily. The wheezings and creakings in the rooms around him have stopped, the Shanghai Bar is shuttered, but still he lies unmoving, he's a sailor made of sticks and heavy stones. Soon enough, he will rise, he will push back the sheet to clear a space on the cluttered bed. Soon the lover will enter. The sailor won't hear her enter, he won't see or smell her, but he will know that she is there. The air will shift and slide beside him: the lover's breath will be heavy in his ear.

Something Shocking

Susan Silver was in the front garden of her house at 24 Walnut Avenue, Caulfield. She was standing on the third top rung of a large ladder. Hanging from a hook at the side of the ladder was a pot of Hot Ochre gloss paint.

She was concentrating intensely as she applied the final touches of paint. She hadn't looked down once in the two hours that she had been painting. Heights made her dizzy. She couldn't sit in the dress circle at the theatre. She didn't even like the stall to have too steep a slope.

Susan smoothed the brushmarks out of the last stroke of paint. She was amazed that she had done it. She had never even stood on a ladder before. She put the brush into the pot. She would get one of the boys to carry it down later. She trembled slightly as she climbed down the ladder, but she was happy. She felt proud of herself.

Her father would have been proud of her if he were still alive, she thought. He had often called her a mouse. 'You are frightened of the dark, you are frightened of strangers, you are frightened of heights, you are frightened of me. What's there to be frightened of? We are living in a free country. Every day the sun shines and the sky is blue. I think your mother gave birth to a mouse, not a daughter,' he would say.

She had loved her father. She knew that he was a coarse man. He looked coarse, too. He refused to buy new clothes. He wore the last pair of trousers that he owned for twenty years. There were brown stains on the seat of the trousers. It amused him enormously that they looked like shit stains.

He refused to cut the hairs from his nose. They protruded from his nostrils like wiry silver brushes. He had a sharp word for everyone. But Susan loved him. She knew that underneath the gruffness and the indifference he was soft-hearted and easily moved.

The day he'd died she'd thought that she was going to die too. Her mother had said to her after the minyan. 'You know, he was very harsh to you. Always. From the time you were a small child. And you loved him. From the time you were a small child you loved him. You could see that he had another side to him. Your brother couldn't see it, and your dear sister couldn't see it, and I, dear God forgive me, I couldn't always see it. But you always knew it, so you can be at peace with yourself, Susan.'

Susan examined her paintwork. It looked good. Hot Ochre had been the right choice. It looked just right against the matt brown brick work. Susan took a deep breath. The air was thick with the sweet smell of jasmine. It was mid-spring and Walnut Avenue was perfumed with the scent of jasmine.

Wendy Fairweather came out of her house across the road, saw Susan and walked towards her. Wendy and Susan had been nodding to each other for nine years.

'Hello, Susan,' said Wendy. 'I noticed you were doing some painting. That sign you've painted on your house, is it religious?'

'It says "My husband is shtooping a shikse". In English that means my husband is fucking a non-Jewish woman.' Wendy Fairweather flushed and rushed off.

'What is that Susan Silver doing?' Malka Berger asked her sister Bronka.

'I think she is painting the outside of her house,' said Bronka.

'What? Is she crazy or something? Her husband doesn't earn enough money to pay for a painter? I heard he is a millionaire. He should be ashamed of himself.'

The Berger sisters continued walking up Walnut Avenue until they were in front of the Silvers' house. They read the sign at the same time. For two minutes the sisters stood, open-mouthed.

'She should be ashamed of herself,' said Bronka.

'It is something shocking,' said Malka.

'Do you mean that it is something shocking that she painted such a thing on her house?' Bronka asked her sister.

'Of course,' said Malka.

'I thought that maybe you thought that it was something shocking that Mr Silver is shtooping a shikse.'

'Everybody is shtooping somebody, dear Bronka, so what is the big occasion?'

'They looked like such a happy couple,' said Chaim Berman to his son Michael, who was visiting from Israel. 'I always saw them walking in Acland Street together on Sunday afternoon. They used to go to the Cosmos bookshop and they used to stop in front of the Monarch cake shop and look at the cakes in the window for quite a long time.'

'Dad,' Michael replied, 'you think that the family who eats cakes together stays together. You're so naive. Harry Silver is having a mid-life crisis. His little dickie got weighed down with chulent and kishke and children and mothers-in-law. He took a look at it one day and thought that he better use it while he can.'

Chaim Berman wondered, again, how he had fathered such a coarse son. After the war Chaim had decided that the only thing worth teaching a child was tolerance. Tolerance for his fellow man. And what sort of a child did that teaching produce? A bigot. A bighead. Michael was living in Israel, Chaim thought, not out of any noble motives but because his American wife's parents needed a family member to keep an eye on the Israeli branch of their family business. So Michael sat in Tel Aviv and ran the head office of an American car-rental company.

Chaim felt sad. He had enjoyed talking to Harry and Susan Silver on Sundays. And despite the fact that he himself had been divorced for more years than he had been married, he still had high hopes for the state of marriage.

'I knew something was up,' said Susan's mother, Minnie Brot. 'That Harry has been looking ten years younger. He walks with a different step. I said to myself, "Minnie, something has happened." It's not a good sign when a middle-aged man starts to look younger. You can make a bet for sure something is up. He is shtooping somebody, but not his wife. Everybody is shtooping their wife. Does it make them look younger? I don't know what you can do, but I don't think this notice that you have painted on the house is going to help things at all. Where is Harry?'

'He's in Sydney on business, but I know that she is there with him,' said Susan. 'I rang the hotel and they said that he was out. I asked if Mrs Silver was in, and they said that she was out too.'

'Oy, my Susan, we needed this like a hole in the head,' said Minnie. 'Trouble with one's children never stops. Small children, small problems. Big children, big problems. And now I've got a son-in-law who's shtooping a shikse. To tell you the truth, Susan, Harry didn't look to me like he was someone who was too excited about shtooping anyway.'

Harry Silver lay in bed next to Diane Burnett. She looked so peaceful. Jews rarely looked peaceful, thought Harry. Her breasts were so pink. There was a pinkish tinge to her hair. He wondered if that was what was called strawberry blonde. He didn't know whether Diane was awake or not. He was in a daze. He could still taste her in his mouth and on his hands. He felt enveloped by the smell of her breasts and her thighs. He could smell her body whether they were together or apart.

She opened her eyes and smiled at him. He had rarely felt so at peace with himself. He could feel the peace. It was a large, still space in his chest. Diane moved her left leg on top of him. She started rubbing his stomach and his thighs. She slid herself on top of him and lay there. They were connected from head to toe. Then she sat up, astride him, and eased him into her.

'Don't do anything,' she said. 'Just lie there.' She made love to him until they both came.

Afterwards, she kissed him on his fingertips, behind his ears, on his feet. She put her fingers inside his mouth, inside his bum.

He felt as though she had entered his bloodstream and was travelling through him.

'I feel insatiable,' she said. 'I feel as though I'm making up for lost time.'

'Tell me about your husband and his special spiritual line,' he said.

'It's called kundilini,' she said. 'He was preserving his kundilini. By not fucking me he was saving his sperm and strengthening his soul. He joined a yoga group twelve years ago. Before that he was so randy he'd fuck anything that moved. When he joined this yoga centre I thought that it was a good move. He didn't know what he wanted to do, and I couldn't see any harm in him meditating. It seemed to give his life a focus. He became completely involved in the centre. He went to India to study at an ashram for six months. When he came back he told me that he needed to be celibate in order to become a higher being. For ten years I cooked and cleaned and brought up the children while he ran yoga courses. Sometimes I used to die for him to touch me, but mostly I felt so fucked by the children and the nappies and the school lunches that I was glad not to have anything more to do at night.

'The day I found out he'd been fucking this Indian yoga teacher he'd met in India, I drove into the centre and walked into the evening meditation group. It was their biggest session of the day, the 6 p.m. meditation session. I was hysterical. I stood in the middle of the rostrum and shouted. I can still remember word for word. I shouted: "John Burnett is an arsehole. He hasn't fucked his wife for ten years. He's been celibate. He's been preserving his kundilini. But some of his fucking kundilini has been leaking into Shanti Shankhar for ten years. For ten years he's been fucking Shanti Shankhar, ladies and gentlemen."

'That was three years ago. When you touched me on the shoulder that night at Florentino's, it was the first time in years that I wanted a man to continue touching me.'

Harry didn't understand why he had put his hand on Diane's shoulder that night at Florentino's. Diane had been there with her father. Harry was having a business dinner with a client, Abe Grossberg. Abe was an old friend of Diane's father, and he had invited Diane and her father to join them for a drink.

Harry had thought of nothing else but Diane since that night. He was addicted. He missed meetings. He didn't return calls. He stood up clients. For thirty years he had had a reputation as one of the best lawyers in Melbourne. Now, nothing mattered. His business, his reputation, his wife, his family. It was as if his desire for Diane took up all of his feelings. There were no other feelings left. He just wanted to be with her, to be part of her.

'I'm hungry,' said Harry. 'You must be hungry too. Let's go to Doyle's at Circular Quay. I really feel like seafood. Let's get dressed.'

As he was getting dressed, he felt a flicker of his old self return to him. The old Harry Silver. The one who until three months ago had worn white boxer shorts, not these black Calvin Klein stretch underpants. The old Harry Silver wasn't interested in underpants. He was a modest, well-spoken, responsible lawyer. He was a fifty-six-year-old family man. He was on the boards of the Victorian State Opera, the National Gallery and the City General Hospital. He was married to Susan Silver. Susan, who was so quiet that her own mother referred to her as having a gentile nature. Harry had been proud of Susan's reserve. He was proud of her English. She had a very upper-crust English accent. 'Mrs Posh', her father used to call her.

It was Susan who had suggested that Harry go to elocution classes. Harry had been nineteen when he had met Susan. He had been in Australia for three years. He had taught himself to speak English in the DP camp in Germany. In 1949, he topped his English class at Melbourne Boys High in his final year of high school.

When he met Susan he was already studying law. He also worked at night as a car-park attendant at the Southern Star Hotel. For five years he had studied for his law exams in the cold, neon-lit attendant's booth. The booth was still there. Harry sometimes visited it. Twice a week in his final year of law, Susan manned the booth while he went to elocution classes. Now Harry spoke beautifully. He spoke as beautifully as any of the men he sat on committees with. He spoke so beautifully he could pass for a gentile. When he first went into practice he considered changing his name to Harold. He didn't really know why he hadn't. Harry was already far enough removed from Chaim. Chaim Silberberg, he had been. He became Harry Silver when he arrived in Australia on 3 September 1946.

He watched Diane put on her bra. She was so pale and pink. Peach coloured. She had peach coloured nipples. He walked over to her and took her breasts out of her bra. He put her right breast in his mouth. She sat there quietly and cradled his head while he sucked.

At Doyles, they sat at a table right on the water's edge, overlooking the Opera House. Harry ordered oysters and crayfish. Forbidden fruit.

'Isn't the Opera House the most beautiful building?' said Diane. But Harry couldn't think about the beauty of the Opera House. He moved his chair closer to Diane. He put his hand under her skirt. He drove himself wild. He felt demented. He wanted to push his hand deeper and deeper inside her.

'Let's go back to the hotel,' he said. The oysters arrived at the table just as they cancelled their order.

He put his fingers inside her again in the taxi. She looked utterly happy, utterly at ease. In the hotel he licked her and fucked her. He felt delirious. He licked her eyes, her feet. He wanted to put his whole head inside her.

At midnight she said she was hungry.

'Should I order some oysters and crayfish from room service?' she asked.

'That's a terrific idea,' he said. He groaned. 'I've got to have a piss, but I'm not sure if I can get up.' They were lying on a black and maroon rug on the floor.

'Don't,' she said. 'Just piss here. On top of me. I'll clean it up later. Go on, just piss. Everything else has flowed out of you.'

'I can't,' he said. 'I'll go to the toilet.'

'Just piss here,' she said. 'I want to see the piss coming out of you. I want to feel it on my body. Come on, piss, piss, piss.'

For the first time in the three months that they had been together, Harry felt uneasy. 'I'll just go to the toilet,' he said. In the toilet he felt sick. He began to sweat. He sat there trying to stem the nausea. What was wrong with him? Probably guilt, he thought. This feeling of infinite freedom was too good to be true. There had to be a price. And this was the price. He had no chest pains; otherwise he would have been sure he was having a heart attack. Didn't middle-aged men have heart attacks if they fucked too vigorously?

Diane came into the bathroom. 'God, you look awful. Let me get you a drink. I'm sorry if I pressured you. It was only a whim. Would you like an Alka Seltzer?' Harry drank the Aka Seltzer.

He still felt sick. He started to cry. Tears ran down his face. He hadn't cried since he was a child. Diane stroked his back. Her touch made him feel worse. 'I think it would be better if I sat here alone for a few minutes,' he said. He sat in the bathroom by himself. He kept crying. Diane came in and sat on the floor. She looked tearful.

'It's not you, Diane,' he said. 'It's nothing to do with you. It's something that happened in my past. Something that I've never talked about.'

'Please tell me,' said Diane.

'You know, not even my wife knows about this,' he said. Not even my wife, he repeated to himself. He had given Susan an importance in that statement that he hadn't accorded her in real life for months. For three months he had been so careless. He had booked hotel rooms on his credit cards. He had sent Diane flowers and books. He had hired cars. He had disappeared. All with no explanation. No subterfuge. He had separated himself from Susan. Now, when he was crying, he was talking about 'my wife'. He bent over the toilet bowl. He thought he was going to throw up.

Diane was crying. She looked lost and bewildered. 'Don't cry, Diane. It's not you, it's me. It is such a messy story, such a heap of shit, that I wouldn't know what to tell you about it. And maybe you're too young,' he said.

'Too young. I feel ancient, Harry. I'm thirty-eight. Please tell me,' she said.

'In the forty years that I've been in Australia I haven't told anyone,' he said. 'When I was ten, my father was shot by the Nazis and my eight-year-old brother and I were taken to Buchenwald. Have you ever heard of Buchenwald? It was a concentration camp in Germany. In Weimar. The house that Goethe used to live in was near Buchenwald. There was a tree that Goethe used to rest under when he went for his walks. They built Buchenwald around that tree. It was a large old oak tree. I often used to wonder what Goethe would have said if he could have seen what was going on around this tree.

'On our first night in Buchenwald, a guard took my brother and me and another boy to his cubicle. He made us undress and lie on the floor. Then he pissed on us. I bit him on the leg and he clubbed me so hard with his rifle that I was unconscious for two days. My brother carried me back to our bunk. The SS and the kapos had their choice of the prettiest boys. They were called "doll boys".

'Buchanwald was a very good posting for the SS. The Commandant, Koch, was fleecing his party. Instead of documenting everything that was being taken from the prisoners, he was pocketing a lot of the loot. He was a multi-millionaire. He had the prisoners build anything that he fancied. Buchenwald had a mirrored riding hall for Frau Koch, who liked to ride horses. The prisoners also built a wild game preserve. They had deer, wild boar, bears, tigers, foxes. Commandant Koch liked to amuse himself by throwing prisoners into the bear cages. The prisoners built a zoo, too. The zoo had monkeys, pheasants, and even a rhinoceros. The SS opened the game preserve to the public. They advertised it locally and made quite a profit from sightseers.

'Frau Koch, Ilse Koch was her name, used to go riding in the riding hall nearly every morning. She was always fucking some guard or other. I heard that she liked to fuck close to her horses, in the riding hall. She liked the band of prisoners to play music for her while she rode. She was so evil that her evil stood out in the middle of all the evil. She loved tatoos. If she saw an interesting tatoo on a prisoner she would ask to have it. The prisoner would be killed and the tattoo delivered. Every prisoner who had a tattoo in Buchenwald was catalogued. The pathlogy department was very skilled at skin removal. They treated the skin in two days. They either made it transparent or they tanned it so that it became tough like leather.

'One of Frau Kock's favourite lampshades came from the skin of a man from our village. It was a tattoo that said "Hansel and Gretel". The base of the lampshade was made from his bones, or maybe they were someone else's bones, I'm not sure. Bones were something else they were very good with in Buchenwald. The scientists in Buchenwald were taught by somebody who had been to Africa how to shrink heads. These shrunken heads were given by the SS as special presents.'

'What happened to your brother?' asked Diane.

'He was transported to Auschwitz in 1944, and I have been on my own ever since,' he said. He felt exhausted. His throat hurt. His eyes ached. How could he say he was alone? He had Susan and he had the two boys. He even had Minnie Brot. As a mother-in-law she wasn't too bad. How could he say he was alone?

Susan had often said that part of him was missing, was not available to her. She only ever said it, he thought, when they were making love. One of the things he had found very attractive about Susan was the quiet crisp way she fucked. She was hungry enough to want him, but she was distant. She didn't drag him inside her. Making love with Susan, he could feel comfortably separate. Intact. In no danger of disappearing.

He felt so alone. His legs shook. His breath smelt. He felt sorry for Diane. He looked at her. She was sitting very still.

'Diane, love, I'm very tired,' he said. 'I've got to go home.'

CARMEL BIRD

Maytime Fair

My wife has died. Six months ago it was, and I still say it like that
— my wife has died. As if it happened a few minutes ago or yesterday. It seems to make the loneliness easier to bear. And letters
still come for her. I wonder sometimes how long it takes for death
and absence to filter through to distant friends and the bank and
the *Reader's Digest*. I went to the bank the other day and said to the
little girl behind the glass in a loud and desperate voice, 'My wife
has died and you must stop sending letters to her about anything
whatsoever. Please understand,' I said, 'my wife will not borrow
money from you. She will not be requiring a Visa card.' The girl
was very nice and got the manager and he apologised and all the
other customers in the queues looked sorry but they looked away.
Then of course the next day the bank sent Marjory a letter about
interest rates. I tore it up.

 I tore up the letter and threw it in the fire and it curled
and went brown and wouldn't seem to burn. Not like the
things from *Reader's Digest* that flare up and spurt out sudden
flames of green and blue and purple. I burned a lot of
Marjory's things in the garden incinerator. Things I couldn't
bring myself to sort or think about. Like Christmas cards and
letters and the half-finished tapestry of the *Laughing Cavalier*.
How could you, Dad, the girls said when I told them. The
Laughing Cavalier, they said, very shocked. I never liked the cavalier myself, and half of him seemed to me to be of no use to
anyone. But Anne said she would have finished it and turned it
into a shopping bag. Then Elizabeth started arguing and said it
should have been framed and hung in the hall just as it was. I
must say I was glad I'd already burnt the thing. Susan had the

sense not to say anything. So nobody knew which side she was on. She's like that.

No nonsense about Susan. Never has been. It's lucky she lives the closest so that it was natural for her to help me with Marjory's things, the clothes. Susan just came round every day for a week or so and folded things up into boxes and then she got St Vincent de Paul to come. 'I'll put the shoes in the garbage,' Susan said, and I was scarcely listening. But suddenly I had a memory of Marjory years ago at a party in her red satin dress and the red shoes we bought in Venice. I went rushing into the bedroom where Susan had what looked like dozens of pairs of old shoes on the bed. They were all sad and brown and grey and black. One white pair and a few pairs of coloured slippers, pastel. 'The red ones,' I said, 'what have you done with your mother's red shoes.' They were already in the rubbish tin mixed up with some celery. I fished them out and Susan looked at me strangely and said nothing. I said the shoes reminded me of very happy times — Venice and the party, and so on — I said. Susan said where would I put them and she looked down at my feet. I had a clear understanding that she wondered in that moment if I was going to dress up in her mother's things. Nothing further from my mind, and my feet are size eleven.

I keep the shoes on the floor of the wardrobe alongside my own shoes. I fancy the ghost of Marjory dances in and out of the wardrobe. I'm sorry I didn't keep a dress or two hanging there. I even looked in the doorway of St Vincent de Paul one day, half thinking I'd go in and buy one of Marjory's dresses, but I couldn't stand the smell of the place.

And I came away from there knowing that the only thing I really wanted was the shoes. She loved them so. For some reason I can not explain, I could not bear to keep Marjory's holy medals. I believed they should have been buried with her, but the sister at the hospital put them in a little box and gave them to Susan. 'Your mother's medals, Susan,' she said, and pressed the box into Susan's hand. 'She was wearing them when she died.' So Susan took them home and in her very sensible and literal way she wrote in pencil on the lid of the box, 'The medals Mother was wearing when she died.' It was a Johnson & Johnson box that had contained six thin oval bunion plasters. And all Marjory's dear medals — Perpetual Succour, Philomena, Miraculous, Scapular, Mater Dolorosa, Little Flower — and two Pius Xs, one attached to a crucifix. All her medals in the thin black drawer that slid in and out. Susan wrote on the lid and came round and gave the box to me. But I said, 'You have them, Susan. Or share them up with your sisters.' Susan said nothing and she took the box away. I can't say how much that box offended me. And Susan's label — 'The medals Mother was wearing when she died'. And the date.

She died on the eighth of November and soon it will be May. I wish the bank and the *Reader's Digest* and the girls would leave me to my thoughts. But Elizabeth and Anne have both rung me today to tell me in their different ways that Susan has done something unforgivable. Nothing, I said, is unforgivable. This is, they said. But what has she done, I asked, what has she really done. 'She has sent Mother's lace tablecloths and pillow shams and handerchief sachets to the second-hand stall at the Maytime Fair.' I said if they had wanted those things they should have taken them. They didn't exactly want them, they said, but they should not have gone onto the second-hand stall at the convent. Actually, Elizabeth said, it's the antique stall. Dealers come with magnifying glasses and snap things up and take them off and sell them for a fortune. I said they should be happy with the pieces of fine jewellery their mother left to them. And the china and crystal. I look around as I speak and think the house is almost empty. The china cabinet used to be so crowded with daffodil-pattern Royal Doulton.

I stop listening to the girls. I close my ears and think of Marjory's bright red shoes waiting for her in the wardrobe. I go deaf. I go stupid. (He is so deaf, they say. So stupid. Susan gets away with anything.)

I learn to cook and weed the borders. Old world pastel pansies that Marjory loved so much. I walk the dog and look up at the sky and think it's going to rain. Marjory's floral bookmark flutters from the pages of the last book she was reading. *Ivanhoe*. She liked to read. Six months and it seems to be a lifetime and I miss her so. I have her shoes. And what I do not tell Anne and Elizabeth is this: I think that with the tablecloths and pillow shams that Susan sent to the Maytime Fair, there would have been some other things. I think Susan sent the medals. Someone, I believe, will buy the bunion-plaster box of medals for a fortune or a song. And the strange thing is — it doesn't matter to me. I don't care.

I Asked the Angels For Inspiration

Last night I dreamed of Rebecca again.

She came in a storm of falling angels. There was a little thunder and a lot of fat rain and the scent of wild roses. The rain pounded down. It beat on my iron roof and made cold waterfalls from the age-rusted holes of the guttering. It made my hands shake when they touched Rebecca's face. She lay beside me in my bed and she comforted me and she said, *I heard you this time.* She cradled my head. *This time I had to come.*

And there was that scent of wild roses again.

I looked at the river, at the sea of roses, at the angels falling from the black sky and into the white river. The wind blew me cold and Rebecca reached out for me. I brushed her hair from her forehead and she closed her eyes.

I said, 'I better answer the telephone.'

Don't, Rebecca whispered, and her voice was as gentle as the song of a choir of Christmas angels. *Don't, it's supposed to be a secret, you'll spoil everything again*, and she was gone into the two-thirty morning.

Through the din of the rainfall, the telephone. Again.

Stumbling through the cold house, wondering why it was a sin to feel such longing, I navigated the darkness — badly. Forehead against a door jamb, knee against a coffee table, and none of it really necessary for the kitchen light was on and Paul and Magda were in there squeezing oranges. Why hadn't they saved me from this; why hadn't they left me to sleep with my

Rebecca? Fuck the casual cruelty of those who help us pay the rent. Paul and Magda were in T-shirts, their bare arms and bare legs brown as cowhide. Among not many other things they shared a passion for beaches.

Sour in the mouth and crabby in the heart I stood by the telephone and stared at Magda's legs — which I do a lot of.

Tall, foreign, dirty as an unwashed potato, I'd had a werewolf's desire for Magda since the day Paul had taken her from a Noosa beach to his New Farm bed.

'Why don't you answer the phone?' I said.

Four hands ran with orange juice.

'Leave the thing,' Paul said. 'They'll give up in a minute.'

But I can never leave it.

On its spindly supports the old house was rocked by rising winds. The wooden walls trembled. I trembled. The place was about to be blown off its ridiculously high stumps and out into the Brisbane River, where we would be washed away until we met the sea. I put my hand on the thrumming receiver and Paul said, 'Go back to bed, you fucking idiot, you know who it is at this time of the night. Why do you encourage them?'

The house quivered.

Why do I encourage them?

Because of the dreams I have, Paul, because I know I carry a stone in my heart, Paul, that's why.

As if I could ever explain that to him — but Magda smiled at me and then she returned to the hand-juicer and a mountain of valencias. Oh, Magda could look into a man's heart as easily as look into a stinking garbage bin. Her gift was to look without curling her lips in disgust. How had Paul managed to keep her so long?

The ringing ran out.

I said, 'Well, I forgot to take the receiver off the hook before I went to bed.' Lingering, watching Magda's legs. She came into better focus. Legs the colour and texture of expensive magazine photo essays. I was no longer sour. But hardly sweet. 'Sorry it woke you,' I said.

They came by with their glasses of juice.

'The telephone didn't wake us,' Magda said. 'We have been sleepless.'

The rain fell hard but the noise was not enough to drown the new ringing of the telephone.

'Tell 'em to be fucked,' Paul said.

They smelled of stale sex and oranges, the sleepless Paul and Magda. Why couldn't I squeeze oranges with Magda while Paul was left to dreams of a ghost named Rebecca? There were goose bumps along Magda's thighs. She knew I was looking. I moved to the windows and pulled them fully shut.

'Go on.' Magda smiled at me again. 'Don't be ashamed. Answer the telephone.'

So I picked up the receiver.

It was as it always was. Silence. Space, the final frontier. Nothingness or eternity in my telephone line. No sense of a Being, but there was a Being. Two-thirty in the morning was this Being's time of day.

'Goodnight,' I said, and put the receiver down.

Magda walked by and put the two empty glasses in the sink. She poured a generous glass of juice and handed it to me.

'This was your stalker?'

'This was my stalker.'

I wanted to lean close for the scent of her hair, for the scent of oranges, for the scent of spoiled sex.

She went to the couch and she and Paul cuddled there. They might very well have been about to copulate there. I took the glass into my bedroom, bolted the door and bolted the juice. I turned out the light and lay down. Outside, the elements howled. I waited under the bedclothes for Rebecca to return, but the bitch wouldn't return. I tried to lure her with randy thoughts but only the rain kept me company. Its insistent fall against the iron roof lulled me. *It is a lie to say I am lonely. I am only alone.* And as longing as my stalker. With every passing night and day, the same sin.

Those two-thirty telephone calls had started a few months earlier. Whose life had I crossed back then? I had no idea. Who was it who wanted me? I couldn't imagine. Was it Rebecca? If only. The rain cried out.

Rebecca. Rebecca.

Holiday mornings. The telephone won't ring. Coffee and news-papers and the sunshine of a Brisbane day. Sit, waste time, watch the minutes drag. Fester alone. This I like.

I have a bad habit.

I like to video-record *Rage* most nights. With the Long Play option you get six hours of old and new music videos. I like to put the tape on when I vegetate around the house. It's my soundtrack for reading the papers, cleaning the toilet inside, sweeping the path outside.

The morning was humid. From the rear windows of my house I could see the river. Ferries quietly steamed against the current; off a jetty a man angled for catfish; at the closest bank a group of kids stood with their bicycles and smoked cigarettes. In a neighbour's weedy yard a fat black cat rolled onto its back and exposed its belly to leaden clouds. I sipped my coffee and read claims about Bill Clinton's sexual appetite.

I blame the endless funk feature on *Rage*.

The house started to sway, this way, that way, this way, that way, just like in the old Smiths' song. Ten-metre supports at the back of an old wooden house will let you feel most vigorous movements. Sylvester was singing in his curiously appealing falsetto and I was at the dining table swaying as if on a rocking ship. The house was moving, moving, moving to an insistent funk beat. Why the fuck was I surprised?

For Paul had the libido of a randy mutt. He was always ready to mount a willing schoolgirl, a tree trunk, any available shin bone. I'd known love once but my housemate had known enough copulation to keep a cricket eleven happy into their dotage. Or was it in fact Magda with the unquenchable fire? The house rocked, the table rocked, my eyeballs rocked. Generations of funk passed. We dabbled in the sixties and the seventies and the eight-ies, even into the Reverend Al Green's current piece of gospel-drenched funk, but the rocking hardly abated. I turned the television up louder and went and stood in the furthest removes of the house.

Nothing worked.

But I guess I had to admire Paul and Magda's dedication. Paul's even more so. Why is it that only the most worthy and undeserving of men suffer from PE? Paul must have been as numb as a gum shot full of novocaine. Even as that thought crossed my mind the screaming started. I know not to be fooled by this. Experience has taught me this only signals the end of Paul and Magda's foreplay.

I packed together a few things and fled before I lost my mind. From a corner telephone booth I rang Henry.

And he arrived at the street corner, at the top of the cul-de-sac that went down to the New Farm ferry jetty. Where I cowered from life and libido.

Henry said, 'G'day!' and I scrambled in.

His ugly Cressida was rotted through with rust, like the guttering on my house, which the landlord couldn't afford to fix. Neither could I. I lost my last job for stuffing up one too many times a Pearl Jam lead break and ending it with an unhappy *ker-plunking* of strings. Now no other band wanted me. Somewhere, sometime, some prick had called me *Leadfingers*, and of course it stuck.

End of a career.

Henry's car picked up speed along Brunswick Street — no prostitutes were out yet — but had to slow down in the Valley. The mall and the streets and the shops had long-since been festooned with lights and coloured streamers and Christmas bells. Families were out in force; where the families prospered the prostitutes failed. As we rattled by the market-day mall we saw crowds and heard music and saw children with their faces to the class of art school Christmas displays.

'Boy,' said Henry. His contacts were giving him trouble and he worried at his eyeballs as he drove along.

I was glad to be out of Fortitude Valley but then there was the City. The City was busier with Christmas lights than I could have imagined. The world was out shopping. What do you do when you're broke and the three-to-five-year-olds in your extended family have no idea what the word 'dole' means?

'Drive faster,' I said.

'Fuck off,' Henry said, and worrying at his eyeballs like a dog at a flea he nearly swiped a grinning pedestrian. 'Should have hit her,' he said.

And what can you do when the marketing men have your name and number, what hope have you got when a database remembers better than you what it is you love?

We went to the RE beer garden and festered the day through.

People came and went from our table, mostly to talk to Henry. Self-deprecating, almost nauseatingly sincere, and the only person I knew under sixty-five who could do the rhumba and the tango, he had the knack of making young women at parties fall in love with him in five minutes and contemplate marriage in ten. He was taller than me, funnier, better looking, and when he played tennis could actually hit a backhand. He didn't have a regular girlfriend. That levelled us a bit.

'Do you know what date it is today?' I hinted, always between drinks.

Henry popped his lenses and put on his glasses. His eyes were big and startled. 'Close to Christmas?'

We sat in the beer garden and listened to a fucked acoustic trio and at intervals rubbed suncream over our arms and necks.

Magda had met Henry once at drinks. During the evening when Paul was out of earshot and Henry was within earshot she had said to me, 'Your friend Henry Carter is a man I will very much like to fuck with.' Maybe I'd envied him since that night. A little later and with a little more vodka in her Magda had said, 'But you are not very old and yet you are very soft in your stomach.' Maybe I'd wanted to smack Henry in the head since then, who knows?

As the sun went down and my head went similarly, inexorably, down toward the table, I remember asking again: 'Do you know what the date is today?'

Henry gave me a strange look. 'What's gotten into you?'

'Too much beer,' I answered.

And both our heads went down and we had a nap and because it was Henry, nobody even thought to throw us out.

By nightfall we were propping each other up in the busy bar next to the Rum Boogie cafe. I can't remember how we got to Fortitude Valley all the way from Toowong.

'What you don't see,' I was telling him, 'is that tennis is a metaphor for Life.'

Henry was watching a young woman in a black dress. Her dress was one or two sizes too small. Her lips were incredibly red. A gaggle of stockbrokers circled her. Because Henry is a polite man he nodded at my meanderings.

'John McEnroe, The Australian Open, 1992, against the German Goliath, Becker. Becker was number four in the world at the time and he'd beaten McEnroe in all their previous encounters. You with me? McEnroe was thirty-three and feeling it and Becker was twenty-four and just about on top of the world. McEnroe, all touch and not much power. That fluidity, that anticipation, that magic, but against the German? Not a chance. But he beat Becker in three sets. That night Becker left the court a humbled man.'

Henry looked pained to have to listen. He said hopefully, 'Want another drink?'

'Wait. Wait. You see, the magic was with McEnroe again. He kept fighting. He refused to die. He couldn't win but he did win. Then he went on to have that fucking amazing five-setter against Emilio Sanchez. And he won, but it took just about four and a half hours. How did he do it? Wasn't he supposed to be worn out? Wasn't he supposed to be at the end of his career? This is what I'm saying. When you're down and out, why do you have to stay down and out? When you're dead why do you have to stay dead?'

Henry's big eyes shifted from the shark-encircled young woman to me. 'What is the matter with you today?'

I looked into my glass. 'I used to play in a rock and roll band. I used to take drugs and write songs and dream about making love to Jean Seberg.'

'Why don't you just find yourself some babe?'

'You find yourself some babe.'

'Okay.'

It seemed a decent idea. So we moved on to find Henry a babe, but first all we did find was some old friend of his.

The bloke was in his twenties and drunk enough on beer and vodka to see past a man's blood and bone, just as Magda could without booze. We were in The Beat and the electro-dance thump was as it had been since 1985. What had changed was that many of the men in their leather shorts and singlets and muscles now had girlfriends. It wasn't a predominantly gay club any more. Anyway, Henry's friend leaned against me, slurped vodka, took one look into my face and said, 'You're the unhappiest soul I ever saw.'

'Who the fuck is this?' I asked Henry.

Henry said to his friend, 'Today has a special significance for him but he wants to be mysterious about it.'

His friend said to me, 'Tell us about it.'

I said to him, whoever he was, 'Why don't you get fucked?' And to Henry, 'You too.' And to the girl standing by me, 'Want to dance?'

So we danced.

She was wearing a sweet white dress that matched her sweet white hair and she looked a little like Madonna from the days when you wanted to fuck her rather than smack her one. But later when I was in the toilet the blonde was in there as well with her dress hitched up around her hips and a quarter-pounder pointed into the urinal. You take your chances. When I emerged Henry and his friend both said, 'Look, just tell us about it.'

I said, 'I'm not telling you a thing.'

Henry said, 'Okay, I've had enough of this,' and he and his friend exited The Beat. His friend fell over once but caught up. I caught up as well. We stopped in at another busy bar. Henry had a job so he said, 'Okay, I know it's up to me. What are you having?'

I said, 'Crown lager.'

His friend said, 'Stolly. Get 'em to give you a double.'

Henry disappeared.

Henry's mate said, 'The problem is you like to carry your problems around with you, but they're only baggage that you can choose to lug or leave behind. You don't want to leave 'em behind. You love 'em. They're what make you. Still, you coulda left your baggage at home just tonight.'

I stared at him, not inviting him to continue.

'You have a choice, a clear choice. You can be weighed down — or not.'

'Thank you.'

'The problem is too many people associate depression or sadness or misery with depth of character. Can you believe it? But you're no deeper than your average check-out chick or grave-digger. This misery of yours is an open invitation for someone to come out of the crowd and save your fucking life. That's why you love it so much. But nobody's gonna save you. Especially not a girl. Unless she's fucked in the head — and that'll really be where your depression starts. Try shaking one of them girls. Can hardly be done.'

'Who the fuck are you?' I asked as Henry returned with our drinks.

Henry said, 'This is Gordon. Gordon's a kind of poet.'

'Kind of a poet,' I said. 'Kind of a fucken drunk. And he smells.' I drank my beer and Gordon drank his vodka. He tried to roll himself a cigarette but it went on forever. I rolled it for him and jammed it in his mouth and lit it for him. I said, 'I had a girl and she left me three years ago today. I met her three years before that, on this day. Six years ago this day I met her and three years ago this day I lost her. She was the first and the only girl for me.'

'So?' Gordon said.

'Tomorrow I'll have been without her longer than I was with her.'

Gordon said, 'Count your fucken blessings. How old are you?'

'Nearly twenty-four.'

Gordon started to laugh. And Henry, expecting me to pour out my heart, or thump Gordon, moved on. We trailed him down the Brunswick Street mall and he couldn't lose us.

It took Henry ten minutes in The Site to find a babe. Or maybe a babette. She was about seventeen and a friend of Gordon's. So it wasn't Henry's pulling power, anyway. Through the cigarette smoke and the smoke machine smoke, and through the neon-lit dark as well, Gordon and I watched the blossoming of nightclub romance. Dancing with the million other dancers, drinks at the bar, covert conversations with each leaning towards the other's ear-hole — Gordon and I drank with heavy bitterness.

Gordon said, 'You know, you should get yourself a new girl-friend. You might lighten up.'

I said, 'I wish I was Henry.'

Gordon said, 'I've never heard so much shit.'

I said, 'Well, what about you?'

Gordon said, 'I don't know about sex. It never made me happy. Sometimes I get obsessed and sometimes I die for a root but most of the time I know it won't make me happy. Women complain with me. Women get pissed off with me. I just come too soon.'

'My housemate could probably give you lessons,' I replied. 'He never comes.'

The name of the young woman with Henry was Helen. She had long brown hair and very trusting eyes. She wore a black halter top and a brown skirt and out-of-date black Doc Martens. She seemed most comfortable with her arm around Henry's waist. I liked her. I said to her,

'What do you do, Helen?' and in the electro-beat she misheard me for she hollered back, 'Oh, Curve and Suede, really. I think the Pet Shop Boys have always been fun but this latest one, it's just the pinnacle. I still love *Died Pretty* though Peno shouldn't enjoy showing his dick so much. Chris Bailey's made a welcome return and who would have thought that after so many years *REM* could make such a beautiful album? I hate Guns 'n Roses

and Nirvana more than anything. I didn't go and see U2 but
"Lemon" is the best David Bowie song David Bowie never did.
And I definitely didn't buy tickets to *The Girlie Show*. How can
that woman have any allure left? And that diamond in her
mouth. It just looks like she's got a really rotten tooth.'

We all agreed that was true.

I said, 'I saw U2's concert. It was a stormy night. Brisbane
summer, after all. All around all that technology and all those
screens and all those people there were all these lightning
strikes in the distance. It was like Armageddon. I remember
thinking, "Gee, they really *are* big." And the duet with Lou
Reed, that was really something.'

Henry said, 'U2 supping at the cock of corporate rock.'

Helen looked at him with the beginnings of that thing that
happens between men and women on nights like these. We got
onto books. Helen said, 'I've been reading a lot of Nietzsche
lately. And Henry Miller. Do you think it's funny they go
together so well?'

Henry was smiling. Well he might. I wanted Helen so badly
I could have thrown up there and then, but he had her all right. A
recurring nightmare I have is that one day I'll really fall head over
heels again, only to find the object of my desire's favourite albums
are *Bat Out Of Hell I* — and *II*.

Henry said, 'No, Helen, I don't think that's funny at all.

I guessed it was love, then.

Everyone wanted to go back to my place.

Gordon said, 'Any beer or vodka at your place?'

'No,' I said.

'Fuck,' he said.

Somehow we knew we'd be crazy to try to drive home. We
counted out our money. I had seven dollars, Gordon thirty-five
cents, and Henry a twenty and some change. Just enough for a
cab fare and one bottle of cheaper fire water. Helen looked at us
as if we were the world's greatest losers, but Henry was already
somewhere near her heart. She came with us.

Out in the street, hailing a taxi for us, Helen's eyes glittered when she looked back at me and said, 'You should cheer up. Think happy thoughts.'

She smelled of roses.

Gordon carried around the odour of beer taps and dolour, Henry the sweet scent of success, me the whiff of death, but Helen, sweet Helen, she just smelled of the world's most beautiful flower. How had we latched onto her?

In the street, with sloping drunks and sad-eyed blacks, with daydreaming cops and sloe-eyed whores, we all latched arms and waited for a taxi.

Magda and Paul were screaming in their room. This time it was the type of screaming normal people do. The house wasn't swaying at all.

I said, 'Let's put *Rage* on.'

Everyone wanted to do that. We turned it on and turned it up loud and over the *The The* retrospective we heard Magda and Paul redefining the terms of their relationship. It went like this:

This Is The Day and Paul was a worm who bolstered his piteous ego with a fat bank account;

The Twilight Hour and Magda was a slut;

Giant and Paul's BMW was an all too obvious extension of his (tiny, she shouted) penis;

Infected and Magda was a fucken slut;

Sweet Bird of Truth and Paul had never come to terms with his emotions or his sexuality. To him love was sex. Sex was life. Life was an epic search for a root. A root gave his life meaning and substance. A good root made him his own personal deity.

'It's the truth,' Henry said.

'You're about to know,' Gordon said.

I said, 'I quite like *The The*,' yet I was only speaking to Gordon because Henry and Helen inexplicably vanished. A wink of an eye and they were gone. The bottle of fire water was down to less than half. Vodka. Very fine. My ears were ringing and there was a discomforting sense of other-worldliness about my own house. How much time had passed? I said, 'Where are —?' and Gordon tilted his head toward the bedrooms.

'Maybe she's giving him a blowie.' Very politely he said, 'Got any beer?' His rollie had gone out and he was having difficulty getting it going again. I lit it for him.

'No beer. Drink the vodka.'

'. . . 's making me sick in the tummy. I smell coffee.'

'You're imagining it.' But I smelled coffee too. I stood up, swayed, staggered. Gordon, lotus position on the carpet, put out his hands and propped me by the thighs until I had my balance. It took a while.

Meanwhile —

Slow Train to Dawn and Magda told Paul the worst thing she had ever done was to give her body to him (this was a line from 'Cruel' by PIL — I never knew Magda was a music fan; yet again, an interesting woman with someone else. I couldn't be more depressed).

— and I was falling toward the kitchen.

Someone had indeed made a fresh pot of my Lavazza. I poured a mug of it for Gordon but Gordon had gone to sleep on the carpet. His rollie had dropped out of his mouth and was burning a small secret hole in that carpet. The bottle of vodka had overturned and the carpet had sopped most of it up. I hated that baby-shit coloured carpet anyway. On the television — *The Mercy Beat* and

I was just another Western Guy
With desires that couldn't be satisfied
So one day I asked the angels for inspiration
And the devil bought me a drink
And he's been buying them ever since

— and I watched a while and straightened the bottle and picked up the burning butt. In his sleep Gordon muttered *Cynthia, my darling, my darling* or maybe it was all just in my romantic imagination and he was nothing but another boozy *disparu* of this world.

I thought of Henry and Helen and the many bedrooms.

The wind was up and the house rocked ever-so-slightly. This meant he was probably giving her a gentle one in my bed. It was two-thirty in the morning. I knew this to be so because the telephone started to ring. I went down the dark corridor and threw open the door to my own bedroom. There, there, there they were, in my own bed. Except that they were over the covers, they were drinking coffee, and they were playing cards. Had I ever come across a more nauseatingly innocent scene?

Helen said, 'Join us for some rummy.'

Henry grinned up at me, 'Come on.'

I pulled the door shut and leaned in the corridor.

Why should I be so threatened by one man who proves himself better than me? Once upon a time Rebecca and I had lain on that bed late into the night, had listened to music, had drunk coffee or coke or champagne, had played mah jong and scrabble and chess. Now — the corridor belonged to me.

And the telephone.

The ringing was insistent. This Being who seemed to understand longing and loss needed me.

I went to the telephone. I knew what would be waiting there. Through the windows I could see the river. I said, 'Hello?' For that's the game we liked to play. I liked too the familiarity of the emptiness and of the silence and of the breach in time and space. It seemed right. Henry and Helen playing cards in my bed, Gordon asleep in front of *The Violence of Truth*, Paul and Magda fighting or fucking their way into oblivion, and my Rebecca, lost forever in lovelessness for me.

I said into the receiver, 'Come on, Rebecca. It's you. It has to be you.'

Silence, and for the first and last time a breath, and the line was dead in my ear.

We went down to the river, Magda and I, for we were the only two left in the house who might communicate. Paul had thrown on some clothes and had slammed out of his room and had driven to parts unknown in that powerful German extension of his penis. Henry and Helen were two sleeping angels in my bed. Gordon, rudely awoken by Paul's departure, was drinking again, bleary in front of the television. I doubted if he took in very much. My last sight of Gordon, at least for that night, was as he tilted in front of The The's elegiac video to *The Kingdom of Rain*. Only the lotus position stopped him from once again falling sideways onto the carpet.

And then there had been Magda, in the dark, in the corridor, crying.

So we walked together in the windy night.

New Farm Park smelled of roses. No wonder, for the southern hemisphere's largest rose garden grows there. Under the fat old moon all the roses were in bloom. Only that moon lit the rolling hills and the sweep of the vast parklands. Magda and I walked amongst the rose beds. Magda ran her hands along the fat blooms and petals. Over the reds and the pale pinks and the whites, Magda's hands danced. Then she picked a rose and stepped on it and led me down the green banks to sit by the winding river.

The surface of the river glittered. The day made it muddy but the night gave it magic. The air was sweet and the river was enchanted and the moon was the colour of snow. There were no stars. Here and there came the sounds of the slapping of water, as if some sad muddy mermaid was climbing from the river to sit on a polished rock and lick herself clean.

Side by side, Magda and me, under a huge tree. I've never learned the names of trees. We leaned together. To me Magda would always smell of stale sex and oranges. She took my hand and she put it on her breast and I took my hand away.

Magda said, 'You know of that song that speaks to Montgomery Clift. That song that tells him to "just let go". This is what you must do.'

I said, 'If I let go, I'm alone.'

Magda took my hand and she kissed it and I took it away again. She said, 'Just let go.'

I leaned my head on Magda's shoulder.

Oh, why does it take as little as a look to make me fall in love and as long as a lifetime to make me forget it?

Magda wouldn't take no for an answer so I let her hold my hand. No sad-eyed mermaid sat on any rock, yet in the space and the silence we watched the dark glitter of the river for a long time, as if we believed she was there. Or about to appear, our mermaid, full of grace, out of the black waters.

A fruitbat flapped overhead and screamed.

Republic of Love

I, Mary the Larrikin, tart of Jerilderie, have loved for roast beef and I have loved for the feather on a well-trimmed hat. In my room above the hotel bar I have felt a squatter's spurs and sucked once on a bishop's fingers. The perfumes of my thighs have greased many a stockman's saddle and kept him company through the lonely nights. Men can nose out my room from thirty miles away, their saddlebags tight and heavy with desire. But of all the men I have ever loved, Ned Kelly, dead three years before they put him in the ground, stole my heart away.

It is hard work loving a dead man: your pillow a gravestone: your arms a confessional. Dead men crawl into your bed at night and evaporate like steam with the rising of the sun. I never saw Kelly even in the light of day. Instead I saw the shadows of candle smoke drift across the smoothness of his hips. I dug my fingertips into the silver squares of window cast upon the muscles of his arms. But I saw enough and felt the rest with my famous mouth and hands. I can tell you that the insides of his thighs had been smoothed by the saddle. He was covered with scars paler than moonlight. He had a foreskin as soft as a horse's inner lip.

Mostly we fucked like greedy children trying to hold on to an Indian summer. Our love had ripened out of season and each full moon hung heavy on the frailest stem of night. But sometimes, in the quiet hour, when his beard rested on my breasts, Kelly told me about the Republic of Love.

In the Republic of Love, said Kelly, there will be no police to eavesdrop on our sleep. We will dream no more in timid whispers but laugh as loud as kookaburras in the dark. Our desires will dive through the hills like flocks of night birds. The dawn will echo with the yapping of our hopes.

In the springtime, when the snows melted, the ground was so damp it rotted beneath a horse's feet. In the morning clouds clung to the roads like sullen cobwebs. By midday they peeled off the mountainsides and stacked themselves like sodden hay in tiered bales that reached towards a hidden sun. It was a time for wet and stumbling love.

I am an indoor girl myself, but I could read Kelly's body like a map and feel what it was like gullying and ungullying through the deep-scored seams that marked those brilliant hills. After three days' ride his stirrups had stained the backs of his heels with orange. His wideawake was filled with melted hail up to the edges of its brim. When he hung his trousers by the fireplace the clouds which had caught in his pockets unfurled and rose up to the corners of the room. His whiskers had been brushed backwards by the stormy winds and stood out from his face. Scratch my beard for me, Mary my love, he said, it is crawling with lightning. I felt blue sparks crackle beneath my fingertips.

I stood naked before him. He wrapped his cool green sash around my waist and came in close to tie the bow. He said he held all the softness of Ireland wrapped up as a Christmas gift. When we lay on his jacket before the fire to make our clumsy love I felt mud slide across the surface of my skin. For weeks it bore the purple scent of Salvation Jane.

In the Republic of Love, Kelly said, we will soak beds thick with emerald sheets and curtains. There will be so much bread to go around that we will scoop out the hearts of loaves and use them for our babies' cradles. They will nestle in the warmth of the fresh-baked centres and rock sideways on the curving crusts.

Shortly before we met, Kelly had begun to rustle horses. He would come to me from the hills at night, his belly full of parrot.

I knew without asking when he had shot and eaten lorikeet. His lips were as soft as feathers. He sweated rainbows. He played with thoughts on the tip of his tongue and mused with the subtlety of a philosopher between my legs.

Each theft, he said, avenged the times the squatters had impounded the Kellys' cattle for straying onto their glutted pastures. They are slick-lipped, swamp-hearted, rough-bellied toads, said Kelly, who begrudge us even the flies that circle round our heads. They would brand the water in the rain-clouds if they could.

I grasped him firmly in my hand and began the movements which would comfort him. He laughed and said the law had squeezed him harder there before. He told me of the arrest when the policeman Lonigan had cupped his fist around his balls and tried to wrench them off, his breathing fast, his face more crimson than a mangel-wurzel. From my work in this room I understood that impulse well. It is police and magistrates, I said, who fall on you like a cattle crush and make each act of love a punishment. They grind you against the mattress until your breath is thinner than a paper-knife. They lust to press you, dry and brittle, between the pages of the police gazette. They threaten to arrest you if you tell.

In the Republic of Love, Kelly told me, you can take any shape your loving chooses. You can fuck like a centaur at midnight and squeal like a poddy calf at noon.

There is one thing I can tell you with certainty. That day at Glenrowan may have been the first time Kelly wore an iron hel-met but it was not the first landscape he had seen as if he was looking up from the bottom of his grave. Before we met he had spent ten years in prison where he had known the world only as a narrow strip of daylight.

He was born in the shadow of Mount Disappointment. Like the other Irish convicts' sons, he grew thin as a weed from the dusty cracks between the squatters' properties. His mouth set into a hard straight line. He had seen his father's body swell with dropsy before his death. He said it was as if Red Kelly's ankles at last had cracked the phantom shackles which had made them ache since those cold years in Van Diemen's Land. He had watched his mother stumble to unlatch the door with a baby on her hip when the police tried to make the Kellys soft by breaking their nights into tiny pieces. He had felt the slab walls quiver as the policeman Flood pinned his sister Annie with his belly, discharging the seed which was to stretch her taut until she died, weakened by the fleshy issue in her womb.

When he was five Kelly's mother explained to him that there were no days or seasons on the wrong side of the law. There were only lucky hours, she said, and nights of swift riding when you could slide in and out of the chilly pockets of the moon.

Later he gave up shearing because the sound of the metal reminded him of a warden's scissors clipping his hair down to its roots. He had stopped sawing wood in the Gippsland forests when the milky sun filtering through the treetops made him think of prison bars.

Before I was eighteen, Kelly said, my arse was polished by the courtrooms' wooden benches. My spine grew straight as a prison bunk. I have nine notches in my forehead made by the butt of a policeman's rifle. I think the granite I broke at Beechworth has passed into my blood for my veins feel as rough as sandpaper.

In Pentridge, in solitary confinement, Kelly spent six weeks with his head covered by a hood. Two slits were cut in the canvas for his eyes. That was when he began to see the landscape inside an angry frame with no soft tomorrows beyond its edges. It gave him ideas. He would turn ploughshares into armour, soldering and riveting the grimness of his gaze.

I stroked his chest and kissed his ear. I knew how it is to feel your body bruise and bend beneath a greater power. To this day my buttocks bear the impressions of floorboards and mattress buttons. I can still read the angry marks made by a grazier's signet ring upon my breasts. I loved Kelly the more for this. I asked him about the Republic of Love.

In the Republic of Love, Kelly replied, the prisons will be emptied and converted into breweries. Their quarries will be thick with waving heads of barley. The husks will drift across the lintels and gateways and wear away their English coats of arms. In the court-yards the smell of hops bubbling will lift away the stench of sweat. Barmaids will trail the scents of their soft perfumes along the dim, grey passages. In the banks, lovers will rut on crackling ban-knotes. They will roll in the safes until their backs are stained with mortgage inks. Sixpences will stick to them until they shine more silver than a blue-tongue lizard's belly.

The day the Proclamation of Outlawry was passed Kelly began to notice clods of grave dirt weighing down his trouser hems. He lost his boxer's gait and began to move as if he wore Red Kelly's irons. He said he could feel his soul trailing like a muddy shadow in his horse's wake, catching and tearing on each roughened patch of bark. When he stood in my room he squinted hard and nod-ded as we talked. He could not see my breasts and face at once.

That Act had closed even those narrow gaps, thinner than horizons, in which he had once moved. Since they had been ambushed at Stringybark the Kelly gang no longer held the rights of citizens. The Act put into words what they already knew: that they were unwelcome in this land which wore a crown. Any man offended by the sight of them could shoot them in the back. Ellen Kelly would soon be put in jail for giving birth to a bushranger. In his Sunday sermon at Mansfield the Anglican Bishop declared them dead already and damned to hell.

Odd to find yourself, said Kelly, staring through a dead man's face. Some days the landscapes he rode through looked as drab and frail as photographs which might lift at any moment from their edges. He had sepia nightmares in which he could not find his way from one image to the next, wandering forever in the soft jigsaw clefts of the Puzzle Ranges. On other days he found the dark blue curves and creases of the hills too beautiful. He lay in the darkness of a cave and saw Aaron Sherritt at the entrance, watching over Joe Byrne while he slept. He could hear Sherritt thinking clearly that the golden hairs on Joe's forearms made them look like angels' wings, while his lips smiled but never opened. Each night more disappointed ghosts joined Red Kelly in the darkness which had begun to press upon the edges of his vision. When he passed a house at dawn the smell of baking bread would nearly break his heart.

He said he thought of going to America, that free land, where he would race steam locomotives on a piebald horse across the plains.

This was the last time Kelly came to me. His eyes focused beyond my head. He mouthed me like a hungry phantom. He felt every part of me to prove that I existed. His fingers were as cool as apples. He took his green sash from my drawer and placed it on his folded clothes.

When he spoke about the Republic of Love his head was as heavy as a tombstone on my shoulder.

In the Republic of Love, said Kelly, there will be no fences. People will find new uses for ordinary things. They will cook toast on the rusting faces of branding irons. They will float down creeks on the discarded doors of shops. The telegraph wires will carry only lovesongs, tapped out in Morse like the rapid beatings of a heart.

Kelly did not see the betrayal in the face of the limping school-teacher with chess-player's fingers who left the Glenrowan Hotel and waved his handkerchief like a salesman's wife at a train full of troopers. In the dock he stared past the crimson face of Judge Redmond Barry, mottling and shaking like a turkey's wattle. I want to believe that he did not flinch as the frail trap of the gallows shivered beneath his feet.

That night the soft head I had felt between my thighs was cut off and shaved bare before the mask-maker's steady hands shaped warm wax around its jaw. The firm muscles around Kelly's lips were torn away and discarded. His heart was stolen by the surgeon as a souvenir. His skull with the five smooth mounds that curved around its base was stroked by an idle policeman's fingers as it weighed down the papers on his desk.

Back in Jerilderie I continued with my whoring, staring beyond the publican's shoulder.

I looked towards the same place as Kelly.

That day neither of us blinked. If we concentrated hard enough we could sense each other breathing: feel the wet cages of our ribs pressing into one another: hear the spines of law books splitting beneath our backs: rolling, beyond our senses, into the Republic of Love.

BIOGRAPHICAL NOTES
ON THE AUTHORS

Francis Adams (1862–1893)
Son of an army surgeon and a novelist, Francis Adams was born in Malta, educated in England, and sent to Australia for his health — he was tubercular — in 1884. In the six years Adams spent in Australia he worked as a writer and journalist; he was a significant figure in the developing radicalism of the 1880s. Three years after returning to England he committed suicide. 'Miss Jackson' was published in the collection *Australian Life* (1892) the year before he died.

Ethel Anderson (1883–1958)
Born in England of Australian parents, Ethel Anderson was educated in Sydney; she returned to Australia in 1924 after spending some years in India and England with her Army husband. She published poetry and fiction throughout the 1940s and 1950s. 'Murder!' is one of a series of linked stories making up the collection *At Parramatta* (1956).

Venero Armanno (b. 1959)
Venero Armanno is a Brisbane writer, and has published a short-story collection and three novels; his most recent book is *My Beautiful Friend* (1995). 'I Asked the Angels for Inspiration' was first published in the anthology *Men Love Sex*, edited by Alan Close (1995).

Thea Astley (b. 1925)
Born in Brisbane, Thea Astley has lived in Australia all her life and worked as a teacher in schools and at Macquarie University in Sydney. One of Australia's most distinguished writers, she has been publishing fiction for almost forty years. She has won the

Miles Franklin Award three times and has been the recipient of many other major Australian literary prizes. Astley was made an Officer of the Order of Australia (AO) in 1992. 'Getting There' is not strictly speaking a short story, but rather a self-contained chapter of the novel *It's Raining in Mango* (1987).

Hugh Atkinson (b. ?1924)
Hugh Atkinson was born in Sydney and has lived in India and elsewhere, returning to Australia to live in 1977. He has written numerous novels, stories and film scripts. 'The Jumping Jeweller of Lavender Bay' first appeared in *Coast to Coast 1958*, edited by Dal Stivens.

Murray Bail (b. 1941)
Murray Bail was born in Adelaide, has lived and worked in India and Europe, and now lives in Sydney with Helen Garner, his wife. His novels *Homesickness* (1980) and *Holden's Performance* (1987) have both won major Australian literary prizes. 'A, B, C, D, E, F, G, H, I, J, K, L, M, N, O, P, Q, R, S, T, U, V, W, X, Y, Z' was published in *Contemporary Portraits* (1975), his first book of fiction.

Carmel Bird (b. 1940)
Carmel Bird was born in Tasmania, a place which figures prominently in her writing, and now lives in Melbourne. She has published two novels and four collections of short stories since 1983; her most recent work is *The White Garden* (1995). 'Maytime Fair' is from *The Common Rat* (1993).

Lily Brett (b. 1946)
Lily Brett was born of Jewish parents in a displaced persons' camp in Germany; she came to Australia with her parents in 1948, and has lived for the last few years in New York. She is a poet and fiction writer who has won numerous Australian literary prizes. 'Something Shocking' is from *What God Wants* (1991).

Ada Cambridge (1844–1926)

Ada Cambridge was born in England and travelled to Australia with her clergyman husband at the age of 26; she wrote prolifically for Australian papers and journals for most of her life, and produced a number of stories and novels, the best known of which are *The Three Miss Kings* and *A Marked Man*, both initially published in serial form in the 1880s. 'The Wind of Destiny' is from *At Midnight and Other Stories* (1897).

Peter Carey (b. 1943)

Peter Carey was born in Bacchus Marsh, Victoria. One of Australia's best-known fiction writers, he has an international reputation and now lives in New York. He has published several short-story collections and numerous novels, including *Bliss* (1981) and *Oscar and Lucinda* (1988). 'He Found Her in Late Summer' is from *War Crimes* (1979).

Marcus Clarke (1846–1881)

Marcus Clarke was born in London and emigrated to Australia at the age of seventeen after the collapse of his family's fortunes. He was a prolific writer, journalist and dramatist, and — after settling in Melbourne — a well-known bohemian-about-town. The Australian literary classic for which he is chiefly remembered, *His Natural Life*, was serialised between 1870 and 1872, and appeared in book form in 1874. 'Poor Jo' is from *Holiday Peak and Other Tales* (1873).

Frank Dalby Davison (1893–1970)

Frank Dalby Davison was born in Melbourne and spent some years living and travelling in North America, the West Indies and, during the First World War, in France with the British Cavalry. He was an early conservationist and an active member of the Fellowship of Australian Writers — in the 1930s an influential, progressive, and highly politicised organisation. He wrote several novels and collections of short stories. 'Lady with a Scar' is from *The Woman at the Mill* (1940).

Robert Dessaix (b. 1944)

Robert Dessaix is a broadcaster, essayist, and translator, best known in Australia for his work on ABC Radio's 'Books and Writing'. He edited the anthology *Australian Gay and Lesbian Writing* (1993), and published his autobiographical meditation *A Mother's Disgrace* in 1994 to great critical acclaim. Dessaix is currently writing a 'fictional autobiography' called *Night Letters*. 'A Clear Conscience' was first published in *Quadrant* (May 1986).

'M. Barnard Eldershaw'

Pseudonym of collaborators Marjorie Barnard (AO) (1897–1987) and Flora Eldershaw (1897–1956). Their best-known work is *Tomorrow and Tomorrow and Tomorrow* (1947). Barnard is also well known for the classic short story 'The Persimmon Tree'. According to the scrupulous scholarship of Robert Darby, the story 'Christmas' was intended to be published around 1932, in a Barnard Eldershaw short-story collection that never materialised. In the end, 'Christmas' was not published until 1988, when Darby included it in his edited collection of Barnard Eldershaw stories called *But Not for Love*.

Delia Falconer (b. 1966)

Delia Falconer was born in Sydney and now lives in Melbourne. She won the *Island Magazine* Essay Competition in 1994 with 'Columbus' Blindness' and the *HQ* Short Story Competition later the same year with 'The Water Poets'. She is currently completing a novel, *The Service of Clouds*. 'Republic of Love' was written especially for this anthology and is published here for the first time.

Beverley Farmer (b. 1941)

Beverley Farmer is a Victorian fiction writer who is most widely known for her 'Greek' stories. Several of her books have won awards. She has written novels, short stories, and the formally experimental *A Body of Water*, a collage of poems, stories, 'life writing', and meditations on reading and writing. Her most recent book is *The House in the Light* (1995). 'Snake' is from *Milk* (1983).

William Ferguson (1882–1950)

William Ferguson, son of an Aboriginal station servant and a Scottish shearer, was Australian's first Aboriginal politician, a union organiser, a Labor Party branch secretary, and a lifelong campaigner for Aboriginal rights. 'Nanya', a story Ferguson had heard as a young man, is written as it was told to him by Harry Mitchell, one of the trackers sent out to bring in the 'lost tribe'; it was published in *Paperbark: A Collection of Black Australian Writings* (1990), edited by Jack Davis, Mudrooroo Narogin, Stephen Muecke, and Adam Shoemaker.

Helen Garner (b. 1942)

Helen Garner is one of Australia's most highly regarded writers. She has lived most of her life in Melbourne; she currently lives in Sydney with her husband Murray Bail. Her first book *Monkey Grip* (1977) won a National Book Council Award, and she has won several other major awards with subsequent books. She has also written non-fiction and screenplays for film and television, and won a Walkley Award for journalism in 1993. 'What the Soul Wants' first appeared in *The Times on Sunday* (14 June 1987) and was later included in the anthology *Reading From the Left* (1994), edited by Wendy Jenkins.

Susan Hampton (b. 1949)

Susan Hampton was born in country New South Wales and now lives on a farm in Victoria. She has won prizes for her poetry and is known for her skills as an editor. She won the Steele Rudd Award for her book *Surly Girls*, a collection of prose poems, performance pieces, and stories. 'The Lobster Queen' is from *Surly Girls* (1989).

Tim Herbert (b. 1959)

Tim Herbert is a Sydney writer who has published fiction in a number of gay magazines and journals, and who co-edited *Love Cries* (1995), an anthology of erotic writing. 'Pumpkin Max' is from his short-story collection *Angel Tails* (1986).

Henry Lawson

Henry Lawson is Australia's best-known literary name. Born in Grenfell, New South Wales, Lawson moved with his mother Louisa to Sydney when his parents separated in 1883. His first poems and short stories were published in the late 1880s, and a decade later he had an established reputation as a poet and fiction writer. His story 'The Drover's Wife' is regarded as the classic Australian short story. '"Some Day"' is from *While the Billy Boils* (1896).

Joan London (b. 1948)

Joan London was born in Perth. Her first book, the short-story collection *Sister Ships* (1986), won the *Age* Book of the Year Award. Her second collection of stories, *Letters to Constantine*, was published in 1993. 'Enough Rope' is from *Sister Ships*.

Olga Masters (1919–1986)

Olga Masters was a journalist for most of her adult life and began writing fiction in 1975. Her first book was published in 1982 and won a National Book Council Award. She published a novel and two collections of stories before her death in 1986; another novel, another story-collection, a stage play, and a collection of her journalism were published posthumously. 'Stan and Mary, Mary and Stan' is from *A Long Time Dying* (1985).

Brian Matthews (b. 1936)

Brian Matthews was born in Melbourne, has lived and worked for most of his adult life in Adelaide, and is currently living in London. He is the author of a critical study of the work of Henry Lawson, and of a biography of Louisa Lawson, which won three national prizes and shared a fourth. He has also published a collection of short stories and a book of 'larrikin essays on sport and low culture' (*Oval Dreams*, 1991). 'Crested Pigeons' is from *Quickening and Other Stories* (1989).

Frank Moorhouse (b. 1938)

Frank Moorhouse was one of several Australian short-story writers involved in the 1970s publishing venture *Tabloid Story*. His first book was published in 1969. Through the 1970s and 1980s most of his work took the form he calls 'discontinuous narrative'. He has published several collections of comic writing and, in 1993, a book quite different from most of his previous work, a long historical novel about the League of Nations called *Grand Days*. He has been an active figure in the Australian literary community since the early 1970s, involved in various campaigns to improve conditions for writers on such issues as censorship and copyright. He has won numerous national and international awards and is a Member of the Order of Australia (AM). 'The Letters' is from *The Everlasting Secret Family and Other Secrets* (1980).

John Morrison (b. 1904)

John Morrison is best known for his short stories — focusing chiefly on the issues of social justice, working life, and family relationships — but has also written novels, essays, and autobiography. He has won some of Australia's most prestigious literary awards, including the Gold Medal of the Australian Literature Society for *Twenty-Three* (1962) and the Patrick White Award in 1986. He is a Member of the Order of Australia (AM). 'To Margaret' is from *Twenty-Three*.

Jimmy Pike (b. 1940)

Jimmy Pike, a painter, was born in the Great Sandy Desert and is a member of the Walmatjarri Community of Fitzroy Crossing in north-west Australia. He has been exhibiting his work nationally and internationally since 1984. 'Mirnmirt' appeared in *Paperbark: A Collection of Black Australian Writings* (1990), edited by Jack Davis, Mudrooroo Narogin, Stephen Muecke, and Adam Shoemaker.

Katharine Susannah Prichard (1883–1969)
Katharine Susannah Prichard's dramatic and tempestuous life, which began in Fiji, included such events as her foundation membership of the Communist Party of Australia, the suicide of her war-hero husband, and her nomination for the Nobel Prize for Literature. She worked as a journalist, travelled extensively, and was a prolific writer of fiction, poetry, drama, and the revealingly titled autobiography *Child of the Hurricane* (1963). 'White Kid Gloves' is from *Kiss on the Lips and Other Stories* (1932).

Christina Stead (1902–1983)
Christina Stead was born in Sydney, left Australia in 1928, and lived most of her life in Europe and the United States. She was a prolific novelist with a unique style; she also wrote short stories, translations, and screenplays. When her husband died in 1968 she returned to Australia, where she lived for the rest of her life. She won the Patrick White Award in 1974. 'Street Idyll' was first published in the *Sydney Morning Herald* (3 January 1972) and afterwards appeared in the posthumous collection *Ocean of Story* (1985).

Dal Stivens (b. 1911)
Dal Stivens is the author of eight collections of short stories, four novels, a book for children, and a book of natural history. He is an amateur natural historian and in his later years has established a reputation as a painter. He was the foundation president of the Australian Society of Authors, and has won the Miles Franklin and Patrick White awards. 'Solemn Mass' was first published in the anthology *Coast to Coast* (1941).

Margaret Trist (1914–1986)
Margaret Trist wrote three novels and two collections of short stories. Like many Australian writers she was involved in a number of the organisations and institutions that make up the country's cultural infrastructure; she worked for the ABC and

wrote for the literary magazine *Southerly*. 'What Else Is there?' is from *What Else Is There?* (1946).

Patrick White (1912–1990)

Australia's most distinguished writer, and a major figure in its literary history, Patrick White won the Nobel Prize for Literature in 1973. He lived in Sydney from his return to Australia at the end of the Second World War until the end of his life. His complex, metaphysical, anti-realist fictions met resistance in Australia in the 1950s, but by the 1970s he was almost unanimously regarded as the country's greatest writer. He is best known for his twelve novels, but also wrote plays, short stories, and autobiography. 'Miss Slattery and her Demon Lover' is from *The Burnt Ones* (1964).

'Amy Witting'

'Amy Witting' is the pseudonym of Joan Levick (b. 1918). Like Elizabeth Jolley and Olga Masters, 'Amy Witting' established her reputation as a fiction writer late in life, after causing a parliamentary scandal in New South Wales in the mid-1970s over her parody of the 'mindless sexism' of some of her fellow writers. She has published poetry, novels, short stories, and textbooks on language. She won the Patrick White Award in 1993. 'A Bottle of Tears' is from *Marriages* (1990).

Judith Wright (b. 1915)

Judith Wright is one of Australia's most widely known and distinguished literary figures, with one of the most substantial and influential bodies of work any Australian writer has ever produced. For over fifty years she has been publishing not only poems, but also stories, essays, criticism, reviews, children's fiction, family history, and three books on Australian race-relations history. In the last ten years she has become almost as well known for her radical stance on the environment and on the cause of Aboriginal people as for her poetry. She has received a large number of national and international awards. 'The Nature of Love' is from *The Nature of Love* (1966).

Beth Yahp (b. 1964)
Beth Yahp was born in Malaysia and came to Australia in 1984 to study. She has written a novel, *The Crocodile Fury* (1992), was co-editor, with Margo Daly and Lorraine Falconer, of the anthology *My Look's Caress* (1990), and was editor of a second anthology *Family Pictures* (1994). 'The Red Pearl' was published in *My Look's Caress*.